MW00892842

WHITE KING AND THE DOCTOR

WHITE KING AND THE DOCTOR

A NOVEL BY

LEE KESSLER

To Kim & Susie,
All the best to new friends.
Lee

Printed in the United States of America

ISBN 1-4116-3400-4

Early Reader Comments

"The plot of ***White King and the Doctor*** unfolds brilliantly at a high-powered pace that captures the reader's interest from the first page to the final scene. Lee Kessler's suspense novel focuses on the War on Terror and reflects her vast knowledge of the terrorists' worldwide modus operandi, as well as of the positive forces heroically battling against them. Her appealing literary talents add to the readability of an absolutely timely, important novel."

—Verna Sabelle, Editor and Publisher
New York, New York

". . . I couldn't put it [***White King and the Doctor***] down. When's Part 2??!! The characters grabbed me—I wanted to see them succeed; I wanted the bad guys to make mistakes. The plot development was great: almost Clancy-ish, but (lots) more coherent. Lee has a real insight on the whole 'PR' thing, and in war it's called, 'Information Warfare.' She has nailed it. This book deserves a WIDE reading. I'm recommending it."

—Russ Smith, Operational Strategy Analyst
Air Force Space Command
Colorado Springs, Colorado

"Great Book [***White King and the Doctor***] and tremendous material for a great movie without a lot of gore. A must read for military and government people. Having a military background with the Naval Security Group and the National Security Agency, I thoroughly enjoyed reading this book. Even though it is fictional, it seemed real-time, and based on factual events and much research. There were so many interesting characters and events to keep track of it was difficult to put the book down. I believe this book presents great insight into the reality of terrorism around the world."

—E. Varner, WDV, Ret. Navy Chief,
United States Navy
Virginia. Beach, VA

"Art mirrors life and life usually returns the favor. In this well-written novel, Miss Kessler has given me a fictional view into the mind and purpose of an all-too-real terrorist. Or is it fiction? In a thriller that is pulled from today's and very possibly future headlines, I was led on a dangerous chase to thwart the terrorists' ultimate goal—destruction of the United States. One of the criticisms of our intelligence community was that it lacked the imagination to foresee the events of 9/11. They would do well to read this book, as would anyone who enjoys more than a good story."

—Michael Fairman, Actor & Screenwriter
Hollywood, California

"TEN STARS! Current events, seemingly unrelated, all become part of one downright scary web. The nagging question throughout is more frightening than the story itself—could it be? Ms. Kessler brilliantly stepped back, viewed the world, and created an imaginative theory that changed the way I view current events forever.

"Society is degenerating and it is not 'just happening.' There is a catalyst—a person or group who is overtly causing turmoil. When I finished the book, I knew that Ms. Kessler had found the answers—the source of this entire decline."

—Marcy Sanders, Internet Company Owner
Los Angeles, California

"White King and the Doctor" opens the reader's eyes and mind as to what the real objective of our enemy is. This book reads like the series '24' views! I was gripped from the opening and couldn't stop. As someone who averages 36-40 books a year, this has been my favorite of the past two years!!"

—Vince Rush, Founder, Rush International
Cincinnati, Ohio

"This book should be a movie. It has all the facets of a great suspense novel. It would make *The Bourne Identity* seem like a TV movie. You can readily see today's events as you turn the pages of this book. The thought processes that went into the writing of the ***White King and the Doctor*** reveal the intellect of Lee Kessler! A must read is not really a true indication of its importance...... replace 'must' with VITAL!"

—Paul Cooper, International Meteorologist
Tucson, Arizona

"Amazing, powerful! Reading this book [***White King and the Doctor***] will cause a paradigm shift. It is truly frightening because every page rings with truth. It is both timely and thought-provoking. It lays out a scenario that explains how we got the War on Terror. Ms. Kessler has used a very creative look to point out what we should have already figured out. This is a page-turner I couldn't put down."

—Shannon Leahy, Internet Business Owner & Mother
North Hills, California

"A genuinely original and thought-provoking novel anchored firmly in reality. Once again we discover that the LOVE of money is, in fact and fiction, the root of ALL evil. As you complete this book, no matter your politics, religion or ethnicity, you'll be forced to view the world from a different perspective. By turning the terrorists from bigger-than-life media images into ordinary people, the author carefully reminds us on every page that it's always all about the day-to-day decisions that each individual makes."

—Marti Baer, Event Production Executive
Los Angeles, California

"Anyone teaching writing should use Dan Brown and Lee Kessler as the two best examples of the use of foreshadowing."

— Bruce Gridley, Trial Attorney
Los Angelas, CA

"This is a book [***White King and the Doctor***] you cannot put down. It makes you think; your emotions run wild. It's **outright scary** and a **wake-up call**. This book is a <u>must read</u> for anyone who breathes."

—Cindy Baas, Marital Arts Company Owner
San Clemente, California

This book is in memory of Jackie Conde Weigand, the bravest person I ever knew; and is dedicated to the “simmering frog.”

AUTHOR'S NOTE

Subsequent to the events of 9/11, I held the paradoxical hope that the devastation of that day might be the saving grace of our troubled country—that Americans would become more united. Instead, we have become more divided than at any point in my lifetime.

I asked myself what could be at work here? Was there possibly a "Fifth Column" in the United States whose purpose was to destroy our solidarity? A visit to the FBI's "Most Wanted Terrorists" site revealed a provocative omission. I decided to probe it.

As a professional actress for nearly 30 years, who has had the opportunity to play historical figures, I challenged myself to figure out what the second-in-command of Al Qaeda was actually doing, and to see if his reach extended into the United States in ways we weren't aware of.

Could I use imagination coupled with basic acting technology to unlock the mystery? I decided to try. *Imagine* that I did an exercise to create the back-story of Al Qaeda mastermind, Ayman Al-Zawahiri. In the process of discovering his driving motivation, I uncovered something so important that the outcome of the War on Terror depends upon it being known—something intelligence analysts, and the media analysts, appear to have missed.

And *imagine* that, as the events of 2003 and 2004 unfolded, my evaluations proved true. It seems I had "reconnected the dots" of current events. *White King and the Doctor* is the picture that emerged. Based on fact, it has been fictionalized in order to tell the story.

CHAPTER 1
THE DOCTOR

The man Usama Bin Laden knew as the Doctor stood unobtrusively at the edge of the compound, virtually unnoticeable, his hands folded prayerfully in front of him. He smiled as he watched Usama with his young converts. Usama's smooth and eloquent voice and gestures were inspiring the Americans who had come for training, and he wondered what the Americans' parents would do if they knew the true intent of their children's sabbatical to Afghanistan.

Usama is our best man at public relations, he thought. *I was right to forge this alliance. We'll use his money and his charisma to bring us the supply of young men we need.* He wondered if Usama had any idea how he really felt about him and what he planned for him. *I doubt it*, he thought. *He's brilliant at business, but blind to intrigue. He will be easy to control for now.*

"I wonder if it's wise to use the Americans in our forces," interrupted Muhammad Atef, Al Qaeda's military commander. The Doctor had not heard him approach and felt that uneasiness he often felt when Atef was near. Despite their collaboration of decades, the stealth ability of his partner unnerved him at times.

"Yes, it's fine—a few at least. They will serve us well in later propaganda. And I'm confident you'll make certain we have no infiltrators from American intelligence among them," he responded, hoping to placate Atef. "All is well. We are winning."

Atef cocked his head and looked with cautious skepticism at this odd remark. Odd, given they had been run out of every country they operated in and were wanted men everywhere. "Well, I came to tell you CNN is covering the China/America situation. I thought you might want to see him. You know, see how his team handles this. It's time we got a measure of the man."

The Doctor laughed. "We can thank the Chinese military for providing this new President with his first crisis. Let's see what the Americans have put in office this time." And with that, the two slipped into a metal shed. They nodded to the guard inside, descended a primitive ladder and went into their underground fortress to assess their newest adversary.

When Usama excused himself from the eager protégés, he joined Ayman Al-Zawahiri, who was known as "The Doctor" in Al Qaeda circles, and his military commander, Muhammad Atef, in the communications center of their fortress. Both seemed unusually riveted to the reporting. The American spy plane was still on the ground, its crew in interrogation. Although the situation was days old now, the news had nothing to report from George W. Bush. Factions of the press that could be counted on to slant the reporting toward criticism of the new President were already skeptical about his silence. To the American press it seemed a sign of the longed-for weakness they hoped to see in this man. To the Doctor it was disturbing.

Zawahiri sat passively watching the National Security Advisor handle the situation, cloaking the intentions and disposition of her boss. *Very shrewd*, he admired. *He's staying in the shadows, letting subordinates handle it. Or is he?* That thought disturbed the Doctor. He had hoped to get a bead on his enemy by watching how he dealt with the Chinese and their unique brand of extortion. But this one was a pretty cool character who was not showing his hand. He sensed danger here; then shrugged it off. Surely 15 years of his psychological efforts had rendered the Americans' top leadership inept when it came to unusual and unexpected confrontations. His only worry actually was that the Chinese had been too overt in forcing the spy plane down.

Bin Laden, on the other hand, was for some reason very worried about this new man in the White House. He excused their aides and confronted his colleagues directly. "What do you make of it?"

The Doctor spoke first, wanting to forestall Atef's take on it. The dynamics among the three of them had changed in recent months. The Doctor knew that to accomplish his master plan, he had to stay in charge. Bin Laden was easily manipulated, but Atef's intransigence when he felt he was right was beginning to threaten their solidarity. The Doctor must remain in control. "We'll have to lure him out—actually get him out in the open—to see what he's made of."

"And how do we do that?" Atef challenged.

"We attack. We need to see if he'll follow the lead of his predecessor, or if he has something else in mind," Zawahiri said matter-of-factly.

Bin Laden, who had been eying both men, turned to Atef and asked, "Which of your plans can be implemented?"

Atef knew exactly what was feasible and not feasible. There were literally dozens of plans they were developing regarding attacks in or upon the United States. But to remove something from the drawing board or pre-planning stages and move it to the front table would require thought and a cost/benefit analysis in both men and materiel. Bin Laden the businessman would want that. His response was terse. "I'll get back to you."

"Good. Be bold, my friend. This is a chance to bring down the Infidel and disrupt his influence."

The Doctor flinched inside as he listened to this sophomoric rhetoric. He excused it by assigning it to the fact his friend had just been propagandizing some American youth and had carried the verbiage over. Lord, how he despised these privileged young. And he knew he was a gift from Allah to Bin Laden, who would have been just like them had it not been for the Doctor.

Confident that Muhammad Atef would recommend an attack upon American assets, private or military, he began to envision the new American President having to come out in the open and threaten revenge. By what that President did next, the Doctor would know which one of his own games would ensure his ultimate victory. And with that to look forward to, he politely excused himself and went to prayers.

The battle plan had received final approval from the Council in March 2001. Zawahiri had expected the attack to be a replication of his brilliant embassy bombings, or the USS Cole, but Atef had surprised him with their most aggressive and far-reaching plot to date. Although the Doctor had strong misgivings about an attack of this magnitude on American soil, he had decided to "pick his fights." What he had needed was a merging of Egyptian Islamic Jihad and Al Qaeda. As the leader of the anemic Egyptian group his entire plan required that his own group survive. And that required an infusion of capital. He needed Bin Laden's money, and now he had it. Even better was the fact that Bin Laden was now completely surrounded by the Doctor's own men. Still resentful of his betrayal by his friend, Ali Mohamed, who had turned out to be a double agent working for the Americans, the Doctor was confident he could avoid a repeat of that fiasco. *Trust no one*, he concluded. *Let no one know how self-correcting I am.* What had been done to him was now being done by him.

He remembered with pride how he had precipitated the split between Sheik Abdullah Azzam and his protégé, Bin Laden. It seemed to Zawahiri that Azzam was siphoning off money and attention from Bin Laden that was needed by the Jihad. He felt no remorse whatsoever about planting the rumor that Azzam was working for the Americans. The man was weak and resisted attacking other Muslims. It pleased him greatly that Azzam and his sons had been blown up in a car bomb the very next night. Bin Laden had killed his own mentor. The speed of that response had convinced the Doctor that Bin Laden was his man—decisive and ruthless.

And so, one by one, all rivals for Usama Bin Laden's money and loyalty had been neutralized. The merger was done. On this unexpected near-freezing night in June 2001, as he watched the sun setting, he breathed in the cold air, enjoying the pain it caused his lungs. The date was set. It would happen in September. While his colleagues gloated in the planning of their surprise attack, he stood alone outside, confident that not one of them knew his true plan. And if his closest colleagues had no inkling of it, he was supremely confident that none of the imbeciles in the international intelligence agencies anywhere would ever guess it, least of all Israel's Mossad.

CHAPTER 2
THE AGENT

Everyone was still on high-alert. It seemed he hadn't slept in weeks, but it had only been three days. September 14, 2001. The President had just finished his heart-felt, supportive message to everyone at Langley. But something was haunting James Mikolas as he made a break for the men's room. Like an itch you can't locate, something was pestering his mind and stimulating his emotions. Sure, everyone was tired and distraught over what had happened. Everyone in America was in grief and exploring their own culpability. But these emotions went beyond that. James was experiencing the sheer terror that he somehow had caused this. *Thirty years as an operative or analyst and I missed it,* he thought as he popped a Pepcid. *But what? What did I do?*

The computer of James' mind was searching his files. It had located an incident. An incident so innocuous that his own mind had discounted it and shunted it to the dust bins of his memory. As it came forward, it was screaming for analysis. "It was just a conversation," he explained to himself, "a simple exchange of information between me and the Israeli intelligence officer." Then he saw it, like a flashbulb going off. There was the information. But there was something else. There had been an added, despondent conclusion drawn by the officer. James had dismissed it as the whining that intelligence people sometimes get into when they're behind in the game. But he saw now that it was that last remark which bore analysis. A germ of a theory was now developing.

He splashed water on his face, as if to help him see more clearly. He had been with the Central Intelligence Agency for 30 years. As he looked at his face, it still had that broad, tanned

Mediterranean look that came from his Greek grandfather. Although James himself was wholly American, his name and his genes had enabled him to pass easily throughout the Mediterranean, Mid-East and points in Eastern Europe and the Soviet Bloc where the swarthy complexion blended in. *Just a little more gray is all*, he mused. *I'm still the same fighting weight I was in college.* He laughed as he realized, though, that the weight wasn't muscle anymore.

Small wonder, he reflected. *I've been inside now since Kosovo.* Although he felt his intelligence had greatly helped the Clinton administration, he was brought inside shortly after the air strikes. Made an inside man, an analyst. He never did know who he'd pissed off. They camouflaged it so well behind their "need for someone of his experience to analyze data, keep a perspective..." It was all part of the CIA bullshit at management levels he had dodged for 24 years. But finally it was his turn.

Oddly enough though, he didn't mind being an analyst. As luck would have it, he was good at it. Turns out the bastards were right to move him in. He could think outside the box, stretch. He could see things others couldn't. That didn't make him popular, but it did make him needed. He knew he had a job until he was ready to hang it up.

He squared off in the mirror. Then he went outside into the smoking area of the garden, found an open bench and sat. The memory of that conversation was now totally forward. He could see it as if it were yesterday.

"I'm glad to see you, friend." Colonel Ari Ben Gurion smiled as he offered a seat to James.

"Likewise. I was surprised to get your call. Is this business or pleasure?" James asked, never one to delay getting to the point. He had learned that much after years of dealing with Aman, the Israeli intelligence service. These guys were hard-core and didn't like to stay out in the open long. And they were precise.

"Well, it's always a pleasure to see an old colleague, but I'm afraid it's business. A drink?"

James motioned to the waiter closest to their table. "Coffee and a croissant, please. And another of whatever my friend is having." He could tell by Ari's waistline that he hadn't lost his appreciation of great pastry. James, too, was happy to see him. The waiter nodded and disappeared out of the sun.

"Do you miss being in the field, James?" Ari asked.

"No," he added, "what I miss is the clarity. When you and I were coming up, the enemy was always on the surface. You knew where he was. And usually who he was. Now we're boxing with shadows. Like there are two worlds. The one that good decent people live in, and the subterranean one full of demons who surface, do some evil, and vanish again. It's shit. We don't even know their names, let alone their motives."

Ari looked at him without speaking as the waiter set down the pastry plate and poured James's coffee. When he was certain no one was in earshot he quietly said, "That's what I wanted to talk to you about. Two men who scare me, more than any I've ever pursued."

That statement rocked James for he never considered Ari to fear anything, let alone the rats he chased through the Middle East.

"And what scares me the most," Ari added, "is they're not even on your radar screen."

"Who, me personally?"

"No, your bosses, your government! They're not taking our warnings as seriously as they need to," he bellowed. "You're old-school. You'll understand. I'm here to give you information about Ayman Al-Zawahiri and Muhammad Atef."

James recognized the names. He knew the Israelis in particular would be interested in these two, given what had happened in Egypt. They were important to President Mubarak, and Mubarak was important to Israel. He knew well how important Egypt today was to Israel's security. But he had no idea relevant to the United States why these two warranted such emotion from Ari.

"Ari, I'm not sure why you are so vehement on this. But I trust you. If you have something to tell me, say it. I'll do my best with whatever information you give me. I promise."

"Okay."

James waited, enjoying the croissant as it dissolved in his mouth. After a moment Ari spoke.

"We've been chasing them for years. They're mixed up with Hezbollah. Zawahiri's been merciless since his imprisonment. We think he's joining Bin Laden, looking for a merger." James, of course, knew of Bin Laden and what a nightmare that situation had been for the U.S., especially with the Bin Laden family living in the United States. And the Saudi connection, too. It was a real mess.

James could see that Ari was struggling with something. He probed, "What about Zawahiri?"

Ari looked at him with eyes of steel. "He's brilliant—a genius. He's refined terrorism into an art. And he's a psychopath. Our guys have given up trying to understand him."

James said nothing. Ari continued, "You know you've lost when the 'mind guys' come and tell you the absurd. They have concluded he's a clinical psychopath driven by uncontrollable psychological reasons, inflamed by his imprisonment and torture in Egypt! James, in my business, that's psychobabble for 'we're not even in the game!'"

"And why does this scare you, Ari?"

"Because none of us can crack him. We don't know how he thinks; we can't penetrate him. He's so far out in front we have no idea what he'll do next, or why. We don't know where he is. We think his military mastermind, Atef, is with him. But we don't know. We don't know what he looks like now." Ari leaned in, his eyes wild. "We don't even know if the DNA the Egyptians have is Zawahiri's DNA. He's a phantom. He could be sitting right next to us for all I know."

"Jesus, what a thought," James exhaled. "You really don't know?"

Ari was ashamed. He lowered his voice and was barely audible. "No." Then he seemed to get a second wind and added, "That's why I wanted to meet: to tell you that if you ever get him in your cross-hairs, take him out. Don't hesitate. Aman regards him as the most dangerous man on the planet. Bin Laden's a school-boy next to him. And we've lost him. If you get him, kill him."

"All right, I got it," James reassured him as he reached into his pocket to pay the bill.

Suddenly Ari's hand grabbed James' wrist. "I mean it, James. We don't know how to go where he is. He's always several moves out in front of the best we've got. And he's going to kill a lot of people."

With that, their meeting ended. They shook hands and went their separate ways at Dupont Circle. The only thing James really thought about their talk was that it was probably time for Ari to retire. Ari had dealt with deadly guys his whole career. And he seemed to have lost his edge.

James stood up. There it was, the thing that was nagging at him. The phrase, "he's always several moves out in front of us..." Looking at it all, from 1993 to Tuesday morning, was it possible? Was that what Zawahiri was doing? Did Bin Laden even know?

A theory was forming. It had been 40 years since he'd played chess. And he wasn't that good when he did. *I've got to do some boning up. And I need to talk to someone.*

He thought of the President's words a few hours ago and, for the first time in three days, he smiled.

CHAPTER 3
THE PLAYER

It had taken him some time to find this kid. But looking at him now, entering the huddle to call the play, James recognized Andrew Weir from the picture in the leading chess magazine, *New in Chess*, he'd been carrying around. The pages were worn ragged from two months of searching for this chess champion who was renowned for beating Big Blue and any other computer he played chess with.

James had to admit the last place he expected to find him was at an Arlington High football game, let alone as their star quarterback. He had always enjoyed a good paradox, so he took a seat in the stands and watched the game.

Andrew was physically not what James expected to find in a world-class chess player. James had fallen victim to the clichés of bookish, nerdish, shy intellectuals, reading in the shadows of their bedrooms. But not this kid. When he first saw the picture, he thought the magazine had done a misprint, or photographed the champion's brother with him or something. But no, the tag-line was very specific. It was Andrew Weir.

As he watched him throw a completed pass before being knocked down, he admired Andrew's poise. They weren't able to get that first down though, and the punt team came on. As defense took the field, Andrew approached the bench and took off his helmet.

Handsome, James thought. *He looks like a soap-opera star!* It was true. Andrew would turn heads. Six feet tall and muscular, his black curly hair emphasized green eyes and a winning smile. James watched as Andrew encouraged the player who had come up a yard short on the last drive. The player smiled as Andrew patted his back, letting him know there was still time.

And there was. Arlington High won the game. James had observed something about Andrew in that last quarter. He was smart. You want a smart quarterback, and Andrew was that. He guessed that most defenses would have problems with an opponent this smart. That pleased James. He felt confident that this kid could help him with the theory. The only problem now was how to approach an 18-year-old football-playing chess champion and persuade him to come help the CIA. Even in Washington that might seem a bit over-reaching. Having watched Andrew though, James decided to be direct. He followed Andrew and a woman whom he guessed to be his mother to a local hamburger joint that boasted it had the best fat-burgers in the United States.

When the boy's mother went to the restroom, James made his move. "Great game today, Andrew," he opened.

"Thanks," Andrew responded automatically. As Andrew looked up to see who had addressed him, James chuckled at the mayonnaise running down his chin. Looked like a good burger after all.

"Do you mind if I talk to you about something?" James admonished himself that he may have been too sudden here. He saw Andrew straighten up a bit and wipe his mouth with his already-messy napkin.

"No, sir, I don't want to talk about chess." Pointing to the magazine in James' right pocket, he said, "I see you've got that article. But I'd rather not."

Geez, this kid is fast—and observant, James thought. That was good. He hoped this boy was as smart as everyone thought. He couldn't afford to blow it, and he knew trying to slide in gradually would arouse Andrew's resistance. He noticed an American flag decal on Andrew's notebook. That gave James some hope. *Here goes what they taught me never to do in recruiting.*

"Actually, Andrew, I wanted to talk to you about 9/11." As he said that he presumptuously sat down opposite the boy.

"I beg your pardon?" Andrew queried.

"September 11th, son." He quickly added, "I'm James Mikolas and I work for the federal government. And I need your help on something."

Before Andrew could even answer, his mother returned to the table, a little startled to find someone already sitting there. She had gotten used to some of the autograph hounds that came up after Andrew won his last tournament. And she certainly was used to pretty girls and jocks wanting some time with him. But somehow, this picture seemed odd to her. She slid into her seat as James rose to greet her.

"Hi. I'm Andrew's mom, Kelly," she said, not extending her hand.

James noted that she was a pretty woman, although he wondered if that red hair was really hers or an attempt to look as she had when she was Andrew's age. She had those same green eyes, though, and was self-confident enough it seemed. Before he could do a polite greeting, Andrew made the introduction.

"Mom, meet James Mikolas. He works for the federal government."

Kelly smiled. The import of that went over her head. After all, Andrew had fans in many professions.

So Andrew drove the point home, "He wants to talk to me about 9/11."

Kelly looked at Andrew blankly, then at James blankly, then back to Andrew. "I don't understand."

"Me either, Mom."

Kelly had the typical reaction people have when confronted with the IRS. They feel guilty, even if there's nothing to feel guilty about. She hoped that, with all the paranoia following the attacks, they didn't somehow think her son was mixed up with the Irish Republican Army or some such thing. But for now, she couldn't quite form up what questions might be appropriate.

James seized the opportunity. "It's a pleasure to meet you Mrs. Weir. I didn't mean to startle you two, but it is a matter of some urgency."

If someone were watching through the window, they would have seen an extraordinary conversation unfold. Andrew and Kelly sat, arms folded, listening without saying a word. James talked, using salt and pepper shakers to illustrate something. At which point, Andrew's arms came uncrossed and he appeared relaxed. Shortly after that Kelly, too, relaxed and nodded to James. The conversation ended quickly when James pulled out his pocket calendar and made an entry. He handed Kelly and Andrew each his card, shook hands with them and left. He was smiling. He had guessed right.

Two days later a Jeep Cherokee in need of a paint job pulled up at the gate to Langley. Andrew was alone in his car. Taking Andrew's ID, the guard checked his clip-board, made a quick call, and then searched Andrew's rear seat area. His partner outside swept the undercarriage with the mirror stick, looking for any explosives while the K-9 unit also checked for bombs. Once the all-clear was given, the guard waved Andrew in and directed him to a visitor parking area.

Shortly after, James came down to reception to pick up his guest and get a badge issued for him. At this point Andrew was still officially a "guest." James had no idea whether more would be needed. It depended on whether his theory proved out or not.

Andrew was taken immediately into what looked like a conference room with pictures on one wall and a mirror on the other. Behind the mirror was Whitney, James' boss. Although he was deeply skeptical about this hypothesis, he knew James' reputation well enough to give him a little wiggle room—just a little. James left the conference room on the pretext of getting a sports drink for Andrew and came into the viewing room.

"So that's the kid," Whitney said with some skepticism. "Sure doesn't look like a chess player."

"Amazing, isn't it! What a great undercover guy he'd make. A real-life 007." He tried to get Whitney to laugh, unsuccessfully. "All right. I'm going to lay it out for him, omitting the actual names and dates, and see what he concludes. If he's the right one, and I believe he is, whatever he concludes will be correct."

"Okay. Let's give it a shot."

James reentered with the drink and set it down. As Andrew took a quick couple of swigs James removed a stack of cards from his pocket. Although they actually had a sequence, he obliterated it by shuffling the deck several times while Andrew watched closely. The last card in the series, however, was not in the deck. James had secreted it in his right side pocket to further test Andrew.

Having thoroughly mixed them up, he spread them out all over the table face down. "Andrew, the only thing I'm going to tell you is that each card has an event on it, some piece of data. This all happened before you can remember, so it won't mean anything to you. I just want you to look at the raw data and let me know if you see anything. Okay?"

"Okay. But can I ask you something?"

"Yeah, sure," James responded.

"Why do you keep calling me Andrew?"

James must have looked puzzled. "I go by Andy." Then Andy flashed that celebrity smile and reached for the cards.

"Okay, Andy, have at it. When you're done signal me through the mirror."

Taking all the cloak and dagger in stride, Andy began. And James could hardly breathe as he exited the room.

James and Whitney observed the boy through the mirror. He had taken off his letter jacket and neatly placed it on the chair closest to them. Was that a smile on his face as he looked into the mirror? Yeah, it was. He winked at them! "Teenagers!" Whitney scoffed.

Andy first turned over all the cards and looked quickly at each one. Very quickly, so quickly they could hardly keep up with his hand movements, he ordered them in a sequence on the table. Then, mysteriously, he picked up each card and pinched it between his fingers. After that, he looked under the table quickly, on his seat, and then toward the door. Not finding what he was looking for, he shook his head and walked over to the mirror.

"Can you hear me in there James? 'Cause if you can, there's a card missing."

"Holy shit!" James exclaimed, rocked by the speed of the confirmation.

"What?" Whitney asked, not seeming to know what to make of it. "Is that good?"

"Yes it is," James answered, trying to get his heart to stop racing.

James entered the conference room eager to hear what Andy had to tell him. "Do you have something?"

"I thought so, but something's missing."

"Tell me what you've got." James had not told his theory to Andy. As far as the Kid knew, he was here because he was smart and could think strategically, nothing else.

"These cards, these incidents and pictures…they're a chess game. You gave me a chess game."

"Go on."

"Well, frankly sir, it was pretty simple. It was obvious at a glance what the sequence was. I've seen this game before. I think the match was in one of my beginning books when I started playing chess. Except for the end. I don't get it."

"Don't get what?"

"There's a card missing. That's why I called for you. The last card is missing. The checkmate move. I don't mean to sound perverse sir, but I call it the 'Kill the King' move. But it's not here, so maybe I'm wrong." Andy looked as if he'd failed. "Sorry to disappoint you. I thought I had it. But without that card, this is all just a bunch of pictures and headlines."

James reached into his right side pocket and placed a card face up on the table. "Is this it?"

Andrew swallowed hard and nodded as he looked at a picture of the assassination of Anwar Sadat on October 6, 1981. James said nothing. After a long moment Andy said in a soft voice, "I remember reading about this in my Modern History class." Then he demurred, "I wasn't very good in history."

The two sat for a moment, then Andy asked, "These seeming unrelated incidents and headlines—the 'chess moves'—are these factual too?"

"Yes."

"Do you know who did this?"

"Yes. We know who actually emptied his machine gun."

"That's not what I'm asking," Andy asserted. "Do you know who we are playing? The shooter was only the Knight. Whose game is this?"

And with that question, posed by one of the world's best chess players, James knew that we stood a chance. He answered calmly, knowing now that the Kid would have to stay. "Yes, one at least. His name is Ayman Al-Zawahiri."

"I've heard of him. The one on the FBI list on the Internet?"

"The same."

"And your theory?"

"My theory is that he is not just a brilliant mind, but also a master strategist who plays chess. Most military men play chess. It develops their mind, helps them to solve problems, and think strategically. I think he is actually playing chess now."

Andy pondered this for a minute. He seemed to be looking at something in the distance.

"And you think 9/11 was part of a chess game?"

"I do, Andy, diabolical as that sounds. I've been praying it was their checkmate move—you know, after the first attack in 1993, the Marine barracks, the USS Cole bombing—their 'Kill the King' move. And that it failed."

Suddenly Andy sat up straight, looked Mikolas in the eye and said like a soldier reporting to his senior officer, "I regret to tell you, sir, 9/11 was not the checkmate move."

"What was it then?"

"It was the first move of the Black King's Knight."

James looked down for a moment and stood silent.

Andrew knew in his gut what James would ask next. He knew the sacrifice it meant. And he also knew how he had felt that beautiful September morning. He wondered what his father would have done. But he knew the answer to that too. Without looking at James, he calmly volunteered, "I'd better go tell my mom."

CHAPTER 4

The day the radio reports had come in detailing the attacks upon the World Trade Center and the Pentagon had been one of the worst in Zawahiri's life. Having to put on the face of joy and victory with his elated colleagues had been more than he could bear.

I wanted to lure him out, Zawahiri thought, *not stir up the entire free world.* What a disaster! He had approved Khalid's plan. Atef had approved the plan. What had gone wrong? It was supposed to be an escalation, a taunt to the U.S., not a blow that would unite them. He had excused himself from their self-congratulatory wallowing in the devastation they were now watching on CNN. He needed to know who did this. For whoever it was had killed them all. *Well, not Ayman Al-Zawahiri*, he vowed to himself. *Not me. I didn't do what I have done to lose now. I'm so close and I'm not going to let some idiot ruin it now. Someone will pay.* He composed himself and reentered the group. Quietly, almost like a snake sliding toward its prey, he approached Khalid Shaikh Mohammed, the architect of the attack plan from an engineering standpoint, and motioned to him to come outside.

Across the room Muhammad Atef saw the two exiting, and decided to join them. He, too, was oddly suspicious during what should have been a time of celebration. After all, the world was made better today, September 11, 2001. Many evil Crusaders had died. And he was sure Allah was pleased. But he wondered why Ayman was not.

Outside in the moonlight, Khalid looked almost ghoulish in the torchlight shadows. He sensed something was wrong. But as brilliant as he was, he could never have imagined what his friend the Doctor had in store for him. As Atef joined them Zawahiri lashed out.

"You were educated in engineering in the United States, were you not?"

"Yes, sir, I was."

"At the University of North Carolina, were you not?"

Khalid Sheik Mohammed was less certain now. "Yes."

"And don't the Americans have the finest engineering programs in the world? The only reason any of us could stomach associating with those swine for even a minute?" Zawahiri hissed.

"Yes, Ayman, they do."

"Then how in the name of Allah could you have not known those buildings were coming down? Are you trying to kill us all?"

The venom in the question was almost more than Khalid could comprehend. His friend was usually soft-spoken and charming. But now, here, he was downright menacing.

"You calculated in advance the number of casualties; you told us three to four floors would be hit, that the fire from the fuel would melt the structure in that area. You said we would kill the enemy above those floors only. We picked the precise floors based upon that. Do you see what has happened?"

For the life of him Khalid could not understand why the Doctor was upset. It had been a great victory. True, his calculations were wrong. But many more of the enemy had died today, leaving fewer for the strong believers to handle on the second wave. And the attack would be devastating to their economy as well. What was the problem?

"You are so stupid, Khalid; you never studied world history, only Arabic history. And obviously they never made you take an American history course while you were in your precious Raleigh!"

"Ayman, please, what is the problem?"

"The problem is that we wanted to lure the President out, to see how far he would go and when he would compromise, as the others have. I needed to see what he would stop short of—how much of him is just talk, and how much is really him. Remember, dear friend," the Doctor seemed to soften, "we want the Americans out of the region so that we can fulfill our mission.

What you have done will bring them in. You left him no choice. And I'm no closer to knowing what he's made of."

"I see," Khalid sighed.

"Now go and secure your families," the Doctor advised both men. "We must all go to our safe places now. You know the drill."

Atef stepped in now. "Yes, we do Ayman. And thank you for putting that perspective on this. I have faith that it will still turn out our way. We will not be defeated. I am sure of it."

The Doctor delayed his response longer than Atef would have liked. They had been brothers in arms for decades and he knew his colleague's every nuance.

"Yes, I'm sure. Goodnight. Tell Usama I am going to talk to my wife."

The three separated. But the Doctor did not call his wife, Azza, nor did he rejoin the celebration. He went to his bunker chamber where he kept his secret plans, opened the cabinet against the wall and pulled out a hidden table-top. And with his right hand, in great anger and disgust, he wiped out the game he had been playing there. And then, on a small pad labeled "Future," he made the note "Demote KSM to pawn. Forfeit pawn."

Calmer now, he placed one phone call—to the head of their film and media production department. He had much to do before he left Afghanistan.

CHAPTER 5

While the Doctor embarked upon the boldest strategic moves in the history of terrorism, a half a world away James Mikolas walked a handsome teenager out of the secured area and to his car. It was drizzling when they stepped outside. James noticed that Andy seemed restless, as if he were trying to get away.

In fact, Andy was just relieved to be out of that building. He had observed a great deal with his quarterback's eyes. Some offices were mere cubicles of glass grouped in a cluster. Some had doors, and authority or secrets behind them. He observed cameras and surveillance equipment, and secured areas which he presumed housed the telecommunications and surveillance personnel. But most of all, he felt confusion there. Reading it like a defensive line facing him, he knew there was a lack of coordination. And something more that he couldn't quite see—yet.

"I never thought I'd be a 'spook,'" he originated to James, trying to make a joke. His hand shook as he fumbled the key in the car door.

"You're not going to be, Kid. You're just going to help me analyze some data." Then he added, "I felt the same way, though, about this place when they brought me in."

"I thought you said you'd been with the Agency 30 years?" Andy questioned.

"Yeah, 31. But only a handful or two here. I was an outside man."

Realizing that James was a "spook," he tried to avoid offending him. "Sorry, I didn't mean…" He didn't get the sentence finished. James waved it off and went straight to the point.

"Kid, you'd better let me explain this to your mom. I'm free for dinner if you'll invite me."

The more Andy ruminated on that, the more it made sense. He was all his mom had now, and he didn't know how she'd take this. *Heck*, he thought, *I don't know how I'm going to take this.*

James was right to have insisted. Kelly's suspicions were up the minute Andy returned with James in tow. She knew when she was about to be ganged up on. After all, she'd fended off enough college scouts trying to persuade Andy to play ball. But she had held her ground. She knew that was owed to Greg. Andy's dad knew that his son had a special intellect. And as much as he, too, loved sports, that was not the life he wanted for his son. Before he died, on a good day when he didn't need so much of the pain drip the D.C. Veteran's Administration Medical Center was giving him for his last battle with cancer, he had insisted that Kelly use his insurance money for one thing only—the best education she could provide for their son. Kelly had agreed, even though it meant she would have to find work of some kind. And it had worked out. She had renewed her beauty license and leased a chair in a nearby salon. Between the insurance and the scholarship MIT had offered, she knew Greg's dream for his son would be fulfilled.

So it was that wall that James ran headlong into—a wife protecting her dead husband's dream and a mom protecting her son. God, what a combination! The fact that they were even talking had nothing to do with James' persuasive powers, quite the opposite. It had to do with the fact that Kelly was the proud widow of a Guard at the Tomb of the Unknown Soldier. And, although most of America was oblivious to it, that was the highest honor that could be afforded a serviceperson. For James knew that it was not just an assignment. It was a way of life involving a discipline for the rest of the serviceman's life. The first day they met, James had noticed the wreath pin Kelly now wore as a pendant. That small lapel pin spoke volumes about Greg—and Kelly. And about the heritage this young man was upholding. He had known at that moment that this kid was the one. He didn't need just a chess player; he needed a hard-core patriot.

Not wanting to patronize her, he subtly commented, "I've never met anyone awarded that lapel pin."

She fingered it suddenly, as if she'd forgotten it was there. She looked at her son for a moment, then back at James. "I know these are desperate times, Mr. Mikolas. I know that all of us will have to make some sacrifice in order to come through this."

"Yes, ma'am, I believe that."

She took control of the conversation. "So I'm not going to argue with you two. It's obvious you need Andy's help with something, and it's also obvious Andy's decided to help you. I think you should tell me, though, if it's dangerous."

"No, ma'am!" he assured her, "just a little time-consuming. We'll need him every day for a time to help us out at Langley on an analysis we're doing. He'll be working directly with me."

"That is the one thing I can't allow," she matter-of-factly stated.

"I beg your pardon?" James was confused.

"Andy can work with you. But I want to remind you this is his last year of high school. He can't miss out on that and still take his scholarship at MIT. And he's the star, I'm sure you noticed, of a football team that is expected to take the Conference this year. There is no way he can mess up his studies or abandon his teammates."

James didn't know what to say next, so he said nothing. He looked to Andy for help, but Andy was just staring down at his empty spaghetti plate. Fortunately, Kelly herself broke the silence. "He can help you, Mr. Mikolas, but it has to be done here."

"But Kelly, if you're worried about MIT dumping him because he misses a few history or geography classes, there's no risk there. We use MIT students often to solve problems for us.

So does the Defense Department. Hell, they'll probably give him credit for the work he does with us."

That was news to Andy. Now he showed some interest. "Are you telling me MIT students are working on classified material while at MIT?"

"Sure, in the technology transfer offices. But they usually don't know they're doing it." James had said more than he wanted to.

"But wouldn't they need security clearance?" Kelly asked.

James had no choice now. *Just tell them*, he admonished himself. Taking in a deep breath, he carefully laid out a secure answer. "They don't know they have clearance. We've done the investigations before we pick the students. All we tell them is that they're working on a confidential theoretical and we need their input." He added, "We don't compromise sensitive data; we give the problem to them in concepts or simulated facts. We conceal it somehow and they proceed to solve it."

Turning to Andy, he added, "That's what I did with you in the conference room. We'd camouflaged the facts so you were looking at the concepts. That's all. Simple."

"And you don't worry they'll tell?" Kelly asked doubtfully.

"No, we don't. As I said, we've already clandestinely done the security check."

"And did you 'clear' Andy?" she asked.

"Absolutely. That's why it took me a few weeks once I'd read about his particular victories. I had to make sure he was the one."

"And you feel he is?" She looked unwaveringly at James.

"Absolutely. No doubt about it."

"As I said," she spoke with less tension in her voice, "you can work here." And then, like a mom, she added, "But, Andy, you have to go to school, do your homework, and not miss a single practice or game."

And that was what forced James to build a quasi-secure area in the basement of Andy's small house. Although he had pleaded with her that, as solid as her foundation was, it wasn't impenetrable to listening devices, Kelly was relentless.

James was distressed about the lack of security at first. He knew it would put a lot of extra pressure on him to maintain the security of any written materials or diagrams they might possess. But the more he thought about it, the more he actually liked the situation Kelly's intransigence had forced on him.

To begin with, it got him out from under the eye of Whitney, who seemed reluctant about this whole theory. In reality, it felt like he was in the field again. That was it. He was actually comfortable having to worry about secure data and snoopy people. Unbeknownst to Kelly, he installed a safe under the floor of the basement where he and Andy could store their work. That eliminated the need for him bringing all of it in and out every day in a briefcase attached to his arm.

It was a small safe, just large enough to hold about 12 inches of papers. The combination lock on it, however, was one of the most complicated ones on the market. And only James knew how to open it. Given where they'd placed it, James was confident that Kelly would never see it, even if she came into their area.

Whitney had fussed at first, but finally had agreed to have the house swept for "bugs" on a regular basis. Ironically, he sent an Orkin truck to the house, so nosy neighbors would just think Kelly's old house needed regular service. Either that, or Whitney had a sense of humor after all.

At first, he was going to give the codes to the safe to Andy and the unusual keys that accompanied the codes. But they looked and clanked so ridiculously on Andy's belt that the two had concluded they would call more attention than they were worth. So, the security of that safe rested solely with James.

There were a few other serendipities as well. Since Kelly's conditions required that Andy be in school, and then at practice, he and Andy had to work at night. So he was usually invited to dinner. Kelly was a good cook and he was a lousy one, and James was fattening his wallet as well by not having to eat out. Further, it gave him "cover." If anyone was paying attention, and he doubted they were, they would just think Kelly had a new boyfriend who came to visit in the early evening, and left properly around 11 p.m. It was cozy, and very workable. It was not the first time in his career that James had had such a cover.

On the nights Andy had a game James picked Kelly up from her salon and accompanied her to the game. *Not bad*, he thought. *Nothing like watching a good team and having somebody to cheer for.*

The only wrinkle, if you could call it that, in the whole set-up was the fact that James very often had to wear a suit. That was not his usual "uniform." Periodically he would transport sensitive materials from Langley for their study. Then he needed to carry a briefcase much like the Hassidic jewelry couriers in Manhattan, and a coat and tie was obligatory to cover up the wrist chain.

But he was confident. And ready for the challenge. He had observed something at the football games that led him to believe that Ayman Al-Zawahiri was in for a rough ride—that he was about to play a game he could lose. The fact was more often than not, Andy's coach did not send plays in from the sideline. Despite Andy's age and relative inexperience, the coach let Andy call most of it himself in the huddle. Andy was also not reluctant to do audibles. He had a poise way beyond his years.

After one of the games James decided to ask Andy about that strategy between player and coach. "I notice Coach doesn't send many plays in to you."

"Yeah, I guess you could say I just trust my instincts," Andy demurred. Then he said something that confirmed for James that he had absolutely picked the right one. "I just *see* what they're doing. Coach knows that."

And so do I, James congratulated himself.

CHAPTER 6

He had thought it through carefully now. It was not as devastating as he first had concluded. In fact, as always, there was a new window of opportunity. Instead of this attack being a death knell, it could just accelerate his time line and bring him to his goal earlier than he had expected.

The Doctor smiled as he reasoned, *I will just have to launch simultaneously. I can do that. Yes, I have the departmental resources to do that. Usama will just have to concur.* He knew that Usama would agree to the first even though it meant an alliance with a man he despised. The more Zawahiri thought about this, though, the more he realized that Bin Laden had become too pious of late and even the first part of his plan could be jeopardized. As for the second part, he knew Bin Laden would disagree, if for no other than personal reasons.

It was at that moment that the Doctor knew he had to do what was considered unthinkable amongst their movement. *No loss,* he justified. *They have both misled me and they have brought this on themselves. I am not going to die here just because they are mesmerized by martyrdom and drunk with delusions of victory.* He knew that the American President would make the opening move—White always opens first. In the military game that would inevitably follow, the United States would move first. He knew what that move would be and he knew further not only how to defend, but more importantly, how to benefit.

With that, he climbed down two levels to the computer and communications area, and entered the classified area reserved for top echelon commanders in Al Qaeda. Here, after entering his personal password, he began to set up a three-dimensional model on the screen. Working only a few minutes, he was satisfied with the basic configuration. He then saved it to a confidential, encrypted folder and logged off. That folder was about to change the course of human history, and no one knew his intention, let alone his plan.

Oddly, though, he could not shake a look that Atef had given him when he dressed down Khalid. He and Atef had endured much together and accomplished much together. There was no doubt in Zawahiri's mind that he was the most brilliant military commander he had ever worked with. And Zawahiri felt he and Atef both had been ill-served this day. Since it was all turning out for the better, however, he decided to dismiss his doubts about Atef's commitment, for today at least, and begin the launch of three separate projects. Each one he knew would confound British and American intelligence and forever alter the effectiveness of their military moves. *This American President may strike first, but he is now playing my game, and the opening move is now mine.*

It was only after receiving confirmation from one of many sites on the Internet featuring chess games that he felt ready to lay out their battle plan to Usama. The message had come to him through his French partner, advising him that his escape route was set, and identifying the code and sequence to trigger it.

There was no way anyone would intercept this communiqué. Zawahiri knew that the intelligence agencies he had to fear were not watching all chess games played on the Internet. There were literally millions, given how popular the game was, and how small the Internet had made the world. And no one certainly could identify the code imbedded in the series of moves that he played out with his partner. Their arrangement was over a decade old now and, since his chess partner did not even know his name, he felt safe. And this man, at least he assumed it was a man, was motivated by money. That was the universal solvent in this type of negotiation. Zawahiri had money, more than anyone knew. How he had acquired it, however, he felt was the most delicious part of his entire master plan. It was his intention that no one ever know, at least not until he had exacted his revenge and was in total control.

For now, however, he turned his attention to the lesser game and to something he regretted doing. The Doctor had played this game long enough, however, to know that sometimes you have to sacrifice a piece—even if it's your Queen. And with that resolve he entered Usama's room to lay out the plan.

"Usama, I need to talk to you this evening," he gently began, knowing by Usama's energy level that he needed his shot. Expertly and quickly, the Doctor administered the nightly test and medication that defined Usama. The leader of Al Qaeda was fortunate to have his own private physician. And even more fortunate still to have that physician be his right-hand man. Once the medication took effect, Zawahiri continued.

"We are all going to need to move higher and deeper."

"You think?" Bin Laden queried. "I doubt if their satellites or operatives know we are here. The missiles will miss us, don't you think?" Then, recalling a very ironic moment from a few years earlier he joked, "How much do you think we'll make on them this time? If I remember, the last time they sent missiles, a lot of their Tomahawks didn't explode. How much did we make recovering them and selling them to the Chinese—$15 million?"

"There won't be any missiles, Usama," Zawahiri broke the news. He paused to let that settle in. Then he continued, "What happened in America will force the President to come here. He won't fire cruise missiles. This time, they will come themselves."

"Let them come. They're just like the Russians. We crushed that empire with our patience, our blessed mountains, our warriors, and with the help of Allah."

"Yes, dear friend," Zawahiri added delicately, "but this time, even if they come alone, they will win. You must tell the Taliban to prepare to defend themselves. And you must prepare to leave. We will be fortunate to have 2-3 hours in each location until we reach our safe harbor and that will require planning and careful selection of your staff and necessary survival materials. You must try to draw as little attention to us as possible."

Bin Laden sat up now, calm in his outward demeanor, but probing in his questioning. "Surely, friend, you don't think the

Americans can stand up to those passes, the temperatures, or our tactics?"

"The Americans only have to stand up to their own resolve. Their soldiers will bear the burden of the other. And believe me, Usama, their soldiers will bear up. They are self-correcting. What they fail at once, they correct. And they have the money to make the correction. I expect they're eager to get in here and unleash some weaponry on us. But, even if they come alone, they will come, and they will win."

Bin Laden looked at his friend, cocked his head a little as if to say, "You're kidding, right?" Seeing that Zawahiri was in deadly earnest, he sighed, "So, what is your recommendation?"

"There are two things we must do. One will secure your safety and provide options for your long-term survival. The second will be hard for you, Usama, very hard. But I believe that if you can get past your immediate loathing of the idea and look at the horizon you'll see that it assures us our final victory. And at the same time, it humiliates our enemies in the West."

"And our friends there?"

"We will tell them what we can. They will act in their own best interest and that will probably leave them standing. If not, they were not meant to survive this war."

Bin Laden was disquieted by the ruthlessness with which Zawahiri laid that out, but he knew the risks of war and he set it aside, assigning it to the fatigue after such an eventful, apocryphal day. With that he motioned for Zawahiri to sit close to him and lay it out.

He could hardly digest the magnitude of what Zawahiri was saying. But he knew this man to be the most brilliant, analytical mind he had ever encountered. Holding his decision in abeyance for a moment, he challenged, "You really think the circumstances will be that dire?"

With not even a millisecond's hesitation, the Doctor fired back, "I do."

"And you think this man will do what we ask? Our liaison advises that he despises us and our goals."

"He does. But he loves money. And he hates America. I believe he will do it."

"Why?"

"Because I would if I were in his shoes," Zawahiri answered confidently.

As was so often the case, Bin Laden didn't verbalize his assent. He nodded his head almost prayerfully. Zawahiri surmised he was, in a way, asking for Allah's blessing on what they were about to do.

Without a word being spoken, the world's two most wanted men had agreed to and launched a plan so original that it would confound not only the United States military and the militaries of its allies, but their governments as well. It would so divide the populations of nations that men and governments would fall. For Bin Laden, the plan was new and this was the opening move. For Zawahiri, who had participated and profited from one of the plan's component parts for decades, it was the checkmate move.

The call was placed. The message was relayed from Afghanistan to North Korea by courier and then from there to Libya. No phone calls were placed. No Internet links were used. No mail that could be intercepted. No agents who could be photographed or interrogated. The message went from Libya to an astonishing conspirator in Europe. And from there, it was delivered to Syria. A lone man on a camel crossed the border, and delivered it in person to the one who hated. A technology of message delivery thousands of years old was used in those few days. And nothing in modern technology could have altered or prevented what happened next.

Meanwhile, while the U.S. positioned its military, secured its allies and negotiated its air strips and flyover permissions for the invasion of Afghanistan, Usama Bin Laden entered Al Qaeda's subterranean production studio to begin what was to become one of the most ironic occurrences in America's War on Terror. All one had to do was note the speed of his entrance to the studios to know that he anticipated these next few days. In fact, if one looked closely, he relished it.

CHAPTER 7

When Andy and his friends turned the corner to his house he could see Mikolas' car parked behind his mom's. They weren't supposed to be working today, so he quickly jumped out of Brian's car, said his see-you-Mondays and went inside.

Usually James would be waiting in the living room if he arrived at the house before Andy. Like a visiting salesman or pastor, James would sit formally, out of the way of the activities of the home. His coat was there on the back of the sofa, but James was not.

Entering the kitchen, he saw James sitting at the kitchen table, hunched over a book apparently deeply absorbed in its content. He crossed to him and peered over his shoulder to get a glimpse of what could be so interesting.

"What you reading?" he asked innocently. James jumped as if he'd been caught completely off guard.

"*The Idiot's Guide to Chess,*" he responded, offering Andy a look at the book. "It's been a long time since I played; I thought I'd better bone up."

"Any good?"

"Yeah, it seems pretty easy to follow. But I'm amazed," he continued. "Did you know chess is now an Olympic sport?"

Andy set his bag down and grabbed the carton of milk from the refrigerator and some Oreo cookies lying on the side table. "Yeah, sure; didn't you?"

James looked stunned. "I had no idea! A sport—an Olympic sport at that!" He wasn't able to compute that at all. And he just couldn't imagine people paying $200 a seat to watch two guys playing chess. But then he didn't get the thing about people sitting home watching people fishing on TV either. Somehow the concept of sport must have changed while he was deployed in Eastern Europe. Changing the subject slightly, "What do you think of Spassky saying 'chess is life'?"

"Actually it was Bobby Fisher who said that," Andy corrected gently. "And I never gave it much thought." He wondered if that was what somebody was teaching in a book on chess. A little bit too philosophical for his taste, and he suspected for that of most people. He added, "Ironic isn't it, that chess is an Olympic competitor and not football? The Olympic Committee came to me last year after I was named Grandmaster and pitched me on the 2004 Olympics."

This was news to James. He was aware of the title of Grandmaster. That was what had caught his eye initially on Andy. That and the comparison the world of chess was drawing between Andy and Paul Morphy, who most regarded as the greatest natural chess player in the long history of chess. If it weren't for the fact that Paul Morphy, the American, lived in the mid-19th century, James would probably be sitting at his kitchen table instead.

He had concluded when he developed his theory that just any champion wouldn't do. Too much training, too much form might actually inhibit the perceptions, which James had a hunch would be needed. He knew somehow that the key wouldn't lie in studied moves or historical remembrances. His gut told him that if this theory were true, only someone operating on pure instinct and intuition would be up to the task. Anyway this Olympic thing intrigued him. He had heard rumors that the CIA recruited there. Putting players in international competitions and using the coded, written material that chess would generate, seemed to him now a likely scenario. After all, who would know what really was written in the seemingly undecipherable notations he had plowed through in this book for dummies? He was curious now about Andy, and even more certain.

"What did you tell them?" James asked, trying to sound matter of fact.

"I told them that if they made football an Olympic event, I'd be glad to oblige; but, no thanks on chess." James and Andy both knew that football would never become an Olympic event as it was so decidedly an American game. Judging by the hint of disappointment in Andy's voice as he answered, James deduced that Andy would have liked to "call the plays" in an Olympic gold medal round. *Hell, who wouldn't,* he thought. *That was everyone's dream.*

"Actually, Andy, I was more interested in the Appendix. Seems there are lists of chess federations and Internet sites." The Islamic one in particular had caught his eye. James had been in the field 20 years. History had taught him that if something caught his eye, there was something there. That was what he was paid to do, have his "eye caught." He didn't tell Andy, but the reason he hadn't heard him come in was that, when he was just thumbing through the book and had come across this listing, his heart had skipped a bit, his breathing speeded up and a little shot of adrenalin caused him to flush. And that was the physical indicator that had always foreshadowed the target, and danger. Today, he decided not to say anything to Andy. After all, the Kid was to help him with the chess part of this. The analysis was James'.

And then Andy said the most extraordinary thing, looking James straight in the eye. "I can see why it is, though." James swallowed. Was this a complete non-sequitur, or had Andy guessed his thought? He said nothing, waiting for Andy to continue. He did.

"Yep, one false move and you're dead." Both let that hang there. Andy grabbed two more Oreos and dunked them thoroughly. He continued, "I remember seeing a book once about dangers in chess. I remember the author said that chess's most dangerous moments are often subtle and easily overlooked." Andy stopped, and appeared to be looking at something. James decided to do nothing but observe. He had no idea how long he waited; it seemed as if he hadn't even breathed. Like two soldiers who observed the same enemy at the same instant and were sizing it up, the two sat at the table. Andy broke the moment by asking, "Do you know what Mom is making for dinner?"

"Nope, but I know she ran to the corner to get something she needed," James answered as he patted the book and slipped it into his pocket. It had not escaped him that Andy, too, had mentioned a book.

CHAPTER 8

A few miles away, as the lights of the Capitol Mall were coming on, a meeting was just wrapping up in the Situation Room at the White House. The green light had been given and the interested parties were quickly dispersing to their offices to inform subordinates and staff of the impending action. The President, National Security Advisor and Chief of Staff were, one by one, informing allies and partners of what was coming next. Everyone in the world knew America's reserve following 9/11 was a reflection of her resolve. The world just waited now to see what her opening move would be.

Seven thousand miles away, another meeting of interested parties was breaking up. They, too, were bunkered. And they, too, had had some hard choices to make. It had taken Zawahiri most of the day to totally persuade Usama that this President was indeed different from the previous ones. Whether he was different intrinsically, or whether their exaggerated attack on 9/11 had left him no option, was now a moot point. In fact, it had taken some days before the Doctor himself had calmed down enough to see that the attacks on 9/11 had, in fact, accomplished what he had intended to do.

Once he was certain, he had to convince Atef and Usama. Both were brave, no doubt, and smart, but both were conditioned to anemic responses from the U.S. They were braced for an attack, but they considered it would be limited and short, albeit intense. The Doctor was convinced that that was a delusion. He had carefully poured over the President's address to the Congress and the world. The full transcript was easily obtainable on the Net. What had alarmed him the most was not the rhetoric or the outrage or the threats of "justice." He had expected that. What he had not expected this President to consider, let alone do, was in the section Zawahiri referred to as the Bush Doctrine. Frankly, he was stunned that the world's leaders seemed to be so caught up in the rhetoric that they didn't recognize a sweeping doctrine the likes of which the U.S.—and perhaps, the world—had not seen in a century or more. This President seemed willing to breach the sovereignty of other nations for his nation's security. That was a threshold no Western leader had dared cross in this asymmetric type of war the Doctor had so painstakingly engineered for more that two decades.

Others could laugh or scoff, but the Doctor knew that if this President meant it, it was the least likely move he expected the U.S. to make, and the one he most dreaded. The game would have to become more complex now. And he was disappointed that Usama seemed oblivious to the inevitable outcome of the plan the Secretary of State had laid out. He did have to concede, however, that it made it easier for him to do what he had to do. No one now would be even the least bit suspicious of his next recommendations.

"Usama, the Taliban will fold in a matter of days. They will buy us time, but they will collapse. Not only must we abandon our primary base, but all other bases as well. In less than two months, the Americans and their coalition will have overrun them," he warned his partner. Atef nodded agreement there.

"He's right Usama. Afghanistan is no longer predictable for us. We've got a few feint moves to make, but in the long run, we must find another state, or several," Atef admonished. "Our purpose now must be to successfully disperse and regroup where no one will find us."

"And you know where this is?" Usama pressed.

Atef hedged his bet. "I have several options. I will advise you when we finish the analysis. Meanwhile, know that we, in fact, will be on the move. Do your part well in the studio tomorrow. I believe the Doctor has provided us a brilliant cover." Then he added, as if to end any debate, "And he most definitely has bought us time."

"Do you have an estimate as to how long?"

The Doctor decided to answer that. "Yes, Usama, three, perhaps four years. And I calculate that is sufficient to establish a safe harbor, build communications and recruit what's necessary to replace what we lose."

Bin Laden seemed satisfied as well, and remarked again how he looked forward to their next few days in the studio. He relished the activity itself, and he especially relished making a fool of the Western press. Characteristically, he stroked his long beard and patted his colleagues on the back affectionately.

That's the best of him, Zawahiri mused, *the part I'm going to miss.*

The next morning, before the sun rose, Usama and Zawahiri entered a motion picture production studio five stories below the surface. Just as the sun came up over the very mountain in which the studio was secreted, the two embraced their producer and entered the recording facility.

No one in America seemed to have known, or remembered, that in an interview given a couple of years earlier to an aspiring Arab journalist, Usama Bin Laden had laughingly revealed the fact that he watched American movies. He had commented that he had particularly enjoyed "Wag the Dog." Gambling on that oversight, Zawahiri knew that the next move would create a classic feint—one for the history books—if they ever guessed.

Given the gravity of the situation which prompted this recording session, the two men seemed oddly joyful.

CHAPTER 9

Knowing that they would need maximum flexibility in their escape maneuvers, and that they would need secrecy and calm to reestablish themselves, Zawahiri had their scriptwriter, one of the best India had to offer, create a series of likely scenarios for the next five years. With the Russia-Afghanistan campaign of the 1980's as a backdrop and source of predicted outcomes, there was ample material from which to theorize.

Many of the players of that war were still around, although supporting different sides now. Corporations that had profited from the earlier war, either in weaponry, construction or oil, were still in the area; and their involvement could be anticipated in any future developments in the region. Also, governments and politicians usually had longevity and rarely changed course. Conjecture was easy for a gifted and imaginative writer.

The screenwriter Zawahiri chose had won numerous awards for war and espionage thrillers before he was ostracized by his country for a political propaganda film that had exacerbated the conflict in Kashmir. He probably could have withstood the firestorm of criticism that created within India had it not been for the sudden revelations about his sexual activities and cult societies that had come to light in the ensuing investigation. His marriage dissolved, his career ruined, he still harbored a dark secret that would result in imprisonment if discovered. And it was that fact that had come into the hands of the Doctor. Once the Doctor had "discussed" that fact with him, it had been surprisingly easy to get him to be the head of their media production facility.

In fact, he flourished in the role. He was so eager to please that his creative juices provided some of the best material ever created for subterfuge. But this project today was his masterpiece.

What most governments did not know, though they tried to, was exactly how much wealth Al Qaeda actually had. The Taliban's religious hypocrisy had greatly enhanced not only Bin Laden's wealth, but that of his group as well. Everyone knew that the poppy fields of Afghanistan supplied enormous quantities of heroin to the world's market. And that heroin brought devastation to every nation that traded in it. Since America was a prime target for drugs, and the marketing campaign had been so effective since its inception in the early 1960's, the current Taliban regime was profiting enormously by simply continuing the marketing strategies of predecessors, both in Afghanistan and elsewhere.

The Doctor particularly loathed the Taliban leaders' pious discussions of religion while they fattened their own coffers. He knew they would fight to preserve their drug supply. After all, no one likes to lose their source of income! And it was the hypocrisy of it all that made them his pawns.

The drug money had other benefits, too. Not only did it enable Al Qaeda to keep their recruits in line with the opium the Doctor supplied, but it also enabled them to purchase and build facilities to run their various departments. The facility they were in today was an absolute wonder. And one the Doctor was sure the Americans knew nothing about.

Five stories underground in the Tora Bora area, a massive complex had been established. The film production department was virtually a corporation unto itself. The best propaganda materials in the world were produced there. Nanda Shinoy was a man Al-Zawahiri relied on. Especially now, since their survival depended on what he was doing today.

As Usama and the Doctor entered the make-up trailer, Usama had questions about the scripts. "Do you really think it could get as far-reaching as this in the next two to three years?" he asked Shinoy.

"Sir, it is not my place to evaluate that. It is just my place to make certain that no matter what America does in the next five years, we have enough scenarios 'in the can' that you can release a tape without having your whereabouts detected. And I believe all of the scenarios are possible."

Usama turned to Zawahiri for confirmation. "Usama, we do not know what America may do, but whatever they do, we must convince them that you are alive and somewhere where you are not. We know now that this President is going to keep coming after us. Therefore, we must be ready with messages to discredit him and force a turnover in the American regime when the time comes."

"Yes, I understand. But how will we make it believable three or four years from now?"

Nanda jumped to answer the question. This was where his interest in history and politics came into play. "We know, sir, that American politicians signal years in advance their intention to make a move for the Presidency. I have compiled a list of likely candidates in their next election. Some are senators; one is a congressman; one a governor; and one or two have stated in their university years their intention of one day becoming President. I have watched their progress economically and politically, and I believe I have selected the most likely group. The only thing I apologize for is that you will need to read the whole speech each time in order for us to insert a different candidate's name. Then hopefully we will have referenced the one that actually is chosen."

"I have no problem with that, Nanda," Bin Laden reassured him. "But what if they choose someone we have not even considered to oppose Bush? What if we are successful in killing Bush before the next election? Can you speculate who his party would select?"

"With respect, I have considered who would be advanced in the event of the blessed death of their President. But I assure you both that, even if we cannot anticipate everything the Americans will try, I do have the capability of editing and overlaying in such a way that I can substitute if necessary."

Bin Laden, who was less technically oriented than Zawahiri, smiled with satisfaction.

Zawahiri, however, now wanted to make certain they were covered. "Nanda, this is excellent news. And do you believe you can fool their intelligence agencies when they analyze something to which you have done this?"

"I do, absolutely!" Nanda seemed uncharacteristically confident.

"And your confidence?" the Doctor pressed.

"To be truthful, and yet humble, I believe I know more about production techniques than they do. In a few days we will be doing video recordings using blue screen technology in order to create the illusions of your various whereabouts. I also can use the same type of technology with sound-only recordings as well—scratchiness, gunfire, ambulances, you name it. I can lay it in. Simply put, Ayman, we have more advanced editing expertise, and Indian filmmakers, in general, are more imaginative. I have studied the Americans. That is their weakness. They are unimaginative."

Nanda seemed satisfied with his own explanation, as did Bin Laden. Usama, frankly, was almost salivating at the proposition of prerecording "talks," as he called them, for his followers. He was starting to get impatient. But Zawahiri needed to be certain. This confidence reminded him of the braggadocio most filmmakers had when they had read too many of their own press clippings.

"And if you don't?" he challenged.

This caught Bin Laden's attention and he turned his eyes to hear Nanda's response.

"Even if they catch it, which I doubt, they won't admit it."

"Why?" Bin Laden inserted himself into the issue now.

"Because it is in their best interest for you to be alive and talking. That's the beauty of this. They need you or they need your tapes. We are not going to give them you. They will grab the tapes instead. I'm sure of it."

Inside, Zawahiri was almost gleeful. Nanda had it exactly correct and the Doctor felt confident they could proceed now. "Usama, our friend here is right. He understands them very well," he reassured Bin Laden.

"Good, good. That's what I thought." Usama smiled and patted them both on the back. This was the delicious part of the plot. The plans of the Doctor had made it possible for them to escape, provided the American forces could not detect their immediate whereabouts. He knew he would sacrifice some of his fiercest fighters to keep up the pretense, but his escape and ability to still command Al Qaeda would surely make ultimate victory possible.

Shinoy's scripts would enable Bin Laden to release recordings, seemingly in response to any scenario the Americans might become involved in. That included military actions in Iraq, Iran, Libya, Saudi Arabia, Syria, North Korea, China, the Philippines, Colombia, Indonesia, and the United States. It was quite a list. Shinoy's imagination seemed limitless as to the types of trouble the U.S. military could get themselves into. From helicopters going down, to kidnapped military personnel, to atrocities soldiers might perform, to the deaths of senior commanders, to alliances fractured, there was a matching response from Usama Bin Laden. And each response was written with pinpoint application to possible futures. The attitudes of other nations in the region were also predictable and could be referenced to supply additional authenticity. A skillful mixing up of time sequences to intersperse past known experiences with fictionalized future ones would lend further believability to the broadcast.

And each created the appearance of the presence of Usama, without actually providing "proof of life." Backup plans were in place should actual "proof" become necessary. In all, they were so realistic that Al-Jazeerah would accept them completely and release them, never questioning the time-line. That would allow the top level of Al Qaeda to effect their escape and, with luck, the military forces would be duped into looking for them in places they had long abandoned.

Of course, in order for that plan to work, several of their best facilities had to be sacrificed. The Americans had to believe they were close. And at least one time, they needed to be. Part of Zawahiri's plan was to use intelligence leaks to lure the U.S. forces into a dramatic battle that would attract the press 24/7. Usama, the Doctor and Atef needed to be believably engaged and would have to escape that one time. After that, it could all be smoke and mirrors. The enemy would now believe, through the ferocity of their defenses, that they still remained in the region.

As Usama watched Shinoy set up the audio recordings, he couldn't help admire his own genius at bringing together such a team. Atef's military set-up was sheer genius. The escape route engineered by the Doctor was fool-proof. And Shinoy's cover was unprecedented. Suddenly he laughed in a way he hadn't in many months.

"What?" Zawahiri inquired.

"I just wish I could see their faces when they fail, time after time, to find us. Each attempt increases our mythical proportions. And that increases our ranks and most certainly our benefactors in the United States and Europe."

"Yes, these swine deserve this," the Doctor also laughed. "But, dear friend, you will be able to see it. I assure you there are televisions where we will be sequestered and you will be abreast of their humiliation."

And with one last admonition by Shinoy to sound exhausted and sick, but not beaten, Usama entered the booth, put on the headsets, picked up Scenario One, and gave the performance of his life. The Doctor waited in the control booth where he could monitor the directions being given by Shinoy. It was important that they be perfect. As he listened to Usama's sincere performance, Zawahiri couldn't help but reflect that their leader had missed his calling. For a moment, he regretted what he was going to have to do.

CHAPTER 10

Zawahiri had another reason for staying in the control booth. In order for his plan to work, and for him to come out of it alive, he would have to convince Atef. And to do that, he had to set the stage. So he insisted that Shinoy and Usama work longer than Shinoy would normally have done.

"This is not America with their powder-puff union rules to follow, Nanda," he admonished the director. "We must finish these quickly. Surely you can imagine how much planning our great leader must do now for the upcoming attacks."

"Yes, yes, I do," Shinoy squeaked. "I, for one, do not need a break. I was just thinking that our commander seemed tired."

"We're all tired, my friend. But I know he expressly wants to push this along. And I will take care of him later."

Bin Laden did not hear this exchange. He, in fact, was wrapped up tweaking the writing of one of the scenarios. He was really looking forward to releasing this one about Saddam Hussein. To use each of the forces he despised against one another and to his advantage, suited his well-developed sense of irony. Although he was beginning to feel faint, he trusted his medications and monitoring to the Doctor. He felt blessed to have such a renowned surgeon as his personal physician. He appreciated the medications the Doctor had provided to ease his anxiety and he was convinced now that the Doctor's scheme would work.

Twenty minutes later, Usama Bin Laden collapsed in the sound booth, cutting his head on the stand as his tall frame slipped dead-weight to the ground. The Doctor was first to come to his aid. Although Shinoy was petrified, the Doctor assured him it was not his fault.

"Do not worry; he will be fine. I must administer his glucose drip."

"What happened?" Atef challenged as he raced into the sound booth.

"His blood sugar got too low, Muhammad. He'll be fine. I should have been paying more attention to the fact he hadn't had a meal break," the Doctor lied as he complimented himself on setting the stage.

Since this was not the first time Usama had required attention for his diabetes, everyone calmed down. Usama was taken to his room, where he could receive the drip and rest a bit before continuing.

One person did not calm down. Shinoy was concerned about something. He decided to take it up with Zawahiri, even if it did risk upsetting the Doctor.

"You know, I have some misgivings. But I don't know how to address them."

Zawahiri hoped Shinoy had taken the bait. He encouraged him to continue and to speak frankly.

"None of us wants to consider this, but it is possible that Usama might become totally incapacitated…" his voice trailed.

"Go on," the Doctor encouraged.

Shinoy sighed wearily. "It is also possible he could die or be killed in the stress of the months ahead. I'm sure that won't happen, but he could. And we must plan for that."

"Yes, I agree, but isn't that why we have so many scenarios? Not just to mislead our enemies as to where he is, but also to make them keep looking for him, even if he is dead?"

"Of course, that's what you asked me to write and record. But I'm thinking now we may want another option or two, just to keep them guessing, or to make them guess wrongly. I would like to do several tracks with you delivering the message. I think that gives you more options, and mixes up the game some more."

He took the bait, Zawahiri thought. In order for this to work, it was better that the idea came from another team member. He smiled fleetingly as he observed how smoothly the set-up of the Queen was going. It would be easier to sacrifice the Queen than he had hoped. "Yes, I see; that's a good idea. So, you're going to write a message or two for me to deliver in the event Usama feels it is necessary?" he covered quickly.

"Exactly."

When they finished the two days of recording, there were 109 separate messages ready for propaganda; 79 by Bin Laden himself, and 30 by Zawahiri. Their video crews had also been busy for days with multiple crews filming settings throughout Afghanistan and its surrounding countries' borders.

Nanda Shinoy had used his blue screen technology to fabricate various locations where Bin Laden appeared to be delivering messages on camera. No one would know that he was just shuffling back and forth off the blue screen set. Later, in editing, Shinoy would add the filmed backdrops to confuse the viewer as to the location of the world's most wanted man.

Nanda was totally absorbed in the editing process. It was his intention to have the final cuts ready by the next day so that the audio and video tapes could be secreted, and copies placed in the safe house that would release them on command to Al-Jazeerah. Since it was Bin Laden's voice, analysis of the tapes by the Americans would authenticate them. He felt confident that would confuse them enough so the rest of their propaganda machinery would make tremendous inroads in the breaking of the spirit of their enemy. *After all, isn't that what propaganda is for?* Nanda mused.

He was most proud, however, of what he had set up for the next day. Shinoy realized it would be necessary to put Bin Laden on camera at least one more time, to reassure his followers that he was alive and to mislead the Americans. For weeks, his set design people had been building an exact replica of the home of Sheik Al-Haby. Since the Americans' invasion of Afghanistan had begun, he wanted to minimize the risk to Bin Laden, so he had sent his set design team to the Sheik's home. They had taken extensive video of the interior and had built what appeared to be his living area on a sound stage in their studio.

As he looked it over, it was totally realistic. The plan was that this video would be "discovered." The enemy would then be looking for Bin Laden in the area of the Sheik, once they ascertained who the Sheik was. Certainly that would provide a few months of amusement! The more difficult part had been to persuade the Sheik, who had been partially paralyzed in the fight against the Russians, to make the trip to an unknown destination. Shinoy had left that up to the extraordinarily persuasive talents of the Doctor.

However the Doctor had done it, the Sheik had agreed to be transported blindfolded to their studio bunker. There they would stage a meeting between the Sheik, Bin Laden and Zawahiri showing the men congratulating each other for their accomplishments on 9/11. The script he had written allowed Bin Laden to improvise his responses. He was certain the Sheik would be so honored to even be sitting with him that he would be lavish in his praise and direct in his religiosity. Since this was Bin Laden's strong point, he felt the message of his religious fervor would be especially inspiring to their intended audience.

Nanda's assistant had just informed him of the arrival of the Sheik. He was resting comfortably in an isolated area of the bunker where no one would see him. They were expected to begin shooting the "home video" right after prayers. His production skills as a cameraman would be tested tonight. It had to appear as if it were being taken by some member of the Sheik's household to be kept for his personal memorabilia. How it would be discovered, or what would prompt someone to go to the Sheik's residence, was in the capable hands of Zawahiri. Shinoy was grateful that all he had to do was create these illusions—not get involved in the intricacies of intelligence and counterintelligence.

Four hours later, the cast arrived on the set to film what would become a pivotal release in the public relations aspect of the war. Bin Laden arrived first. He was excited about being on camera again. In fact, he was almost obsessed with being on camera and especially looked forward to this subterfuge. Since the Sheik had undergone considerable inconvenience and pain in making this long trip, Bin Laden wanted to personally welcome him to his "home." He couldn't wait to see the old warrior's expression when he walked into the replica of his own home. He was supremely confident that the Sheik would be impressed and that he could pull off the deception.

The Sheik arrived with little or no make-up on. Special lighting and make-up effects had been designed by Shinoy's team to give the appearance of absolute home-video quality. Bin Laden and the Sheik were genuinely glad to see each other. Their warm embrace gave Shinoy confidence. *No one will detect that this is a staged event,* he complimented himself. The emotions were real. Only the location was a deception.

The next part was trickier. If anything were to go wrong, it would be with the addition of the next character in his "play." He was experiencing genuine fear, knowing the jeopardy to the actor if he failed. He didn't dare show any fear, however, as Ayman Al-Zawahiri was in the control booth with him, hidden behind a two-way glass—to hide not only his presence, but also his identity.

In the next moment, something they had done many times before was about to be repeated, but with a new wrinkle. Before, it had only been Zawahiri and Bin Laden together. Today there would be additional people and he feared the deception might be discovered. He secretly said a prayer to his own God.

The actor playing Zawahiri stepped onto the set and warmly greeted the Sheik. Like others around the world, the Sheik had only seen video of Bin Laden and Zawahiri together. He, therefore, had no idea that the short, round man who greeted him as the Doctor was, in fact, Nanda's father. Zawahiri had been using him as his camera double for the years he and Bin Laden had been making public appearances. The press of the entire world had fallen for it. Only the most cautious of reporters couched their commentary with "the man in the video with Bin Laden is believed to be his right-hand man, Ayman Al-Zawahiri." The others accepted this short, rotund, cherubic, and scholarly-looking man as the Doctor.

Nanda feared for his life, not just because his father might fail in the performance, but also because he might succeed. Everyone in the world was looking for Zawahiri and they mistakenly assumed this man he loved was Zawahiri. It was a terrible no-win situation. His only comfort was that his father had insisted. When Zawahiri had spotted in Nanda's father a resemblance to uncles on his own mother's side, he had concocted the idea of a double, and offered it to the father and son as a means of freeing Nanda from the blackmail Zawahiri was holding over his head. Nanda believed that Zawahiri valued his own life, and that he was sincere in striking a deal to end the blackmail. Still, he felt shame sometimes for involving his father in a ruse that was so dangerous.

But his father loved his only son. His mother had died years earlier, and Nanda's father had doted on him. The man's particular features and coloring did enable him to pass for an Egyptian. It was not difficult to imagine that the Zawahiri of years ago, in prison photos or intelligence film, could have matured into middle age with this look of a gentle scholar. Certainly, the turban worked to further confound a positive identification. So in every film the enemy had, the person identified as Zawahiri was, in fact, an Indian taxi driver who was simply trying to save his son from prison and disgrace.

Only five people knew that the man on the videos with Bin Laden over the past few years was not Ayman Al-Zawahiri. In 1998, Zawahiri's brother, Mohammed, had been captured and had disappeared after extradition to Egypt. The Doctor was certain he had been killed by the Egyptians and they had his DNA. To save himself from identification in the event of capture, Ayman Al-Zawahiri had devised a deception, and Shinoy had aided him in perpetrating it.

Shinoy had to admit it was one of the most brilliant moves he had ever made. It was almost existential, for it had left the entire intelligence community not knowing what the second most-wanted man in the world even looked like. And that was a fact not one of those agencies could admit to their bosses.

The Doctor, too, had appreciated the sheer audacity of it. The file he had on Shinoy was secreted away in a bank vault. As long as the producer/director/screenwriter delivered his particular brand of cinematic deception, the file would be given to him later. He would have earned it.

Shinoy felt he could trust Zawahiri on this. He had always seen him follow-through on promises if the people delivered. He had no reason to believe otherwise now. So, on the back side of the glass, a much taller, angular man watched as the drama unfolded. The actor playing the Doctor performed his subdued part perfectly, barely speaking. If the Americans ran an analysis of the voice, however, they would assume it was Zawahiri because, just two days earlier, the same actor had read the new scripts Shinoy had prepared for Zawahiri. And it had been the actor who had been videoed in the many previous tapings of Bin Laden and Zawahiri, showing them with recruits or giving speeches. Of particular delight to the Doctor, was the fact that the DNA would obviously not match, nor would any fingerprints that might be secured from Nanda's father. It was only remotely possible that Zawahiri would be detected and captured, but if he were, his fingerprints would not match those of the man the intelligence communities thought to be him.

To further secure himself, a sympathizer inside the Egyptian intelligence forces (for a handsome fee) had substituted DNA slides and fingerprints of a John Doe for those of Mohammed Al-Zawahiri. The sympathizer later drowned in the Nile quite mysteriously. The Doctor smiled as he reflected, *It is all about money, after all.*

After Sheik Al-Haby had left the set and returned to his room, the Doctor returned to the security room, logged on to the computer he used, and pulled up the encrypted file he had created a short time before. Briefly, he studied the three-dimensional model he had created. Then with his mouse, he highlighted the fourth level of the model. He studied the object which resembled a castle for a moment, labeled it "the Sheik," hit "save," and closed the application. Then, he downloaded the entire file to his personal laptop. He would have preferred the security of the safe vault of the underground computer, but this would have to do. It was time to move.

He knew that this entire complex would soon be destroyed. If luck were with them, the Americans might never find the computer. Perhaps their own bunker busting bombs would be so powerful as to obliterate everything. But, if they were found intact, he remained confident that, even if they reconstructed the contents of the hard drive, no one would have any idea what the model actually represented, let alone what its purpose was.

No need for any medications tonight, he mused, as he bathed and prepared for bed. Ayman Al-Zawahiri slept soundly that night.

CHAPTER 11

Andy had plotted every military move he had access to. He and James scoured every cable news network, every foreign television network they had access to, and all of the military data the Pentagon released as sensitive, but not top secret. This alone occupied hours daily. James' job was to review data and extract anything which his analyst's mind told him might be significant. He understood well that you should never believe what you read in newspapers or hear on the news. At best, it is a partial truth. He further knew that in times of war, the news would be deliberately manipulated by the government to fool the enemy. Generally, the press themselves did not know they were part of the deception.

So, for James, this was an excruciating but challenging task. He had to identify the reports that were not only true, but also likely relevant to the probable American strategy and tactics that would not be revealed to the enemy in some chummy press conference. He knew very well, after years in the Cold War, that war is deception. He just prayed that America was perpetrating some deception here.

Whatever he found, he turned over to Andy. Andy's chess board was on computer and also on the table. He preferred to work with the actual chess board, though. All moves were meticulously documented traditionally so that any chess player could follow the progress of the game. White was their team and Black was Zawahiri. If the U.S. moved, he would identify what piece the move most resembled and move it. Then he would wait to find in James' later materials what move Black did in response. All the while, he was looking for patterns of past games. Since Andy was a natural chess player, he had to actually study the history of famous chess matches to see if there was anything there. It was when he was studying danger areas that he had his first big realization. And that was painful.

It was December and every news channel was competing for a ring-side seat for what was expected to be the show-down with Usama Bin Laden in the mountains near Tora Bora. The Taliban had fallen. Their precipitous collapse had been almost too easy. Despite the fire power brought to bear against them, something rang untrue to Andy. The quarterback recognized that the defensive line collapsed uncharacteristically. It haunted him, but analysis wasn't his job. He told himself he had to address it with James.

Before James could even set his coffee down, let alone get his coat off, Andy confessed. "I think we've done the whole game backwards, James." There, he had said it.

"What do you mean?" James eased in.

"We've plotted our moves, and waited to plot Black's response. I think it's the other way around."

"Kid, I don't know what you are talking about."

"The line is not a defensive line. It's offensive." It tumbled out now. "They have been making the first moves, and the U.S. actions have been the response. We have done just what Black wants us to do."

"You're joking," James challenged, knowing the Kid wasn't, by the look of him.

"No sir, it's a set-up. He's provoking us and then making it look as if we provoked him." Andy got out the computer record of the moves from the very first moment of the invasion of Afghanistan. He then changed the sequence to make Black's move the first move. Now, instead of America's breathtakingly rapid destruction of the Taliban military structure being the offense, every move was actually in response to a move the enemy was making. The effect was shocking to James. He almost felt his head jerk as the paradigm shifted. Making Black the cause point, rather than the response point distorted everything. Until that moment, he thought the U.S. had the initiative. Now it was evident the United States was merely reacting to the enemy's initiative. And to make matters worse, it appeared the enemy was setting the United States up to win.

Andy could see James was working with it. The grimace on his face told him he probably should have at least waited until James had had a cup of coffee or two. Too late now. They replayed the game, starting with Black. James sat back dumbfounded.

"I don't get it. This makes no sense. Surely they can't be setting us up for a victory. Their lives are at stake here. Why would they do that?"

Andy hesitated for a moment, and then advanced his theory. "I don't know the why, James. But it confirms something that has been gnawing away at me."

"What?"

"For some days now, I've had the feeling that Black forfeited the game."

"Jesus!" James exclaimed. "When?"

"Early, maybe even with their first move." Andy let that sink in. "I think Zawahiri forfeited, deliberately and early. The rest has all been a feint."

James had come to trust this bright young man. He dreaded asking the next question."Then, what's he doing?"

"You remember when you told me about the Israeli you spoke with who said he's always several moves out in front?"

"Yes, I do. So?"

"Well, I don't think he's several moves out in front." He stopped, and then decided he'd better tell James. "I think he's several games out in front."

"Games? Did you say games?" James was almost shouting now.

"Yes, sir. He forfeited the first game and has been playing another. And the Americans don't know that. They think he's still playing a military game and that they are winning."

"Well, what kind of game is he playing if it's not a military game?"

"That's what we're going to have to figure out, James. What game is Ayman Al-Zawahiri playing?"

Then, as if that weren't enough, Andy added, "We'd better figure it out, and we'd better get on that game board." And with that, Andy wiped the first chess game board clean. And as he did so, American and Coalition war planes and ground forces closed in on Tora Bora. And all the American media watched.

CHAPTER 12

The milk flowed; the beautiful Virgin disappeared into a pastel haze of flowers and leaves. Her fragrance, and that of the flowers, intoxicated Ayman. He reached for her, but she had vanished.

Suddenly the knife-like pain in his stomach ended his hallucination and brought him up out of the deep sleep. It was the first time he had slept without medication for his ulcer in quite awhile and he was disappointed to be haunted still by the Virgin. During his imprisonment in Egypt for complicity in the assassination of President Anwar Sadat, he had started having these hallucinations. It was reported that many of those who were being tortured suffered these dreams. That was what had given him the idea of drugging new recruits with heroin, and staging a replication of these hallucinations he remembered so well. Then he would implant the idea into the neophyte that, if he performed a suicide attack, he would be rewarded by a return trip to this Heaven he had just experienced. And it had worked. With a modicum of expense for drugs, and a set that could be used over and over again, he was able to keep these young men passionate and willing to commit suicide missions.

He had learned much in those three years of imprisonment. He had learned that no one could be trusted, and that his particular vision of religion must take over the world. He had concluded further that he was the rightful leader and, despite the fact that he had been regarded as one incapable of leading, he had concluded that he was the ruler—and no one else.

It was his torture that had brought him to this. The superficial investigator would have concluded that three years of daily torture had radicalized him. But that was not it. Ironically, his torture had led him to awareness about the mind that caused him to believe he could pull it off. By rights, he should have died there in that prison. The beatings, the naked humiliations, the mad dogs, the terrifying hoods, the electric shocks—all should have made him deranged, at the very least.

But Ayman Al-Zawahiri was too smart for that. Instead, he had used the beatings as a chance to understand the mind and how to control it. Whether it was one of the electric shocks the Egyptians were prone to inflicting, or divine intervention, he had found himself one day outside his body. The guards were beating him mercilessly one afternoon in the late autumn when Ayman suddenly found himself disengaged from his body, watching the torture. His mind had separated from the incident and was somehow protecting him from experiencing the agonizing pain.

That resurrected his interest in psychiatry—most especially a particular brand of psychiatry which specialized in pain, drugs, hypnosis and the subsequent planting of instructions or predilections in the victim. However he had stepped outside his body, he was grateful, for it enabled him to watch what the interrogators were doing, without being immersed in the pain and control they were exercising. Oh yes, he had learned a lot during those three years!

And, he had discovered how to neutralize a force. Almost by accident, he had learned how to make himself immune to the power of his interrogators. When they were not physically torturing him and others, he observed that they engaged in a process of rendering a person incapable of making decisions. By doing that, the person was made powerless. The mechanism was so simple it was almost diabolical. First you persuade the individual over time that nothing is either decidedly "yes" or decidedly "no." You persuade him that there are two sides to any argument, and only two, and that they are equally balanced. He moves toward the middle, where maybe something is desirable or maybe it isn't. When the individual is finally in the middle, he cannot decide. When he cannot decide, he commits no action. And, when he commits no action, he loses self confidence.

Ayman thought that was a brilliant way to handle enemies and dissidents. Find a way to render them actionless. Their lack of action would then cave-in their confidence. Their lack of confidence would come full circle and make them incapable of deciding. *You almost don't need a guard or counterforce,* he had concluded. *The person renders himself impotent in this constant circuit of indecision, inaction, and lack of confidence.* All one had to do was become expert at how to get people to always and equally look at both sides of an issue, and they would move themselves to the middle where everything was a "maybe."

The moment Ayman Al-Zawahiri had discovered that, albeit through the pain of three years of harsh incarceration, he knew that he could rule the world. Ruling Al Qaeda was now only a matter of hours away. Ruling the world of Islam was assured. No clerics could successfully challenge him. All that remained was the United States.

He and Bin Laden were in complete agreement that the United States was the true enemy of their movement. Its corrupt, self-indulgent, hedonistic culture had created a world-wide monster that would destroy their strict religious rule, called Shari'a. The people could only be controlled through strict application of religious law and the one enemy of that control was freedom. Both clearly understood that it was America's freedom that made her so dangerous. Her people were free to pursue Hedonism; to act selfishly and godlessly; to satisfy their greed; to participate in, and glorify debauchery and sexual perversion. It was their freedom that allowed all this to exist and spread like a venereal disease, continent by continent.

On that they agreed. But that was all. Bin Laden felt that the United States had to be destroyed and he was planning one ill-conceived attack after another. Zawahiri had had enough of ill-conceived plans. After all, he had had no real part in the assassination of Sadat. He felt it was impetuous and ill thought out. Nothing but devastation could ensue from it. He had been right. And he had reaped the whirlwind just by being connected to the plotters and assassins.

September 11th was the same in his mind. It was rash, and they would all reap the whirlwind. Only this time, he was not going to prison or endure torture for anyone. This was his opportunity to take control and handle America in the simpler, safer way. As a result of the torture he had endured, he had betrayed his closest friend in that prison in Egypt. And he had been betrayed. That was the way of their cause, he concluded. Only one thing was for sure: Ayman Al-Zawahiri was never going to be the soft-spoken, jovial poet his movement was used to. No one would ever think of him that way again. He knew the Israeli intelligence agencies sought him. He relished the idea that they regarded him as a psychopath, so dangerous they didn't even know what to do with him. That reputation, like that of the Hashashin one thousand years earlier, insured his survival.

And he felt his plan for the United States was fool-proof. He did not have to destroy the United States. He knew that was a military impossibility. All he had to do was neutralize them. And since the early 1990's he had been in the process of doing just that. What was even more gratifying was the fact that he was certain they would never guess what was being done to them—until it was too late.

He remembered a story his father had told him one day in their home on the poor side of Maadi, on the banks of the Nile. His mother's family discussed radical politics, and was active in the revolutionary changes taking place in secular Egypt. He had never forgotten the day at the dinner table when his father had asked him if he knew how to cook a frog. Ayman was only 11 at the time and had no answer. Without even interrupting his eating the dessert Ayman's mother had prepared, his father had coached, "You place him in a pan of cold water on the stove. Then you turn on the heat. By the time the water is hot enough that the frog knows it is in danger, it is too weak and dulled by the heat to leap out." He had never forgotten that.

Four years later, unbeknownst to his family or friends, Ayman Al-Zawahiri formed an underground cell, and began his plan to bring down the Egyptian government. He was 15.

And now, 35 years later, it was all about to culminate in the mountain passes of Afghanistan. He shook off the pain of his ulcer and swallowed another of the alkaline tablets he kept for such a need. He despised the nightmare of the Virgin. But there was no time to dwell on that now.

He and Usama, along with Al Qaeda's doctors, department heads and Atef, were about to escape from the American trap. The Khyber Pass was not an option. They would not go to Peshawar this time. The alliance Musharraf had struck with the

Americans made the situation in Pakistan too unpredictable. They knew their cave complexes in Hindu Kush would be overrun, or demolished by bombs. So they prepared to escape on foot through rough terrain, to separate safe houses. It had to appear as if they were in Tora Bora in order for this to work. And that meant sacrificing some of their best men in order to lure the enemy's forces into the area and to convince them that the "big catch" was at hand. The fighting would be fierce that day, and in the days to come. Their colleagues would die, pretending to protect Usama. The world press would follow every move. In the end, Usama would have left long before, eluding the Special Forces in the same way he had eluded the Russians two decades earlier.

For the military, it would be just a disappointment. They would regroup. But for the media, it would be a humiliation and they would need a scapegoat. American intelligence would be discredited once again. That was the plan.

The Doctor had prepared Usama for an arduous journey. He had persuaded him to send his family out earlier, ostensibly to prevent any possible injury to them. The trail would be treacherous, the weather forbidding and the possibility of detection and ambush constant. Zawahiri administered Usama's meds making sure he had sufficient hydration to keep pace. Then he shouldered his medical pouch and his laptop, adjusted his turban, and followed Bin Laden out of camp. As they left their cave compound and inhaled the sharp cold air, Zawahiri could see Bin Laden brace himself. Atef led. Zawahiri stayed always where he could observe any nuances in Bin Laden's movements. In fact, he was waiting for the physical sign that would enable him to administer a particular drip to Usama.

Today was the day. He regretted that he had to do this. But Usama's determination to make everyone on Planet Earth embrace Islam was not only ill-conceived, it was insane in the eyes of the Doctor. He had no desire to conquer the world for Islam. He intended only to rule. And for that goal, Usama was now a liability. That, and the fact that he truly was deteriorating physically, was the justification the Doctor used in his own mind to make the next deeds palatable.

CHAPTER 13

The traffic on Interstate 66 was agonizingly slow. Washington, D.C. was experiencing one of its never-prepared-for snow storms. It had always fascinated James that, despite the fact that the city had regular snow fall during the winter months, it was never prepared with the equipment necessary to handle the situations. To him, it seemed as if the city had an identity crisis and viewed itself as a Southern city, incapable of being disrupted by anything as mundane as regular snowfall.

So tonight's creeping pace on the Beltway and I-66 was no surprise to James. He laughed as he saw drivers waving to each other with one finger, and wondered how they could possibly think that would make a difference. He could see that America was slipping back into its old habits of incivility. The weeks following 9/11 had aroused a kindness in the American people, one that James had not experienced since his boyhood in a small town in upstate New York. It had gone beyond a shared grief. He believed it was a shared decency, and for a moment, he remembered why he had taken his life in the direction it had gone—to preserve that decency.

It seemed only yesterday that he was a sophomore at the University of Wisconsin, studying Eastern European languages. He, like so many of his generation, had been inspired by John F. Kennedy's invocation to "ask what you can do for your country." He was not even a teenager when he and his family sat in front of their black and white TV and heard that President address the nation during those treacherous 13 days in October.

Funny, but as he looked back now, James could see that it was then that he had decided to save the world. His voice had not yet changed and he didn't even weigh 100 pounds, but he had decided to defeat that enemy because he never wanted to see his mother so afraid again. And he never wanted to feel that helpless again.

It had been his intention to study languages and then secure a job at the United Nations, where his abilities as an interpreter could contribute to bringing about peace and stability. But in 1969, all that changed. "The War at Home," as it was called, was occurring on the Madison campus of the University of Wisconsin. Under siege, and under martial law for nearly two semesters, James was struggling to even complete his courses. The main street was boarded up. Merchants had given up trying to keep store-front windows in the face of almost weekly anti-war protests, breaking glass, and occasional fire-bombings.

During one of those protest marches to the Capitol at the end of State Street, James had decided to follow along to see what was happening. Whether it was because he was standing outside the protest, or whether it was because it was just his time to see, that night he had spotted it. The presence of demonstrators too old to be graduate students, and too experienced to be "just kids" caught up in the violence. That night he *knew* that those agitators had come from somewhere else, and that they were using these thousands of others for a purpose. That night James decided to chase the "enemy within" back into its hole. The next day, he quietly packed up his things, left the University of Wisconsin, and drove to Washington, D.C. Two weeks later, he was in training with the Central Intelligence Agency.

Now, 30 years later, he felt that decency he had tried so hard to preserve slipping away as people fought for their 30 feet of concrete. He had heard a news clip on the radio where the President had told Senator Schumer from New York if Americans forgot 9/11 by the Super Bowl, we were going to lose this thing. It bothered him, not as a concerned citizen, but as an analyst. And he was reminded of Andy's warning that they had better figure out what game Zawahiri was playing and get on that game board.

He took a long, deep breath; sucked it up; and resolved to do battle with his own boss. Meanwhile, he noticed a Walgreen's off the next exit and decided to stop. Twenty minutes later, he pulled up in front of Kelly and Andy's house with a shopping bag in hand.

As he approached the front door, he could see the two of them setting up a modest Christmas tree in the living room window. *Two simple Americans celebrating a tradition,* he thought as he rang the bell.

Kelly answered. "Hi James; we're running a little behind. Christmas parties, you know. I always have unexpected clients at the last minute."

"No problem." He handed her the bag a little awkwardly. "I thought this might save you some time."

Kelly looked inside and eagerly pulled out the two boxes of Christmas tree lights. She had been complaining the night before that one or more of her strings were out and that she didn't look forward to having to find which bulbs were at fault. She looked relieved to see all new lights.

"Thank you," she smiled. James thought she looked pleased. She definitely looked tired, though.

"Let me and the Kid do that," he offered. "I can see you've put in a long day. What do you say I order in a pizza?"

"Really?" She thought about it for a minute. "Andy loves pizza. Me, too."

Andy had overheard, and as he grabbed the light boxes, he said, "Great!" James didn't know whether he meant the lights or the pizza. But it didn't matter. He could see Andy was happy. And, for the briefest moment, James felt as if he had a family.

Later, when the lights were up and the pizza box was empty save for one piece, he sat quietly watching Andy and Kelly carefully pick ornaments out of a box and place them on the tree. He could see by how tenderly they each handled them that every ornament must have had a story. That's what made families, you see, little stories. James never had that. What he chose to do during the Cold War and after left no room for family. His own parents had passed away years ago while he was in East Berlin. He was not even contacted about it, and only learned of their passing when he came "out." In his heart, though, he knew they would have understood.

So tonight, as ordinary as it had been, had been a highlight for James. And he was resolved to protect this for others. "Time to work, Kid."

"Okay." Andy always seemed game. James noticed, however, that he had dark circles around his eyes and that the phone hadn't rung as often for him. Usually the girls called every night, turning Kelly into a virtual secretary. He wondered just how far Andy had withdrawn from his normal life.

Their team had won the conference title. It had been quite a game, and Andy, quite the hero. James had been there in the stands cheering like the rest of the community as their team took the first conference title in 25 years. Now that the rigorous practice schedule was over, James would have expected Andy to look more rested, not less. He knew this project was taking its toll. And he dreaded bringing this up.

"Kid, let's go to the basement. I need to talk to you."

"Sure. See you in the morning, Mom."

Once they were safely inside their compartment James broke the news to Andy. "What you were talking about yesterday…I think you're right. And I think I know what game he is playing now. I've seen it before. But I didn't realize it until my drive out here tonight."

"Great. What's the game board?" Andy seemed invigorated.

James pulled a small piece of paper out of his pocket. He was famous for jotting ideas down on scraps while he was driving. The writing was unsteady, obviously done hurriedly in traffic, but Andy could read it. He studied the sheet for a minute; then he whistled. "This should be challenging," was all he said as he sat down to pull the latest press clippings.

"We're going to have to brief Whitney on your conclusions," James added. He wondered if the Kid was up to doing his first briefing to a CIA chief, and he wondered if Whitney's imagination was up to the task. This one was going to be a stretch.

"You have got to be kidding!" Whitney bellowed, as Andy finished telling the boss what he had told James. The Kid flinched, but held his ground.

"No sir, I wish I were."

"James, what in the hell do you think I'm going to tell the guys upstairs? What makes you think they'll believe this?" he challenged angrily.

Very matter-of-factly James answered, with steely resolve. "I don't know how you're going to tell them, but I do know what else you're going to tell them. We didn't get hit on 9/11 because of lack of awareness of their intentions. We got hit because of a lack of imagination. And we had better get goddamned creative if we are going to win this thing!" He waited for a moment to let that sink in and added, "That's what you're going to tell those old farts, you old fart."

Whitney didn't know whether he had been insulted or not. He decided to take it diplomatically. "All right. All right. I'll figure it out. I'll do my best."

James accepted that. But if he had not been so tired, he, as an analyst, would not have missed the significant clue. Imbedded in Whitney's comment was the reason the United States was behind in the game, an endemic flaw. And no one noticed. The consequences of not noticing would prove to be catastrophic.

CHAPTER 14

"Is he ready?" Bin Laden asked, sinking to the cold ground for a rest.

"Yes. He's waiting for your orders," Atef answered as he lowered himself to a sitting position beside Bin Laden. "I believe we should stop here long enough for the Doctor to administer your drip."

Bin Laden agreed. While Zawahiri squatted next to him and began the ritual of the glucose drip, it was obvious to the group that their leader was weaker today than usual. It had been an arduous climb, mostly in the dark and bitter cold, without the aid of night vision equipment.

What was particularly disturbing to Bin Laden was the intensity of the bombardments. He was miles from where the Americans were bombing and shelling, but the repercussions and reverberations were so intense they had trouble maintaining their footing. No one wanted to discuss the unspeakable horror this must be creating at the ground zero point. Each knew that at prayers they would pray for the souls of their fellows who were dying today in the charade.

"You were right, dear friend," Bin Laden volunteered suddenly.

"About what?" The Doctor queried as he prepared the needle.

"The Americans." He seemed to want to say more, but instead he merely stroked his beard, which was now thinning and gray. He was still young in years, but the actions they were dramatizing now were a thousand years old. And Bin Laden looked as if he had walked every step of those years.

As if to punctuate that, the earth jolted again just as Zawahiri prepared to insert the needle. He hesitated, then tried again. Again the earth reverberated in response to the bombardments in the distance. Small rocks and sand loosened inside the cave and slid down the walls onto their heads.

Finally Bin Laden joked, "Perhaps if you stop trying to stick me, the Americans will stop the bombing." And as if on suggestion, there was a pause in the aerial assault. They all laughed and Zawahiri successfully inserted and taped the needle. Then he stood and personally held the drip. Their treacherous escape route did not really allow for hospital stands. They were bulky and awkward and would be easily noticed by any indigenous people they came in contact with.

Meeting people on their path was not the problem. Being recognized was. So the Doctor had explained to Usama that the last four to five days would be crude, but effective. Bin Laden had no worries whatsoever, as his colleague was not only a brilliant surgeon, but a pharmacologist as well. He knew he was safe in the care of the Doctor.

Once the glucose had taken effect and normalized his blood sugar level, Bin Laden wanted to finalize their plans. "I want principals, no seconds," he announced. With that command all but Atef, the Doctor, the public relations officer and the Doctor's double were excused from the crude cave and literally sent out into the cold to post watch. Then they summoned him.

As Zarqawi stooped to enter the cave, he noticed Bin Laden holding a piece of paper. Just before they had departed their main complex, a messenger had returned with the answer they had expected. Their enemy would be their ally in this next plot. Bin Laden had calculated correctly this man's greed and his hatred of the countries they were about to bring down.

"Zarqawi, please sit," Bin Laden graciously offered. "We are traveling light, as you know, but I am sure we have something we could offer you."

"I require nothing, thank you. To be honest I'm most anxious to know how I may be of assistance." Zarqawi was respectful, but all knew that he was an intelligent, hot-tempered and ambitious terrorist. Tonight he sensed that he was about to be given an assignment that would elevate him in the levels of command and enhance his position in the folklore. And he was ready.

"We do not have much time," Bin Laden began softly. "Your assignment is imperative to the successful establishment of new host countries for Al Qaeda."

Zarqawi stared only at Bin Laden. He did not blink. But, he was listening intently.

"Our stay in Afghanistan is coming to an end. We will need new bases and we will need infrastructure. Sometime in the next few days we will send you to Iraq."

Zarqawi was stunned by this, but he knew enough to just wait. There would be more and he must show no signs of weakness now. Bin Laden continued, never taking his eyes off this young firebrand.

"Shortly, we will reinsert you into the hot zone. Our public relations team will put out the word that you have been injured. You will be transported to Iraq, where the Dictator there has agreed to give you asylum in order to be hospitalized and heal your life-threatening wounds. Your recuperation will require you to remain in Iraq for sometime. While there, you will be in the care of a hospital run by the Dictator's two sons."

Bin Laden paused for a moment, as if to inhale his next idea. Then he added in an almost fatherly fashion, "Do not trust either the father or his sons. We will dispose of them as part of a larger plan that you will never be privy to. But make no mistake: they will be taken care of." The steely resolve in his voice was something Zarqawi had never heard before. He knew not to even try to guess the greater plan, rather to just concentrate on his part in it.

"In the coming years, you will be in a position to disrupt and recruit and establish vital training camps for us in the country of Iraq." Bin Laden painfully leaned across and handed Zarqawi the piece of paper he had been holding. "This is your contact person. When we wish to send instructions or changes, we will use this contact. Should you need to contact us, use this person. Memorize it and we will destroy it before you leave this chamber."

Zarqawi did as he was commanded. Quickly he memorized the data and returned the paper to Bin Laden who burned it.

Zarqawi felt dizzy. Al Qaeda was cellular in structure. No one cell knew what the other cells were doing, or the membership in each cell. He knew he could not know the whole plan, but he was staggered to discover that he was being put in charge of his own cell. And it appeared to him as if his cell was the nucleus of an entire country. For a fleeting moment, he saw his name in the headlines of CNN.

"One thing you should know," Atef added, "It will be perhaps a year or more before the Dictator is no longer there."

Imprudently Zarqawi asked, "Where is he going?"

With no noticeable change whatsoever, Atef ignored the question and continued, "Do not engage in any activities until he is gone. That is imperative. You are to wait; you are to report to us what you see and hear; but you are not to act in any way to draw attention to yourself. Understood?"

"Understood." Zarqawi felt rebuffed. "I am honored and humbled that you would entrust me with this. And I assure you I will not let you down."

"We are confident of that, son. And we know that in the years ahead our cause will be advanced tremendously by the work you soon will do in this new country. Meanwhile, enjoy Baghdad. We understand it is a beautiful city. Allah be with you."

And, with that, Zarqawi was excused. He was proud and ready for the challenge. Little did he know the controversy and confusion his name would stir up in the years ahead. For now, he was giddy at the opportunity he had been handed. Surprisingly, he went right to sleep, confident that now his career was truly beginning.

A few hours later Zarqawi was awakened, taken by two second lieutenants and reinserted into the hot zone. Immediately, an ambulance arrived to pick him up and begin his journey into the annals of terrorist history. Bin Laden and Zawahiri were confident that this would work. In fact they were jubilant, given the information the Iraqi intelligence officer had given them when he returned with the Dictator's answer.

Shuttles had been going back and forth between Baghdad and Kandahar for more than two years. It was clear to everyone that the Dictator had a stake in the game, would use his money liberally to acquire weapons, and aid other neighboring states in acquiring weapons systems that he would later want. No one doubted that, when he had enough of the materials he needed, he would launch a lethal and devastating attack upon Israel. Knowing Israel's response capability, those who dealt with the Dictator knew also that the Dictator would need to be dealt with. And it appeared this was his time. Certainly no one would mourn, and no one would object or intervene. This man was feared and despised. And his bullying days were almost over.

What Al Qaeda knew, but they doubted Western intelligence knew, was the Dictator had been secretly destroying his chemical and biological stock that was out of date and unusable. Some of the materials were so unstable that the Dictator knew his own army would not be able to deploy them without killing themselves. The fact that the Dictator was doing this secretly, taunting the UN, and playing games with their inspectors, was actually deliciously diabolical from the point of view of Ayman Al-Zawahiri. He watched with admiration as the self-professed disciple of Stalin submitted to UN resolutions, then violated them, then submitted again, and then expelled inspectors altogether.

There was only one conclusion intelligence officers would reach and that was the Dictator still had the weapons the UN wanted destroyed. The reality was the Dictator had destroyed the worthless ones and was using them as bait in his game of cat and mouse. The actual biological strains necessary to resume biological warfare had been sold to another country and transported through Syria for a handsome commission. One needed only the chemical formula to restart a chemical program. And those formulae and materiel specs were safe in a vault a long way from the nation of Iraq. Even more dangerous weapons were now already in the hands of the enemies of the West, and the Dictator had set his sights on becoming the wealthiest man in the world. For some reason, he acted as if he wanted his picture in Forbes Magazine.

Of particular interest to Al Qaeda were their intelligence sources reporting France, Germany and Russia were so deep into taking bribes from the Dictator that they would stall or kill any serious UN interference. And that would facilitate Al Qaeda's plan against the U.S. Meanwhile, the Dictator's accounts around the world were bulging as he took European money in exchange for Iraqi oil. If the UN verified the weapons were in fact gone, the sanctions would be lifted. That might be helpful to the Iraqi people, but it would stop the flow of cash into the pockets of the Dictator and his select conspirators who benefited enormously from the charade.

The Doctor knew that the one thing he could count on was the Dictator would act in his own financial interest, no matter what the consequences to his people. Zawahiri despised this boorish man for that trait, and, at the same time, admired his audacity.

And, for that reason, they knew he would take their bait.

After Bin Laden had gotten over his dizziness and was feeling a little better, he, Atef and Zawahiri held what they knew might be their last planning meeting together for some time. The cave was cold and damp now, and the light they allowed themselves was minimal. The fireworks of the American aerial bombardment in the distance had tapered off and they were able to speak softly to one another.

"Are you sure the Americans will take the bait?" Bin Laden asked, oddly needing reassurance. He looked long and serenely at his military chief, Atef.

"Most definitely," Atef responded. He exuded that sublime confidence he had when he had created a masterful military strategy. Their cells would execute what he created. And there was no doubt in Bin Laden's mind that Muhammad Atef was the most creative and original military commander he had ever worked with. He was grateful to Zawahiri for bringing this kind of talent to their alliance.

Atef was laughing now, something he rarely did. "I doubt if we even needed to set bait. The Americans were planning on

Iraq anyway. It was just a matter of sequencing. This will just be the justification they need to garner support."

Zawahiri wanted to add something. "You see, Usama, it was inevitable that the Americans would come. You see now that their response in Afghanistan is quite predictable?" Bin Laden nodded his agreement.

Atef resumed, "What you have to understand is they will want Iran and Iraq if they are to secure themselves. If I were them, I would want the same three. And there is no way on earth I would overthrow the government of Iran with a madman like the Dictator next door. With his army and weapons systems, he would swoop into that vacuum and seize the nuclear facilities before the Americans and their allies had a chance to stabilize control."

"So the issue for them is truly one of timing?"

"Exactly," Atef assured him. "What our attacks on 9/11 did was to precipitate their response and force the sequence. Afghanistan first. Then, with our help, Iraq. Then Iran."

"Surely, we won't lose Iran, too?" Bin Laden sounded alarmed.

"No, Usama, I'm merely laying out what I believe their Joint Chiefs will recommend to their President. That's why I'm confident they will move into Iraq. Ayman has made certain that their grounds will be the weapons and that our friends in Europe will see to it that they are isolated."

Usama was satisfied now. To be honest, he had never conceived of a plan this far-reaching. He had been told that Ayman was one of the most brilliant men on the planet, and tonight he was sure of it. Their strategy was to discredit British and U.S. intelligence, damaging them, and placing them under siege for years; to isolate the U.S. and Britain by extorting their normal allies into abstaining, or even turning on their former cash cow; to eliminate the madman from Iraq and his malevolent sons; to take Iraq for Al Qaeda, using its bases and resources for their own purposes, while the local clerics fought over territory; and to continue their alliance with Iran, having dramatically increased the real estate they held influence over—all this done graciously with American tax dollars.

To accomplish this would necessitate perhaps the finest public relations campaign ever engineered by Al Qaeda. In fact, as Bin Laden mulled this over, he could see that very little of this would play out militarily. The bulk of it would happen through masterful manipulation of information. He smiled as he anticipated the field day his world-class public relations team would have with this assignment. He genuinely looked forward to watching the Ambitious and the Stupid delude themselves, as they fought for their national interests. *Yes, it will be a fascinating next phase,* he reflected.

Feeling a little dizzy again, he indicated that their meeting was over and asked the Doctor to stay to assist him. "Do you want to have the head of our public relations department brief you, as well, on the tactics he will use?" the Doctor asked. "I'm sure Samir would not mind spending a few minutes with us."

"No, I'm confident you'll see to the tactics. I only wanted to review and approve the strategy. You have done a masterful job, Ayman, and I apologize for bringing this on us so fast."

"No need, dear friend, none of us knew the towers would collapse. We, as always, have turned it to our advantage."

"Excellent." Bin Laden paused for a moment, looking straight in front of him. Then, "So, what shall we do about this dizziness?"

"I have something that should relieve that."

As he had done so often, Bin Laden rolled up his sleeve and waited for his Doctor to inject him and let him rest. Zawahiri opened the bag he carried on their walk-outs and retrieved a small vial. It took only a moment to fill the syringe and give Bin Laden the shot. He didn't even think about it as he administered a medicine which would sky-rocket Bin Laden's heart rate causing an apparent heart attack, and then dissipate leaving no trace. In the morning, it would appear that their leader had simply succumbed to the combination of illnesses he had endured for years. The stress of the bombardments and their treacherous escape route had felled him. He knew the others would accept this. The only thought the Doctor had was that Bin Laden had served his purpose, and his illnesses were now actually becoming a liability to their survival. Bin Laden had performed well. And he would be remembered. That was more than most men could say. The Doctor felt no remorse.

He watched for a minute as Bin Laden's breathing changed dramatically. Then he quietly exited the cave. Hunched over his battery-driven laptop, he opened an encrypted file and removed the Black Queen from the second level of a three-dimensional grid. A more experienced eye would have recognized the 8x8x8 cube. Zawahiri, however, was confident no one would put it together. Closing the file, he decided to rest an hour or so until someone would sound the alarm. *After all, I will have much to do to reform our group after the demise of our great leader. I should sleep,* he admonished himself. And he did.

CHAPTER 15

"Ayman, wake up," Atef commanded the Doctor in a tense and whispering voice. "Ayman!" The Doctor was awake and sitting up as quickly as his stiff muscles would allow. Sleeping on the ground in this cave was a far cry from the climate controlled chambers of their bunker systems.

"What is it?" he asked, as if he had no idea why Atef was kneeling beside him.

"Something's wrong with Usama. I can't wake him." Atef said. Both men had seen too much dying to not know what a body feels like when the spirit has left it. The cooling down is unmistakable. The Doctor could tell by the eyes of his friend that the words were more public relations than anything else. He could tell it was done.

Nonetheless, both men hurriedly entered the small cave Usama had spent the night in after receiving his last medications. Bin Laden was seated cross-legged as he often did, but his torso was bent over to the ground as if he had fallen face forward. There was no rigor mortis yet, but his face and hands were cool to the touch. The body heat was slipping away.

The Doctor laid him out quickly, continuing the charade, and tried to take his pulse. "Usama, come back. Usama, can you hear me?" the Doctor shouted. He wept and turned his face directly to Atef who was hovering on the other side of the prone Bin Laden. "Muhammad, he is gone! There is no pulse and he is cold already."

"I know. I can feel the chill of death."

Zawahiri stood up and stepped backward, never taking his eyes off Bin Laden. Except for the fact that his eyes were open and he looked surprised, nothing looked unusual. There was silence for a moment or two as both men walked around their leader, as if changing their perspective on him might change his "deadness" somehow. Finally, Atef spoke.

"What do you think happened to him?"

"I would guess a heart attack. When I left him, he was complaining of dizziness again. I gave him something for that."

"And what did he say?" Atef asked with something uncharacteristic in his voice.

The Doctor wondered what that mechanical-sounding voice indicated. Was it just the shock of Usama suddenly and finally no longer being with them? Or was it suspicion about the circumstances? Zawahiri couldn't tell, but it did not escape his notice.

"He said he was feeling better and that he would rest here." He added mournfully, "I felt he would rest better alone, without my snoring in the night, so I moved to another cave. If only I had stayed…" his voice trailed off.

"What?"

"I don't know for certain, but if I had been here, there are things that could have been done to revive him. Even in this crude environment, there is much I could have tried!" The Doctor was convincing in his grief and remorse.

"Ayman, he is with Allah now."

The Doctor nodded and bowed his head. Then he volunteered without thinking, "I'm afraid his illnesses finally caught up with him. It was only a matter of time. My guess is that he had a heart attack, and that it was over quickly."

"Perhaps," Atef replied. There it was again, something mechanical in his voice. He seemed to be looking at something in his own mind that was more real than the answer he gave the Doctor. Unfortunately for Atef, the Doctor noticed it.

Why did it have to be this way? I should have known that of all the ones, he would be the one to guess. That changes the plan. He quickly reprioritized and decided he'd deal with Atef later. Now, however, they had to decide what to do with Bin Laden's body. The sun was coming up, leaving them very little time to handle it. Every moment now mattered.

It had seemed like hours, but had been no more than 20 minutes since Atef and the Doctor had informed the other party members of what had happened. There was no hysteria amongst these disciplined warriors, but there was almost unspeakable grief over the loss of their visionary leader. Not wanting to lose any momentum or time, each seemed to recognize that sooner or later we all come to the end. Surely this was something each had contemplated in his heart. Only the insane would not have considered this possibility, given that the best enemy warriors ever fielded were in constant and deliberate pursuit of them all.

On that sobering thought, almost in unison, each of them took dominion over their personal feelings and began deciding what to do with their fallen leader that would at the same time foil the enemy's goals.

It was Samir, their Public Relations Department head, who spoke first. "It is imperative for our worldwide operations that no one but us knows that our dear friend has died." All were in agreement on that point. Their recruiting, their finances, their war plans, the enemy's priorities, all hinged on the belief that Usama Bin Laden still lived.

Zawahiri decided not to tell them now of the masterful work he, Usama and Nanda had put together. There would be time for that at the meeting he would call this evening. Fortunately, all the survivors turned to him automatically for guidance. He was the *de facto* head. That was certain. That was the plan. And he knew now that the rest of his plan would be fulfilled. This once-young teenage rebel had risen to the heights of his "profession." Having forged an alliance with Al Qaeda, he had maneuvered himself into the number two position. With no one of any magnitude in a position to challenge him now, he would automatically assume control of Al Qaeda, and Al Qaeda's money.

And with great, solemn authority, he devised a plan for the disposal of Bin Laden's body. Departing from tradition, Bin Laden was to be cremated. Zawahiri's security chief and his top aide were to stay behind and bury the ashes deep in the bowels of the cave system they were using. Even if the Americans found the cave, it is doubtful that they would find a deep and carefully camouflaged grave containing only ashes. The rest of the company was to advance as quickly as possible to their next location. Since they were moving away from the direction the enemy assumed they'd be heading, they knew that they could, for a few days, occupy one of their inland hideouts. From there, they would make their final exit in different directions. The cell of top-echelon Al Qaeda was about to go mobile, and individual. They were very certain of their security measures, and of the viability of their communications network.

As the others disappeared over the first rock formation, the Doctor hung back, ostensibly to verify that nothing was left and that Usama would be properly handled. No one was looking as he went to the security detail that had been with him for some years, and provided new instructions to them. For a moment, they each looked puzzled. They looked at one another and then, with the discipline they had always demonstrated in the years they had followed the Doctor, they reached out and took a small vial and syringe that Zawahiri offered them.

"I know this is not what you expected," the Doctor said placatingly. "But these are desperate times and Usama, above all others, knew that extraordinary measures would be required." The two men remained silent so the Doctor pressed on. "The antidote will raise the body temperature and reverse the coma." He then leaned in to them and handed them a handwritten note with the remainder of their instructions. His security chief nodded his agreement.

"Allah be with you," the Doctor responded.

With the Doctor standing on guard, the two men took Bin Laden's body into one of the caves. It was clear they had set a fire deep inside the cave when a small wisp of smoke escaped from the chambers. Fortunately it was not enough to call attention to their location. Some time later they emerged with what appeared to be ashes and tossed them to the winds of the land in which Usama Bin Laden had hidden so effectively for 20 years. The Russians had never found him. The Americans had never found him. And the Doctor smiled knowing no one ever would.

As he hurried to catch up with the company, he affirmed to himself, *Samir will make great use of this. He will make pawns of them all.*

Two hours later, three men emerged from the cave. Zawahiri's security chief seemed to be supporting a lanky man whose legs were weak. Verifying that the area was clear, the second man returned to help his colleague. Though they moved slowly and carefully, in a matter of minutes they had vanished into the landscape.

James woke abruptly as if someone had shaken him. He could swear he had been moved. The clock said it was 1 a.m. and he had a chilling feeling something had happened. Throwing back the single sheet he slept under no matter what the season, he first looked outside. The street light revealed only the snow melted into slush. As was common in the District, any snowfall was minimal and lasted just long enough to tie up traffic and raise the hopes of school children. Then it would begin to melt as the area returned to its normal temperate climate.

Certain that something had happened that affected him, he turned on the television. CNN was repeating their reporting of the Tora Bora battle from earlier in the evening. The "live" field reporter had been distant enough from the action and the expected capture or killing of Usama Bin Laden that his replay only served to illustrate his dispassionate coverage. James had no idea whether that was the editorial policy of CNN in this war-journalism, or whether they actually had a weak-Willy covering the hot zone, or whether the U.S. military had intervened and kept this poor guy so far from anything that he had nothing to report.

Still, James was quite certain that something out of the ordinary had transpired. He felt lighter somehow, as if a blackness had lifted somewhat. Channel surfing, he hit Fox News with Geraldo Rivera live. That was riveting. It was obvious Rivera had gotten himself closer than prudent, and he was practically salivating over the prospect of the demise of Bin Laden. He was passionate, which was uncharacteristic of a journalist. *Well, I can't blame him. Why go 8,000 miles to act like a hypocrite, by pretending you're doing unbiased reporting of this event?* he mused. *I'd like to be in the action myself. What I wouldn't give to see that monster leave this earth! Hope he has an asbestos suit.*

Whatever it was, the battle at Tora Bora was still going on and the level of commitment of Pakistani troops on their border resembled the best of goal-line defenses. *Maybe I ought to wake the Kid and see if his football experience provides something more fruitful than his chess.* James reminded himself that that was uncalled for. The longer he looked at the screen, the more nervous he became. The more Rivera talked about the troop build-up, and the net, and the movements that would close the noose, the more James was certain that he had already slipped through. He, now, was absolutely certain that neither Bin Laden, nor anyone else who held information or command, was anywhere near Tora Bora. He felt sick to his stomach and really did want to call the Kid.

Reason got the better of him, though, and he realized they would address it tomorrow when they got together. Surely this was some kind of move where the King escapes. Then it hit him, what the Kid had said, "We're doing what he wants us to do. Our moves are merely reactive." James then remembered that the Kid had gone further in his briefing with Whitney. "There are secrets here. Zawahiri has forfeited the military game. He has a reason to do so, and we are executing every move he wants us to make." And then, as if that weren't enough to say to a deputy director, he added, " I am quite sure he is playing another game altogether, and he is moving to checkmate in that other game. I, sir, would like to know what his real agenda is."

If it hadn't been so very insubordinate of Andy, James would have laughed. As it was, he was responsible for this project, and he couldn't afford for Whitney to think some flippant, high-IQ teenager had the audacity to think he knew more than the Joint Chiefs, the NSA and MI-6. *Still, the Kid had balls.*

He knew, of course, that Whitney didn't have any, and that Whitney wasn't going upstairs on a theory. He and the Kid would need to do better than that. Still, certain that something had shifted in this invisible chess game that was being played, he went to the refrigerator, grabbed the carton of milk and some Fig Newtons and turned off the television. It wasn't long before the calcium took its effect and he dropped off to sleep.

Andy was just coming out the front door when James pulled up. He had his jacket on and was flipping his scarf over his neck. Before James could turn off the ignition, Andy hopped in the passenger side and said, "Sorry about this, but I need to get my mom a present for Christmas. This is the only time she's not around. So I was hoping you could take me to Fair Oaks Mall."

James didn't see any point in protesting. The Kid deserved a little break. And they could talk in the car. "Sure, Kid," James said in his best chauffeur's voice. "Is there some particular store, or are we just browsing?"

"Lord and Taylor," Andy answered proudly. "She's always wanted to shop there, but, well, you know, with work, and my travel and all…"

"Great idea. She won't expect it." Then he added, "I'll take care of my shopping too. One less thing to worry about on Christmas Eve."

Andy had been working for two months now with James, and he had no idea who James would be buying Christmas presents for. It bothered him a little that he knew so little about this soldier. Andy knew soldiers—true soldiers—and in his eyes, James was one, though he knew almost nothing about him personally. He told himself he'd pay more attention.

As their car turned the corner, the familiar Orkin truck pulled up. Mrs. Standish across the street noticed it as she went to her mail box, but paid no special heed as she had seen it several times. The usual technician got out of the driver's side and entered the house. What Mrs. Standish didn't notice, because she also hadn't paid much attention to her neighbors of 15 years, was that no one was home. This Orkin man entered a home when the owner was not present. Furthermore, if she had looked closely, she would have seen he had a key.

Once inside, he immediately opened the door to the basement and descended. His field was stealth, and it didn't take him long to plant the "bug" in the overhead light. He had been here before sweeping for "bugs," but his orders today were different. Very professionally, he restored the light fixture.

Then, as unobtrusively as he had arrived, he left the area. James and Andy were just entering Lord and Taylor.

CHAPTER 16

They were all exhausted by the time they arrived at their safe house. A network of believers guarded them now. Although rest was in order after the arduous trek through the mountains, Zawahiri knew it was imperative that the three of them meet. Samir and Atef looked almost shell-shocked as they wearily loosened and dropped their packs. It was quiet here; no shelling, no war sounds whatsoever. But the whole troop had suffered from the shock of Bin Laden's death, and the Doctor could tell that they were jumpy and probably frightened, as the reality of their situation sank in. He had known the night of September 11 that their lives in Afghanistan would come to this.

He felt no sympathy for his colleagues. *After all,* he thought, *we've had to flee in the face of capture many times before.* He actually felt disdain for any of the senior Al Qaeda who had deluded themselves into thinking that somehow the Taliban could repel the Coalition forces. As for himself, he was physically weary, but mentally almost exhilarated. Although he was disappointed that he had had to do what he did, he did have to do it. Usama Bin Laden was no longer capable of leading the organization, and in order for the mission to succeed the Doctor had concluded that he, himself, had to assume control. And Ayman Al-Zawahiri had made a point of never regretting what was necessary in order to accomplish a mission. Right now, everything was going as well as expected, and it was time for him to establish his authority over the organization and lead it on.

Only Atef worried him. The others were manifesting a natural grief at the loss of their mentor and leader. Usama's vision had carried them far. No other group on earth was as feared as his warriors. That had left them in a tremendous position of negotiation despite the fact that they physically had to implement extraordinary security measures. But Atef seemed more suspicious than sad. It was not what he had said. But rather what he had not said that perplexed the Doctor. As they had left the area, leaving the Doctor and his security detail to bury Bin Laden, the Doctor had observed Atef watching them from the top of the hill. He stood there suspended in silhouette in the dawn's light. To the Doctor, his fixed gaze at the burial detail seemed like an eternity, for Atef never took up the rear. He always led from the front. His lagging at the rear was out of character, and had not gone unnoticed.

Nonetheless, Zawahiri concluded that Atef would fulfill his military obligations to the organization. He was cause-driven and the Doctor was confident that, if there was something there, he could address it later.

"I know we are all weary from the pace and the loss we have incurred," he said softly to Atef and Samir, "but before we sleep, I suggest we attend to prayers and do our strategic planning. If the last few days have shown us anything, it is that we must not take our time here for granted. We must put ourselves last now, and make certain that all plans are meticulously laid out and communicated. Agreed?"

They both agreed. It was as he had planned. Their escape had to be harrowing in order for it to be believable. That alone would ensure that the world would believe Usama Bin Laden had miraculously escaped the Americans' lair, eluding and defeating them in their public relations war, if not their military one. They could almost see and feel doubt creeping into the minds of politicians and press as Bin Laden seemed to have defied and beaten their *best.*

The death of Bin Laden would, oddly enough, strengthen their position and make them almost mythical in the minds of others. He would never be found. Therefore, he would always live. And if he lived, others would always second-guess themselves. And second-guessing is a way to vanquish oneself. It was for this reason that the Doctor expected all the senior Al Qaeda leaders to fall in step. Like him, they would know that whatever the causes of Bin Laden's death, it worked to their advantage.

I will deal with Usama later, he coached himself. *No one will know his whereabouts, let alone that he lives, unless I choose to reveal it later. If it turns out he is never needed again, he will remain where I have secreted him.* He laid out his prayer mat, confident that there would have been in-fighting if the transition of leadership had been handled any other way. Though each member of the team was gifted in his area, the Doctor knew that not one of them had the brains to do what they were about to do. Calmly, he attended to his prayers.

The senior three bathed, ate and then reconvened to set the stage for the next round. What they plotted would confound nations and weaken the resolve of governments in the months and years to come. Zawahiri was the first to speak, "I think we should begin with a report from the department heads."

Atef concurred and then made an odd request. "I think we should include Mohammed in this session." Mohammed Makkawi was a gifted military operative. Zawahiri and Atef had known him from Special Forces in Egypt. Years earlier, he had conceived of a plan to hijack planes and fly them into government buildings in Cairo. Nothing had come of it then, but Mohammed was almost feared for his smoldering ambition and temper.

To include him now was not ridiculous, just odd timing. The Doctor decided to pursue it a little, "You think so?"

"I do," Atef answered without looking up.

"Why?"

"Because he has exceptionally bold ideas. And we may need him soon. I also would prefer to have someone back me up."

"All right; you're right. Your function is so vital to us; it would be unwise to leave the post with no second."

Zawahiri sent for Makkawi. While they waited, he indicated that he wished to receive a report from their finance officer first. Zawahiri, an exceptional businessman, was interested not only in how much money he now controlled through Al Qaeda, but more keenly in how their investments were doing. Despite what the press promoted regarding Al Qaeda being financed by Bin Laden and by contributions from sympathetic mosques around the world, the organization actually was a highly diversified corporation, and its holdings and activities were immense. With some 30 corporations in Switzerland alone, only Saddam Hussein matched the number of locations Al Qaeda had that held money. It had been a simple matter for them to move money to him in Jordan, Syria and Switzerland as compensation for his upholding his end of their deal.

Zawahiri made a mental note to himself to send a coded inquiry to his own financial advisors. He was particularly interested in a type of stock and was most interested in tracking some trends since September 11. Ironically, although the United States and its allies were investigating heavily the financial backing of Al Qaeda, and intending to seize all bank accounts that were flowing cash to the group for sustenance and materials, no one had any inkling of the actual area the Doctor was targeting. It was a failure that would prove catastrophic to the United States. No one knew that the Doctor was even in a position to undermine any and all strategies of the U.S. government, let alone how he had done it. The Americans had no idea of the direction of the attack and did not even recognize it as such. That certain knowledge bolstered Zawahiri's spirits and his desire to complete this next phase.

The finance officer arrived, and a detailed briefing commenced.

Zawahiri was very satisfied with the increased flow of arms into South America. Their relationship as a supplier to FARC in Colombia was one that both organizations valued. Al Qaeda had always had a policy of being liquid. In order to perpetrate the terrorist attacks they planned, they needed to be able to move money around easily and effectively.

The current report that Hamza al-Qatari, their finance officer, provided to the remaining council members showed that Al Qaeda continued to be the primary seller of heroin in the region. Most of Afghanistan's poppy crops were under Al Qaeda control.

Through long-standing and lucrative deals with disaffected Russians, Libya and Syria, Al Qaeda had procured massive armaments. Some were used for their own engagements, and the rest were secured in caves inside Afghanistan itself. The trading of arms with groups who needed weapons in order to destabilize their governments was one of Al Qaeda's major businesses. It was through such arrangements with Colombia and other South American groups that Al Qaeda secured much cash, as well as escape routes for their operatives in the United States. They had learned long ago that an Arab can resemble a Hispanic. What was especially brilliant was their realization that Americans would be suspicious of someone coming or going from the major coastal ports in the U.S. Their language and speech might give them away. On the southern borders of the U.S. however, the agents were used to Hispanics not speaking English and paid almost no attention when their questions went unanswered, or were answered in a pantomime motion rather than words. As such, their operatives crossed easily and made their way south to negotiated escape routes.

But what Al Qaeda wanted most from their South American conspirators was a safe place to run one of their major industries. It generated lots of cash, had almost no overhead, and was noticeably not dangerous. Their Telephone Fraud Department turned in an astonishing report to Zawahiri that night. By establishing call-cell setups in the Philippines, they had acquired an estimated $250 million in profits and had never been caught. For two and one-half years they had stymied law enforcement in the United States and Philippines. Then, to the astonishment of those countries, they had folded their operation and vanished. They were wealthier by huge sums and they had perfected their game.

After that they had begun set-ups in South America. In the coming two years an operation in Brazil would amass another $50 million in just six months. They were established conveniently in a corner where they could dismantle and cross the border into Uruguay in a matter of minutes. From there they could move to a third country. This round-robin would keep them out of the hands of any one law enforcement group should their business be compromised in some fashion.

As the Doctor reviewed the last six months, he felt vindicated that he had persuaded Bin Laden to expand this type of business.

Other than the rental of the storefront to run the call-centers, their only expense was the fee they paid the hackers to penetrate a PBX or voicemail system. Not only were these hackers gifted, but there was discretion among thieves. Not one of them was going to turn himself in, let alone reveal his cash cow. These phantom warriors were costing telephone companies hundreds of millions of dollars and no one had any idea who they were.

"I see we owe a debt of gratitude to the Telecommunications Reform Act of 1996," Zawahiri joked.

"Exactly," Atef added. "It opened a broader field for competition and gave us a much broader hiding place. Notice, Ayman, that the amounts are spread out through more than a dozen telephone carriers."

"Yes, I see. We expected that." He reviewed the numbers for a minute and then added, "Spread out through that many carriers, they had no idea how big our attack was, let alone that it was coordinated. Sadly for the United States, they are just now discovering that our cell activities in any of our businesses are capable of being coordinated, and that the result is devastating."

"What's delicious, Ayman, is their lawmakers have no idea how they opened the door for us!" Atef snorted. It was obvious he took pride in the almost Trojan-horse-type strategy their fraud department had deployed.

Each of them paused for a minute to ingest a little additional supper before continuing with the updates. The size and secrecy of the group prohibited anyone from cooking for them, so they were getting by with some bread from their days of escape, some dates and a bit of goat cheese. It raised their energy, however. And they continued.

"What do you have from the United States?" the Doctor queried his financial officer.

Hamza replied quickly. "There you will be most pleased. Our ATM businesses and credit card fraud businesses are creating a steady cash flow of $15 million per month."

"$15 million, did you say?" Zawahiri was almost disbelieving.

"Correct." Then Hamza added, "It seems the Americans are more and more reliant on their technology. Our companies have experienced a 33% increase in ATM locations, and the amount of data we are collecting and using to penetrate people's accounts is staggering. The same is true of credit card skimming. The only problem there is recruiting truly trustworthy personnel to take jobs in retail establishments. But, if you'll look at the recruiting report on the last page, we are improving there as well."

At this point Samir jumped in. As the Director of Public Relations for Al Qaeda, he usually had nothing to say at these meetings. He mostly just listened and formulated PR strategies based upon what the other men discussed. Later, at a discreet time, he would bring them to Bin Laden and Zawahiri for approval. It was rare that military strategy personnel were around when he gave ideas on PR.

But tonight, whether emboldened by Bin Laden's absence or whether he wanted to assert his position with this newly-formed command team, he spoke up somewhat assertively. "That is a particular victory for the marketing campaign we ran in the United States. It was fairly easy to get the Americans to go to ATMs in convenience stores and hotels, rather than their banks."

"Yes?" Atef responded.

"Yes, the Americans have a Convenience button that can be pushed in marketing." He smiled, as if proud of himself, and added, "It just took me awhile to figure out how to punch it." He waited, knowing someone in the chamber would take the bait.

Atef responded, "I don't follow."

"They didn't respond to our efforts to persuade them they needed something that would provide more convenience." He paused for dramatic effect and smiled broader. "They responded to the opposite—something that would afford them less inconvenience. The real button is Inconvenience! The Americans have a real sense of self-importance and anything that inconveniences them lowers their status." He let that sink in. "They expect to be catered to as they succeed, so anything that reinforces that they are important and shouldn't be inconvenienced will be appealing. That's what I discovered and used."

Atef and Makkawi exchanged looks. Makkawi spoke first. "We can use that. We can definitely use that to offset what the U.S. government will do at airports following our attacks. They will make it too *inconvenient* for their people and will have to ease their own restrictions." Suddenly both men laughed. The others watched, not quite getting it, but amused by their colleagues amusement.

The Doctor was the first to put this into real play. "Exactly, Mohammed. You will not have to devise military strategies on how to get past U.S. security in crowded areas. Samir has just given you how to do it. The Americans themselves will find it *inconvenient.* Turning to Samir, he added, "All you have to do is select who will be the one to start delivering the message to the American people and, in enough time, they'll solve our own problem for us."

Samir was thrilled to have what started out as a story turn into a coordinated military/PR move. He had some worry about what his role would be after Bin Laden's sudden death. Now, he had no anxiety whatsoever. He had good ideas and he was capable of implementing them. No one knew PR as well as Samir. Educated at Princeton, he had a minor in Russian languages, but was a Phi Beta Kappa with the highest grades ever given in Public Relations. He had a particular gift for understanding how to market to the American public and had had seven years of experience with one of the leading advertising agencies in the United States and five years with one of the finest public relations firms in Manhattan. And tonight he was happy, for he already knew who to call to plant the seed of doubt that would germinate in less than two years into a revolt of almost Constitutional proportions in the United States. That revolt would, on its own, undermine the department that the U.S. President was setting up to secure America and coordinate homeland defenses.

Not even Samir could have guessed that as the months went by, the fiery Constitutional debate that threatened that department would actually be precipitated by the Inconvenience button in marketing.

For now, however, Zawahiri seemed satisfied on the financials. He was in fact secretly gleeful. Al Qaeda's wealth was greater than he had known, and growing monthly. It was the steady and steep upward graphs in all categories that emboldened him now. He excused all but Atef, Samir and Makkawi. The future strategies and activities of Al Qaeda were about to be determined.

"That was all good news, don't you think?" the Doctor offered.

"Decidedly," Samir said without hesitation.

Atef was silent for a moment and then added, "Yes, most definitely. We'll be in Red Alert for quite some time. This will give us resources."

The Doctor noticed two things. The first was that Atef had delayed as if contemplating something. He was Number Two in command because he had no delay. His decisiveness and ruthlessness were legendary. And he had never bothered himself with moral or philosophical issues. His game was war, and his goal the obliteration of whatever enemy his organization was attacking.

The second was his reminding them all of the obvious regarding the Red Alert. That was a term for maximum hiding and identity subterfuge. Through the years there were times when their whereabouts and identities had to be completely camouflaged. To be spotted even by local sympathizers could be dangerous. It was at these times that their plastic surgeon and anesthesiologist were utilized. Although expensive, their services had facilitated their escape in the past. It was also during these times that their maximum safe houses were used. In various locations in Afghanistan and in Pakistan, they had compounds where they could stay hidden for weeks and months if necessary. They were in one now in Kandahar. There appeared to be only one approach down this narrow dirt street to the small house at the end. The residents were all poor, living the life of most of the citizens of Taliban Afghanistan. People could come and go and be observed easily by an outpost in the first house on the street. Tunnels connected the first house and an outhouse in the rear of the safe house. It was through that outhouse that an escape could be made.

What concerned the Doctor was Atef's bringing up the obvious.

"Was there something you wanted to say about the Red Alert?" he asked Atef directly.

"Yes." This time there was no hesitation. "If any one of us is spotted and identified, and Usama is not seen with us, people will wonder where he is and they will talk. Before, Red Alerts were temporary until the pressure was off. But with Usama dead, our strategy must change."

"How do you mean?" Makkawi asked.

"Neither Ayman nor I can be seen again, or people will guess that something has happened to Usama. We must disappear as completely and believably as Usama has 'disappeared.'"

"Yes, that is correct," Samir chimed in. "From a propaganda standpoint, our objective can only be accomplished if the world press and governments believe he is still alive and has eluded capture."

"That was my point. We are now in a state of permanent Red Alert—and I'm glad we have the resources for it." Atef finished.

For once, the Doctor hesitated to speak. He needed to think about this for just a minute. Then it came to him. "Muhammad, you are wise to point this out to us. And, save for one thing, we would be permanently in Red Alert."

"What one thing?" Atef challenged.

"Your height!" the Doctor laughed. For a moment everyone was quiet and then they realized why Ayman was laughing. It was in fact deliciously ironic. Muhammad Atef was almost the same height as Usama Bin Laden. Both men stood out hugely in their culture as both were nearly 6' 5" tall.

He continued, "All we have to do is make *you* disappear in the eyes of the intelligence community and then, if we're spotted, they will conclude it is me with Usama."

Atef missed altogether an underlying hostility in the words of the Doctor. His smile camouflaged a hidden possibility. But then Atef had always been blindly loyal. Deceit was not really his game despite the fact that he was trained and gifted in psych ops. He would pay dearly for that blind spot.

But tonight, for the moment, everyone in that room felt a sense of relief. It was almost dawn and the Doctor suggested they sleep a few hours before tackling the exact planning that this new situation would demand. They agreed.

James had purchased an MIT jersey and a photo album. He hadn't decided when to give them to Kelly and Andy, but he had wrapped them himself and placed them on his dresser. It had been a long time since he'd needed to buy Christmas presents for anyone, let alone a teenage boy and his mother. Not having a clue what would be appropriate for Kelly, and having a typical man's aversion to shopping malls, he went on-line to a comprehensive site he'd heard about. It serviced hundreds of stores.

In one of the sports stores, he found T-shirts, jackets and paraphernalia from all the major colleges and universities in the U.S. He liked the idea of keeping the Kid's dream alive with a jersey from his future alma mater. *And,* he figured, *you can never have enough jerseys.*

Choosing something for Kelly was harder. For a few minutes he had wandered around in women's clothing stores, and ended up in aroma therapy sites and other areas he regarded as way too personal. Remembering how proud she was of her son, he decided on a photo album for her to keep pictures of his graduation and years at MIT. Being as practical as he was, he also figured you can't have enough photo albums. Even if she had to wait a few years for a grandkid or something, sooner or later she would use it. So he was happy with his purchases, and actually enjoyed wrapping them up when they arrived.

Of course, he had no idea if he would even be invited into their personal lives for the holidays, which made the gift choice even better. It was sterile enough. He decided to just take them along when he went to the house tonight. *No big deal,* he admonished himself. *It's just a little something.*

He was just getting out of his car and trying to avoid stepping in a residual puddle from the melting snow when Andy opened the front door and shouted, "Hey, partner. I got some good news."

"Yeah, what's that?"

"I'll tell you when we get downstairs. What's that in your hand?"

James offered the gifts up feebly, a little embarrassed. "Just a little something for you and your mom for your tree."

"Gee, thanks," Andy gushed. "That's great!"

"It's nothing, just something for under the tree, you know."

"Okay, but it's still great."

One of the things James liked about this Kid was his transparency. What you saw was what you got. For someone who got as much attention as Andy was used to receiving, the Kid was actually humble. And he was always upbeat. James Mikolas didn't want to admit it, but he was pretty fond of this handsome young patriot.

Kelly was looking through the mail and handed Andy a letter. Andy handed her the gifts saying, "Look what James brought us." Kelly was too busy admonishing James for bringing gifts to notice Andy eyeball the return address on the envelope and slip it surreptitiously into the kitchen trash. Andy was pretty sure neither his mother nor James had paid much notice.

"Mom, we're going straight down. I'll take out the trash when we finish."

"Okay." She waived them off as they opened the door to the basement. Trying not to shake her gift too hard, she placed it under their tree. James' presents were the only ones under the tree. But Kelly knew her son had purchased something for her. Why else was he so secretive about his room recently? He must be hiding something there. The only thing she couldn't figure out was how she was going to find enough time to get to the mall to find something for him. Her feet were so tired now from working on haircuts and frostings all day that her head actually hurt. So while the guys were down there doing whatever it was they did down there, she decided to soak her feet.

The table in the center of the basement that James and Andy used was covered completely with sheets of graph paper. Andy had a pad of paper graphed to 8x8 and used these to plot moves. Corresponding to these was a notebook he used to write down the chess moves he was working on. That way he could replay any game or exercise by recreating the moves he had so meticulously logged. This notebook was secured in the safe every night, as were the graph paper sheets he used.

Surprisingly, Andy did not like to sit at a computer and create these models. James thought that would be a whole lot easier, and certainly easier to preserve them for future use and evaluation. But Andy would have none of it. He was an old-fashioned, hands-on guy who liked to study and practice chess the way it had been done for hundreds of years.

Next to the log book of chess moves was a code book. It was this book that was so very sensitive from a security standpoint. Although James never brought it up with Andy, they were playing a very real adversary. Both knew that the events of September 11 were real and that the enemy was very deadly. Since they hoped their work would shed light on how that enemy was performing while providing clues to his thought process and intended actions, James knew the work was, in fact, dangerous, if anyone had any idea what they were doing.

He no longer was uncomfortable pouring over information in a basement of a home in Alexandria, Virginia. After all, much of his field experience had forced him to do secure work in insecure areas. Nonetheless, he was grateful for the bug sweep that Whitney had provided. It did make it easier for the two to brainstorm.

"What have you been working on, Kid?" James asked, amazed at the quantity of paper on the table.

"That's what I want to show you." Opening up the code book, he added, "I've updated it, by the way."

The code book was creative, to say the least. Every day James and Andy listened to the news and read newspapers to pull out any occurrences that caught their attention. Since James was the analyst, he was the one who usually spotted an event in the news that might have something to do with the War on Terror. Some were obvious like reports of U.S. military attacks or movement in Afghanistan. Some were less obvious, like a report of missing explosives in a mining camp in the Pacific Northwest.

James read the obituaries in every major city daily to see if the death of anyone caught his attention. The cessation of negotiations in political or economic arenas also caught his eye. The vacationing of heads of state was a source of interest to him, as well as the political tribulations of U.S. allies. Gas and oil mishaps never escaped his notice, and mergers of corporations that involved infusions of cash from foreign sources intrigued him.

Whatever the piece of data, Andy would evaluate it from the point of view of a chess master to determine whether this "piece" was a pawn or Bishop or Knight. The easiest to label, of course, were actual people rather than incidents. But either way, they could be loosely categorized and placed on a chess board. On a chronological timeline, James and Andy could then track to see the next time this person or type of incident appeared.

From there, a chess game would emerge. Although the opponent was invisible, they could surmise his move by what appeared in the newspaper. James had theorized that not only was Zawahiri playing a deadly game of chess, but that he was mimicking earlier Grandmasters. What they had been looking for was proof of Zawahiri's copying recorded games played by various Grandmasters in world championship tournaments. If he were, they could then identify patterns and predict what his next move would be with the person or scenario. And they could also look for encoded messages within the "writing" of chess moves—anything, basically.

All these were logged in the code book, and from that, Andy would construct various games on the graphs. He then entered the chess moves themselves in the "Moves" log for future recreation. Tonight, Andy was both flushed and subdued. This contradiction puzzled James.

"What you got, Kid? That's a lot of paper there."

"Yeah," Andy paused. "What I got is good news and bad news."

"Give me the bad news first."

"He's not playing recorded games from tournaments or from famous Grandmasters."

This caused James to reel a bit. He had been so sure of this. "Are you sure?"

"Yes, absolutely. I've reviewed every game that I could find. None of the games we have set up here match, in any way, a game played previously."

James was deflated now, "And is there good news?"

"Most definitely." Andy added quickly, "I was afraid that would be what we would find. No one would really be capable of controlling all of the responses of his opponent—especially not the responses of the President of the United States—so I knew he couldn't be copying an exact game."

James couldn't see any hope in that at all. It all seemed so unpredictable. "The good news Andy, please." James struggled to remain optimistic. "I thought at Langley you spotted a game you recognized."

"Yeah, just coincidence I guess. Killing a head of state, capture of Knights and pawns—it's all pretty regular for a great chess player."

"You lost me, Kid."

"He's a natural chess player, James, and he's playing one move at a time. He doesn't play like anyone else. It's not formal; it's natural. He's unique."

"And that's good?"

As if trying to explain this to a child, Andy laughed. "Yes, James; it is good. It means I can play him, this Mr. Ayman Al-Zawahiri. He's playing like a regular person and I can play him. And like any other person, I can beat him." He paused for a moment and then patted James on the back. "James, trust me. That is good news." And Andy smiled.

James wanted to believe. After all, the Kid was a world champion chess player—a Grandmaster, and a young one at that.

"Isn't that why you hired me?" Andy joked, knowing that this was a labor of duty. He was not, in fact, a paid employee of the CIA.

"And why are you so confident?"

Without even a fraction of a second's hesitation, Andy said, "Because everyone makes mistakes. With a canned game, the outcome was already determined. With an actual real-time game, he'll make a mistake. Sooner or later he'll make one. Everyone does. And when he does, I'll be waiting."

Something in the way Andy said that gave James chills. It was the first time he had ever seen the predator in this sweet-looking Irish kid. And it was also the first time he truly understood that chess and war were the same—at least to the serious chess player. And he remembered now an odd thing Andy had said at Langley. He had referred to the "Kill the King" move. James' cursory reintroduction to chess had taught him the goal was to capture the opponent's King. No one referenced killing the King, no one but Andy. At that moment James realized there was a great deal he didn't know about his partner.

Just as James and Andy were winding up downstairs, Kelly finished soaking her feet. As she got up to empty the water, she fumbled the pan and spilled water on the kitchen floor. She quickly wiped it up with paper towels and opened the trashcan to discard the wet towels. Kelly didn't know why she looked into the can that night. Certainly it wasn't to snoop. She just looked, that was all. And in looking, her eye caught the envelope she had handed Andy just two hours earlier.

Seeing that it was unopened, she assumed Andy must have been distracted and accidentally discarded it. So, being Mom, she picked it up out of the trash and cleaned it off. She went motionless, however, when she saw the return address. Knowing full well who the addressor was, she could not imagine why this letter was in the trash unopened. And she wondered if this had anything to do with Andy's recent secretiveness.

The stairs creaked as the two came up from the basement. Not wanting to deal with this now, Kelly pocketed the envelope and quickly closed the can.

A moment later James had left and Andy had grabbed the trash as promised. Hurrying back in from the side alley where they kept the trash cans, he rushed upstairs calling, "Goodnight, Mom," as he closed his bedroom door.

CHAPTER 17

The Administrator barely noticed the dozen or so rats that scattered on the walkway as he entered the hospital. For 20 years he had endured the rats and insects and inferior quarters, and now barely noticed the conditions he was working in. To be sure, he did his best to keep the interior of the dilapidated old boarding school sanitary, but that, too, was a never-ending task.

In the days of the Shah, the buildings and grounds had been a vibrant private school where some of the state's wealthiest children came to learn. But after the revolution the Ayatollahs had refused to even use the school, lest they remind everyone of the lessons they had learned there earlier. All schools were now run by the state where the indoctrination of the pupils could be carefully monitored.

The collapse of the education system, however, had been good fortune for the Administrator. He had worked with some officials and volunteers of the World Health Organization as a young man, and they had planted in him the dream of running a healthcare facility for those with mental illnesses. The volunteers had long ago returned to their countries where the care of such people was a jewel in their resume. He was left to struggle with his dream in a country that regarded any such impaired people as lepers.

Finally, just to shut him up and get rid of him, an official in this town had said he could use the abandoned school, but he would have to provide funding and the staff himself. The man had been very clear that no one in authority would give any money to the care and feeding of such defective people, and especially not to the female population under his care.

It wasn't much, but it was something, and he had started with that. For 20 years now, he and a small staff of sympathetic individuals had been running an asylum. The Administrator's background had been business and management, and he had no formal training in medicine or psychiatry. Although he, from time to time, was able to hire a professional in those areas, they were mostly has-beens or beginners who jumped ship as soon as a better opportunity came along.

Because of that, he had found the care of these resident patients to be a great burden. Not only had he forfeited most of his inheritance to just keep the doors open, he had to spend a great deal of time begging for money from citizens who already were struggling to care for their own families. There was little food and little heat. He almost never had money for new clothes for the patients and, since they had been abandoned by society, they had no resources of their own. The result was that most of the inmates were mal-nourished, unclean and improperly clothed.

He had discovered that people's appetites decreased when they were on psychiatric medications. Since he had no real training to help anyone there with their problems, and since he needed to save money wherever possible, he had resorted to drugging all patients as a matter of routine. It kept them quiet and controllable, and reduced his food and medical budget. He had long ago ceased justifying this treatment of people as animals. In fact, there were days he felt he was walking around in the same sedated daze most of his patients were. And there were days he wished he was catatonic.

But he had some hope this morning, and there was almost a spring in his step as he opened the door to his office. A few days earlier he had received a large amount of cash from a messenger. The accompanying letter had said he should expect a new patient within the week, and the money was for the care of this man. The letter also made it clear that excellent care was required and that, as long as he provided that, the benefactor of his new patient would pay for all the expenses of the facility.

It had seemed almost too good to be true, but a subsequent note informed him that the man would indeed be arriving today. He had no idea who the man was, and he had no intention of trying to find out. All that mattered to him was that there would now be money for food and clothing, and perhaps a little extra for him as well. *Should I not prosper as well for all my trouble?*

He never answered his own question because three men suddenly appeared in his office. Silently, the third man sat down upon entering the room. At first glance, he seemed sedated and unaware of his surroundings. *He'll fit right in,* the Administrator thought. Quickly, the other two, who were intimidating to say the least, laid out the requirements for the care of their charge. Watching them, the Administrator realized that it would be unwise to fail to follow through.

Instructions were already prepared. The folder contained the man's name, history, information about his medical condition, and the various medications that would be needed in order to keep him stable. A required diet was included, as well as the strict regimen of psychiatric medications to be administered. It was this piece of paper that shocked the Administrator. He was mystified as to why anyone would spend so much money on the overall care of a man, and then would medicate him to this degree. The patient would be so sedated by these dosages that he was confident the man would be virtually unaware of his surroundings. He would be able to hear for sure, but it was doubtful he would be able to communicate effectively, and he certainly would be incapable of causing any trouble.

Five years earlier, the Administrator would have been torn about what to do. But he had succumbed to more base needs in the last harsh winter and decided at that moment that whoever these people were, he was just going to take the money and keep his mouth shut. There was more money here than he had seen in his life, and he was going to make certain now that it kept coming. Whoever the silent one was, he was going to receive the best cell the Administrator could set up in this hospital.

He explained that carefully to the two men who had brought their charge in. They seemed satisfied that he was sincere and said they would check in from time to time. As long as their friend was in the condition he was in now, the money would continue. They didn't even need to articulate the threat of what would happen if the man was mistreated; the Administrator could imagine that all too well.

The two men prepared to leave and made one last statement to the Administrator. "This man's personal physician wants the glucose drip commenced at 3 p.m. this afternoon, and he wants you to keep the Thorazine drip ongoing at the levels he has prescribed. If he wishes to change them, he will do so himself. Understood?"

"Perfectly. Rest assured I will follow the regimen his doctor has prepared. And please assure his doctor that he will receive excellent care here."

"The Doctor is confident of that."

With that, the two left, after each had kissed the third man on both cheeks. The man, however, was too sedated to acknowledge their gestures of affection and respect.

CHAPTER 18

In his dream he was blindfolded, but he could smell the stench of urine accumulating in his cell. And he could hear the breathing of his friend, Isam. Only the diabolical Egyptian interrogators would humiliate so completely by placing Isam Al-Qamari in the cell with the man who had betrayed him.

Ayman Al-Zawahiri had, at first, lamented that he had lured his friend and co-conspirator into a trap, but as the months and years went by, he had justified it in his own mind as what he had had to do to spare his own family any more harassment and shame.

Even Qamari had forgiven him. "I pity you for the burden you will have to carry." That was all he had said. And now the two sat in virtual silence, waiting. Each day brought new tortures and humiliations. Once they had talked as brothers and planned a glorious Islamic state. They had debated and philosophized long into the night in the street cafes of Cairo, and now they shared a cell. Neither man wanted to say anything that could be wrung out of the other in their private torture sessions with their hated keepers. It was no surprise then that Qamari had not informed Ayman of his plans to escape the prison, let alone not offered to take him along.

All Ayman heard was shouting and raging and steel gates banging. He was cold, yet sweating in fear. When he heard no breathing in the cell, he feared Qamari had been taken as he dozed. He feared the worst. When the door opened once again suddenly, he wet himself. And added to the shame of this lack of control, he was informed tersely that Isam Al-Qamari had been killed in a gun battle during an escape attempt. He vomited and collapsed back into his own urine.

The Doctor woke abruptly. He knew it was one of those dreams he had been plagued with for 20 years. He knew that. But each one seemed so real. He never knew when one of the dreams would occur, and they were different each time. But each time, he was transported back in time to those years of imprisonment and experienced them over and over again, as if they were today.

It was that particular phenomenon that had aroused the Doctor's interest in psychiatry. He had, of course, studied the field of psychiatry, along with pharmacology, during his years as a medical student. Few knew that in addition to being a brilliant surgeon, he was masterfully indoctrinated into the history of psychiatry as it had been introduced into Europe. Even fewer knew that he practiced psychiatry and that Usama Bin Laden was one of his patients.

Those closest to Bin Laden knew that he suffered from anxiety attacks—particularly after they were chased out of the Sudan and were truly men without a country. Although Bin Laden joked that that was why he had surrounded himself with Egyptian commanders and lieutenants, no one but the Doctor knew that he was delivering medication to Usama Bin Laden to take the edge off the anxiety. True, they were all men without countries, but the Doctor took care of Bin Laden and through the years, Bin Laden had become dependent on the Doctor not only for the extraordinary and brilliant vision and planning of Al Qaeda, but for his mental well-being.

That form of study was rather mundane and academic compared to what Zawahiri had seen and experienced in prison. He had managed to survive the physical beatings and had begun a therapeutic study of mind-control and torture techniques that involved the use of drugs, hypnosis and pain. At first his study had been by observation alone. Without benefit of any books or research material, he had deduced the entire mechanism of the mind by observing what was done by the interrogators, and what happened to each and every one of the "experimental rats," himself included, that these swine tried it on.

Over time, he had formulated a theory of how the mind worked with regard to painful and traumatic experiences, and what responses the mind dictated to the body. It had become clear to him that there was something to the cliché of "mind over matter" and anyone who knew that could "rule." Patiently, he endured. He observed that a current threat could remind someone of earlier threats and experiences and could, in some instances, even provoke the same emotional and physical reactions—even to the point of experiencing pain in the exact areas of the earlier abuse. And with that, he had stumbled onto a strategy that would literally make it possible for one man to rule the entire world.

Even to this day, he smiled as he thought how powerless armies and leaders were in the face of this one simple piece of information. And now he understood how his ancestors a thousand years earlier, the Hashshashin, were able to dominate the region for 300 years. Even though he understood his own thirst for power and domination was a virtual rerun of incidents long ago, he relished experiencing the replay, including the pain. He knew that if he understood it, he could use it.

Freud had tipped it in his theories of repressed childhood memories influencing the individual's behavior later in life, but that was all he had done. To the Doctor, it was clear Freud had not researched deeply enough. But he was at least right that our behavior today is influenced by hidden experiences from our past. And so he had become expert at mind control. He did not need to torture. He did not even need to be near his adversary. He needed only to identify what was an area of weakness—an area of fear or pain—something the adversary could not deal with. Then, like a master marketing executive, he would punch that button again and again and again until the adversary's own mind would cripple him with emotional and physical pain.

Even to this day, he believed those years in prison were the most important years of his life. He had experienced and watched interrogators use drugs combined with painful torture to reduce the subject to a state where hypnosis was possible. The hypnosis was nothing more complex than making the victim susceptible to suggestions or commands. They would then obey their captors easily in the future. But what the Doctor had discovered was that this could be used in a "normal" setting. It was, he concluded, the basis of successful marketing. Find a way to make the target susceptible to suggestion, and then use the button over and over again to get him to do what you want or buy what you want.

This body of knowledge had made Ayman Al-Zawahiri very powerful and he knew it. Before prison, he was a dedicated, but ineffectual leader. After prison, he possessed a power, and demonstrated an ability to lead and control that had led to his becoming the commander of Islamic Jihad. And now, Al Qaeda.

The Doctor was particularly proud of the vision and foresight he had demonstrated in establishing and training the suicide bombers. He had fought hard for that as part of the military strategy, for he knew how horrifying and upsetting that would be to the Jews and the West alike. Furthermore, his years in prison had taught him to trust no one. That had led to his creation of the blind-cell structure of Al Qaeda. No one cell knew the personnel or missions of the others. That made them almost invulnerable to penetration. The capture of a cell did not compromise the rest.

Icing on the cake was provided by the brilliant suggestion of Nanda, that they videotape the suicide bombers the night before their mission. He knew precisely what trepidation and revulsion those videos would arouse.

As he got up off the hard floor they were sleeping on, his body reminded him of the areas he had been beaten. His knees and shoulders were suffering from the previous days' efforts in escaping Tora Bora. Nonetheless, he looked forward to this meeting with Atef and Samir. He felt some discomfort with Makkawi there, but he also felt sure he could control the situation. He faced two military commanders against the one emir. But he had no fear. In fact, a plan was germinating in his mind. It was his hope that he would not need to implement it; but, one thing was for sure, Ayman Al-Zawahiri would not be caught off guard.

Whatever Atef and Makkawi might be plotting, he was several moves out in front of them. Taking out his laptop and opening the encrypted file, he methodically moved the White Knight on the second level of the cube to the Black Rook's square and captured it. He decided it was a wise trade-off, given the havoc it would later produce. And in setting the stage for that havoc, he moved the White Knight that was two levels up from there in the three-dimensional model, making it vulnerable to the Black Bishop on the same level. Levels two and four were highlighted and in play. Two separate games were being played. The White Knight bore an identification label, the same in both games. The label on the Black Rook's square was a location that would become infamous, the conquering of which would later come to haunt the Americans. The Black Bishop's label on the fourth game level would remain a mystery and source of denial for years to come.

He had a few minutes before their meeting, so he allowed himself to linger over these last few moves. *After all*, he thought, *it isn't as if there is a timer running. This game is mine to play, and mine to win.* One of the characteristics of Ayman Al-Zawahiri that was reported in the press following 9/11 was his secretiveness. Ironically, the press had no idea.

One of the carefully guarded secrets was the fact that he played chess at all. He actually held the game in some disdain, but it was a form of mental exercise, and for him, a method of testing his strategies and tactics. He thought it ridiculous that anyone would use a computer as an opponent. In his mind, man is far superior to the computer. Man can plan, he can think, and he can exercise judgment. A computer can not. He had heard that some Grandmaster had lost to the IBM computer, Big Blue, and he had thought, *What an idiot! Losing to a computer!*

He wondered what could have convinced the world-wide chess community that a computer would possibly be superior to a man. *They should have known that the thinking mind would always win out.* It was that conclusion that had led to an almost lightning-like revelation. He had concluded that all you had to do to become master of men, was to get them thinking like a computer, mechanically devoted to whatever was programmed into them. In answering his own question, how do you get man to think like a computer rather than a rational, reasoning person, he had effortlessly formulated the plan that would bring the United States to its knees—and with it, the rest of the free world.

And that began one of the most insidious fifth column attacks in history. As he looked at his simple model on the computer, and reviewed the implications of his last move, he smiled. This would work. He was certain of it. Now he looked forward to sitting with Atef and Samir and planning the military and psych-ops aspects of the campaign. In his mind the Battle of Afghanistan was only the beginning. And only a true appreciator of irony could know that this quiet man, seemingly on the run, holed-up in a modest house in Kandahar, was, in fact, the victor.

He signaled his associates to enter. He had good news.

"Kid, why don't we put this onto the computer?" James complained to Andy, as they poured over the pages Andy had printed off with news headlines from 1994 – 1997.

"I told you, James, I use the computer for research, not for playing," Andy retorted. He was testy for some reason. James concluded they'd been down there too long. Nothing was surfacing and he could feel Andy's tension.

"Let's take a walk."

"I don't want to take a walk. I want to find something!" Andy replied, cranking up the volume a bit.

Andy reminded James of the search and rescue dogs they had watched on TV at Ground Zero. Every day the dogs would go to this dangerous site and in a playful spirit, seek to find bodies. Every day they found nothing. As the grim reality of what that signified sunk into the recovery teams and the dogs' handlers, the dogs still had no idea of why. They were merely despondent over a day's work, coming up with nothing. To the dog, it felt as if he were failing. And that was no fun. It almost made one cry to watch those beautiful, brave animals so dejected and depressed.

James remembered what had brought the dogs out was something their handlers dreamed up. In the gymnasium where they were brought to eat and rest, they set up an area filled with piles and piles of cardboard cartons. Inside these cartons were dozens and dozens of treats for the dogs to find. As the dogs prepared once again to face failure, instead, they were met with success after success. And their spirits rose.

Not that the Kid's a dog, James mused, *but he could use a few "hits."* He had an idea.

"Hey, Andy, when was the last time you and Brian threw some balls around?" Brian was Andy's star wide-receiver. The two had made some history for Arlington High in the Conference Championship game, but hadn't seen each other since. Come to think of it, James hadn't heard Andy refer to anyone recently. And he began to wonder if this Kid was down here even more than he knew. It had been his intention that they would work a few hours each day. That is what Kelly had demanded. Now he suspected that Andy had overdone it. And one thing you learned as an analyst was when to "take a walk."

"I haven't seen Brian since the game."

"Something wrong?"

"No," Andy answered without hesitation or regret. "I've just been busy with studies and this is all." Then he added, "Why do you ask?"

"Now don't take this wrong, okay?" James said.

"Okay."

"It's called 'take a walk' in our game." James kept an eye on Andy to see how this was going down. "You almost get constipated, focusing too long on something, and you can miss it."

"Constipated?" Andy asked, turning that word over in his mouth.

"Well, you know what I mean."

Andy thought about it for a second and then said, "Yeah I do. It happens all the time in football. You cramp up is all."

"So what do you do to fix it?" James asked.

"You take a walk," Andy joked. "Just kidding, you just go throw some balls around."

"So, let's get Brian over here and throw some balls."

Just the prospect of seeing his teammate seemed to release the tension. They went upstairs and started to make some popcorn. After all, if they were going to be throwing and catching passes at midnight in the streets in front of Andy's house, the least they could give Brian was a little refreshment!

While they were sitting at the kitchen table James decided to make small talk. "What was it like defeating Big Blue?" he asked innocently.

"No big deal, really."

"Seriously?" James asked. Andy had received such notoriety for defeating Big Blue after Kasparov's loss to the IBM computer game that James figured it must have been a really big deal. IBM must have figured it was a big deal too, because they retired Big Blue shortly after that. There would be no rematch.

"Seriously. What a joke!" Andy offered. "Any significant player ought to be able to beat a computer."

"So what was the deal with Kasparov?"

"I honestly don't know. He must have been having a bad day or something." Andy seemed so unimpressed with something that had shaken the chess world and introduced a whole industry of computer chess programs. To many, it was a status symbol to be able to defeat a major computer chess program.

James was curious now. "Why isn't it a big deal?"

The answer was disarmingly immediate. "Because a computer can't think. It can't plan and it can't reason. That's all. It can evaluate the weight of a choice or option. It can calculate best moves and the points on captured pieces. But it can never understand forfeiting a Rook to capture a Knight. I, on the other hand, can think."

"And that's all?" James asked. It seemed too simple.

"Yup, that's all. As I said, it's no big deal." Andy poured the popcorn out into a very large bowl and then, with that signature grin, asked playfully, "How much butter do you want?"

"A lot," James answered. The doorbell rang. As Andy ran to let Brian in, James had that same feeling in his gut he had had with Ben Gurion. He had a nagging feeling he was on to something, but he didn't know what. Dismissing it for the moment, he decided to just enjoy the kids and eat some popcorn. Andy wasn't the only one needing a break.

CHAPTER 19

His years of commanding operations in the Balkans had brought Zawahiri closer to an understanding of Russia and, most importantly, of Stalin. Zawahiri had a keen sense of enemy identification and, in fact, he had persuaded Usama that it would be Ayman Al-Zawahiri who would determine the enemies of Al Qaeda and Islam. Though the group had military advisors and a brilliant military commander in Atef, it was vital that Zawahiri control the targets list. He trusted only himself these days. The others could go soft; they could become reasonable and tolerant. And if they could not spot an enemy, they could be undermined.

There was one thing Zawahiri admired in Stalin. That was his total willingness to kill innocent people in order to maintain his rule and impose his will on the world. The brutal, direct style, however, he did not like. As an educated man who spoke three languages, Zawahiri had acquired a taste for Shakespeare at University. One side of his family had art in their genes and, from time to time, he enjoyed the theater. Perhaps that is why he was so good at disguise, and why he had secured Nanda and created their production company.

Personally, though, his favorite character was Iago in Othello. He could relate to the quiet, demeanor of service that masked the cunning determination for revenge. Zawahiri had that same desire for revenge and he knew the best way to do that was to be to Bin Laden what Iago had been to Othello.

As for the rest of Stalin, Zawahiri considered him a brute, and a coarse peasant at heart. It was well that they had fought the remnants of his dying ideology in Afghanistan. And it was for that reason he was certain they were making the right moves with Saddam Hussein. He knew the White King's next move would be Iraq. It had to be. One didn't have to be an expert in Soviet or world affairs to know that anyone whose hero was Stalin would have to go.

The fact that the United Nations had lingered for more than a decade on the hope that Hussein would abandon his ambitions, was a joke in the terrorist communities. It was one of the reasons they felt emboldened. If they would appease and secretly deal with that Stalin-like thug, surely they would crumble easily in the face of the surgical precision of their brand of terror.

Zawahiri had been disappointed in recent months with the reports from their Weapons Department. Their cache of combat weapons was impressive, and their purchase of the suitcase bombs was a coup. But they were behind in the areas in which he was most interested—chemical and biological. Most of the trips between Baghdad and Afghanistan in the last few years had been his attempt to secure weapons from Iraq.

Now, however, with the invasion of Iraq by the United States a sure bet in his mind, Hussein was right where he wanted him. Saddam would take the money and revel in the embarrassment of his enemy. Zawahiri would have the weapons and Saddam Hussein would not be looking for the double-cross. He was smart. But he was greedy. And he was falsely confident as a result of the incompetence of the diplomacy of the 1990's. False confidence had been the downfall of all leaders. That was something that would not plague the Doctor. His confidence today was not delusional. He was absolutely certain he knew how to bring down the White King.

After all, the Soviets themselves had begun the attack long ago. All the Doctor need do now was reinforce and enhance a strategy the Soviets had put in play before their demise. And the Americans had no real idea that it had been deployed, let alone that it was residual. For more than a decade the United States had prided itself in outsmarting the Soviets in the Cold War. Everyone knew they were the victors—everyone except the psych-ops team that had injected the plan into the United States. Zawahiri had discovered it in prison in Egypt; he had seen it reinforced in his service of terrorism in the Balkans; and he would simply ride it in now.

For that reason, he was looking forward to the invigoration of their planning meeting. The room smelled musty from lack of use, but the home itself would serve their purpose well as a safe house. This inner room allowed them private conversations, while the outer rooms allowed for, and certainly created, the atmosphere of a normal, small home in a city surrounded by the enemy.

Their breakfast had been light, but Atef, Samir and Makkawi also seemed to be renewed by a few hours of sleep away from the incessant shelling reverberations they had recently endured.

Their host was a taxi driver whose right arm had been lost in a mortar attack in the war with the Russians. He had fought with Usama Bin Laden and was one of the men Usama could count on for aid. To the Doctor's surprise, this dedicated man had accepted without question their story that Usama was not with them because he was safely secreted in yet another house. A testimony to the man's humility and loyalty was his complete acceptance of this. The Doctor had seen not a hint of disappointment or hurt feelings. That was good. Hurt feelings, feelings of being slighted, were the seed that the Doctor had seen mature into a full-blown revenge motive. No one likes to be demoted. A friend can become an enemy over just such carelessness. But the Doctor felt confident that this man only wanted to serve. He was a true believer. Usama was wise to have chosen this humble house.

The four mats were arranged in the room in a way that allowed the men to sit comfortably in a circle. Each could address the other easily. In the center was an earthen pitcher with nectarine juice and a bowl of fresh fruit. The Doctor spoke first, ready to take the lead.

"I want you to know that nothing has changed in the face of the death of our brave leader." Each man nodded politely. "We have all known that, at any time, we could be gone. The success of our cell structure is evident. Muhammad, I'm confident that the plans you have laid for military attacks in the coming years are not only workable, but they are virtually infallible. You and your lieutenants just remain flexible."

"Yes, sir. I understand."

The Doctor continued. "What I want to concentrate on today is our basic strategy regarding the United States, and most specifically, what our fifth column plan will be."

Zawahiri knew he had the interest and agreement of all at this "round table." After all, their own survival depended on this as well. At the close of this meeting, each would begin the second journey, to their individual safe houses. This was a vital time for each to make certain they were perfectly clear on the mission.

"The mission of neutralizing the United States' influence in this region and elsewhere is well underway. But never lose sight of that. In everything you do and in everything you say, remember that the purpose is to bring down U.S. influence, to render our enemy totally ineffective. Understood?"

It was. He decided to speak boldly now. In order to get an alignment of these top leaders, he invoked their fallen leader. "Usama and I had laid out careful strategy and tactics just a few weeks back. As I give them to you tonight, please regard these instructions as coming from Usama himself." He paused for a moment for dramatic effect and to catch a glimpse of their reactions. Each was appropriately subdued and attentive.

"Our strategy will be to simply attack the Americans where they are weak. Muhammad, your military actions always must be targeted at vulnerable areas. Do not attack the United States in strong areas. Remember, they will be pitting their best against us at all times."

Atef responded immediately. "Agreed. I believe our best opportunity to do that will be in the next arena. Once Saddam is toppled and they begin both reconstruction and the search for the weapons, Zarqawi will have almost limitless targets." He stopped for a moment and asserted very professionally, "I do want to be very clear, however, on what we regard as their areas of weakness."

"Unquestionably, the Americans in particular are vulnerable to 'body count.' Since the Vietnam War, they have a wound like an abscess that has been band-aided. We're going to rip that band-aid off and throw those bodies at them, and make them wallow in images of their dead, disfigured, precious youth."

Zawahiri had said this with dispassion. He might as well have said, "Make sure you put napkins on the table." And that alone produced a chill in the room. Knowing that they were all in agreement on this, he added, "And Samir, your job is to feed this. At every opportunity punch that Vietnam button. The Americans pride themselves in being the land of the free and the home of the brave. But they're not. Somalia showed us they are not. Kobar towers showed us they are not. Their offer to me of Egypt for Herzegovina proved one thing to me. The White King cannot endure a body count. So punch that button."

"I understand. But I will need the fifth column for that."

"Yes, definitely, use our U.S. assets. The French can be counted on in that arena, too, I think."

Samir hesitated for a moment and then decided to dive in. "To pull this off, I'm going to need more than Al-Jazeerah."

The Doctor laughed. "For sure, and that's why you were selected, Samir."

"Yes?" Samir didn't seem to be tracking.

Friendly, the Doctor embellished, "Dear friends, Samir here is too modest. He knows Usama specifically chose him and I specifically approved him because of his education in the United States. That Princeton pedigree, you know. That, and the fact that he knows everyone in the media. Samir, here, is a very worldly fellow!"

The others laughed as well. Samir, however, just waited.

"Samir, Samir, who better to market our U.S. mission than someone who knows the Americans well? Tell me. Have you ever made a list of your enemies' strengths?"

Samir admitted he had. The Doctor seized on this to make a point. "Exactly. One of the ways to find the weakness is to find the strength. It would be a foolish combatant who doesn't research and determine his adversary's strongest points. Then he can prepare based upon a reality of what may be thrown at him. Right, Muhammad? Makkawi?"

The two military commanders nodded simultaneously. "See, it's simple. Samir, your job is to take each and every strength the United States has and turn it against them. Make it a weakness. And then sit back and watch the implosion."

The air in the room was noticeably chillier. A brilliant, relentless adversary was laying a plan and everyone there could feel it. "And Atef and Makkawi here will exploit every weakness you give them. Do you understand?" He directed the question to all three.

"Perfectly," Atef responded. "Samir will hammer away at their strengths until they convert to a weakness, and Makkawi and I will attack every newly identified weakness. I have just one question."

"Yes?"

"How will we know when they are neutralized?" Atef asked. And then, somewhat clumsily, he added, "In case you are not here to evaluate."

Zawahiri wondered if the question was as sinister as it sounded. He would be speaking to Atef afterwards and would address his indiscreet comment then. For now, the Doctor smiled and answered, "They will not just be isolated; they will no longer be able to move. You will see indecision. When they are stalemated on decision points, you will know we are there. By the way, it will be obvious. No decision, no action. Just remember that. No action, no confidence. At that point they're done. It's very simple. Don't complicate it."

"That's it?" Makkawi asked.

"Yes, that's it. The burden, of course, is on our friend, Samir, here. But he'll have help."

"Who?" Makkawi asked, not knowing if it was even appropriate to do so.

"His fifth column," the Doctor answered. "The one he has already, and the one he will create. And before you get your hackles up, Muhammad, about our Personnel Department and us usurping their authority in recruiting, let me assure you this will not be done in any way that the world has experienced before."

The mystery was considerable even for them. He took it even further. "We are entering new territory. And this recruiting will be like none you have ever experienced. At an appropriate time Samir will fill you in, or you may figure it out on your own as events unfold."

"That's all you're going to tell us now," Atef interjected abruptly. "Right, sir." For a moment Zawahiri wondered why he had commented. But he let it go.

"For reasons of security, Makkawi, after this meeting you are to separate from Atef. Use the normal communication channels, but we need you in separate locations in Afghanistan. No one raid by U.S. forces must be able to take us all out."

"Understood."

The Doctor continued, "Samir, have you received all new releases from Nanda and his team?"

"Yes, I have. I also have been provided with our contact person in each market for distribution of the propaganda releases. And I have the communication channels and equipment necessary for accomplishing all this."

"Good. You, of course, will be nowhere near Atef or me. Do you know your escape route?"

"Yes, a bit hot right now, though."

Zawahiri responded kindly, "I know. You'll wait here with me until it settles down. Our people across the border in the tribal region will house you until your move to Peshawar. It should be interesting for you there. Nice opportunity to play Musharraf, don't you think?"

"He's in an awkward position right now. I should have an opportunity or two." Samir winked at the others.

"He'll save his own skin. He won't be looking for the likes of you at all." Then, as if to reassure his propaganda officer, "You know, gentlemen, Samir is the only one of us who is completely off the radar screen. No one is even looking for him. Nice position to be in, don't you think?" They did.

The significance of this did not escape Atef. "Imagine, a man whose face is not on a Most Wanted poster!" With that they all ate some fruit and prepared to leave. Atef, however, disturbed the ending by voicing one final question.

"Ayman, since the Spanish Civil War, a fifth column has typically been what General Vidal referred to as an enemy in your midst, a subversive that engages in sabotage or espionage to aid the enemy without."

The Doctor was listening intently and didn't seem to mind the rudeness of someone overriding his control of the meeting. Atef continued, "How does public relations fit in here?"

"Simple," the Doctor answered. "There is a bit more to the definition of fifth column. I am specifically referring to subversive agents who attempt to undermine a nation's solidarity. And that, most definitely, is in Samir's territory."

The Doctor waited for a minute. He contemplated whether to speak further, and decided it would be best to inspire even the senior commanders at this time. *After all, isn't that what great commanders are expected to do?* Zawahiri thought. Very purposefully he continued, "My brothers, we are going to break the solidarity of the United Nations. We are going to break the solidarity of the United States and its allies. And when America is alone and maligned, we are going to break the solidarity of the Americans themselves. This is their final hour. The scourge that they and their Western allies have brought to this fair earth is ending. The pollution of Islam and the Holy Land is ending. We will wipe it clean, and we will wipe it clean in the next five to ten years."

This was Samir's moment to impress and he seized it, "Yes, and for that I have prepared two lists. One is 'Witting Fifth Columnists' and the other is 'Unwitting Fifth Columnists.' The U.S. will be expecting and looking for the *witting*. It's the *unwitting* list that will break their resolve. You bring in the body count, Muhammad, and I'll break their resolve."

"Clear now?" the Doctor asked.

"Yeah, for now."

Atef could not have known it, but that simple statement sealed his fate. The Doctor sensed a fracture coming. And his mind was made up.

"May Allah be with us. Safe journey." Zawahiri prayed. As Atef passed him to exit the close quarters, the Doctor gently pressed his forearm and whispered, "Please stay, I need you to arrange a meeting for me."

The two men stood silent for a moment as the others cleared the room. The sound of a cart's wheels on the rock-strewn street outside was the only external noise they could hear. The Doctor was about to speak when Atef began.

"Ayman, before we get into this, there are a couple of matters I did not want to discuss with the others. Decisions I feel you should know about."

"Yes?"

"I have issued an assassination order for President Musharraf. He's made his bed now and he has endangered our people and our goals. No one can double-cross Al Qaeda and go unpunished."

"I agree. Do you know when it will be done?"

"As soon as he lets down his guard. Right now, I'm sure he has maximum security around him. He knows this will mean his death. So we'll wait until we have him. I would guess a year, maybe longer. But we will get him."

"All right. What is the second?"

"I'm sorry to have to advise you of this. But Peshawar is no longer safe. You should remove Azza and your children from the villa and bring them to your safest point in Afghanistan."

The Doctor did not want to hear this. As best he could, he had kept his loyal wife and children from harm's way. Unlike Bin Laden who was always parading his wives and children around, subjecting them to the possibility of assassination, he had allowed his wife to live in relative comfort and security in Peshawar. True, it was far from her home and her beloved mother, but Azza had always known her duty. Her place was with her husband, no matter what.

Zawahiri was not a sentimental man, but Azza had represented Islam well. She was devout and had impressed him as a young man by wearing the niqab to cover her face. At a time when other Muslim women were being encouraged by the West to expose their faces and many other parts of their body as well, Azza had found favor in his eyes. She had served him well as a wife and took excellent care of their five girls and one boy.

Though they saw each other rarely, and though she knew what her husband was doing, Azza had resisted the temptation to return to Egypt and live comfortably with her family, who were mostly lawyers.

So it was with a sigh of resignation that the Doctor agreed with his military commander that it was time to bring his family into the Keep. "Very well, and I thank you for your advice. I can see it is done with respect and candor. Will you do the same with your family?"

"Yes, it is being done as we speak."

"I see. Well, this ties in with my request of you."

Atef seemed forthcoming and most ready to serve. It was too bad he had lost his edge.

"Muhammad, I want you to arrange a meeting between me, the Dictator and his two sons. The meeting can be in Baghdad, but you must have the sons with him."

This request appeared to stun Atef. He couldn't disguise his opinion that this was just too dangerous. "May I ask why you would do such an imprudent thing?"

"Yes, of course. In order for the Dictator to take the bait, he must believe we are absolutely sincere. My doing something as outrageous as traveling to Baghdad at this time should convince him of our sincerity. Moreover, never forget that he is an arrogant man and he will puff himself up over a face-to-face with me. He will regard it as a coup to be meeting with Bin Laden's second."

That made sense to Atef. Then the Doctor continued, "His sons must be there. Do not let him send his sons in his stead. It is all three of them, or nothing."

That was a taller order, but Atef knew immediately why that would be necessary. They were about to double-cross one of the world's great double-crossers. Saddam Hussein would like nothing better than to send just his sons to negotiate. Then he would feel free to break the deal later, claiming that his two headstrong sons had made a deal he was not in agreement with. The Doctor would not allow that.

"Tell him, I will speak only to him, personally."

Insuring that Hussein did not deceive them with one of his famous doubles could be forestalled by making certain that Hussein had to negotiate the deal himself. It was risky, but he was also greedy. Atef knew Hussein cared nothing for his people, but he did like leverage. And they were about to give him some. There was only one thing that Atef was now unsure of.

"Tell me, Ayman, once we know you have the real Hussein in the room with you, how is the real Ayman Al-Zawahiri going to be in the room? He will be expecting Nanda's father, will he not?"

"I will take him with me. He will introduce me as Bin Laden's personal emissary who has the knowledge of chemical, nuclear and biological weapons necessary to pull off the intelligence fraud of this magnitude. It will be me talking, with

Nanda's father nodding agreement and assent. Do not worry. I will take care of that."

Atef trusted the Doctor on this point. After all, the whole intelligence community had already been fooled by Zawahiri; why not Saddam Hussein? Then the Doctor continued, "When we leave, I will accompany my double to my home in Peshawar and prepare my family. He will stay behind to facilitate their departure and I will return to the Keep by myself. Can you handle security on all that?"

"Absolutely. Where will you go after your family is secured?"

Given the decision the Doctor had already made, he was unwilling to tell this to Atef. All he would say was, "I will leave the country. I will be more effective outside of Afghanistan. That is all I will tell you, Muhammad, as I do not want to endanger you in the event of capture. From now on, each of us must secure our survival separately. We must not leave Al Qaeda headless."

"No, we certainly wouldn't want to do that." Atef spoke quietly, unable to hide the sarcasm.

The Doctor knew this was his opportunity. They had served together for many years. They had won many great victories. Atef deserved a straightforward question. "Is there something you mean to say to me, Muhammad?"

Atef looked away for a long moment. He wished it had not come to this, but he recognized that he had done an incompetent job of concealing his feelings of late. Without any preparation he blurted, "I know what you did."

The Doctor did not flinch. Nothing gave him away, he was sure. "What do you mean?"

"Usama. I know you killed him." There, it was said.

Taking a deep breath, the Doctor looked directly at Atef. "Muhammad, our friend was a sick man. His health was failing, his mobility diminishing. The stress of these moves was weakening him and those around him. It was only a matter of time. He knew that."

Atef had to admit that was a masterful answer—a non-confession confession. He was quick to spot that it was above all a circumspect justification for what he knew the Doctor must have done.

"Surely you can see, Muhammad, that as regrettable as it is, our cause is strengthened by the fact that he can never be captured or placed on trial. He is larger than life now. He would have wanted it this way."

It was not until that moment that Atef really understood how much Ayman Al-Zawahiri had been changed by those years in prison. As quiet and serene as his outward demeanor was, Atef knew now that the man was as cold and calculating a warrior as he had ever encountered. But, in his heart, he also knew that the Doctor was right. As perverse as it might seem, Usama Bin Laden had become a liability. And they were, in fact, better off militarily than they were a fortnight ago while he lived. The military commander that Atef was overrode the friend he had been.

"I just wish you had told me, Ayman, is all."

"I understand." And with that, the two men parted for the last time. The Doctor quietly took out his computer and made a note to himself to make a phone call. He verified the number he would need and made the entry for two months from that day. Logging off, he rose and called once again for Samir.

Samir came quickly, always seeking to please. "Yes? You need me?"

The Doctor smiled warmly and embraced the man he called his Information Officer. "Yes, Samir, if you can make time, I would like to discuss with you how we are going to literally drive the Americans insane."

CHAPTER 20

Kelly didn't know what to do with Harold Danforth. His appearance at her front door just days before Christmas was disquieting. She had a terrible feeling that this had something to do with the letter Andy had thrown away. Or perhaps with the four other letters she had found in his sock drawer, unopened.

All five letters were from the U.S. Chess Federation and Mr. Danforth was the chairman of the organization. She had met him briefly, of course, at tournaments in which Andy played. In fact, the photo that James had spotted in the magazine featured Danforth and Andy. Under other circumstances she would have welcomed a visit. After all, Andy's victories had earned him his MIT scholarship, or at the very least, had attracted their attention. And Mr. Danforth's glowing recommendation of Andy to his alma mater had cinched it. That was why it was so disturbing to Kelly that Andy was discarding letters from this man whom he highly regarded.

Although Danforth had politely asked if he could speak with Andy, Kelly didn't handle mysteries very well. Finally, she had coaxed out of him that Andy had forfeited defending his World Chess Champion title by failure to respond to the formal invitations to participate in the U.S. Masters Championship and in the Chess Olympiad for the World Chess Federation. Fearing that he might have another Bobby Fisher on his hands, and being genuinely concerned for Andy's well-being, Danforth had come from Philadelphia to see what the problem was.

Unfortunately for Danforth, he had come in the evening when he assumed he would have a better chance of catching Andy. Andy and James were downstairs and Kelly knew there was no way she could interrupt. That was the rule. So she had tried to stall for Andy, and then finally had encouraged Mr. Danforth to return to Philadelphia with the promise that she would have Andy contact him.

Danforth had just left, but with misgivings. The chess community at the top is a small one and it wouldn't be long before rumors would float about Andy. Unbeknownst to Danforth or James or Andy, a chess fan by the name of George Nasser was paying very close attention to tournaments and their attendees. Living quietly by himself on the Upper West Side of Manhattan, Mr. Nasser was a professor of history at Columbia University. He was one of the most popular professors there and had been tenured for over 20 years.

He loved to play chess and was conversant about every major tournament and every major player in the world. Those who knew him surmised it was just some form of hobby with Mr. Nasser. In fact, it was more than a hobby. It was a profession. Mr. George Nasser was a paid operative of Al Qaeda, with long-standing ties to the University of Cairo, and to one bookish medical student he had met some 32 years earlier.

His job was to review all significant play occurring in the world of chess and to spot anyone who might be CIA. The Agency was known to use it as a recruiting source, given the analytical abilities of the high-level players. The fact that these players were making tournament appearances in countries all over the world provided excellent cover as well.

Just as Harold Danforth was returning home empty-handed, George Nasser was reviewing the contestants in a number of tournaments. One name caught his attention. Not for its presence, but for its absence. He had spotted that Andrew Weir of Arlington, Virginia was not in attendance at a key national tournament. That alone would not mean anything. But a quick review of the players in the upcoming World Tournament revealed a glaring omission. Andrew Weir was not on the list.

And George Nasser decided to find out why.

Kelly had planned to speak with Andy after James left, but Kelly wasn't much of a poker player. James took one look at her look of consternation and innocently asked, "Kelly, is something wrong?"

She would have preferred to confront her son alone, but it didn't seem to her that she had a life with her son much anymore. Since James had come into their lives, they had this odd new "family," and there were secrets. So she figured, *What the heck; he's probably in on this somehow,* and decided to confront the two of them.

"Yes, James, I had an unexpected visitor while the two of you were sequestered down there. Andy, Mr. Danforth came by." She paused to see what Andy would do with this. He looked sheepish. Looking down, he ran his hand through his hair and then finally looked up at his mom.

James didn't know what this was about, but figured it was best to just listen. So the three of them just stood there in the front hallway, looking at one another.

"I'm sorry, Mom, I should have told you," Andy broke the tension.

"I would understand if you didn't want to play in tournaments anymore; I wouldn't necessarily agree, but I would understand. What I don't understand is your rudeness in not even responding to the committees. These people have been very good to you—especially Mr. Danforth—and I raised you better than that."

She hadn't spoken harshly. In fact, her words revealed more hurt than anger. It was clear to James that there was a kind of openness between Kelly and Andy that went beyond the normal mother/son thing. He guessed that they had needed each other after his father's death in order to survive at all and they had been confidants ever since. This time Andy had left her out and it was clear she didn't understand why.

James knew all too well that intelligence work made its participants withdrawn and secretive if they weren't careful. You have to monitor so much of what you say and do that eventually it just becomes easier to stay by yourself. Yes, he did know that, and he chastised himself that he hadn't been paying close attention to Andy. Looking back, he could see some symptoms, but frankly he was so committed to getting answers that he just assumed this well-adjusted kid could handle it.

"Mom, you did raise me right. I don't know why I didn't respond. I'll call Mr. Danforth and straighten it out. I promise."

"And you're going to play if he'll let you?" she asked, as if his playing could somehow restore normalcy to their lives.

"No, Mom, I don't want to play."

"But why?" she asked, genuinely confused.

Andy wanted to tell her that he was living chess everyday now. Even when he was at school finishing his last year, every spare thought would wander back to trying to identify what his opponent was doing. Before, the games were just games, but this man was a mass murderer and would destroy everything Andy loved if he could. This man was playing for keeps. The thought of playing chess to just play chess now was unbearable to him.

"Andy, I asked you why?"

"Because I don't want to, that's all, Mom." He knew that would hurt her even more to not tell her why, but he couldn't reveal to her what they were doing down there. She knew it was classified; she knew the house was swept for "bugs." It hurt him, but he could not tell her.

Kelly looked so awkward, standing in the hallway. It was clear she wanted to say more, but withheld it with James there. Andy continued, "Mom, trust me. I'm okay; I just don't want to play." Stooping down a little, he looked into her downcast face. "It's okay, Mom; I promise. I'm not trying to hurt you, but I just can't explain. You'll have to accept that." And then Andy said something that must have been characteristic of his father, "You did raise me right, Mom, and I'm a man now. I have a reason to do what I'm doing, and you're just going to have to let it go at that."

Kelly looked at him a little warily for a minute and then suddenly laughed. James didn't know what to make of that. "You're just like your father. He used to do that to me, too." And she laughed again. "But you apologize to that man. The poor guy drove all the way from Philadelphia!"

"I will. You're totally right on that."

James hesitated to say anything but thought he should.

"You know, a little break might help. We have been spending a lot of time cooped up down there. What do you say we take a breather? Remember, take a walk."

Kelly didn't seem to mind being left out of an inside joke, especially since James was suggesting just what she wanted. She agreed. Andy surprised her by asking if he could speak to her in the kitchen. They left James alone, still standing in the hallway.

"Mom, I don't think James has anyone to spend Christmas with. I don't think he has any family," Andy whispered. She knew what was coming next. Her son had always brought home orphans and strays, just like his dad. During the all-too-brief 11 years they were married before he had passed away, there was not one holiday they had spent together without some Army buddy who didn't have a place to go on the holiday. Her husband was just one of those kind people who didn't want anyone who served his country to eat alone, especially at Christmas. It was so predictable, in fact, that she had always stashed a few extra gifts away in a box, just so she could put something under the tree for them as well. Any anger she might have felt with Andy's recent secretiveness vanished when she realized he was just like his dad. He was kind, and she was grateful for that.

"I'd like to invite James for Christmas." He was almost apologetic.

Taking her son's handsome face in her hands, she squeezed his cheeks like she'd done so many times when he was little and said, "Just like Dad. It's fine. Go ask him."

You would have thought James had been made to stand in the hallway outside the principal's office the way he looked when Andy returned.

"Sorry, Kid; your mom's right. We can take off through Christmas."

"Yeah, great. James, Mom and I want you to come over for Christmas dinner."

James was surprised, but the Kid said it so emphatically that he didn't really leave room to refuse. "Sure, okay, I'd like that." And that was the truth. For the first time in a long time, this shadow warrior wasn't going to be ordering the turkey dinner special at Lucy's Coffee House in the District. He would spend it like normal Americans spend it.

He felt a sense of relief somehow.

After he left, Andy kissed Kelly, said goodnight, and bounded upstairs. "I'm going to sleep in a little Mom, if that's okay." It was.

"What've you got for me?" Ayman Al-Zawahiri asked Samir as he quietly entered the room they had met in earlier.

"The basic strategy laid out, and most of the plans. And I've got the list of personnel I'll be using," Samir answered confidently. He had learned never to appear hesitant in the presence of Bin Laden or the Doctor. "If you'll allow me, I'd like to review it with you and have you side-check it for me. You know, to see if I've implemented the pivotal viewpoints as you intended."

"Of course."

Samir had his laptop with him. He sat quickly and logged into a top security file. If the American forces could ever find this file, he doubted they would believe the possibility of anyone accomplishing the scope of what was included there. Frankly, he doubted if they would even comprehend it. And if they did, they would dismiss it as sheer madness. That, he was counting on. In fact, that was why he knew this campaign would prevail. Al Qaeda was patient. They were long-term. Seeds planted long ago were being harvested by them now.

"Frankly, I'm looking forward to this. This is the most aggressive public relations campaign I could ever have imagined. It is a credit to you and Usama, and it is a privilege for me to be entrusted with it. I promise you, Ayman, I will succeed."

"I know you will. We've already had some sizeable help from our friends in Switzerland." As the Doctor said that, he was looking forward to leaving Afghanistan and to the pleasure of reviewing his stock portfolio. This "war" was making him a wealthy man and it was booming an industry that he was a "player" in. It was all according to plan. Tonight he was quite serene and he had confidence in Samir. He was the best.

"Let's take a look," he gestured as Samir opened up the first file.

The Doctor couldn't help but note that Samir always looked out of place in these settings. Although he was wearing the type of robe and apparel that they all wore when they were in Afghanistan, it never looked natural on him. People joked about the Doctor wearing a business vest over his caftans and what a dichotomy that wardrobe represented.

Samir didn't do that. He actually tried to look like a Muslim. He was one of course, but his years in the West had left an indelible mark on his bearing and his personal wardrobe style. He was in fact the kind of man who looks most relaxed and natural in a business suit. One would guess he would wear laundered shirts with heavy starch. His silk ties would come from the finest mills in Italy. Shoes would be immaculately polished, and his hair and manicure would reflect a man who was careful to details—neat and conservative. Yes, he would fit in perfectly in New York, Paris, Berlin, Milan, Geneva or Singapore. These were the cities he frequented and his cover was effective. But here, with his Al Qaeda brothers, he looked out of place.

The Doctor noticed that he had wavy black hair. Samir usually kept it so neatly cropped that no one would have guessed that it was so thick and wavy. But weeks of being on the run prohibited Samir his usual hygiene and grooming. Today he looked more like an artist than a public relations guru. Zawahiri smiled, trusting that Samir would be an artist in the work ahead. He personally relished the idea of the destruction that he and Samir were dreaming up.

Samir asked suddenly, "I need to know, how important is regime change in the U.S. and Britain?"

With no hesitation whatsoever the Doctor answered, "Very, but not vital." Then clarifying, he added, "We'll take care of Bush and Blair in the next military theater. But it is not vital to our plans to have them gone. Whoever their people offer up now is really of no consequence. We've got them either way."

"Then do you want me to expend resources to take them down?"

"Absolutely. In general, it is my view that any time you can get the enemy to change its players and game plans in midstream, you are better off." He continued enthusiastically, "The Americans are particularly vulnerable here. Their military is not, but their civilian congressional leadership is stupid beyond belief. They actually believe that every new regime almost has an obligation to change the programs, plans and strategies of the predecessor."

Samir concurred. Zawahiri added, "And that is one of the great pitfalls of trusting the selection of leaders to the people themselves. Their selfishness forces the leader to change direction. That's our advantage."

"What are you referring to?" Samir asked, more to affirm his own thought process than to learn something new.

"We have patience, and continuity. They do not. Even if a good leader follows a good leader, it still produces inconsistent actions. Notice the difference between them and us. Our great Usama is gone, but there is no breach of continuity whatsoever. We know our purpose and none of us will deviate from that."

"Yes, I agree, and that is why I am especially pleased with this project. It should drive the Americans away from their purpose. At the very least, it will obscure it."

Zawahiri laughed and joked, "That shouldn't be too hard. The Americans strayed from their purpose long ago. And we will take advantage of that, right?"

"Absolutely," Samir confirmed. "In fact, let me show you the plan."

With that, he brought up on the screen the "Areas of Attack" list. It was impressive. Samir had laid out on one side of the page a list of things the United States and its people regarded as their strengths. The arrogance and misguidance of it almost made him gag as he had drawn it up. But he was confident that in this repugnant list was the ruin of America, if he could turn the asset.

On the right-hand side of the page was what he intended to turn the strength into—how it would manifest itself as a weakness. Various attachments then laid out the specific marketing approach he was going to take and the list of people who would participate in accomplishing it.

Samir graduated first in his class because he, like Zawahiri, understood that things are as you consider them to be. The same event from different perspectives looks differently. Samir called it the Rashomon Effect after a popular Japanese movie about an incident seen through the eyes of four different people. Each one saw the same set of facts differently because each one saw the event through his own emotional filter.

Therefore, he knew that regardless of the "facts" as they were about to unfold in the coming months and years, his assignment was to get people to see them through the "emotional filter" he picked for them. That was why he enjoyed his time with Zawahiri so much. He had never met anyone who understood the mind as well as Ayman Al-Zawahiri, and he knew that the particular type of mind control through propaganda that he was about to create would require assistance from this master. So, with pride, he opened up the list to his mentor.

Zawahiri asked, "What do they regard as their greatest strength? Let's start there."

"I would have to say their freedom."

"Then we will use their freedom to entangle them to the point they are enslaved. Their 'freedom' will become their worst enemy. Do you understand?"

Samir did. In fact, he had begun the planning already. "Yes, Ayman, I do. I've even taken this into the sub-categories on which they hang their superiority. By that I mean their Constitution and precious Bill of Rights. They are most vulnerable on the freedom of speech. By the time I'm done with this, their speech will sound like the cantankerous ranting of fools. The dissention will be huge, and the volume and hysteria will make them appear ridiculous."

"Good, very good."

"Their pride in their justice system is another point of vulnerability. One of the things, Ayman, that repulsed me the most while I lived in the United States, was their sanctimonious raving about their justice system. The fools never even looked at the result of their indulgent cry-baby system—more and more criminals and perversion."

Samir spoke with such venom here that the Doctor admonished him slightly. "Samir, your observations are brilliant as usual, but I caution you to monitor your own emotion in this arena. Be like me. You identify the target and then dispassionately attack it. Emotion can cripple you at a key moment. Remember that."

Samir took it well. "I will. In any case, my plan will eventually render them helpless in the trials of those they capture. By the time I'm done, they will be so confused; it will be easier to just release the ones they capture than to confront the animosity and morass of trials."

"Their right to bear arms will be turned to our right to bear arms. We will enjoy and exploit every freedom they offer and we will use it to trap them."

At this point the Doctor interrupted. "Excuse me, Samir. You are on the right track, but I want you to make one adjustment."

"What is that?" Samir asked sincerely.

"I want you to regard the Americans' great strength as their goodness and their sense of fair play. I think if you look at this for a moment, you'll find that they regard these as their strengths. And that you will be able to punch the 'Good' button and 'Fair Play' button with each of the other areas you attack."

Samir looked at that for a moment, turning his head to a cocked angle as if that might help. He smiled. "I see. I see. We can turn their goodness into indecisiveness and weakness. That would cause them to treat a true enemy like any other accused, and will entangle them into the morass. I get it. Use their goodness against them."

"Exactly. With everything that Atef and I and the others in the years ahead bring to the table, ask yourself, what would an American who wants to be *good* do, in order to remain Good and Right?"

"So, whether it is Respect for Life, Courage, whatever it is, I look for the opposite and encourage them to that."

"Yes. That's the best way to neutralize the Americans. Get them to do the opposite of what they normally consider the right thing to do, in the name of doing the right thing, and they will implode."

The Doctor could see that Samir was already creating on that last five minutes of instruction. He decided to elevate the level of information for Samir a bit. "Did I ever show you where I learned this, this turning right into wrong, this stalemating effect?"

"No, never."

"You remember my imprisonment. It was there that I began a thorough study of the mind. It was obvious to me that just playing war games would only lead to more centuries of give and take, victories and defeats. I concluded that the way to win was to use the mind, to bring the mind of your enemy under your control. And I had to learn to do it remotely, as I doubt if I will ever be invited into the White House." They both laughed heartily at the idea of Ayman Al-Zawahiri walking into Number 10 Downing Street or 1600 Pennsylvania Avenue.

The reality was the Doctor could very well be on the guest list for such prestigious locations. For no one in the world, save for a handful of his colleagues, knew what the Doctor looked like. And no one except Samir knew the true location the Doctor called home. This fact would bring the United States to the brink of collapse in the coming years.

But the Doctor had no intention of delivering blows directly himself. No, he had found a much safer, more effective way of undermining the effectiveness of his opponent. Tonight, he decided to let Samir have a peek at the origins of his transformation from unknown militant to the mastermind of the deadliest group on the planet. That was something he was proud of and didn't mind sharing with a fellow as bright as Samir. In fact, he was confident Samir would know immediately how to use this data.

"May I?" the Doctor asked as he logged on to his own computer and pulled up a file. The file was not confidential. It didn't need to be. The Doctor knew his enemies would fail to understand the importance of the information even if he personally handed it to them. They were already too far gone. For that, he was grateful. His colleagues would guess at the ramifications, especially with the help of Samir. And that is why he showed it to him now.

The file was under the name of G. Brock Chisholm. As Samir scanned it, he observed that Dr. Chisholm was a Canadian psychiatrist trained at Yale and in London. He was once the Director General of the World Health Organization and resided in Geneva until his death. Samir laughed as he remembered who this gentleman was. He was the guy who had said children should not be encouraged to believe in Santa Claus. They had studied that at Princeton as an illustration of how to blow an analysis of your marketplace! Santa Claus, it seems, is important to the children of the West, and Dr. Chisholm had not taken that into account. His statement inflamed the world. It had become a kind of reverse public relations.

For the moment Samir didn't understand how this PR blunder could be relevant. Then he saw some random quotes attributed to Dr. Chisholm that Zawahiri had highlighted. Dr. Chisholm and a Dr.Rees had gone beyond just the World Health Organization. They were cofounders of the World Federation of Mental Health. That didn't particularly stand out. One would expect two psychiatrists who were committed activists to perhaps create an organization fostering their field of interest. It was the quotes, however, that caught Samir's eye:

> The re-interpretation and eventually eradication of the concept of right and wrong…these are the belated objectives of practically all effective psychotherapy…. If the race is to be freed from its crippling burden of good and evil, it must be psychiatrists who take the original responsibility…. And lastly…psychiatry must now decide what is to be the immediate future of the human race. No one else can….

Amazing! Samir thought. Puzzled, he asked, "This World Federation of Mental Health? Is that what their charter says?"

"No," the Doctor paused. Then he added, "You wouldn't expect it to, would you?"

"No, I can't imagine their being that bold."

"They weren't. I found those amongst his writings. He was a pretty outspoken fellow and it was not difficult to find. But I got some very good ideas from him. Ones we can use now."

Samir was deep in thought. This was clobbering even his mindsets. Nothing he saw at Princeton prepared him for what came next.

The Doctor took a unique pleasure in offering up this treasure to his disciple. He did view Samir as such, and he knew this young man would eventually grasp this and deploy it in his PR tactics.

"…Public life, politics and industry should all of them be within our sphere of influence…." *That's harmless enough,* Samir thought. The next quote, however, chilled him. He had not thought of this. "…We have made a useful attack upon a number of professions. The two easiest of them naturally are the teaching profession and the church[;] the two most difficult are law and medicine…."

"Samir," the Doctor interjected, "remember this was written some time ago. A lot has happened in law and medicine since 1940. It certainly opened up my eyes and gave me ideas, however." Samir wasn't quite sure what the Doctor meant by that.

"Read what comes next. I think you'll find this most useful to you."

It was somewhat dark in the room. The greatest light came from the computer monitor itself. There were odd shadows on Samir's face as he read, "If we are to infiltrate the professional and social activities of other people I think we must imitate the Totalitarians and organize some kind of fifth column activity! ... Let us all, therefore, very secretly be 'fifth columnists.'"

"Amazing," Samir exhaled. He actually was a bit numb.

Jokingly, the Doctor nudged his student, "So Samir, I suggest you reexamine your experience with the West and its current culture, and you go and find your fifth columnists."

"They're already there," Samir said under his breath. And then as if to convince himself he repeated, "They're already there."

"For 60 years they've been there. Do you see now why I know we can wrap this up in just a few years? They have already created a psyche in the West that will enable you to recruit your own fifth column quite easily. Delicious, don't you think?"

Both men appreciated irony. For it was Christmas season in their enemy's camp.

CHAPTER 21

December 2001 ended innocuously and disappointingly for some. For the United States and Britain, it was hard to endure the reality that Usama Bin Laden had slipped through. How much easier it would have been for them and their television generations to have been able to wrap up that storyline quickly. The Doctor was right. The seed of impatience was planted and it would reap a full doubt. And, a long night of agony was beginning for Pakistan.

In different parts of the world, men plotted. Andy and James, perhaps the only two people who had any real idea of what was happening, enjoyed a quiet traditional Christmas with Kelly. It seemed to James that his bosses were missing the picture, and he had a gut instinct that the Kid would tumble onto something in the New Year. To his surprise, he wasn't the only "orphan" Kelly and Andy were taking care of. Before they enjoyed their Christmas dinner, the three of them went to the Tomb of the Unknown Soldier, and presented a full dinner and token gifts to the squad that had drawn duty that day. They eagerly took the food and cheer down into their barracks under the Tomb and thanked Kelly once again for being so thoughtful to fellow comrades. Before leaving Arlington Cemetery, Andy showed James his father's grave and placed a poinsettia on it.

James later learned this was a ritual with Kelly and Andy, one they had followed since their husband and father had passed away nine years earlier on Christmas morning. As James looked across the Potomac to the Capitol, he whispered to his friend Abe, whose monument was the first to greet people who crossed the bridge, "I won't let you down." And with that solemn promise, he sucked in the damp air and prepared to feast on Kelly's delicious dinner.

Farther north, a Columbia University professor made plans to take a short trip to Washington, D.C. in order to deliver a lecture on the history of the Hashshashin to the Central Intelligence Agency.

In Peshawar, in one of the city's finest hotels, a respected businessman from a European public relations firm was putting finishing touches on his battle plan. His strategic planning section would have made interesting reading had it been seized or discovered. But it was worded in such a way that it could apply to any ad campaign. After all, business was ruthless. Wasn't that common knowledge? The plan was simple: make every right a wrong, and every wrong a right. Use this to promote two-sidedness and hang them up in maybes. Once they were steeped in "maybe we should and maybe we shouldn't," then make them wrong, even when they are right. *The Americans were right to attack after September 11. We weren't prepared, is all,* Samir thought to himself. *We won't let that happen again. This one slipped by us. The world agreed with the U.S. and made them right. Next time they attack and defend, we'll make them wrong.*

And with that, he completed his list of "The Fifth Column." He added the name of a U.S. Marine private to his list of "Witting" and made a pending note. This is one that would get utilized later in the game, to be sure. And on the list of "Unwitting," he circled in red the name of one of the most prominent media people in the world. *This should be fun!* he mused. *Of all the ones, his own arrogance will make him one of the easiest to turn.* The man was good. That was not the issue. And he was fair-minded. That was not the issue. The issue was that he was conceited. And he was ambitious. This man would make the perfect man to turn the United States into a giant, paralyzed "maybe." All Samir had to do was take the man from righteous to self-righteous. Confident in his plan to do that, he logged off and allowed himself a delicious dinner.

Muhammad Atef was in his safe house with his family. Presumably there he could coordinate the upcoming military activities in Afghanistan, Philippines, Indonesia—he had quite a list, and a lot of homework to do. But he took some pleasure in the fact that his family was with him, where they too could be safe. And he looked forward to activating Zarqawi.

In their villa in Peshawar, Azza and the children were waiting for Ayman, Nanda and his father. Ayman, of course, was coming separately, but she knew they would be united soon. This place had been a nice home, and she knew somehow that her next quarters would not be as pleasant. *At least the children will be near their father,* she thought. *When he arrives to help us move I will speak to him about our littlest. She needs some special attention.*

Outside a village in Iran, the inmates of a decrepit asylum were enjoying a better meal than usual. Money left over from the care of one of their fellow inmates was responsible for their good fortune. The man himself, however, was oblivious to that fact. He sat alone in a room, drugged, looking out the window at the barren trees. He spoke to no one.

Hundreds of miles away, Ayman Al-Zawahiri completed two moves on his three-dimensional chess board. On the Public Relations game, he labeled the Black Queen, "Samir," and advanced the Queen on the White Bishop. For the Doctor knew which piece Samir would move on first. *After all, he has had a great teacher. Certainly better than Princeton!* he gloated. The Queen is boss and is free to move in any direction. That was a good designation for Samir. His passport would not be challenged and he had access to everyone needed to bring the United States down. *And he is truly gifted,* the Doctor reminded himself.

Turning to his Military game, he labeled the Black Bishop, "Ayman," and advanced it on the opposing King. Choosing to think of himself as the Standard Bearer, the Italian's name for the Bishop, rather than Fool, which was the French name, he prepared to leave that night under cover of darkness to meet with Saddam Hussein. Accompanying him would be Nanda's father and a new security detail. On the Queen's side of the board, his Rook, labeled "Atef," was watching his back. He was responsible for the completion of this next crucial phase and Atef's chief of security was regarded as invincible.

The last things he did were make a note to "forfeit Queen's Rook," and place a phone call to a satellite phone outside of Kabul. He closed his notebook and prepared to usher in the New Year.

CHAPTER 22

Professor Nasser was especially pleased to accept the speaking engagement in the Washington, D.C. area. The Central Intelligence Agency had been quite anxious to accept his help in the War on Terror. His specialty in history was in the origins and development of extremism and the use of suicide terrorism. His doctoral thesis had been one of the more interesting reads of the early 1980's. And no one knew more about the Hashshashin, the assassination squads of 1094 A.D., than Dr. Nasser.

He had drawn astonishing parallels between the appeasement tactics utilized with Hitler prior to World War II, and the submission tactics used by the Lords when their fortresses were threatened by the assassination squads. The thesis caused controversy in New York City when he ended in present time by comparing the extortion tactics of the Mafia to the tactics of the Hashshashin.

Given the revelation that the young suicide attackers on September 11 had believed they would be rewarded in paradise, he knew the CIA would sooner or later want to talk to him about the methods used by the Hashshashin to drug and implant their young followers.

He would speak at Langley in their auditorium, and had been told it would be an historical briefing to bring the team investigating this area up to speed on the subtleties and historical context. It was too bad he had had to wait until February in 2002, but he knew that this speech would provide a very valid cover for his absence from Columbia.

All he had to do now was find out the address for one Andrew Weir, and he would take a ride over to Arlington,

Virginia after finishing at Langley. The secretary who had made his travel arrangements was very accommodating in giving him an extra day in Washington following his engagement.

Given that he was a well-known attendee of all major chess tournaments and a contributor to any fundraisers they held, a well-meaning and accommodating secretary had provided Andrew's address. Frankly, it was easier than he thought it would be. She wasn't suspicious at all when he said he wanted to mail a fan letter to the young star. Mapquest did the rest. *Nothing like getting directions right to the door!* he scoffed.

There was a damp chilly wind blowing across the parking lot at Langley. He was sent through the same security measures as all guests at the headquarters. Whitney was walking James out of his office when his secretary informed him of the arrival of his guest speaker. The two had been having a heated discussion about James' lack of anything concrete to contribute to the team's discussions. He felt this idea—predicting what Al Qaeda might do next by using this chess champion—was beginning to test his faith in James. The fact that James was sticking to his guns and had upped the ante to suggest they might even identify individuals through their analysis was intriguing to Whitney, but seemed like just BS to him at the moment. He was not in a good mood and blew James off verbally as they walked out of the secure area.

So when Dr. George Nasser extended his hand to greet Whitney, he introduced Nasser quickly to James Mikolas and indicated that Mikolas was one of their team but would not be sitting in on the lecture today. The two men shook hands and went their separate ways. As for James, he was relieved to miss another lecture. He needed to take a walk and think about Whitney's reactions. They were not optimum, and he was feeling the pressure.

It was already dark when Nasser left Langley and began a slow trip to Arlington. Somehow he didn't mind the dreariness of February in New York City, where the activity of the city itself provided color and interest. But staring at the taillights of the thousands of people in front of him on I-495, he felt almost disconnected. *This is probably a wild goose chase!* he thought, wanting to turn the rental car in and head for Dulles.

It's on the way to the airport, he debated with himself. From his vantage point, it would take just as long to continue on to the address on the seat beside him, as it would to turn the car in. So heaving a sigh of impatience, he decided to just do what he had intended to do. He was going to see if he could find out why the reigning World Chess Champion was not scheduled to compete.

Finally, after what seemed like hours, he pulled onto the quiet street where Andy and Kelly lived. Nasser realized then that he had no plan whatsoever, and moreover, he had no training whatsoever for this type of work. He was an analyst and spotter. But no one had ever trained him for field work.

Nasser, however, had a healthy self-image and figured it couldn't be that tough. He could figure it out. And if he came up with something, maybe Al Qaeda would promote him into something more than just one who scans chess tournaments looking for CIA moles. If he were really honest with himself, he had to admit that he was eager to get in the game.

Like so many other "sleepers" in the United States, he had no idea an attack was imminent that day last fall. And he had no idea what part they expected him to play in the ensuing war, if any at all. *This will make them notice me!*

Deciding not to do something as obvious as walk up to the door, he figured the best way to start was to park near the house, where he could keep an eye on the front door. And then, just wait. He anticipated that, if for some reason, someone questioned why he was parked there, he would just say the traffic had been so bad that he had pulled off the Beltway to read and miss the rush hour.

It was 6:30 when Dr. Nasser pulled up under a cluster of leafless maple trees and parked. His book was propped up in front of him on the steering wheel and he had his reading glasses on. Over the bifocals, he could easily keep an eye on Andrew Weir's house while appearing to be reading.

Hour after hour went by, with nobody even coming out onto the street, let alone out of Andy's house; and he was getting discouraged. He couldn't figure out how to proceed, since he didn't live in the area. Deciding that it had been just a pipedream driven by his own ambition, Dr. Nasser started the ignition and set the book on the seat.

Just as he put the car in gear, the front door of Andy's house opened and a man exited. He turned and waved goodbye to someone in the door who was just out of Nasser's eye-line. Although the man wore a coat and had turned his collar up against the wintry dampness, Dr. Nasser recognized the man. He had been introduced to him briefly that afternoon, just before he spoke.

Although he couldn't remember the man's name, he was sure he was the man with Whitney, and that meant he was CIA. *George Nasser may be lousy with names,* he admonished himself, *but I am very observant to detail. And I remember that man's badge was the same as Whitney's, and Whitney said he was on the team.*

He was almost giddy with excitement when he realized he had actually succeeded. Surely it could not be a coincidence that a CIA employee in the area of counter-terrorism would visit with his target for a long period of time. This man and Andrew Weir must be connected. And, it was his guess that was the reason Andrew Weir was absent from the list. He was working with the CIA. And Nasser concluded that was what his handlers, whoever they were, would want to know.

It was 11 p.m. and James did not notice the rental car as he got into his own car and drove away. For a moment, Nasser considered following him to try to get the man's name. But he decided against it, as he personally had no connections in Washington D.C. who would check license plates for him. He guessed it would be simpler to just innocently ask Whitney who the man was.

And it was. Before he left the next morning, Nasser called Whitney to thank him for the opportunity to speak to the team and, self-deprecatingly, mentioned to Whitney that he had trouble with names. "For example," he said, "I forgot the name of the man you introduced me to at the entrance, as soon as I shook hands with him. What was his name, by the way?"

"James Mikolas," Whitney answered without any hesitation.

A few hours later, from the privacy of his own apartment again, Dr. Nasser logged onto a chess game. If one had examined it closely, they would see that the game had been going on for some time. Moves were very sporadic. Then tonight, he logged a chess move into the game and pressed "enter." The symbols recorded were "26.Nf6." No one would have known that that particular move of the White Knight was an encoded message, indicating a penetration and threat to the opposing King and requesting direction on what to do.

Nasser had no idea who his game partner was, let alone where he was or how long it would take for the message to reach anyone in command authority. After all, he doubted that Usama Bin Laden and his lieutenants were anywhere near an Internet connection at this stage of the war.

He was wrong.

CHAPTER 23

Mikhal was stunned to receive the call from the Doctor. Ayman Al-Zawahiri had saved the life of his daughter following a car accident. The Doctor was quite a surgeon, and had taken pity on the poor father who couldn't get any help from the Taliban for his stricken daughter. He knew she was just going to die, because they cared nothing for the young women. But she was his only daughter.

On that night, when the Doctor had left Bin Laden's side to come and save her spleen, Mikhal had pledged that if the Doctor ever needed him, he would do anything for him.

So it was with a feeling of honor and with a willingness to repay a debt that Mikhal did something he never would have considered doing, had it not been as a favor to the man who gave him back his sweet little girl.

Excusing himself from the quiet of his home after dinner, he let himself out and made his way to the quarters of an American Special Forces Unit that was operating inside the city. The sentry saw him coming, clearly in violation of the curfew. But the young sergeant behind him recognized Mikhal from the neighborhood.

Signaling to his men that he was going outside, he stealthily slipped out the door and hugged the building. Mikhal nodded and the young sergeant motioned for him to approach. Looking at the man, he did not in any way suspect a trap.

As Mikhal got close enough for the sergeant to see him clearly, he recognized him as the teacher whose family lived a few blocks away. He wondered what the man was doing out here now, and why he would want to talk to Americans. Both men stepped back into the shadows and Mikhal leaned in close to deliver the message. In a moment, they separated. The sergeant watched Mikhal disappear around the corner before stepping inside again.

Immediately he got on the phone and informed his Colonel that they had a tip on the location of a high value target and he was waiting for instructions.

Muhammad Atef was hunkered down in his safe house in the outskirts of Kabul, directing military operations. He was in communication with Zarqawi who was safely ensconced in Baghdad. Zarqawi had recovered from his "wounds" and had been set up in business in northern Iraq by Uday and Qusay Hussein. What his ultimate activities would be were determined by the Doctor, and would be relayed to Zarqawi once the Iraq War began.

For now, however, Atef was planning attacks in Indonesia and Saudi Arabia, laying out a timeline for the next five years. He had been taught well by the Doctor to stagger the attacks and vary the locations. It had the effect of keeping the whole world off-balance.

They had successfully trained the Palestine Liberation Organization to never let more than seven days go by without some new insurgency or attack. Atef didn't know much about this mind stuff. But the Doctor did, and he had explained to them all that once the mind is dramatically upset by an event, it will settle down in about seven days. After that, the people sink into complacency again. So part of their tactics globally was to never let more than seven days go by without some form of attack to upset people again.

The Doctor was counting on Samir to exploit that, to guarantee it had the front page coverage and the lead story in the evening news. So far, Samir was right on top of it. Whether Al Qaeda claimed credit for an attack or not, the whole world was giving them credit. That was good for their resumé! And it confirmed once again the uncanny ability the Doctor had developed to pick the right people and tactics to keep people emotionally unstable.

Now that Atef was in his safe house in an ordinary neighborhood, he had access to news and the Internet by using a satellite phone. He tried to use what limited opportunity he had to access anything that might be important. The safest site for him to access innocuously was an Islamic chess site that had thousands of legitimate games going on around the world. Buried in amongst them was their code site, which enabled them to communicate with their "sleepers" around the world. Atef had reminded himself to check that site as soon as it was safe to do so.

He was dangerously close to American forces now, and he knew it was only a matter of time before he and the family would have to vacate. So for now, he was working long hours, trying to set and dispatch as many plans to their cell commanders as possible before he might have to disappear again.

Tonight, he frankly was overburdened by the plans he had to make in Chechnya. Zawahiri's brother, Mohammed, had been the primary person responsible for recruiting and training the Chechen rebels. But Mohammed had been kidnapped by Egyptian intelligence in the United Arab Emirates, returned to Cairo and had disappeared more than two years ago. He and Zawahiri knew that meant Mohammed was dead. But it also left that area headless in its military activities, so the burden of planning had fallen to Atef. This was a vital area, but their immediate problem brought on by the September 11 attacks was forcing Atef to place the execution dates well out into 2004. He figured that, between now and then, he would develop a devastating plan. He just wanted to watch the political landscape for a while and see what would develop.

So, closing the Chechnya file, he opened up the Chess site to see if there were any messages. Not really expecting to find any, he was a little lackadaisical, much like people who log into their email not really expecting anything but spam. But tonight, there was a flag indicating the presence of a message.

Opening it he could see immediately it was from the New York professor whom he and Ayman had known at university. Actually, Ayman had recruited him. He felt he might be useful in

New York, a sort of "eyes on the ground" person whose credentials gave him access to more than most.

The message disturbed him. He forwarded it to Makkawi, hoping to discuss it with him when they next met. He was composing an answer to Nasser, asking for more details on names and events in order to evaluate the seriousness of it, but he never completed it. There is nothing more unmistakable than incoming fire, and in his last moments, Muhammad Atef recognized the sound of missiles. His last thought was: *how did they find me?*

CHAPTER 24

Saddam Hussein recognized a good deal when he saw one. And he also recognized a double-cross. One thing he was certain of was that his game of stringing along the UN was nearing an end. He was making a lot of money selling oil to European nations illegally, but that could only continue as long as Iraq was embargoed. Once the embargo was lifted, the Iraq economy would return to a free market instead of one held captive by Hussein. His people would receive more money to be sure, but not him. And that was just not going to happen. They existed to serve him, not he to serve them.

Frankly, he was surprised the UN had dragged the resolutions out as long as they had. This was why he had nothing but pure disdain for any foreign minister who came to him. He knew full well that they represented men who were basically cowards. But he knew the time had come when he would need a new source of revenue for his personal coffers.

The deal Al-Zawahiri had presented through the "science" man he had brought with him had much to entice him. He mused that Bin Laden must be distracted, however, to think he would not be looking for the double-cross. To be sure, he was happy with the money he would receive for secretly selling off his chemical and biological material. And he relished the idea of disgracing the United States and Britain. He had a long score to settle with the Bushes, and he thought Tony Blair was eloquent, but pretentious.

It would be a stunning coup to put those two in their place, he thought. The plan called for Saddam, his two sons, and any other top echelon Cabinet personnel to vanish just as the United States attacks. He was to bluff with every available means until they attacked, but once they made their opening move, he would disappear into the elaborate network of escape tunnels and safe houses they had in Iraq. Everyone figured it would confuse the enemy when it appeared Iraqi forces were now headless. The apparent lack of a central command would work to their benefit.

Saddam particularly liked the Benefits List that Nanda's father handed him. Not realizing, of course, that the man he thought was Zawahiri was, in fact, an imposter, he thought it a bit odd they had written this down in this format. Seemed like an insurance salesman's pitch to him. The list had been drawn up, however, to make it easier for the imposter to maintain the disguise of Zawahiri. This way he wouldn't forget any key points, nor appear uncertain.

It worked. Saddam laughed decisively at one point, and the Doctor knew he would take the deal. What struck his sense of irony was that his country's infrastructure had virtually been destroyed by him and his policies anyway. There was nothing more he could squeeze out of his own people. But, once the Americans were through with their war, they would have to pour billions of dollars into reconstruction. *What idiots,* he thought. *The U.S., Britain and the UN will pay for the rebuilding of my country. When I return, I'll have a brand new source of cash!*

Saddam could literally see his nuclear weapons dreams materializing before him. Rich with cash, his enemies identified by who allied with the American forces, he could purge them easily when he returned to power. And this is where he would outsmart the great Usama Bin Laden.

Appearing to believe the escape route they had planned for him and his sons to Syria, he knew very well that, at the last minute, Syria would reject him. He knew Bin Laden was planning then that Saddam Hussein would be trapped and killed in Iraq. Why else would they be asking that this Zarqawi, who was being given asylum, be allowed to set up terrorist training camps in the northern part of Iraq?

He didn't buy for one minute this grandiose new alliance between him and Bin Laden. Obviously, Bin Laden was being driven out of Afghanistan and was looking for a new country to set up his operations in. What better country than Iraq, with the elaborate bunker system Hussein had created. But he would fool them.

Saddam Hussein reasoned that even with Zarqawi operating in his country, there would be an advantage. That ought to confound the U.S. and Britain even more. Certainly it would open up some public relations opportunities as well. While his activities would decoy the United States and force them to handle the hit-and-run tactics he assumed Zarqawi was concocting, the disruption and carnage would flush out a complete list of clerics who would need to be dealt with. *They'll write my target list for me.* He now calculated that Zarqawi could do that for him. Al Qaeda would attack anyone who allied with the U.S. *What a way to get rid of your enemies and have bloodless hands,* he smirked. *And the people of Iraq will hold me blameless.* If Usama Bin Laden was stupid enough to give him such a gift, he was going to take it.

Without telling his sons of any of his thoughts or plans, Saddam Hussein agreed to the deal. He would keep them on a need-to-know basis. No one but Saddam, however, would be privy to his plan of escape. When the moment came, he would double-cross the double-crossers. He would not go to Syria. He would, in fact, disappear into the Iraq that would protect him. And he would wait.

Certain that Zarqawi would distract the Americans, and the absence of chemical and biological stockpiles would discredit them as well, he knew he would return to power. His army and the loyal members of his party would regroup. He had only to wait it out. Zawahiri had assured him that the U.S. would lose the propaganda war, and this he did believe. He was very certain that they all had the means to have the United Nations put the screws to the United States, just like they had in the first Gulf War. It would be more intense this time, but then again, the money made it worthwhile.

If he handled it right, Zarqawi would help him get rid of all religious opposition. This appealed to him specifically. Being a man with no faith in anything but himself, he envisioned that the next Iraq would be a totally secular Iraq.

The man Hussein assumed was just a scientist, along to facilitate the briefing of how to break down and transport weapons for sale, kept a close eye on the Dictator as Nanda's father reviewed the document with him. He was looking for the double-cross and saw the exact moment Saddam decided to try it. No one else did though. Unfortunately for Uday and Qusay Hussein, it never occurred to them that their father would sacrifice them. That lapse in judgment would cost them dearly.

For now, it seemed to the brothers a great way to make $1 billion and, at the same time, end this United Nations weapons game they had been playing. They, like their father, felt that the real game was nuclear weapons. And for that, you need cash. They had the contacts; they needed the cash. Al Qaeda needed weapons and safe haven. It seemed a fair trade to them. In fact, it seemed as if the time when they could end Israel's miserable existence was at hand.

What was interesting was that no one in that room cared about the people of Iraq. They were merely an expendable resource. For every participant in this deal expected to live out the rest of their lives in wealth and comfort in some other part of the world.

Once the first installments of cash were transferred into Hussein's accounts in Jordan, Syria and Switzerland, the deal was done. The Doctor and his stand-in rejoined their security detail and made their way to Peshawar. Once there, they were greeted by Nanda. He had been of great assistance to Azza and the children in their preparations to move to a safe house.

If the house had been under surveillance, Zawahiri's enemies would have seen that a few hours after the man known as Zawahiri entered, another man joined the family. He was taller and thinner and, oddly, the children seemed to know him well. No one was watching, however. And Ayman Al-Zawahiri and his wife and family made their way out, in the company of Nanda and his father.

While Zawahiri was setting his family up in their new quarters, Saddam Hussein began to escalate his rhetoric against the UN inspections. The gradual deception was taking shape. As he gave the order for facilities to refuse the surprise inspections by the UN scientists, he knew exactly how that would be viewed within the intelligence communities of Israel, the U.S. and U.K.

What really tickled him was the ruse they were developing for the satellites that passed regularly over Iraq's known weapons facilities. *This will give them something to take pictures of.* He wished he could listen in as the analysts reached their conclusions about the significance of the photos. He knew they would see what they wanted to see. And that was why he was certain Al Qaeda's plan would work. Double-cross or no double-cross, it was a good plan.

And Saddam Hussein will, once again, prove who deserves to be Ruler of the Middle East, he affirmed to himself.

While Zawahiri was working the Iraq angle and securing his family, he got the word about Atef. The air strike had killed him and his aides and family. Makkawi was the one to break the news. Although they had policy about how often they could use the satellite phones, and what kind of call to make, the Doctor didn't mind this time. He would not admonish Makkawi for emotionally relaying the news of the U.S. strike and of the devastating consequences of the raid.

Knowing full well that the U.S. was listening in on every satellite phone transmission they could, he kindly advised Makkawi to calm down. Reassuring Makkawi that he was totally qualified to step into Atef's shoes, he then proceeded to commiserate with Makkawi about the price one pays for victory.

"We all know it could happen at any time, my friend."

"I know. It was just so unexpected. I just didn't think it would be this soon," the new military commander of Al Qaeda lamented. "The fortunate news is that he had transferred the plans to me just before. I have them and will see to it that they are executed."

The Doctor complimented him, "I have complete faith in you. And I suggest that we not discuss this any further on the phone."

He had no sooner begun the sentence than Makkawi jumped in, "You're right. I will be in touch." And then, he hung up. The call, however, was picked up and had been monitored. The tape of its content was relayed immediately to Langley and became one of the confirmations they needed to declare a probable "kill."

It was a good day for U.S. intelligence. Certainly the President would be happy that one of the world's most dangerous men had been eliminated. Further, intelligence files on Makkawi indicated that he was brazen and deadly, but nowhere near as brilliant as Muhammad Atef. He was known to have a terrible temper, and they were hopeful they could use that uncontrolled emotion against him. Between ambition and temper, there was opportunity.

And that was exactly what the Doctor had planned. Since the U.S. wanted this man so badly, this was a perfect chance to inflate their ego. Confident that his plan was materializing, he kissed his littlest girl on the forehead as she slept, and returned to the plans for his own escape from Afghanistan.

Whitney was ecstatic. If they had any champagne at Langley, he would certainly have broken it open. By the time James walked in, the best way to describe the normally dour Whitney was to say he was "aflutter." James couldn't help but smile at this change in his boss. He knew something had happened.

"What's up?" he asked.

"We got the son of a bitch!" Whitney said, pounding his fist into his other hand for emphasis.

"Bin Laden?" James asked hopefully.

"No." Whitney deflated ever so slightly. "But we got his military mastermind, Atef."

"Jesus! Really?"

"Yeah, we got it confirmed by a satellite call between Zawahiri and Makkawi. All we're waiting for now is for the ground team to confirm. Looks like a bloody mess, however."

"Where was he?" James asked.

"In his house, of all places. We got a tip. We confirmed the target individual and hit it with everything we got."

"Any pictures yet?"

Whitney was a little more vague now. "No. Given the size of the strike, no one made it out. We're going to have to call this one on DNA. But they're working on it. We should have something to give to the press in about four hours."

"Excellent."

"That ought to make up a little for Mullah Omar giving us the slip, don't you think?" The feigned negotiations and cease-fire deception that Omar had pulled off was still a source of embarrassment for the CIA and the military commanders in the field. The press, fortunately, had been so interested in what was starting to develop in Tora Bora that they had commented on the blunder, but not given it much airtime. For the moment, it had seemed they had dodged the bullet.

But the United States had not yet figured out, in a public relations way, how to ignore a cease-fire request, and then kill everybody there. It just didn't match people's concept of the Geneva Conventions, let alone their inherent sense of fair play. It would not be long before the Doctor would capitalize on the moral dilemma this presented.

For today, however, the people of the United States would be given a good headline. The press that day was looking for a victory, some good news. The death of Muhammad Atef fit the bill. It wouldn't be long before all of that would change, however. For Samir was hard at work on his part of the plan.

CHAPTER 25

When James had returned to Andy with the news of Atef's death, Andy had gone to the military chessboard he had laid out on the center table. Somewhat reluctantly, he removed the Black King's Knight from the board and set him on the side.

James knew enough by now to just let the Kid think. Something in the way Andy was still fingering the Knight made James wonder what Andy was thinking. He was silent for quite some time and then said, "That's it."

"What?" James asked.

"He'll advance a pawn. He has to."

James's understanding of chess was rudimentary at best, so he felt no embarrassment in saying, "Where are you going with this?"

"Zawahiri can't play without a Knight. If Atef is dead, he'll have to get another one. The way he will do that is to move a pawn across the board to the other side. If the pawn can avoid capture and arrives at the other side, he is promoted to whatever piece Zawahiri needs." Andy paused to let James catch up. "He needs a Knight, so he'll pick that. The next person we hear about will be the new Knight."

Andy was certain of it. And the young Grandmaster was right. The Doctor highlighted a layer in his model on his laptop. That layer, the second from the bottom, was labeled "Military." Then the Doctor moved a black pawn past a White Knight and Bishop and easily placed him on the other side of the board. Promoting his pawn to a Knight, he returned his Knight to the board and labeled it "Makkawi." Zawahiri, however, needed two Knights. So, on another part of the board, he advanced another pawn to the opposite side and promoted that pawn as well to Knight. Labeling the new knight "Zarqawi," he logged off.

Andy missed this last move initially. It would be months before he caught his mistake.

There had been another flurry of excitement in March of 2002. The U.S. got a report that Zawahiri and his whole family had been killed in an air strike. Then it was amended to a report that his family was killed but Zawahiri, badly wounded, had managed to escape. Later it was amended to his family presumed killed and Zawahiri definitely not killed in the house. The press doesn't like to be wrong and they began to look for someone to blame for "our inability to catch the top guys," as they called it.

In fact, Zawahiri's family was killed. Zawahiri, however, was nowhere near the home he had sequestered his family in. Staying with them to provide cover for the Doctor's escape was Nanda's father. It was a natural mistake that the informant thought he saw Ayman Al-Zawahiri in the yard of the home. After all, he had just recently seen him in a video that had been released by Al-Jazeerah.

When the attack began, Nanda and his father both were thrown clear of the home. Sustaining injuries, they were able to crawl away and were picked up by a sympathizer in a home near by. By the time the military got there to assess the strike, Nanda's father had been removed in an ambulance. It was thought that would give him his best chance of escape. The Red Crescent would have, in fact, deterred an attack by the Americans or Canadians.

Unfortunately for the man, Pakistani mercenaries in the area saw an opportunity to seize a vehicle. The driver, his "shotgun," and Nanda's beloved father, who was willing to risk his life for his son, were all shot and buried in a snow bank. Some weeks later a tip to the Canadians caused them to return to the area. There was enough of a break in the weather that they could exhume the bodies from their snowy graves and begin the identification.

Because the bodies had not been properly buried, they had decomposed enough to require DNA analysis for positive identification. The skull of the body believed to be Zawahiri was flown to Washington's FBI lab. The Egyptians had given them samples of Mohammed Al-Zawahiri's DNA in order to assist in a positive identification.

The samples did not match, and the people at Langley were deeply disappointed. Once again, the Doctor had eluded them.

It was fall now. Today, in fact, seemed as clear and beautiful to James as the morning of September 11. He had never been a man to feel he had much joy in his life. But he was certain he had none now. More than a year had passed since that fateful morning. Except for a developing pattern of Andy's being able to anticipate what move would come next in this imaginary chess game, there had not been any real breakthroughs.

The fact that they were alive at all in their project was credited to Andy's spotting the ascension of Makkawi as the new Black Knight to replace Atef. Andy had called the play, and in a matter of weeks it was evident that is what had happened. Whitney was reluctant to say it confirmed their theory. As far as he was concerned, it was a logical military move, not a chess one.

But, he was embarrassed enough about taunting James regarding the discovery of the body people hoped was Zawahiri. When word had come in, Whitney told James it was a good day for the good guys and he jabbed at him mercilessly about the chess theory.

"This should pretty well rap up your little project," he had joked. "No need for this nonsense anymore."

Whitney was a career bureaucrat, for sure. It never occurred to him that James would have been happy to have Zawahiri dead in some morgue. James was not advancing this project to secure a promotion for himself. Whether Zawahiri was dead or alive,

James didn't see any lessening in the threat of Al Qaeda. He just prayed that Zawahiri was not bright enough to have launched something that would have a life beyond his own and Bin Laden's. Anyway, when the final word came in from the FBI, they were all disappointed and just quietly returned to their routine.

Today, as he stood in Whitney's office to brief him on their latest analysis, he was eager to be done with it and get out to Andy's. The prospect of a war in Iraq was causing him some anxiety. The adrenalin rushes he was having signaled him that something was afoot. He was just jumpy, that was all.

Finishing up quickly, he excused himself and hurried to his car. As James pulled out of the parking lot, the President of the United States was taking the podium at the United Nations. He was preparing to warn the nations that their actions were rendering the UN unnecessary as a world body. The drums of war were beginning to beat. James caught a portion of the speech on his way to Arlington.

In Baghdad, Saddam Hussein and his Cabinet heard it all. Saddam Hussein had always been a consummate actor and that day he was proud of his performance before his own team. No one would have guessed how inwardly pleased he was that the world appeared to be taking the bait. He did have to admire, and couldn't help wonder, how Zawahiri had persuaded the French to stand in the gap. *Amazing what a thief will do to avoid getting caught,* he thought. Every dictator knows that his blackmail list is his most precious tool. *Bin Laden must really have the goods on someone!*

Though President Bush gave a forceful and compelling speech, Saddam Hussein was secretly gleeful about the fall the young President was about to sustain. *Serves him right.*

At the same time in New York, Professor Nasser was taking the morning off to watch the address at the United Nations. Watching the television, he was overtaken with an anxiety attack.

He could not understand why his message had had no response. It had been months.

Six months ago he had seen the news about Atef. Since that was at the time he had sent his message, he concluded now that the attack must have disrupted his communication somehow. He was fairly certain now that it had never gotten through.

A helpful "leak" revealed Makkawi as the heir-apparent to Atef. When Nasser read that in the New York Times, he decided he should try again. He had no idea who was supposed to intercept and read the encoded messages on the Internet site, but he felt his message was important enough that someone over there needed to read it.

Logging on, he entered the game. The last move had been his. Once again, there was no response from the other side. So he just repeated the move again. Even if someone did spot it, it was logical that a player would repeat a move when his opponent was so obviously irregular in his responses. Satisfied that it was correct, he logged off and returned to the television.

Makkawi, on the other hand, was neither watching television nor logging on to the Internet. He had, in fact, inherited the entire dossier of responsibilities from Atef. But he had had very little exposure to chess and even lesser interest in the game. Frankly, he was having to plan so much so rapidly that he had time only for the top priority projects. Foremost on his mind right now was the completion of the training camps in northern Iraq. Their graduates would be needed in the very near future.

He saw the reminder on the checklist to check the chess site and was just opening it when his second came in with bad news. Two more of their commanders had been killed and 12 captured. These 12 had information that was very sensitive and if they spilled it under interrogation, Makkawi's location would be compromised.

So, just as the site came up, Makkawi logged off. He seemed to catch a flash of a flag on the opening page, but he had no time to deal with it then. It was evident to him now that the United States was serious about capturing or killing them all. He had been a hunted man before, but nothing like this. It took every bit of his wit and cunning just to figure out ways to stay ahead of the Special Forces units that were pursuing him. The Doctor had made it clear their best chance was in the mountains between Pakistan and Afghanistan. That was proving to be correct, but it also made communications difficult. What little time he had with technology had to be used for the urgent. He would just have to deal with the Internet game later.

Some months had passed and a new year had begun. It was clear as they moved into the spring that war in Iraq was imminent. The atmosphere in Washington, D.C. had turned strident and harsh. Not even the early arrival of the cherry blossoms softened the mood that prevailed.

Andy watched the neighborhood children heading off to school. His own graduation the summer before had been fun but uneventful. He had found it increasingly difficult to lie to his buddies and classmates as to why he wasn't headed off to MIT the following fall. To forestall conversations that would only be dangerous, he had invented some story about needing to help his mom for a semester or two. That seemed to satisfy them.

Today, however, he felt a twinge of remorse that he was at home, holed up in a basement instead of nearing the end of his first year of college. Although he tried to work out, he just couldn't afford to spend time with friends or even with any former gym partners. He was thinner and less fit, and he knew it.

Kelly had observed the circles under his eyes and challenged him on the amount of sleep he was getting. In reality, Andy was getting enough sleep. What seemed to be sucking him hollow was an awful, nagging premonition that something terrible was about to happen. He couldn't shake it loose. He slept, but awoke with almost an obsession to identify what his opponent was doing. Today's dread was worse than ever.

Remembering a book on dangers in chess, he logged onto Amazon and found the exact title and author. Sure enough, he had it in his collection of unread chess tomes. Study of the game was never his thing. But today he hoped this thin book would offer some comfort.

He got no farther than the "Author's Note" when he spotted it. He had actually warned James about it months ago. Pouring through the book, he found something. And the minute he read it, he understood why he had been so anxious. Now he had to prove it.

Chapter 26

The Doctor learned of his supposed death and the death of his family the same way the rest of the world did, on the nightly news. It was an event noteworthy enough to produce news alerts with Reuters, Associated Press, all of them. He had just come into his flat from the market when he heard the French-speaking news anchor interrupt her broadcast for a live report from Pakistan.

He knew it might eventually come to that, but frankly, he thought it would take the Americans longer than that to find him, if at all. His hopes were that Azza and the children would be safe for years, protected by a loyal network in the cave complex they were sequestered in. Nothing would have pleased him more than for both Zawahiri and Bin Laden to disappear so completely that the Special Forces and intelligence agencies of the world would look like incompetent oafs.

Placing Nanda's father with the family had seemed like a perfect escape cover for him. Anyone who might be interviewed would unknowingly point to this man as Zawahiri. That would give him more than enough time to make his exit. He had to admit he had expected the Canadians, Brits and Americans to approach his location differently, knowing his wife and children were there. Their natural aversion to harming women and children, he thought, would keep his family safe, and slow down any pursuit of Zawahiri himself.

I misread them, he thought. *I didn't think they'd kill the families to get to Atef and me. I guess they've made an adjustment after Mullah Omar escaped.* Although he would miss seeing his children, Ayman Al-Zawahiri was a practical man, not a sentimental one. He knew full well that, in war, children die. And he felt the families of great leaders must automatically be prepared for and share in the fate of their men. Azza had been loyal. He couldn't have asked for more.

Knowing that he could not change what had happened, he began to calculate immediately how long it would take the FBI to determine that he was not dead. He concluded he had a few months at most. After that, they would be on the hunt for him again. But for now, they didn't even know he was at large, let alone that he had escaped through Iran to Turkey, and from there, he had flown without incident to Geneva, Switzerland.

Years ago, through his family's connection in pharmacology and medicine, he had recognized Switzerland as the place to be. Impenetrable to invasion, the Swiss took the same approach to banking and commerce. One could hide in plain view. With three languages spoken throughout the country, the somewhat odd accent he had when he spoke French was accepted as an influence from some other European state, not Egypt.

From the time he was a young man, he had spoken French fluently. Though Arabic was his native language, his life in Cairo and his education there had opened the door to travel, study and business in both France and Switzerland. The idea of a second identity, not just an alias, had come to him when he saw how the Swiss protected the identities of any of their prosperous "visitors." Expelled from Egypt, hunted and on the run, he had decided to "hide in plain view."

For more than 15 years now, the people in his neighborhood had known him as Phillipe Monet, a quiet, studious financier who had established and built a financial services business in their district. His thin frame and receding hairline were reminiscent of the men in a section of France close to Geneva, so he had blended in quite easily. No one had ever really checked on his actual origins. Why would they? He was just a nice man who lived quietly.

Through the years he had seemed to grow in financial prosperity. His contributions to projects in his district of Geneva had earned him the respect of the mayor and had resulted in his securing some very important introductions. No one knew, of course, where his money came from, and the bank was never going to reveal it. So, although Islamic Jihad was sorely lacking in funds, the Doctor was not.

The people in his neighborhood guessed that he had an uncanny way of assessing investment opportunities and that he must have a very exclusive client list. Once, a number of years earlier, a wealthy jewelry store owner had asked Phillipe to assist him with some evaluations of companies and their stocks. Phillipe had graciously declined, telling the man that he handled very few clients and that it was not his wish to offend but that the man, though wealthy, did not meet the minimum portfolio requirements to warrant Phillipe taking him on. He then was kind enough to refer the man to a legitimate investment firm, and that firm was grateful for the referral.

His reputation grew considerably after that. And so did the invitations to parties and events. It would be rare indeed for Phillipe Monet to not be invited to the most prestigious affairs in Geneva.

The Doctor had always had a flair for pharmacology. During his imprisonment in Egypt, his interest had taken a turn toward psychotropic drugs. He had seen firsthand how effective they were in interrogation and in control. Taken to their logical extension, he could see why the Nazis had experimented so much in that area, and why the Soviet Union had followed suit. You could get anyone to do whatever you wanted him to do if you drugged him properly.

Thus, a study of drugs and their effects had become a part of Ayman Al-Zawahiri's life. He knew that Al Qaeda would need them. Bin Laden had known that heroin crops were a great source of income and that drugs of that type would assist in controlling the assassin squads they were training. But the Doctor had spotted a far more effective and insidious use of pharmacology. He had concluded that it was a vital part of any effective fifth column strategy that one might deploy in the 21st Century. If one could be persuaded to submit to being drugged, then that individual could easily be turned into an unwitting member of the fifth column. Ignorant of the mind control aspect of it all, the person would become an unwitting ally of the one promoting the drug. Those realizations had precipitated the Doctor's rise to wealth.

Turning off his television, the Doctor sent an email to his contact in Afghanistan. The man was to relay the message to Nanda. First, in order to appear sympathetic, he expressed his sorrow at the loss of the man who had loved Nanda so well. He spoke in a heartfelt fashion of their mutual loss and the deep bond of their grief. Then, he authorized Nanda to be ready to release the first of the tape-recorded messages of Ayman Al-Zawahiri. Once it had been determined he was not dead, he wanted to strike terror by being defiant. And that had been the subject of one of their tapes. He knew Nanda would know which one.

Then he logged on to his investment site to track the latest on his own personal portfolio. He was especially interested in following the trends of two types of stocks since 9/11. He could tell by his experiences in the war in Afghanistan that they would most likely be trending upward. After all, it had been a difficult time in history.

Makkawi had notified him that Zarqawi was readying the attack, and that he himself would attack once the Americans had done their part. The stage was now set for an escalation in all arenas and the Doctor knew that the escalation would cause the stocks that had been up trending to surge dramatically. He smiled as he contemplated the exponential leap his personal wealth was about to take.

As he opened the mail his secretary had placed on his desk, one envelope caught his eye immediately. The logo was stunning and prestigious. Everyone in Europe coveted communication from the Director of this organization. His humanitarian activities were renowned and his commitment to the health and well-being of all people had earned him a Nobel Prize nomination. If the Doctor had played his hand correctly, no one would have noticed his year-long absence, and they would be eager now to reward him for the contribution he had made to the people of Geneva.

Opening the envelope, he took a deep breath and read its contents. Smiling, he took out his Mont Blanc pen and wrote a short note on the parchment enclosure. It read simply, "I accept most appreciatively." And with a simple signature, Phillipe

Monet accepted an invitation to be on the Board of Directors of the World Health Organization.

Lastly, he called his barber and made an appointment. Without the beard of his religion, he wanted to make certain that his moustache was properly trimmed. *After all, I'm back in the West,* he commented to himself.

From the time of the death of his family in the cave complex near Jalalabad to the autumn of 2002, the Doctor was acclimating himself to life in Switzerland once again. He had learned during his time in prison, and from subsequent study of the philosophies of great dictators, that one of the ways to deflect someone off your trail was to tell a truth so outrageous that it was automatically dismissed as a lie. There was a curious phenomenon in the human psyche. People had a level of acceptable truth. If you went beyond that, even if it were true, they would assume it was false. Much of the deception in warfare of the 20th century had understood that.

Therefore, it had not surprised him that no one had ever really looked for him in Switzerland. Years earlier he had told friends in Cairo that he was going to live in Switzerland. It had become obvious, with a death-sentence-in-absentia on his head that he could never return to Egypt. He had been expelled as well from the Sudan. So he had leaked information that he would settle in Switzerland.

When an Egyptian newspaper published that in later years, he had laughed and felt no peril, whatsoever. It was obvious the Swiss themselves would consider it impossible that a terrorist could be living in Switzerland. The "mistake" the Egyptian journalist had made was to suggest that the Swiss had given asylum to Zawahiri. Nothing could have gone beyond their acceptable truth more than that. So they rejected the whole article as a lie, and said he had never even been to Switzerland, let alone been given asylum.

And so it had died down, and he had begun his career as an investor in the pharmaceutical companies that dotted the countryside between Geneva and Zermatt. His commitment to the health of his province and to the charities of his area offered him the opportunity to travel, and seek out prices and deals for medicines and other materials that might be needed by these organizations.

It was that alone that had saved him in Russia in 1997. He and his top two lieutenants, Ahmad Mabruk and Mahmud Al-Hennawi, crossed into Dagestan en route to setting up an Islamic state in Chechnya. There they planned to add Central Asia to their target list for jihad. The Russians, however, had captured them. They were extremely suspicious of why these three had entered the country illegally. With false passports, it took some sorting out, but the Russians had eventually released him when they came to believe that the man they were holding was in their area looking for the price of medical supplies and medicines.

They had been released, and the cover identity he had set up had worked. "God blinded them to our identities," he had told friends. That was when he knew the wisdom of his second identity. Shortly after that, though, he had commenced the plans to secure some kind of double for himself, so that no one would know what Ayman Al-Zawahiri would actually look like.

The only disappointment of their near miss in Russia came when he had returned to find that Bin Laden had only given a measly $5,000 to Islamic Jihad in their absence. But he had given millions to his mentor, Azzam, and his moderate organizations. From that moment on, getting rid of Azzam had become a great priority and was accomplished easily. But the Doctor had never forgiven Bin Laden for his lack of loyalty. That had made it easier to do what he had to do in the hills of Afghanistan.

Now, however, sitting in Switzerland, the irony was that he could move freely about Europe. But he could not return to Afghanistan or Pakistan. Today he was very pleased with his wisdom in setting Al Qaeda up in its cellular structure, and in the establishment of its suicide squads. He knew for certain that, even if he were not there, those he had trained would not only know what to do, but would know how to do it.

And he was grateful to Nanda for taking the bait and recording tapes of Zawahiri himself to be released if necessary. It was obvious by listening to the BBC and the European stations that the United States was stymied by their inability to find Usama Bin Laden. Now they were stuck with having lost Ayman Al-Zawahiri as well. He was laughing at the predicament this placed them in, and he prepared to maximize use of it in the next arena.

Only one thing gnawed at him a little bit as he dined on a salad and some pheasant. That was, the press was covering Lebanon's Hezbollah and seemed to be scoring points by pointing out that its head of overseas operations, Mughniyeh, was reported to have become unrecognizable following plastic surgery. Frankly, he had no interest in where the man was, but he didn't want too much attention put on people changing their appearance. He knew that if the press talked about it too long, some smart young intelligence officer would get the idea to look not just at changed appearance, but also at changed identity.

Still, I'm safe, he told himself. Even if Mughniyeh and others changed their appearance or identity, they would still be involved in criminal activity, and there was a danger that sooner or later they would be picked up. Confident that he had created something far superior to their crudities, he added, *After all, my business activities are totally legitimate. No law enforcement agency in the world would look at me twice.*

That was true. Ayman Al-Zawahiri was about to skate past all of the investigative agencies because he was not involved in money laundering. None of his businesses were a front for Al Qaeda, and, therefore, would not attract the attention of even the most seasoned hounds. The Swiss would glance off his accounts too, as they tried to help the United States ferret out the accounts that were laundering money for terrorists. To the Swiss auditors, Phillipe Monet was just an investor who had made money in pharmaceuticals.

Calmer now, he decided to just relax with the prospect of being out in public and speaking in French. *No one is looking for me here,* he thought.

While the Doctor finished his evening meal, Andy sat at his computer in Arlington, Virginia staring at the FBI's Most Wanted Terrorists list. Anyone in the world could log onto the FBI site. Andy himself had done so many times. But today he was fixated on the picture of Ayman Al-Zawahiri, or rather the description below the picture. He was haunted by the reminder in the chess book that the "most dangerous moments are often subtle and overlooked."

He had logged on again to just take a look at his opponent. It helped him to imagine the man and to get into his mind a bit. He instinctively knew that if you could see things from your opponent's angle and choose good moves for him, you could more easily defeat him.

James had just come in. They were starting early today. Once Andy had graduated and fulfilled his commitments, Kelly had lifted any restrictions as to when they worked. To be honest, it was easier for both to work in the day. James hoped Andy was enjoying some time with girls or friends. Whatever, the Kid was surely engrossed in the computer, so James had quietly removed the clippings they were going to review that day.

Suddenly the Kid commented, "Did you ever notice that the FBI site lists Zawahiri's height and weight as unknown?"

"It does?"

The Kid then scrolled through the other wanted terrorists. Their descriptions all included basic physical data. Only that for the Doctor was "unknown." That seemed to bother Andy.

"What's up, Kid?" James asked. "Our job's to figure out what he's doing, not how much he weighs." He was attempting to joke, but that didn't lift Andy's mood. James' voice changed now. "What is it, Andy?"

"I just think that's odd. And my gut tells me it has something to do with what he's doing. I just can't quite put it together."

The two sat silent for a minute and then Andy added, "I thought if I could just get a clue, I could figure out what games he's playing now. It's been months you know, and he's clearly not in the war game, or at least not all the time. He's in intelligence or propaganda, something…" his voice trailed off. "I just can't get a sequence here."

"What do you mean?"

"Well, is he playing the war game first and left that for the propaganda game and left that for the intelligence game, or is there a different sequence? It's all jumbled up to me. It's almost as if he's got a move going in all of them, like he's playing them all simultaneously or something."

"Hmm, I don't know." James was about to ask if they should take some time today to see if they could identify how Zawahiri was sequencing his games when Andy exploded.

"What did I just say?" he shouted. For a moment James was speechless. Andy repeated, "What did I just say?"

"You said it almost seemed like he was playing them all simultaneously," James repeated.

Andy jumped up, causing his chair to tip over. "My God, that's it! No wonder it all just seemed like a jumbled mishmash. That's it!" He was grinning.

"You lost me, Kid, but I can see you're excited. Fill me in, please."

"There is no sequence. He's playing them at the same time, not one following another. He is not thinking linear."

"And?" James was waiting with his mouth hanging open.

"Raumschach! Son of a gun, he's doing a Raumschach. He's gone three-dimensional. He's folded his various games all into one space and he's moving pieces from one game to another in that space."

"What's Raumschach?"

"It's German for 'space chess,'" Andy responded.

"I never heard of three-dimensional chess. Is there such a thing?"

"Yeah. Lousy game though, I think." Then Andy added, "Some German doctor by the name of Maack invented it back at the turn of the century. He started out with an 8x8x8 cube, but later changed it to a 5x5x5 game. I think they had chess clubs playing it up until World War II."

"Is it still being played?" James was fascinated by this.

"Yeah, I think so, but it never interested me. Last time I saw it was in a Star Trek movie. They didn't know how to line the boards up either."

For a minute, James just let that sink in and then he ventured a question. "Star Trek? The TV series Star Trek? You're telling me Ayman Al-Zawahiri is playing a chess game made famous by a TV series?"

Andy looked at it for a moment and commented sardonically, "Kind of ironic." Then he amended his explanation, "When I was a kid I used to read Isaac Asimov's science fiction short stories. One of his stories had a 3D chess game in it; only his was a true 8x8x8. I remember I was fascinated for awhile."

"Is it hard to play?"

"Yeah, I guess," Andy exhaled. "To me it's just a brain tease—a way to try to distract an opponent by making the game more complicated. Me, I prefer to play a game of confronting and just plain outmaneuvering my opponent. I keep things simple."

Both seemed to know that after many months they were onto something which might explain why they had never gotten a clean through-line on the Doctor's intentions. They were silent for a long time. Each was working the problem.

"We've got to go to Wal-Mart right away," Andy broke the silence.

"Why?"

"I got to buy something right away," he hollered over his shoulder as he bounded up the stairs three at a time. James grabbed his coat and followed. Unbeknownst to either, their complete conversation, like others before it, had been recorded.

CHAPTER 27

More than two hours later, James and Andy exited Wal-Mart empty-handed. They had been looking for chess sets, which Wal-Mart had, but Andy wanted something in particular. They had to have eight sets, all identical, and they had to be transparent. That was not something that such a mass merchandiser would be apt to carry. Andy seemed stumped.

James, however, remembered there was a specialty game shop in his neighborhood in the District. He'd never gone in there. It was too full of scruffy intellectuals for his taste. So he figured that might be just the place.

He was correct. The owner had a wonderful selection of antique chess sets, including the Art Deco period. It seems that Americans had liked to decorate their apartments with chess sets that reflected the décor of that era. Finding eight the same was almost miraculous as far as James was concerned. In reality, what seemed so extraordinary and unique now had actually been a common chess set 70 years earlier. Andy played with wood sets. Generations earlier had played with inexpensive glass sets.

More problematic, however, were the eight boards. All eight were glass and quite heavy. The shopkeeper wrapped the whole collection up carefully and helped James load it into his car. James was still stinging from the price he'd had to pay. He just knew he was not going to be able to put this on an expense requisition, and he knew this was way beyond the Kid's budget, so he hoped this paid off.

By the time they got it all, they were both hungry so James suggested they were close to his apartment and they could make a sandwich or something there. That was fine with Andy.

Just as he was moving aside a stack of newspapers he'd left scattered on the small eating table, James realized he'd never had a guest in this apartment. Andy was the first visitor he'd invited in. *Jesus, what I life I chose,* he reflected for a moment. Andy was, of course, oblivious to all that and was just grateful for the sandwich.

"Got any pickles?" he asked. "I like liverwurst with pickles."

James smiled. So did he. And the one thing the Kid requested, he had. Maybe this would be their lucky day.

Finishing up quickly, Andy indicated they needed to go to a bakery that specialized in wedding cakes, big wedding cakes. That was a tall order. To be honest, James never paid attention to bakeries so they had to find one in the Yellow Pages. It was just before closing time, so they raced over to one near Dupont Circle.

Andy purchased 25 half-inch plastic columns that cake-makers use to separate the tiers on tall, heavy wedding cakes. Each column was five inches tall. He asked the owner, "I don't suppose you have any rubber bases for these, you know, to prevent skidding?"

The idea was actually preposterous, and all three had a good laugh over that. So James and Andy made one final stop at Home Depot and found rubber bases for each end of the plastic columns. Andy was tickled and couldn't wait to get back to their basement office.

Just as they were unloading, Kelly returned and offered her help. The sets were, in fact, heavy and took up quite a bit of space. Andy immediately started to unwrap them and Kelly started upstairs. "You guys hungry? I can make something."

"No thanks, Mom; I ate at James'. He's a good cook, it turns out!"

James just shook his head at this and didn't know what to say. So he kept it simple, "No thanks; we just ate."

Now it was Kelly's turn to shake her head. She left the two to their unwrapping. What Andy had in mind took only a few minutes to assemble. He had layered eight boards on top of each other, separated by the cake pillars, and began to place the chess pieces in their appropriate places on the first board. Although he had eight chess sets, Andy used only one set. It was his intention to move pieces of just one game into different game levels. His theory was that Zawahiri was playing with only one chess set of pieces or players, and that he was moving them into whatever game he wanted to play at a given time. This was a mistake—a costly one.

"Kid, wouldn't this be better on a computer?"

"Yeah, eventually, but right now, I need to feel it and walk around it. Okay?"

"Sure, Kid; you're in charge." James watched as Andy deftly moved pieces in their ranks and files. That was usual. But he perked up when he watched Andy begin to move those same pieces into other layers of the 8x8x8 set-up. He was beginning to see that a Queen in one game could move to another game on a different layer. By going into three dimensions, the player could play multiple games simultaneously. Each layer was obviously a game. And, more importantly, it allowed the player to play in all games at once, with a move in one game being the response to a move in another game. So something that might seem like a non-sequitur was in actuality a lucid response to a move in another arena.

Frankly, James was stunned. It disoriented him at first until he finally got the perspective. And he couldn't wait to assemble data and get this to Whitney. This should change their perceptions.

"So…" he opened.

"So now all we have to do is figure out the eight games Ayman Al-Zawahiri is playing," Andy exclaimed. "This should work."

James could be of help here. He offered, "One would be Religion or, at least, a particular brand of religion."

Andy took out his paper labels and wrote "Religion" on one and attached the label to the side of the bottom board of the eight-board chess game. "And?"

"Obviously, there is a Military game."

Andy agreed. "Obviously." Again he wrote a label for "Military"and attached it to the second tier up. Then he stopped. The world was in agreement that this was a religious conflict that had been developing for centuries and had now spilled over into 21st century warfare. The rest they were going to have to guess at. Ayman Al-Zawahiri was known to them only as a man of religion and terrorism. They were having trouble putting words and labels to the other six labels.

Andy said quietly, "I have a theory as to what might be another one of the games."

"Let's hear it."

"Well, we've talked about public relations or intelligence or propaganda, right?"

"Yes; what are you getting at?"

Andy answered quickly, "Well, I don't know which it is or if it's all three, but something has been bothering me and I think it's relevant." James leaned in. He could tell by looking into Andy's eyes that he was looking at something. And that "something" was real.

"James, did you happen to hear the news in the last few days? I mean live, not on replay like we're listening to it down here?" The question took James a little off-guard.

"Yeah, I guess. I turn it on before I go to bed. What were you looking at?"

"Something my mom was looking at. She made a comment in passing while she was washing dishes. It didn't mean much to me at first, but it's nagging at me now." He swallowed and continued, "Some news anchor was doing a short piece on some organizing going on out on the West Coast regarding an anti-war protest on Iraq."

James didn't make a connection. "What about it? You know those types; they didn't get enough of it back when I was in college!"

"Well, it's what my mom said in response. She talks to the TV sometimes. She yells at the news."

James smiled. He bet she did. He had long ago discovered that Kelly's red hair was natural, and so was her Irish temper.

Andy added, "She said, 'You'd think those idiots could wait until there was a war at least.' Then she turned off the TV." James felt a rush of adrenalin. It was huge actually. And he knew what that meant. He reminded himself that he was paid to have something catch his eye, and this did. He was breathing heavily when Andy completed the thought.

"James, doesn't it seem a little odd to you that there would be anti-war protests going on before the war even starts?" There it was; something so obvious they'd all missed it. The sequence was wrong. And the Grandmaster had spotted it. As the adrenalin-effect dispersed, James was truly glad to have this sweet young man on his side.

Grabbing the pen, James wrote "Public Relations" on one of the labels and showed it to Andy. Andy nodded and turned his attention to the glass cube. Neither knew it, but they had just arrived on the same page as Ayman Al-Zawahiri.

Five time zones away, the Doctor rose early to take the web-conference with Samir. He had something urgent to relay to him. Serene and confident in his approach, it never entered the Doctor's mind that someone had, for the first time, penetrated his mind.

CHAPTER 28

Samir had asked for a meeting. His stay in Peshawar had been productive. Getting the Arab press to report critical news was not difficult. They, after all, were not the least bit interested in presenting both sides of anything, nor did they hold themselves to a standard of non-biased reporting. So it had been a good place for him to "cut his teeth" on releases and leaks that would enhance Bin Laden's popularity, and strengthen support for Al Qaeda and for their mission.

Once he returned to his offices in Paris, however, he hit a wall with regarding how to initiate his campaign. He knew his message, but he wanted to make certain that it launched with the impact they needed for the timeline they were dealing with. As he looked at the calendar now, he knew time was short and that he needed a far-reaching public dissemination campaign, not a word of mouth one—at least to start.

The secretary at Monet and Associates had graciously set a meeting for the weekend. This would give him time to make travel arrangements and secure his hotel. She had said that Monsieur Monet could make more time available if they did it on Saturday, and that he suggested they meet in his offices.

Landing at the airport he had been surprised to be barely able to see the ground. They were in for a heavy winter in Geneva, judging by the sleet and bone-chilling temperature. He knew that the Doctor could handle these temperatures, having spent so much time in the Balkans and the Hindu Kush mountains.

Samir, however, was grateful that the weather in Paris was rather temperate. Once he had left the United States, he never wanted to do "winter" again. And it didn't help that today he was having trouble with a cab. Finally, he resorted to something he had learned in New York; share a cab.

The office building in this neat, older section of Geneva was mostly dark. In the lobby, the attendant had left the area and simply left the sign-in book out on the table for guests to sign in. Quickly, Samir logged in and took the elevator to Monet and Associates' floor. The door was unlocked and Samir could hear the copier going as he slipped in.

"Monsieur Monet?" he called out. "Are you here?" He still had to remind himself to use the Doctor's alias whenever he spoke. He'd been practicing that for weeks by addressing the Doctor in imaginary conversations frequently enough that he wouldn't slip up when other people were around. Not knowing who might be in the office, he made certain to keep up the charade as he entered.

"Yes, I'll be just a moment, Samir. Please have a seat in my office."

The Doctor's office was very tasteful. Samir couldn't help but admire the contrasts in this man he knew. Their last contact had left them battle-weary, tired and running for their lives. But he would never have known that sitting in this elegant, but conservative, office. It was clear that Monet and Associates was prosperous, but there was nothing ostentatious. What struck him was the collection of poetry volumes that were bound and displayed on the white mahogany bookshelves. He remembered now that the Doctor was quite a poet. *How ironic,* he thought, *in better times he might very well have been a poet, enjoying the Seine and the Danube.*

"How was your trip?" the Doctor asked, sitting quickly at his desk.

"A bit choppy on landing, thank you."

"I meant the other trip," Zawahiri corrected.

"A bit choppy," Samir answered and they both laughed. "I was grateful to get out of there, frankly. He is preparing for quite a fight, I sensed."

"Yes, he should be. After betraying us like that, he knows what's coming for him." The Doctor hoped the President of Pakistan, Pervez Musharraf, would meet his end quickly. The executive order had been out for some time now and Zawahiri knew that Makkawi would take his shot as soon as he could penetrate the Presidential security. Musharraf might think the Americans could protect him, but anyone could be taken down, if the assassins were patient enough. If there was one thing Al Qaeda was noted for, it was its patience. Musharraf knew that.

"I agree. Phillipe, I appreciate your time and I trust I may speak freely."

The Doctor indicated he could and that there was no one here to overhear anything, so they did not have to waste attention on getting the names right. For Samir to have asked for a face to face meant he needed some specific help.

Samir began directly. "I remember, at Princeton, studying the writings of William James. And something he had commented on in a psychology treatise was discussed at length by my fellow students. Do you remember, Ayman, his talking about telling a lie?"

"Most definitely. He said that if you tell a lie often enough, people will come to believe it is the truth, or words to that effect."

"Yes, that is it. And I must do that now with our PR campaign. The lie is not what has stymied me. I know exactly what I want to say; I just don't know how to get it repeated often enough in a short period of time. And, in order to be of help to Makkawi, this has to saturate very quickly."

The Doctor knew immediately how to handle this and was appreciative of Samir's candor regarding his uncertainty, because certainty was one of the ingredients necessary for this to work. So he patiently coached him.

"Samir, you have an advantage given that we are doing this to the United States. You may have slightly more difficulty with Britain, but I doubt it. It's quite simple. Never forget that the U.S. media has ratings to get, and 24-hour programming to fill. They are so proud of their competitive market that their news agencies are forced to compete with one another, and therein lies your solution."

Samir didn't quite get it and frowned slightly. The Doctor continued. "All you have to do is get one—one credible one—and the rest will fall in line to copy it. They can't stand to be scooped, and they will repeat almost immediately what you tell the first one. So pick your first target. Make it a large, reputable one. Get them to take the bait and you're home free."

Samir was well aware that the American press has a, what he called, "Self-Importance" button. They viewed themselves as the guarantors of liberty planet-wide and they mistakenly believed their journalists were infallible. They were not. By the 1990's they had turned out of their journalism schools a group of men and women with personal ambition larger than a vision of service.

Tempted by the money and fame of modern-day journalism, he knew that most of them saw "Pulitzer" in their dreams. He further knew that they were trained to be competitive, even if it meant cutting corners. And to get the readership and viewers, they had to attract the attention of an audience with a lurid appetite for sex and violence. That meant "sexing" up their pieces.

The advent of 24-hour news and big powerful news cable companies had put more money on the table for the lucky few who rose to the top. And every one of the ambitious newscasters he had met were concerned about their "contract" more than they were about "truth."

His scorn for journalism in the West and its pretentiousness was shared by Zawahiri, but the Doctor had a much better understanding of how to manipulate the press, and that understanding would create havoc in the United States in the months and years to come. Samir was frowning.

The Doctor interrupted, "I can see your disdain on your face. I sympathize, but work your way through the problem." Samir looked at him and the Doctor asked, "Who do you view as the most ambitious and unconventional of their media moguls?"

Without any hesitation Samir answered, "Bud Walker of Walker News Group." Samir had just named a man who had built his empire into one of the largest, most comprehensive news and entertainment groups in the world. He owned TV stations, newspapers and cable broadcast organizations, and had built his reputation by beating the pants off the network organizations in global news coverage.

He was a somewhat rough, self-made billionaire who cared very little what people thought of him. He was mercurial and unpredictable, except in one area. And that was the area the Doctor was about to strike. He had something to prove, and a master was about to play him like a violin.

"Good. He will be a perfect choice. Was he on your list?"

Samir smiled because the man was, in fact, at the top of his "Unwitting" list. He nodded.

"Samir, don't doubt yourself here. He has to prove that he is better than anybody else, and he will take the bait. Remember, he is a simple man, but he is not a great one. Great men know that simplicity is admirable. Less than great men think that complexity is something to be admired and rewarded." He paused for a moment to take a sip of water from his Waterford crystal glass and added, "You and I know that the more complex you make a thing, the easier it is to control people. Never forget, when you want to control people, make it complex. When you want people to control themselves, make it simple."

This was a variation on make wrong right and right wrong in order to confuse people and render them incapable of action. Samir had watched the medical establishments practice this for years. Some of the more argumentative classmates he had had discussed it in class. The argument had gone something like, "Doctors make health and the body complex. The poor schmuck thinks he can't possibly know anything about it, let alone do anything about it, so he let's the 'expert' completely control him. On the other hand, those doctors who made the body and its maintenance seem simple gave control back to the individual. And those individuals were rarely sick." Samir remembered the debate vividly, so it didn't take much for him to nod agreement with the Doctor on the underlying principle.

Without knowing it fully, Samir had chosen the one man whose self-importance was such that he would make all news issues complex, rather than simple. He would promote the "two sides to every story," forgetting that just because there are two sides, it doesn't mean they are both right, let alone of equal weight. This man would forget that, and he would tell both sides, even if telling both sides distorted the truth.

As a man who pulled himself up, Walker had developed an almost sanctimonious viewpoint about victims. Now that he was at the top of his game, he was prone to see people as victims.

His brand of journalism was leaning to promoting victims by always covering them, always promoting their viewpoint, and almost never challenging their responsibility for what had happened to them. In his mind, he was now their advocate. He was the redeemer of those less fortunate.

And, Bud Walker needed to be right.

That one trait had been identified and singled out by Zawahiri. He knew his kind. And it was about to be exploited to such a degree that the average American would wonder if he had somehow entered *Alice in Wonderland.* There was in fact no limit to how deep the rabbit-hole would go.

The Doctor knew that, and with a fatherly pat, he touched Samir's arm. "Samir, you picked the right man. Find him. Get close to him. Tell him what you want him to tell others. He will do the rest. His ego will demand it. Then, my friend, sit back and watch the chain reaction."

The Doctor seemed almost serene, knowing they were about to use good men for such destruction. By the time they were finished, these good men would have destroyed logic, shattered trust and almost dismembered the cohesiveness of a great people. And these good men would do this, thinking they were following workable and long-standing operating procedures in their profession. Their hands would be clean.

Suddenly, Samir laughed. "I just got it." He laughed again. "I didn't get it until you said 'chain reaction,' then I understood."

The two men just looked at each other. "Whoever gets the story first, the others will scramble to repeat it so as to not be left out. Once they have committed on the story, they will dig in to defend it. They will need to be right. So the 'lie' will automatically be repeated over and over and over again until accepted as true. And I won't have anything to do with any of that." He looked at the idea of someone else doing the work for him for a moment and breathed a huge sigh of relief. "Amazing."

"Do you feel better now?"

"Immensely. I felt overwhelmed, not knowing how a small firm like mine could accomplish such a vast penetration quickly enough." Then, almost apologetically, he continued, "Ayman, until this moment, I did not fully understand what an unwitting fifth column would look like, or how it would get created."

Reassuring him, the Doctor gloated, "Well that took me some years to learn myself. Never forget that once you know what they regard as their greatest strength—nation or man—that is where you attack. Plant your lie there. Remember, my brother, 'Goodness' and 'Fair Play.'"

Samir rose, and embraced the Doctor. He did not know when he would see him again. But he was confident now that he could initiate the sequence and the chain reaction would follow. As he closed the door to Monet and Associates, he stopped at the elevator to make a note on the small pad he always carried inside his breast pocket. The note read simply, "ratings" and "feed the beast." Those two phrases alone would bring the United States to a dead stalemate, and land it at the brink of losing its War on Terror. Two simple phrases. He looked forward to getting started now. He felt as if a huge weight had lifted and his mind was clear.

Turning the page, he wrote one reminder to himself. It read, "Figure out how to meet Bud Walker." As he came out onto the now quiet street, the sun shone fleetingly.

Chapter 29

Saddam Hussein was particularly worried about his older son. He had had enough trouble with daughters and their lamentable husbands. No one likes to have to murder their own sons-in-law. But he had had to. As the years had gone on, it had become painfully clear to him that only two of his children could be trusted. And he had given them much responsibility and much authority as a result of his belief that they wielded power in an even more frightening way than he did.

Now he had concerns. Both Uday and Qusay had seemed reluctant to tie in with Bin Laden on this next project. Although both had understood the desirability of declawing U.S. and British intelligence, he sensed that Uday was so deeply entrenched in the lifestyle of drugs and parties and debauchery that he had developed, that he would blunder at a critical moment in their escape. He, frankly, did not know what to expect, and that made him nervous. So for a few months, he kept Uday on a short leash and asked his younger brother to reason with him.

Qusay was confident now that he had his brother under control. Besides that, he was the one who really controlled the money, and more importantly, their elite security people. He was confident Uday would follow along if for no other reason than to protect his personal financial interests.

It had been harder to convince Saddam's Cabinet. They really had no choice, but there were many of them, and in order for the charade to work, they all had to exit in unison and remain undetected until the Americans and British had been finished off. Saddam did not trust Bin Laden to make these arrangements since this is where he expected the double-cross. There was absolutely no reason to believe the new young King of Syria would be able to hold up under the pressure. Saddam could smell that the plan was to turn him and his people back, refusing entry, or to kill them at the border. But either way, he was onto them.

The reality was that Saddam Hussein had far easier escape routes he could create. He didn't have to debate one minute in his own mind to pick the country that would capitulate the fastest. After all, the four countries he had been trading with had made fortunes selling him armaments. Since this was in violation of their own laws, let alone the UN resolutions, each had a reason to either cooperate with him now, or at the very least, turn a blind eye to what was about to happen.

Years of surviving in the blackmail game had taught him instinctively who to squeeze. There was one government of the four that he knew would co-operate the most. In fact he had taken great care to cultivate them over the years. Knowing that they had an ax to grind with almost everyone in Europe, as well as the United States and Britain, his offers of cash for weapons and oil for cash were seductive to them.

There is one thing dictators understand if they are to enslave a people. That is, they have to find out what wrong the people of that country want to right and then promise to right that wrong. That group can then be counted on to promote the most extraordinary lies and misrepresentations in order to secure justice in the area they feel they were wronged. They will, in fact, promote and spread the lies and rumors so effectively and so frequently, that they fall victim to believing them themselves. And when that happens, the dictator can enter, and promise to free them from the clutches of the enemy they themselves have lied about and vilified.

As far as Saddam Hussein was concerned, his hero, Stalin, had been one of the most gifted he had ever seen at that. But perhaps the best example in modern history had been the takeover of the German people by Hitler. Once the German people were persuaded that they had been wronged after World War I, and once they had been convinced it was Jewish businessmen who had done it to them, the people themselves spread the most exaggerated lies and did it so often that they came to believe the Jews were, in fact, an enemy. Hitler stepped forward, offered a solution and the people amassed to execute his solution.

Hussein was not only fascinated by the effectiveness of Hitler's tactics, but admired him for the number of Jews he had eliminated. He intended to complete what Hitler was unable to do. The purchases of materials he was engaged in would put in his hands the means to finish the job. He needed only to find a way to create a breach between the United States and Israel, or get the United States strung out so badly that they left the area.

And it was this one common goal that Al Qaeda and Hussein shared that made this unlikely alliance possible. In fact, Saddam concluded that the very open-minded European press would never believe such an alliance possible and would foil U.S. efforts, if the United States did put it together. *This Bush will be as weak as the father,* Hussein had concluded. That conclusion emboldened him and was actually the key selling point that had persuaded his Cabinet that they could pull it off.

That, and the fact that he knew no one in the United States would actually believe France was an enemy, rather than an ally. Even if someone in their White House did figure it out, he knew they could never effectively voice it. His own public relations team, let alone Bin Laden's, would annihilate them for it.

So Saddam Hussein put the squeeze on his allies inside France. They were so deeply involved in the arms sales and contract kickbacks by now that they would do whatever he demanded to stay hidden. What he demanded was French passports for each and everyone of his top echelon. They would exit, not through Syria secretly, but openly through Jordan. The Americans would not be looking for an enemy to escape through a country they regarded as an ally. And neither would Bin Laden. They would all be out before his assassins could strike.

Once in Jordan under false identity, his people would go to France. They would wait there until Iraq had been cleared of the United States military. From what little he had seen of this man Zarqawi, he had no doubt the United States would rue the day they had tackled with that ruthless son of a bitch. Once the U.S. was disgraced and demoralized, he would take care of Zarqawi and appear, once again, as a necessary hero for his people, ridding them of the murderous foreign fighters. By then, they would know for certain that they *needed* him; that they were incapable of living without his making decisions for them and providing security for them.

"At that time," he promised his people, "you will return from France and we will resume our rule here, without the thorny interruptions some of our own tribes and clerics create through their ridiculous preaching about an archaic form of Islam." All of them laughed, save one. Unfortunately for Saddam Hussein, he did not notice that one of his men did not laugh. There was, in fact, one patriot in the room, who knew now that the time had come. He would have to take sides.

But for the moment, the traitor would remain hidden, for he had already decided that Bush II was not Bush I and maybe, just maybe, he could come out of this alive. The discussion had turned, however, to an elaborate deception regarding the baiting of Hans Blix and his team of UN inspectors. If they did this correctly, Blix would become an unwitting ally.

Saddam had concluded the meeting by exhorting his colleagues to remember that, for them to become the most powerful nation in the region and to expand their territories, they had to eliminate Israel. He reminded them this was just a detour, but that the target was still Israel. "There are just a few players that have to be gotten rid of first."

In the end, they had concurred. Not that they had much choice. Each one had witnessed Saddam's murderous and instantaneous response to disagreement. Besides, a year in the French countryside didn't seem like such a bad idea. Perhaps they could even enjoy some of the delights of Paris itself. So, they had agreed. Not one, however, knew that Saddam had no intention of going to France. No, he planned to escape to yet another location. He was far too smart to wait this out in the arms of the men he was blackmailing.

Bud Walker, too, was preparing to partake of the delights of Paris. Only, he wouldn't be coming in under the cover of a false passport, trying to remain unnoticed until the storm had passed. Quite the opposite. He and his wife loved this city, and they both enjoyed the celebrity their wealth and position brought them in Paris society.

So, while his wife made preparations for an annual shopping trip to her favorite shops in the "city of lights," he and his personal assistant were picking and choosing from a variety of invitations to soirées. This media man loved media attention, and since he was a man of humble origins, he was especially gratified with the reception he always received in this city.

And Bud Walker had an ego healthy enough to take pride in the fact that the people of this city welcomed him, while at the same time they demonstrated disdain for the President of the United States. His own personal opinions had clouded his insight, for he thought the French meant it personally. They did not. There was, in fact, an underlying anti-Americanism that was residual from the time of de Gaulle. There was a perceived wrong that needed to be righted, and the French frankly felt that way about the man who occupied the White House, whoever he might be. They just manifested it differently with George Bush than they had with Bill Clinton.

But to Bud, he embraced it as a sign that he was more popular than the President. And that was a misconception promoted by his wife on an almost daily basis. So the two were ready, of course, to attend the reception the President of France was holding during the Christmas holidays.

Also on the guest list was the head of a small, but rising public relations firm that had donated generously to a favorite charity of the First Family of France.

CHAPTER 30

Samir was adjusting the studs on his tuxedo shirt. Tonight's affair was black tie and he frankly liked to dress now and again. Knowing that he looked so very European eased the tension in his abdomen. Tonight was a very important night for him. Getting Bud Walker to play ball would launch a devastating public relations campaign. *The Doctor was right. If he takes the bait, he will launch the campaign. And no one dares attack the press in the United States.*

The more he thought about it, the greater his admiration was for the Doctor. The people of the United States had been educated since their beginning to revere freedom of speech and dote on the freedom of the press. That worked as long as the press was trustworthy, but if it could be corrupted, the Americans' reliance upon a corrupt press would be the undoing of the country. That was the reasoning he was using with his plan tonight.

Getting an invitation had not been difficult. He had done some great work for several French ministers assisting them in delicate public relations matters concerning their mistresses. True, his firm had helped secure major contributions to significant French charities, but he knew that this invitation was payback for his covering up their little indiscretions.

Samir knew that he would have an opportunity to meet Bud Walker, but he had not worked out how he would deliver his message to him. The message was worked out, but not the delivery mechanism. And this had him more than a little anxious. Bud Walker was the perfect target and time was short. He had to launch this campaign or risk jeopardizing the mission altogether. Too many of their colleagues were dying in Afghanistan. The money lines were disrupted and they had a serious lack of training locations to replace what they had lost in manpower.

Iraq, then, was very important to their recovery. He had not understood why Bin Laden had struck in such a way as to guarantee an all-out war, but it was not his place to question military strategy. He had no way of knowing that no one had been expecting that type of attack. Even if he had, he would still have remained loyal. It just made his job so important now. Something had to distract the United States from its relentless assaults upon their positions.

Years of travel with Zawahiri had taught him that in order to win a war of this type they would have to win the propaganda war. They had been doing that in Eastern Europe, the Mid-East, and Eastern Asia, but the attacks of 9/11 had forced them into a type of propaganda war unlike any he had seen. They must somehow persuade the victims themselves that they had in some way deserved it. And he must do it so effectively that the victim was not only weakened and doubtful, but changed course altogether.

Samir was confident that he could do it eventually. After all, he had been educated at Princeton. He had watched firsthand what the Americans value and what causes them to flinch. And he had observed in the last decade in the United States almost an obsession with being liked and agreed with. This, of course, was something he could not even discuss with his classmates because they were the ones who somehow had accepted the idea that, to be a true American, meant you never offended anyone about anything. This surrendering of decision to the opinion of one person he felt was a perversion of their very values. The ultimate outcome would be that the one rules the many, and he had no idea how America had arrived at that inversion.

The Doctor knew, however. In fact, he had become wealthy in the process. But it would be sometime before Samir would come face to face with that reality. Tonight, all he had on his mind was Bud Walker.

"I just have to redirect him, that's all," Samir said to himself in the mirror. He paused and then smiled. "Redirect." Suddenly he had it. He knew what to do. It was quite simple actually. He had long ago learned that if you want to make something quite small appear large, you generalize the discussion. You make it appear as if everybody is saying something, even if it is only one person. He had laughed because this was the oldest trick in the propaganda book.

To take a generality even further, you attach it to a gossip line. That really obscures the source of the statement and overwhelms the reasoning ability of the person. Knowing that the press wants to report the truth, he was about to overwhelm Bud Walker's reason with gossip and generality. Then Walker would do the rest.

Like a warrior ready to do battle, Samir exited his apartment and had his doorman hail him a cab. He was ready; nervous, but ready.

The party was in full force when the Walkers arrived. The President of France was genuinely pleased to see them, and was most complimentary of Mrs. Walker's gown. He seemed the epitome of charm. Their escort from the Ministry of the Interior saw to it that they were properly introduced to everyone, including Samir.

Walker didn't seem to take much note of Samir's introduction. Judging by the fact there had been at least 80 people in front of him, Samir was looking for an opportunity to speak with Walker alone. Samir watched him cautiously throughout the evening. Without calling attention to his watching, he was careful to observe the man he was stalking. It seemed the media mogul had a healthy respect for fine Scotch, but not much regard for wine. Given that he smoked cigars, that was fitting. And that gave Samir an idea.

He knew it was only a matter of time before Bud Walker would excuse himself for a smoke outside. Despite the time of year, the weather that night in Paris was very pleasant. The lights of the city and the simply dazzling view of the Eiffel tower in its Christmas resplendency made a stop on the terrace quite palatable. So Samir exited to the terrace with a brandy and waited by the door.

In a matter of five minutes, Bud Walker slipped away from his wife's side and out to the terrace. He and she had many disagreements about what she regarded as a disgusting habit. The only thing she hated more was his chewing tobacco when they vacationed at their ranch. If he would just settle for a cigarette she wouldn't have nagged him. But the smell of a cigar made her nauseous. So they had compromised. Though most men do smoke cigars indoors, Bud Walker and his third wife had an agreement that he would engage in that nasty habit outdoors, and outdoors only.

That simple little solution to nagging led Bud Walker to the terrace that night. It was late afternoon in the United States. No one in the United States had any idea that the future of their country was about to change. In years to come experts would wonder where they had made the turn. They would be mystified as to how they had bogged down in a quagmire of rancor and indecision. The simple answer was: a nagged husband decided to smoke on the terrace.

As soon as Samir saw Walker slip onto the terrace and head toward the railing, he knew he had him. He had guessed he would do this. That was what he was paid to do, know what the opponent would do in various circumstances. His confidence riding high now, Samir felt invincible and moved over to address Walker.

"May I?" he offered Walker a cigar. It was a fine brand and one he knew Walker would try.

Looking at it, Walker commented, "I understand these are especially fine."

"Yes, please, try one. I would be honored." That did it. Bud Walker puffed up just knowing that the simple act of his taking a cigar from someone was an honor to that person. He knew how all celebrities must feel when people want their autograph, or desire to keep something of the celebrity's. Bud couldn't help but marvel at how far he'd come in life that he was in an apartment of the President of France, overlooking the city of Paris, taking a cigar from someone who was "honored" to serve him.

"Thank you." He took the cigar. Then he decided to make the man's night by actually talking to him. *A little small talk wouldn't hurt.* "So, I gather by your accent that you are not French."

"That is correct," Samir answered, easing him along.

"Where are you from?"

"I'm originally from Egypt, but I was educated in the United States. I reside in Paris now where my PR firm is."

Hmm, I thought I detected a U.S. education here, Walker thought. "Where'd you go to school?"

"Princeton."

"Great school. I understand their Public Relations department and program is exceptional."

Samir answered conservatively, "Yes, most definitely. That is what attracted me."

Wanting to compliment this man and honor him even more, Walker added, "I've hired men from Princeton myself to promote some of our projects. First rate. You made a wise choice."

"Thank you, sir. I know my father has been proud of my alma mater." Samir watched to see how Walker responded to the voicing of respect. He puffed up. He was just where Samir wanted him.

"It's interesting living here in Paris," Samir ventured. "Especially being in the public relations field. It gives one quite a perspective on world opinions."

Bud Walker didn't want to be known as just some rich guy. He wanted to be respected as the head of the premiere news empire in the United States. His ambitions included even global news agencies. In order to live up to that, he was automatically interested in the opinions of the rest of the world. After all, he was going to be senior to it all. He wouldn't be just representing the United States; he would be reporting on and for all the people of the world, eventually. He envisioned himself as the wise mentor to them all.

And it was that ego that asked the next question. "What have you learned recently from the French, you know, about the state of affairs?"

With no hesitation whatsoever, Samir began his prepared launch. Using the oldest trick in the book he subtly overwhelmed Bud Walker with a series of generalities. He leaned in to speak in confidence, "To tell you the truth, people here are surprised at the United States and how reckless Bush has become." He paused to let Walker digest that. He knew now that if Walker asked a next question he had taken the bait.

"You mean with regard to Iraq?" There it was. He had him!

"That, yes. But frankly, everything. Everyone is talking about the importance of alliances now and of agreement. The French are very interested in creating alliances, not breaching them. Everyone here is very respectful of the United Nations and the conscientious work it has done in this matter." Walker was inhaling his cigar and looking out over the city. Samir calmly turned to look out over the city, too and added, "The consensus seems to be that this is a mistake. The United States should not be fussing at its allies. It should be attacking the right target."

"And they feel we are not?" Walker asked. Samir's heart was racing. The question itself revealed the victory. Walker had taken on the generality and spoke of "they" without questioning once who "they" were.

I was right. It seems Bud Walker has an ax to grind too. "From everything I've been able to gather, you're right." Now he went for the jugular. "And they're a little puzzled too, frankly."

"About what?" Walker asked quickly.

"I don't want to be critical. I'd be the last one to want to cast doubt here. I mean I know the pressure you're under."

Now Walker was really curious. "What are you referring to?"

"Well, again, this is not what I feel, of course. But they're a bit surprised you'd be taken in by your Government so. The French can't understand why the American press, of all the world's press, would let themselves be used as a propaganda tool. That's all."

"What do you mean?" Walker sounded a bit belligerent.

"From what I've heard, the people here and everywhere in Europe frankly, feel the press is being used to bang the drums of war when it isn't necessary to do so. Now they are beginning to wonder what's being covered up."

"Covered up?"

"Yes, the word in the cafes is 'what did America do to invite the attack?' It's terrible, of course, but the United States must have done something to bring this on, and they must be trying to cover up something—money deals, oil, something—if they've duped the press into just covering the United States' point of view and ignoring the rest of the world's."

Walker was silent, but his brow was furrowed. He was glowering now, but said nothing.

"If I may say so, sir, the French, to me, have always demonstrated themselves to be fair. They look for the other side of the issue. Germany, too, I think. They know that there are two sides to any story. And I think, frankly, they view themselves as superior to you because they will try to take responsibility for what they have done, but you don't."

"Me? You mean me?"

"Oh, no, sir. Not you personally. Good lord, no. Your government is what I meant. And that's what puzzles them about your press. They expected more is all. They expected you to be better."

"Humph. I see." That was all Bud Walker said. The two continued smoking until they both felt a chill.

"I appreciate your candor, Samir. It isn't often you find anyone who says what he really thinks. Wars get started that way you know; good people saying nothing. I appreciate you setting me straight."

"That wasn't…I didn't mean…" Samir feigned an apology. "I just answered your question is all. You're too important in your field for me to do any less. I thank you for the opportunity to share with you what I've learned."

"You're welcome." With that, Walker rejoined his wife who was starting to debate with a diplomat about France's involvement in Southeast Asia. Sensing that would only lead to trouble, the couple prepared to leave the party. Samir remained on the terrace. Tonight he would log in to a chess game and show that the White King's Knight had been moved.

Two hours later, the Doctor logged in to the game and spotted the move. He then opened up his encrypted file. The cube had four layers highlighted. On the fourth from the bottom, the Doctor relabeled the White Knight. Although the

Knight was still on the same side of the board as its King, the move of a "mouse" spun the "rank" on the board the Knight occupied by 180 degrees. The Knight was now facing in the direction of its own king. The Doctor smiled, pressed "save," logged off and went to bed.

Back in the penthouse suite of a grand hotel overlooking the Champs Elysees, Walker was telling his wife, "I have a responsibility, you know. It goes beyond just our government, our people. I have a responsibility to all the people of the world. And by God, I'm going to fulfill it."

She nodded and went to bed while Walker emailed his staff that he wanted a meeting of all editorial chiefs first thing on Monday morning when he returned. Bud Walker was about to make his move.

CHAPTER 31

The decoded report on his desk was worse than he had expected. He had anticipated that there would be delays and disruptions in communication coming out of the theater of operations. He had expected fragments of emails and satellite phone messages; he had expected direct damage reports by their support base in the area. But he had not expected the degree of devastation of their command structure.

Now Makkawi's report was indicating that Khalid Sheik Mohammed himself had been captured. Turning to WNG, CNN, BBC, no one was reporting it. Whoever had him was keeping it under wraps for a while. The Doctor congratulated himself on demoting Khalid right after 9/11. His failure to properly anticipate the damage of Atef's planned attacks had led to disaster for them. He had known it would and he did not want Khalid in a position where he would have any information, let alone any involvement in the plans they were deploying now.

Despite Makkawi's fears that Khalid might reveal information to the United States or Canada about attack plans within the U.S., the Doctor felt they were unwarranted. He had, in fact been declawed more than a year ago when he was banished to Pakistan for his own protection. At worst he might reveal the truck bomb plan they were working on. The only thing really uncertain was when the United States would reveal they had him. *He'll expose him when he feels it will do him the most good,* he concluded about the U.S. President. *Probably just before he attacks Iraq. Good.*

Although the Doctor was convinced that would ultimately work to Al Qaeda's advantage, he was very angry with George Bush. He could see their analyses of him had been deficient. The son was not following the form of his father, neither were his advisors. He wondered how much that black woman he despised had to do with this. She dressed demurely, but he saw in her eyes that she would relentlessly pursue the goals of her world vision. To Zawahiri, the rise to prominence of Condoleezza Rice was further demonstration of the corruption of the West.

We'll catch him in Iraq. Meanwhile, he concluded that the United States' President was pursuing too relentlessly and inflicting too much damage. Hundreds of their commanders and seconds-in-command had been captured or killed all around the world. Their support base was loyal but tied down by incessant surveillance. He doubted that the American people had any idea how many Special Forces units were operating in that arena. These reports in front of him painted a bleak picture of everyone being on the run. Makkawi himself was exhausted just trying to avoid the forces tracking him. The Americans wanted Bin Laden and the Doctor, and they wanted them badly.

Cave structures and computer communications can be rebuilt easily. They can be commandeered, as they would be in Iraq. Weapons were easy to come by, especially once they had access to Saddam's massive stashes of weapons. The Americans themselves would soon help them with that. But good people, trained people, were harder to replace.

It had taken years to develop the kind of talent the enemy had wiped out in just a little over a year. And for that, Zawahiri now hated George Bush. He picked up the phone and placed a direct call to Samir.

Since both men were off the radar screen of intelligence in their cover lives, it was possible for them to converse by phone without being too circumspect. They could talk. They just needed to camouflage the actual subject material so that any casual listener who might happen to overhear would not think anything of their conversation.

"Samir, I have rethought my position on a change at the top. I now have concluded it is vital." That statement was ambiguous enough even if someone was listening. For all they would know, he was talking about a corporate reshuffling. He continued, "I want you to call our man in France and I want him to publicly call the man at the top out for recklessness. Then I want you to ensure that the opportunist you have cultivated runs with it. Is that clear?"

"Perfectly." Samir understood the reference to Walker immediately. "Do you have a timeline?" Samir asked, trying to determine the urgency.

"Before he opens his second theater. I want our man in the hospital to have a head start."

Samir exhaled noticeably. He knew the "man in the hospital" meant Zarqawi who was waiting for orders. That was quick. He was thinking of a plan already when he answered, "No problem."

That ended the call and the Doctor felt better. Every once in a while he experienced the same physical manifestations as when he was imprisoned. Watching so many good men tortured and killed had left him with the sweats and high blood pressure. The ulcer that had plagued him since that time was a chronic source of irritation. He was still being treated for that. And seeing these reports of what Bush had authorized caused him to want the man gone. He knew it didn't really matter. In the scheme of their operations, it didn't matter whether Bush remained or was ousted in 2004, but to the Doctor, it now mattered. It had become personal.

Samir knew exactly what to do. Deep inside the French government, close to President Chiraq, was a man who had the ear and respect of his President. He also had committed crimes of bribery and espionage. He had personally benefited from governments and businesses alike, and his secret had to remain a secret. This went way beyond indiscretions with a mistress. Samir's knowledge of this, and his cover-up of it, had earned him the indebtedness of the man. To be sure, it was motivated by fear. And that is why Samir knew the man would do exactly as Samir told him to do.

Like any good advertising director, he now had a channel to plant the seeds he wanted planted. He knew eventually he would use this man, he just hadn't known when. But this was perfect. It blended their overall strategy with a chance to please the great Doctor.

A few days later, the President of France made an uncharacteristically harsh criticism of the United States. At first, the U.S. government was merely puzzled, wondering if he was posturing to handle an internal faction. Their puzzlement would soon turn to dismay. Within weeks, France and Russia together would threaten to veto a measure brought to the UN by Secretary of State Colin Powell. He had worked hard to diplomatically forge a coalition and cause the United Nations to take responsibility for its ultimatums. The mere threat of veto signaled a shift of alliances.

The players in the War on Terror were deviating from the script the United States and Britain had in mind. It would be months before they truly noticed that an ally had started to look and act like an enemy. Their best analysts would come close to spotting the truth but would glance off. After all, a truth like that was so outrageous it had to be false. The Doctor had known they and their news media would react that way. What the Doctor didn't know, however, was that a young chess player was coming dangerously close to figuring it out.

The meeting Bud Walker had with his chiefs had been less confrontational than he had expected. He knew that these experienced journalists, editors and directors held him in some disdain. To be sure, they knew he was a gifted businessman, but they had lived in their ivory towers long enough to regard him as a rich "wanna-be."

That didn't particularly turn them off, however. Having an ambitious boss like Walker guaranteed them the best staff, and the best salaries. As his empire had grown, it had also given to them great lifestyles. Their shared biases enabled them to attach themselves to Walker's goals.

So, when he explained that he wanted them to start taking another view on this whole War on Terror thing, there was very little dissent. He had been persuasive; they did not want to be known as a network or news agency that was a mouthpiece for the government. He had punched all the right buttons about "Journalistic Integrity" and "Daring To Take the Lead."

Walker was, in fact, teaching them to do the unconventional. Watching his colleagues begin to salivate at the idea of some voice-of-opposition investigative journalism, a lone news chief had argued that a time of war precluded them from attacking the way the Government was prosecuting the war. He feebly reminded the others that disinformation was part of the waging of war, and they needed their relationship with the Secretary of Defense and the Pentagon to be impeccable. He had suggested that if they were not careful, their actions could be considered to be aiding and comforting the enemy.

The man was a Korean War veteran who had covered numerous war theatres during the Cold War. He was keenly conscious that one has to balance the freedom of the press with the security of the nation. "Some discussions and debates, though appropriate, need to be held behind closed doors. And some stories should never see the light of day in news print," he had argued.

The others, however, were either too inexperienced or too ambitious to really appreciate the subtle ethical issues he raised. No one else in the room had any doubts whatsoever about their own ability to navigate these dangerous waters.

Walker sensed the tide was turning his way when he delivered his main statement. "We are going to be out in front on this. I'm telling you, there is more here than meets the eye. This government is withholding something, and I, for one, intend to find out what that dirty little secret is. Gentlemen, I'm a country boy, as you know. But one thing we countries boys know is that if there is smoke, there is a fire somewhere. And I can smell some smoke in this fixation on going into Iraq."

They were all silent, but attentive, so he continued, "And months from now, when it surfaces, we are not going to be looking at the ass of CBS or CNN or anyone else that had the guts to tackle it first. No, sirree! They will be looking up our ass this time." He decided to hold out his final carrot. "And this is our chance to overtake Fox and end this monopoly they hold on 'fair and balanced.' By God, we'll show them 'balanced.' We're going to take the lead here and come out the gate as the first network to talk about the other side of this. The American people aren't going to hear just one side anymore. We'll give them something to think about."

The idea of smashing the competition in a bold, if not controversial, editorial move was too enticing. They all nodded agreement and commenced the instruction of their editors. The change in course was subtle, almost unnoticeable at first. But like a boat leaving harbor one degree off course, the deviance is unnoticeable at harbor's edge, but potentially fatal a thousand miles out.

And no one in Washington took much notice when the ACLU got some coverage that read "Antiterrorism Laws Endanger Our Rights." The gathering storm was dismissed as just the ACLU doing what the ACLU does. It was perfectly predictable. For a public relations man in Paris, however, the clippings were a sign that the seeds had taken root.

Back in New York, George Nasser was becoming desperate that his message had not gotten through. The more he listened to the news and the more he heard of his brothers being killed or captured, the more certain he became that the CIA had somehow penetrated their complex communications networks through this Grandmaster, and that whatever Usama Bin Laden was planning was being foiled by these covert efforts.

Why else would they be operating off the CIA premises even? he challenged himself. In his mind, whatever was going on in that house in Arlington had some bearing on the events he saw on the nightly cable news. By the New Year's break, he could no longer sit in his apartment waiting for some response out of the war theater. That would come, he was certain. But George had concluded he needed to be ready with more than just his observation of some kid hanging out with a CIA analyst.

He didn't know exactly what he planned to do, but he knew he had to be on the ground in Arlington. So he reserved a room at the Holiday Inn in Fair Oaks for two weeks. Using a Budget rental car with Rhode Island plates, he parked the car a few houses down from Andy's home and watched.

Disappointingly, he saw very little. The one good thing about the cold damp weather was that no one was on the streets to observe him. He was able to confirm the pattern, however, of James Mikolas and Andrew Weir spending each and every day together in that house. He noted that twice an Orkin truck came by. *Sure wish my super was as diligent*, he mused.

One day he noted that Andrew Weir was apparently driving for Domino's Pizza. His rusty jeep had their sign on it. Nasser didn't know why he hadn't noticed it before. That gave him an idea. It was an easy task to follow Andy one night to the exact pizza location he was working from. George then went back to his hotel room and looked up the Domino's closest to his hotel. It was the one Andy was servicing.

He was emboldened by this. *Perhaps I can turn myself into a field operative and do some real good in this war.* He picked up the phone and ordered a vegetarian pizza, knowing that Andy had arrived at the Domino's Pizza location just a few minutes earlier. Then, he waited.

One half hour later, there was a knock on his door. As he opened it, he saw up close the handsome tall young man he had been following. Andy smiled and said, "Hi. Got your vegetarian pizza here. It smells great!"

George smiled and responded cordially, "Great. I was getting hungry. Please. Step in. How much do I owe you?"

"Twelve-fifty."

Having lived in New York for the better part of his adult life, George Nasser knew that the best way to get great service and to get things you needed was to tip heavily. Anyone working for tips automatically would go out of their way for you and be appreciative. So, he handed Andy $5 instead of the expected $1 tip.

Andy grinned and said, "Thanks, much appreciated."

Watching Andy out of his window, George thought, *I wonder just how many nights I can stand to eat pizza!* An idea was coming to him. The more he thought about it, the more he was proud of himself. He was quite certain now that he could get close to this Andrew Weir, even into his house if he played it right. George

Nasser experienced a flush of personal ambition, a sense that he was in the right place at the right time. He was determined not to let Ayman or Usama down.

Over the course of the next week, Andy received a ticket to deliver a vegetarian pizza to room 1201 at the Holiday Inn in Fair Oaks every night. He knew exactly who it was for and was starting to look forward to his conversations with the visiting professor. After all, the man had no family and he seemed to be cheered up by the few extra minutes Andy spent with him each night.

On the seventh night the professor made a proposal to Andy. "You know, I have another week yet, and I'd like to see some of the sites of the city. But I don't much like going alone. I have an offer for you."

"What's that?" Andy asked innocently.

"I'd like to hire you to tour me around." Then he hastily added, "Not the whole day, of course; I have work that prevents that. But I was thinking maybe two to three hours in the mornings. I'd pay you $20 a day."

It didn't take Andy long to decide. He'd been delivering pizzas because he and Kelly needed money and it was one of the few things he could do on his odd hours. But $20 was about all he made on a great night, so the idea of an extra couple hundred dollars was appealing. He really wanted to take some of the pressure off his mom and he knew James wouldn't mind. James had been pestering Andy about getting out more and was trying to limit their work time to afternoons.

"Yeah, sure. That'd be great. Tomorrow?"

"Tomorrow," George answered softly. His heart was beating fast and he wondered if that was true of all field operatives.

The next day George Nasser and Andrew Weir commenced the next phase of their relationship.

James pulled up in front of the house and was surprised to see Kelly sitting on the front step. *Bit cold for that. What's up?* James asked himself. As he got closer he could see she was crying.

"Kelly, what's wrong?" he asked sincerely.

She was holding what appeared to be a dozen or so response cards to some type of invitation. Clearly, the contents were upsetting. James just stood there, waiting for her to answer.

Holding the cards up to him, she dropped a few. "Andy's 21st birthday is in two weeks. I thought I'd surprise him with a party."

As James picked up the cards that had dropped to the pavement, the ones he looked at all had "unable to attend" checked off. They didn't even appear to have a note. He didn't know quite what to make of it.

"They're all the same," she offered, choking back tears. "None of his friends are coming. A few are away at college. But most didn't even respond. I don't know what to tell him. I don't know what to do." She broke down again.

James just waited. She looked up at him and he hoped she wasn't going to blame him. He deserved to be blamed, but he hoped she wasn't going to. Frankly, he had no idea the Kid was about to turn 21. He thought he was maybe turning 20. A little at a loss for words he stalled by saying, "I thought he was 19."

"He's 20. I held him back the year his father died. He lost so much time trying to help out near the end I thought it best to give him a rest. It's his 21st birthday, James. That's special. And I wanted it to be special for him, something he'd remember always." She paused and added, "And no one wants to come."

Since James had never had a family, he was a little tentative about stepping into this obvious trauma. But he sucked it up. After all, he reasoned, he had precipitated this by turning the Kid into a spook, of sorts. And he couldn't stand to see Kelly cry. She was a brave and hard-working woman, and she deserved better. After a moment, he got an idea.

"Tell you what, Kelly; I think I've got an idea. Should be fun for Andy and he'll never have to know no one wanted to come."

"What?" she asked hopefully.

"I have a place down on the Cape Fear River. It's actually pretty nice down there, even in the winter. Why don't we all go down there, spend a few days? I'll treat him and you to one of the greatest dinners the South has to offer at Sadie's." He made it sound so great that Kelly laughed. She had no idea what Sadie's was, and had no idea if the dinner would be great, but she appreciated the solution.

"Accepted."

James smiled shyly. That was good. He'd done something right. *Maybe this family stuff isn't so tough after all*, he thought.

CHAPTER 32

Their time on the Cape Fear River proved to be just the right thing. James had persuaded Whitney that they needed to take a break for a few days and that the Kid deserved something out of their cash funds. He had argued that if they had cash to pay informants, they ought to at least get a little money into the hands of someone who was trying to help them get into the mind of the master terrorist.

Whitney clearly recognized that Ayman Al-Zawahiri had stymied the best analysts in all the intelligence agencies they were connected to. If there was any hope of figuring out how to anticipate his next moves and find him, he was willing to toy with it. It wasn't costing them anything. So he coughed up a few hundred dollars so that the Kid could take a break from pizza deliveries long enough to celebrate his 21st birthday.

As James left Whitney's office though Whitney watched him through the glass and thought, *I hope he's not going soft on me.*

James hopped into his car and handed Andy some money.

"What's this?" Andy asked.

"A birthday present from the boss, Kid." Knowing that seemed out of character, he added, "Every once in a while that guy has an emotional thought. So enjoy it. It might be the last money you see from him."

They all laughed. Andy had noticed that Whitney didn't seem to enjoy life much. He had that same hollowed-eye look that George Tenet had these days. Both men, to him, seemed to be struggling with resentment and anger. He had seen it opposite him as he looked out over the defensive line when he played a team that had lost its confidence, and he had seen it in the eyes of some of his chess opponents. It was almost a pre-death type of look, as if the person knew he was about to lose.

That was why Andy was relieved not to have to go to Langley every day. He was afraid he'd catch that look, and he wondered when President Bush would replace the man at the top. *He ought to talk to Coach,* Andy concluded. *Coach always knew when to take a man out.* And Andy could see that the Director of the CIA was in that zone now.

Turning his attention to the road, it was a crisp clear winter day. Having never been to Cape Fear, he had no idea what one would do there in the winter. Somehow, he couldn't see himself fishing on an icy river. But he welcomed the time away, and James and his mom seemed determined to do something special for his birthday, so he was game.

The three days passed by quickly and easily. James' cabin was just that, a cabin. But it had a woodburning stove that heated the place easily, and the bathroom facilities were more than adequate. Kelly seemed content to make Andy's favorite cake—white cake with coconut frosting—and had bought him an ivory chess case. It was obviously expensive and at first, he thought of telling her she shouldn't have, but he quickly reminded himself that it was his 21st birthday; his mother was trying to give him something lasting for him and his family in the future.

The carving of the eagle on the lid was beautiful, and it surely would be a great box for his best set. Truthfully though, Andy was having some difficulty ever imagining himself with a family. The events of 9/11 had obscured the vision of the future for most Americans. That was compounded with the intense focus he had on penetrating the mystery of Zawahiri. He couldn't see anything in front of him but the task of defeating this man. If he could end Zawahiri's game, then maybe he could think about the normal things young people look forward to.

Meanwhile, he would settle for letting his mom dote on him a bit. As he opened the box, his eyes teared when he saw the pin his father had worn. For years Kelly had worn it around her neck, and today she was handing it off to him. It was, indeed, a symbol of the young man assuming the role of his father. Each generation hands off to the next, and Andy knew it was his turn. He hoped he wouldn't disappoint his father now. Sports, chess, those were the ordinary activities of young men. But fighting in this war was a challenge. So much depended on the outcome.

The fire was down to embers now. Andy added a log to the fire and stoked it. As he did, he looked at Kelly asleep on the sofa. She had been reading and had fallen asleep with her book still open on her chest. Gently and fondly, he covered her with an antique throw James kept on the back of the worn furniture.

The air outside was remarkable. Andy only needed a scarf to keep warm and he joined James who was sitting on top of an upside-down canoe along the bank. "What you doing?" he asked.

"Nothing, really," James answered. He was looking at something in the water. "Actually, I was watching a mallard under that bank over there."

"Yeah, where?" James pointed it out, and for a few minutes the two shadow warriors sat quietly enjoying the elegant movements of the duck as it grabbed insects off the water. Each knew the other was thinking about Dr. Ayman Al-Zawahiri, but each was content to let the other have a day of peace.

Saddam Hussein was just finishing a lavish dinner in one of the apartments of his palace. He had left explicit instructions to have a television turned on 24-hours a day, so that he could catch any breaking news regarding the United Nations' weapons inspections.

He had kept his part of the bargain regarding the inspectors. Some days they would come with the international press. On those days he usually signaled the ground commander to let the inspectors wander at will in the facilities they wished to inspect. He had no trouble anticipating where they would appear. *The idiots remember where they last found materials from years earlier, and will just return to the sites they wanted to visit when they were thrown out five years earlier.* He smirked at how pious and cocky the inspection team was.

The team had in fact decided to visit previous sites and, most specifically, the ones they were scheduled to visit in the late

1990's before their expulsion. None was bright enough to guess that Saddam would anticipate that. He only had to guess at what order they would inspect.

Frankly, it didn't matter, because all the facilities had long since ceased to be weapons facilities or stockpile dumps. So it didn't matter to him what order the UN chose to swoop down on him. But he did enjoy these little games and looked forward to the evening news coverage of the day's events.

Whenever the team showed up without the press, his commanders were ordered to be obstreperous and to obstruct the inspections. If the press were there, they would film and show the whole world that Iraq was a good world citizen and had complied. The obstruction at the other sites was guaranteed to raise the suspicions of the inspectors, but more importantly, those of U.S. and British intelligence. After all, what possible reason would Saddam have to prevent an inspection unless there was something there to hide?

This tactic was proving so successful that by January 2003, the U.S. was saying that proof was not necessary, given the obstructionism. Their patience was growing thin and the whole world could feel the tension. It felt like a caged animal, pacing, waiting for the chance to pounce on its tormentor outside the cage.

The plan called for Saddam to open the door of the gate just a little and, at the same time, let the world press watch as the caged animal of the United States heaved against the gate. Knowing the timing of satellite flyovers and guessing they would target sites where he had presented the greatest barriers to inspection, he staged a stunning deception. It would come to haunt Colin Powell and President Bush, and embarrass all of intelligence.

The satellite photos that MI6, and the Russians, as well as the U.S. were examining clearly showed tractor trailers arriving at a warehouse facility and leaving that facility. The only conclusion they could logically draw was that Saddam was rattled now with the imminence of an invasion, that he did, in fact, possess stockpiles of weapons, and that he was loading these trailers with the weapons he wished to hide.

Standing in front of one of the TV screens, relaxing in an exquisite green and silver silk robe, Saddam laughed openly at the monitor. All the channels were falling over themselves to broadcast the United States displaying the photos and offering them as proof of concealment and defiance. The trucks had indeed been sent to the facility and ordered to stand by for some hours, and then leave. They, in fact, were empty. And the U.S. had fallen for it. They clearly believed his refusal to allow some inspections was covering up facilities like these and that he was removing weapons to safe places now.

Not only would that add fuel to the fire, but it would also press the urgency. If, in fact, the U.S. believed that he was now moving weapons, they would attack early. He had them now where he wanted them. The U.S. had backed away from trying to get a UN resolution to authorize them to invade. France and Russia's threatened veto had caused them to disengage from a confrontation at the Security Council. He knew what they would do next. They and the British would act on their own. His own lawyers were telling him they would use the last resolution as the justification for the invasion, claiming that its authority was implicit.

He wondered if the Americans had any idea how deeply involved France and Russia were with kickbacks, and money laundering, and fraudulent use of UN funds. They seemed to be oblivious. The French had assured him the United States would be unable to regard France as an enemy, and the British would not allow them to even entertain such an idea, let alone publicize it globally.

Watching countries try to jockey for position and try to coordinate their various constituencies confirmed for Saddam why a dictatorship is the best form of government. And he clearly understood why Stalin and Hitler had been so wise in destroying anyone who voiced a different opinion. *What a colossal waste of time and energy,* he reflected. *And all of it for the illusion of countries being good little boys and girls. They deserve what they are about to get.*

And he felt nothing but disdain for these Americans. Hadn't anyone taught them history? His own recollections of how the Americans had trapped the Soviet Union in the Cuban missile crisis gave him the idea of presenting something for the United States to photograph. He guessed they would try now what had worked for them then, a dramatic disclosure of incriminating photos. Only this time the photos would boomerang on them. *It's their arrogance that makes them think I would not outfox them on this one and use their own history against them.*

Finishing his cigar, Saddam reentered his inner office and confirmed the movement of cash to three of his European corporations. He was pleased with the percentages he was receiving and knew that he would come out of this wealthier than any one could have expected. Then he compiled some detailed notes on the sequence of events of his escape. Opening the door that connected his bedchamber to his office, he disrobed and went to bed.

Samir meanwhile was pouring over the news headlines in all major U.S. and British papers. The Internet allowed him to review all the transcripts of news broadcasts as well. His office, however, resembled a communications command center. He had televisions in separate compartments on bookshelves especially built to hold their weight. From his desk he could monitor seven channels in the United States: the three major networks and four cable news channels. He had been watching WNG's coverage 24/7 and was waiting for the duplication process to begin.

He knew their strategy was working when he saw the seed of doubt he had planted with Walker appear in the copy of Walker News Group's lead anchorman. At first it was just a change in tone, the addition of an edge of skepticism in his voice as he read the releases related to the War on Terror. It would have gone unnoticed by the viewing public, but Samir discerned that the anchor was straining a bit, trying to distance himself from the piece.

Within a few weeks, their producers had grown bolder and were inserting language that implied the possibility of deception on the part of the Administration. At that moment Samir knew the seeds of doubt had taken hold. He could honestly say he looked forward to coming into his office these days. For he knew it was only a matter of time before the seeds would sprout into an open challenge from some member of the press to the Administration. And once that open challenge occurred where the motive of the United States regarding Iraq was questioned, he knew that he would watch a virtual cross-pollination of it from his desk. He was certain it would cross-over to all other networks.

It actually occurred before he expected it. An alert producer at the United States' leading cable news channel had apparently picked up on this subtle change in reporting and begun to wonder why. Not wanting to be scooped and not wanting to lose the ratings game, he had alerted his staff and journalists to begin digging. He specifically told them to keep an open mind here, and not be swayed by their emotional response to 9/ll. Reminding them that great journalists never swallowed Pablum spoon-fed them by governments, his admonition escalated their own natural bias and appeared to give them permission.

Everyone in journalism knew of Bud Walker's ambition and intentions to take over the lead in broadcast journalism, so no one wanted to get flanked by him in a journalism war. He appeared to be going in another direction and, by God, they were not going to be left out.

The beginnings were innocuous enough and infrequent enough, but Samir observed with delight the spreading of the doubt from screen to screen in his office. It began as just some nagging doubts and assertions of "what's the rush?" The editorial reasoning of the networks was inserted to imply that since the world had gone so long as it was, why didn't they just let the UN inspectors finish their job?

Soon it was snowballing into questions of "recklessness" and at that moment Samir knew he had won. Not only had the ideas he had planted in Walker's mind been duplicated, but the actual words he used were as well. Within weeks it had escalated into suggestions that the United States was alienating everyone by attacking and weakening the United Nations. And in an attempt to be fair and balanced, the U.S. media began to print and give voice to the viewpoints of France, Russia, and Germany. Soon

Samir's TV monitors tracking broadcasts on the BBC and on the television networks of France and the Arab world revealed they had picked up on the idea and were empowered to insert their own bias.

And that was what the Doctor knew would happen. It didn't matter whether the issues were valid or true on anyone's side. It only mattered that doubt was spreading and he knew that once it reached avalanche proportions, the media would have to escalate it to another level to feed the beast.

What the Doctor knew was that extremists wait for any incident that allows them to cast aspersions and drive wedges. Sooner or later, everyone makes a mistake. And at the moment of the mistake, the extremist viewpoint seizes on that mistake and impugns the very motive itself.

Though it was clear the United States, Britain and Spain were going to invade Iraq, that did not fluster Samir; quite the contrary. The Doctor had messaged him with a "bravo, well done." They would invade, but they would invade in an environment of division and hostility in the very circles they would normally count on for support. Polls were beginning to show a shift from a "decided yes" to "not certain." It was perhaps the pinnacle of Samir's public relations career. In just one campaign, he had shifted the United States from certainty to a "maybe." And with the "maybe" came the loss of confidence. It was just a crack, but *after all, we're just beginning,* he reminded himself.

One of his happiest days came when he emailed several Internet links to Phillipe Monet. He thought the Doctor would relish the fact that the mainstream journalists swallowing the bait had now brought out of the woodwork all the conspiracy theorists that were looking for cover-up and gain. Though it was just the beginning, the speed with which unsubstantiated garbage can be passed and disseminated on the Internet gave him certainty that, sooner or later, that too would surface to the mainstream.

He could hardly wait to see who it would be that would elevate Internet "bathroom wall" writing to mainstream status in their attempt to stay ahead of their competition. The wall of journalistic integrity and common sense had been breached, and the West was now hurtling toward a Sweeps.

In the middle of it all was Bud Walker. He had no idea he had been set up. Nor did the first political challenger in the 2004 election in the United States spot it. His own personal ambition blinded him to the possible consequences of pursuing this line of reasoning, but he did it anyway.

Watching this on television in his offices overlooking Lake Geneva was the Doctor. All he did was smile, for he knew enough of American politics to know that if a candidate was floating this trial balloon, the public had made it possible. He was certain now that the viewing public had no idea they had been taken. Believing that all journalists of major repute are fair and balanced, that one goes to the press for the truth and facts, they never noticed that none of this passed the common sense test. The Doctor was right. Once you provoke the memory of a painful experience again, a once-rational mind becomes irrational, and can be manipulated. It becomes easy then to hang a lot of lies on only one truth. But the irrational person can't differentiate the truth from the lie.

And so he authorized Phase Two of Samir's plan. It was simple really. He placed a hold on the plan for approximately six months so that he could coordinate it with his orders to Zarqawi. Once Zarqawi was in place and in business, he would unleash Samir with one of the most brilliant mind-control operations ever perpetrated on a free people.

For now, however, he was content to open up his three-dimensional block and on the same level as the White Knight facing its own King, he labeled a White Bishop. Rotating the Bishop's rank 180 degrees, the White Bishop also faced its King. Then he boldly highlighted the top layers of his cube, opening them also to play, and logged off.

Five minutes later, he called the president of Decu-Hehiz, an immense pharmaceutical manufacturer, and asked for an appointment. As Phillipe Monet was the leading shareholder with the corporation, the call was taken by the president himself and the appointment set without hesitation. The meeting was set for March 13, 2003—one week before the invasion of Iraq. The opening pawn move of the final phase had begun.

CHAPTER 33

Rudolf Iseli was the youngest president in the history of Decu-Hehiz. He was also the most ambitious. The corporation was a staple in the Swiss economy and transacted business all over the world. During the ten years he had headed the company, they had grown from being just another manufacturer in Zermatt to one of the giants to be reckoned with. Their revenues were on an upward graph that would cause a novice to think the trajectory was the moon! Their profit margins were the best in the industry, and they had honed in on a particular market that had proven to be huge. Their various divisions were enjoying anywhere from a 9% to 22% increase since the beginning of the new millennium.

Abandoning most of Europe for the fat and juicy marketplace of the United States, they had been doing battle with other European manufacturers and those in the States as well. Iseli himself was not only gifted, but was developing a reputation of being one of the most ruthless CEOs in Europe. He lived, breathed and ate "compete and destroy." And if he continued to escalate Decu-Hehiz's reputation, he knew that the choicest positions in the world would be offered to him.

Already he enjoyed a lifestyle greater than Youssef Nada, whose Swiss financial empire was legendary in his country. Nada's palatial estate in Lugano was the envy of many a European. But for some years, Iseli had surpassed the tasteful, yet lavish lifestyle of some of his peers. An invitation to one of his parties on Lake Geneva was the sign that an individual had arrived in Swiss society. His ski lodge in the foothills of the Matterhorn was resplendent with artifacts he had acquired in his travels throughout Asia and the Middle East.

Most of this was owed to the man who was about to meet him in his office. An investor who had not only risked a great deal of capital, Phillipe Monet had proven to be a brilliant strategist with regard to Decu-Hehiz tackling, and now dominating, the U.S. market. He had persuaded Iseli years earlier to pursue the United States, and to avoid the murkier and less fruitful waters of Europe.

Monet had been right. The United States had a vast population and one with a very dominant medical establishment. The American people placed their trust in the family physician as much as they trusted their pastor. Their doctor, therefore, had enormous control over what they took and how often. And their doctors, despite the most advanced technologies in the world, were sorely in need of help. There was not enough time in the day to stay abreast of all the advancements, and they were turning more and more to pharmaceuticals for solutions, and to the pharmaceutical rep for his expertise.

Training the reps of Decu-Hehiz to a level of medical and medicinal expertise above and beyond that of any competitor had been an expensive proposition. But Monet had insisted this was the way to go, and that it would yield a return on investment that would catapult this company to the head of the class. Although he had never directly said it, Monet had implied that a refusal on Iseli's part to take this tack would result in Monet investing his money with a more pliant competitor. Iseli had always been a gambling man. He not only was a regular high-roller at the finest casinos in Europe, but he had a sense of adventure as a businessman. He was capable of exploring new territory and had actually understood the wisdom of the strategy. And now, ten years later, he was a wealthy man with his own stock options.

Monet now wanted to speak to him, and he wondered what new idea the man had. He was just adjusting his tie to present his best appearance when his secretary announced the arrival of Phillipe Monet. The two embraced as old friends and immediately settled in to expensive leather and teak furniture Iseli used at the end of his office. From where they were sitting, the two men could enjoy the sailboats on the lake. The day was too chilly, however, and the only boats moving were the ferries that connected the metropolitan area with the outlying towns along the lake.

Iseli had ordered an exquisite lunch for them and motioned for Monet to help himself to anything from the buffet. Usually Monet had a fine appetite, but today he selected only a few seafood items and some strawberries. *He's got something on his mind for sure,* Iseli thought. He waited for his investor to begin.

"Thank you for taking time in your busy day on such short notice," the Doctor began.

"It is my pleasure. You know you are welcome here at all times."

"I appreciate that, so let me get right to the point." The Doctor paused for a second and then let out a deep sigh as if mourning something. Then he began in earnest. "You and I have made a great deal of money off our U.S. market, haven't we?"

"Most definitely." Iseli wondered where Monet was going. "Is something troubling you, my friend?"

The Doctor gloated inside that Iseli had grabbed that explanation for his sigh. It would make this easier. "Yes, most definitely. You know I suffer from ulcers and they have been bothering me of late."

"I'm sorry to hear that. I assume you're better today." Then realizing that his entire spread was acidic, he offered, "I'm so sorry. Would you like me to order something a bit more benign?"

"No, no, the medications have it under control today. But it caused me to think," the Doctor continued. "You and I have gained so much, and our friends in America, that is how I view them, have lost so much recently. It disturbs me daily to think of the agony of those towers collapsing, and the fear and uncertainty they are living with on a daily basis now."

"Yes, I understand," Iseli offered politely. He didn't understand though. He had no idea where Monet was going with this.

"And now, all the uncertainty and debate about what their next move will be. They're losing their friends and face those colored terror alerts every day when they rise and turn on the TV. Frankly, I don't know how they are coping, given how vulnerable they are to attacks on almost any level. The anxiety level must be enormous."

"Yes, I see your point. I had not given it much thought, truthfully. They seem to be coping."

The Doctor seized the moment. "Actually, I think not. My recent bout with my ulcers caused me to reflect on how much damage stress does. I have observed in my life that when people are afraid, they get sick; and when they lose something dear, they become depressed."

The Doctor had spoken slowly and deliberately to make certain Iseli would follow him. Now he paused to see Iseli's response. He seemed to be in mild agreement. So the Doctor continued, "I was feeling guilty, actually."

"Why?"

"I know this may sound sentimental from a ruthless old businessman like me, but I have become a wealthy man selling our product to the people of the United States and it pains me to see them suffering." He inhaled deeply and added, "So I came here to suggest a change in our strategy toward them. I want to help them."

"Of course, I too," Iseli responded obsequiously, "but what did you have in mind?"

"I believe we are well prepared to handle the physical illnesses that may accelerate due to the stress of the current world, but I believe we can do much better in providing something for the anxiety and depression they must be experiencing—which I fear will grow much worse as time goes by. This will be a long war for them, and I fear the price will be immense. Anything we can do to alleviate that I believe is not only a good investment, but is the most compassionate thing we can do."

Iseli said nothing for a moment.

"Do you agree with me, Rudi? Are you willing to help our friends?"

"Yes, certainly." Iseli had taken the bait. Iseli had never really looked upon Americans as his friends. If anything, the United States was just another challenge, a place to make money and catapult his company. He never did anything for altruistic reasons; his decisions were always driven by the cold reality of money and return on investment. So he didn't really have any understanding of what Phillipe Monet was saying. But he was not going to run the risk of offending this man even though Monet was certainly talking like an eccentric today. To humor his investor he asked, "What did you have in mind?"

The Doctor then laid out an innovative plan for the development and marketing of some of the most powerful antidepressants ever invented. They would represent a new generation of psychiatric medications and would find their way into the hands of Americans of all ages. Iseli was impressed. He wasn't quite sure why Monet was so empathetic toward the Americans and wanted so much to help them, but the businessman in him recognized that there was a huge door opening to them. He might not identify with Monet's reasons, but he could smell profit. The terrorists it seems had spiked the demand for a category of pharmaceuticals. And what Monet laid out would make it possible for Iseli to arrive at the forefront of this market. *And strike a blow at terrorism as well,* he thought. *Good idea. We won't let our best customers suffer from anxiety and depression.* He could see the industry accolades already. And he could see his portrait on the cover of Forbes Magazine. That was a feather he did not yet have in his cap.

He rose to escort his friend out and was greeted with yet another offering from Monet.

"I'm glad you see this as I do, Rudi. I always knew you were, at your core, a kind man," the Doctor lied.

"Thank you Phillipe; you are most kind."

"I'm going to recommend an advertising firm to you that I believe is especially suited to handle this campaign. You select the product, and I can guarantee this man will penetrate the market place faster than anyone I know."

Iseli had no idea who he was talking about, as Monet did not mention a firm, but rather just alluded to a man. "Who are you referring to?" he asked.

"There is a public relations firm in Paris that is stellar and creative. They are small, but the head of the firm, Samir, is one of the most brilliant people in his field, and he was educated at Princeton. I don't believe there is anyone who understands the American and his buying buttons better than Samir. I recommend him most highly."

"I'll take that under advisement. Thank you," Iseli commented nonchalantly. He was startled then to feel Monet's hand grip his forearm. The grip was such that it actually hurt.

"No. Not under advisement. He will handle the campaign for you," Monet stated flatly. There was no room for disagreement here and Iseli quickly understood that this was another one of Monet's terms that was not negotiable. Like before, he knew that to ignore this "suggestion" was tantamount to blowing the investment. Rudi Iseli was a realist.

What the hell do I care what advertising agency we use anyway? Rudi asked himself. *Agencies like that are a dime a dozen. If Phillipe has to have this Samir, whoever he is, so be it.* He nodded his complete agreement with Monet's demand. "Absolutely, whatever you say."

After Monet left, he grinned. He could see the quarterly reports already. And whatever bug Monet had up his rear was all right with Iseli. He wondered for a minute if this bachelor investor of his had something going with this Samir guy, and then he dismissed it completely. *Who cares? He doesn't get into my affairs. I won't get into his. Besides, he's never steered me wrong before.*

A thousand miles away another meeting had been hastily arranged. The Doctor knew he was going to need a face-to-face with Zarqawi to spell out the exact tactics he wanted deployed in the coming months. While Zawahiri was looking forward to introducing his next attack upon the United States, his security detail was working out his passport and identity for a hasty trip to Damascus.

Syria had become the crossroads of the terrorist world. There was no place better for messages to be passed, or for meetings to take place than in Damascus. Not only did the indigenous military turn a blind eye to the use of their city, they often helped the various organizations with recruiting.

With the invasion of Iraq imminent, the Doctor had to move quickly now. Saddam Hussein was following the script very neatly. The U.S. President had issued his last ultimatum, and Iraq had one last chance. In about ten days, Zawahiri guessed, the U.S. would attack.

Getting the Doctor into Damascus was easy. He had any number of innocuous identities he could deploy to justify a trip to this ancient city. His team in Switzerland was confident he would not be on anyone's radar screen; that was as long as Zarqawi was not spotted. Getting Nanda into the city from his hiding place was also quite easy. As far as they could tell, no one in intelligence had any dossiers on Nanda Shinoy. Once he received the messenger carrying his new orders, he was free to arrange his own transport.

It was far more difficult to get Zarqawi out of his hole in northern Iraq and across a monitored highway from Baghdad to Damascus, and then get him safely into Syria. Intelligence operatives from every country in the area had some personnel tracking the movement of key supporters of Hussein. The Doctor was fairly certain, however, that they had not made a solid connection between Al Qaeda and Hussein. One existed. But the public relations campaign they had run for years about the animosity between Bin Laden and Hussein had worked. *The lie told repeatedly becomes truth,* the Doctor reminded himself.

Further, his choice of a relative newcomer to the stage of terrorism was, he felt, a stroke of genius. He and Usama had been grooming this young man, but Zarqawi had yet to strike a blow that would cause his face to be appearing on wanted posters. There were no rewards offered on him yet. No one but the Doctor knew the role Bin Laden and he had selected for Zarqawi. The young man was fearless and he was ambitious. He was also inexperienced. And it was for that reason that the Doctor felt the instructions needed to be conveyed in person.

He had not been in his hotel room more than ten minutes when he received word that a package had been delivered for him at a house at the edge of the market. Walking easily through the market square and into one of the side streets, he stopped occasionally to look at wares and offer a feeble bid. When the merchant naturally rejected his offer he would move on. Near the end of the street, he entered a rug and copper shop and continued on behind the counter to the home in the rear.

Entering a private dwelling two blocks away, Zarqawi was escorted to an earthen tunnel under the floorboard. He had to stoop to navigate it, but the exit was clearly lit. He climbed a rickety ladder and emerged in a closet in the rear of the home. Immediately he recognized two of the voices and he quickly moved to the kitchen area to greet them.

Nanda turned quickly when he heard Zarqawi enter the room. The Jordanian terrorist, who was a fugitive from his own country, was still a relative unknown in the global world of terrorists. He was a handsome enough young man. Only the serpent-like eyes might have betrayed his deadliness and gruesome creativity. As he removed his head covering, Nanda was somewhat startled by the coldness he felt now that Zarqawi had entered the room. The months of waiting in Iraq had aged him. He showed no signs of debauchery like Saddam's son, only the icy coldness.

"Nanda," Zarqawi acknowledged his presence. "I did not expect to see you." Zarqawi had not been in the inner circle on the Doctor's identity deception. The man he knew as Zawahiri was reported dead in the attack upon Zawahiri's safe house. He had no idea whether Zawahiri had actually escaped. When Makkawi had sent him the message to attend a meeting in Syria, he frankly had no idea who to expect there.

His ambition caused him to want to meet face-to-face with the Doctor. Knowing that Atef had been killed, he reasoned now that a major assignment was looming for him. He was not prepared for what came next.

The man whom he knew as Zawahiri's assistant spoke to him, "Do you know who I am?"

"Yes, of course. We spoke briefly in the cave near Tora Bora."

"Correct," the Doctor affirmed. He had misgivings about revealing his identity to Zarqawi, but he realized that this man would soon become one of their top commanders and that it would be necessary for him to be included now. That is why he had risked the in-person meeting. He had to be sure of Zarqawi. And he had found through the years that the only way he could be sure of a man was to look him in the eyes. Without taking his eyes off Zarqawi, the Doctor continued softly, "Regrettably, you were laboring under a misconception."

"And what would that be?" Zarqawi spat back. The question was legitimate, but the tone was insubordinate. The Doctor chose to ignore it. After all, he knew the man was a cunning and defiant hothead. That is precisely why he had been chosen.

"I am in fact Ayman Al-Zawahiri." The Doctor stopped to let that sink in. Zarqawi reminded him of a leopard with its lightning speed and turning ability. His eyes darted immediately to Nanda for confirmation. Without saying anything Nanda nodded that this was true. For a moment it looked as if Zarqawi suspected a trap; then he seemed to relax a bit.

Had he never seen this man who said he was Ayman Al-Zawahiri in the company of Usama Bin Laden, Zarqawi would have killed them both right there. He would have concluded Nanda had been compromised somehow and was leading the enemy to the top leaders. But his mind flashed on that last meeting before he was reinserted into the Tora Bora theater and whisked away to Iraq.

Zarqawi remembered how tired and drained Bin Laden looked. While Zarqawi was being briefed by Atef, he had noticed this man who was in front of him now reach over and very expertly adjust Bin Laden's drip. At the time it had not registered; he had been so intent on his promotion. Knowing that the real Zawahiri was Bin Laden's personal physician, this subtle automatic gesture assured him now that the man in front of him was, in fact, the master terrorist sought around the world.

"I must say, I didn't know," he offered respectfully now. "I'm glad to see you are well and that the planning is still in your hands.

The Doctor smiled kindly at him and proceeded. "Thank you. We were on a 'need-to-know' basis then, and you were not in the loop. Now you need to know."

"I understand."

The three then sat on some pillows in the far end of the room and began the briefing. Zarqawi had been told to recruit and train, but to wait for further instructions. He had been told very explicitly not to do anything until Saddam was gone. It appeared he had done just that.

"It is my estimate that the Americans and British will strike imminently."

Zarqawi concurred, judging from the rhetoric he was hearing on the news and in the streets.

"I came here because I want you to have no doubt as to exactly what you are expected to do."

Zarqawi smiled. *This is it,* he thought. *This is my chance.* Wanting to impress the Doctor, he started to lay out an elaborate plan for the use of suitcase bombs Al Qaeda already possessed and ones that he could acquire if the Doctor would just provide him with the funds. He explained that one or more could be detonated in the Baghdad area, eliminating the bulk of the U.S. forces in one attack. It would be blamed on Hussein and his sympathizers, yet strike a terrible blow to the U.S. and its morale.

Emboldened by the Doctor's silence, he embellished his plan to include simultaneous explosions in Tel Aviv and Jerusalem. He cited carriers from his forces in Jordan who would be able to penetrate the border through Jordan. He had heard on the news that the crossing point between Iraq and Jordan had been abandoned. The increasing expectation of Iraqi refugees had lowered security measures in the whole area as countries hastened to try to feed the Iraqi people if large numbers of them became refugees. Zarqawi reasoned that this would offer a simple way to begin to move the bombs through to Israel.

The Doctor seemed fascinated. He nodded his head oddly as he listened to this rash desire to make another bold, devastating attack upon the United States and its allies. This was the same impetuous, self-righteous lobbying that had gotten them in these straits in the first place. When he had had enough, he loudly interrupted. Since the Doctor was normally very refined and soft-spoken, his belligerent delivery stopped Zarqawi cold.

"You will do no such thing; and you will not entertain any such thing!" the Doctor yelled. "Do you understand me?"

Zarqawi did not, but he was too intimidated now to challenge. "Yes, of course, whatever you dictate. I was just relishing the idea of following the events of two years ago with an attack even more dramatic. I apologize if it was ill-conceived."

The Doctor reminded both men that a large attack that kills many in one location and in one instant would no doubt be a part of their tactics in the future, but for now it was out of the question. It didn't take much persuasion for Zarqawi to see that the outcome of a localized lethal attack is devastating for a moment, but it is quickly forgotten or faded. And it strengthens the determination of the opponent.

What the Doctor had in mind was a variation of the Chinese water torture he had experienced in prison. Brave men could brace themselves for a brutal beating, but none could stand up under a relentless, measured, light tapping. The duration of the tapping and the focus of it produced both pain and the terrifying anticipation of the pain. Men cracked, and went mad. Some gave up their information just seeing the water rigging being set up.

Zarqawi was a good student. As he mulled over the plan, he could see it would produce a gradual erosion of the effectiveness of the military opposition, and that it most decidedly would undermine the resolve of the people who sent the military. Instead of strengthening their resolve, it would, in fact, weaken it. A continuous series of small lethal attacks; it was simple really. Moreover, he couldn't help but laugh vigorously at the idea of letting the Americans lead his forces to the stockpiles of conventional weapons that would enable him and his men to fight a guerilla war for years if necessary.

"I want you to be very clear on this. That is why Nanda will stay with you," the Doctor explained. "Once Hussein is gone, follow the Americans. Raid what they find and use the weapons against them and the Iraqis. Your primary objective is to create a body count, not all at once, but sustained—a little at a time. This is very important for you to understand."

"I do, but why do I need Nanda?"

"Nanda will film what you do and see that it is released. I am relying upon you to stage an especially vicious, bloody type of assault. Use kidnappings and car bombings. As before, we will video the suicide bombers and deliver their heroic speech to the press. But I want you two to video the kidnap victims. Use anything you can—their begging, their urinating—anything to lure the attention of the media and the audience."

"What audience?" Zarqawi asked naively.

"We'll create the audience. You just make sure that the beheadings you do are on video. Our own community will not flinch at these tactics, but the Americans and the Europeans will not be able to stand up to it. One-on-one butchery they cannot seem to stomach. And, as Allah is my witness, you are going to turn their stomachs until they almost retch their own guts out. And when they do, we'll show that, too!"

Then he added, "And I want you to keep at it. Never let more than two to three to four days go by without some unexpected death or disappearance. This is important."

"I will. Every 48 to 72 hours. I will."

"The next thing is to vary the target. Choose people as Nanda guides you. He will know which nations we are working on. Victimize their citizens." Turning to Nanda he asked, "Nanda, you do understand that?"

"Yes, absolutely. I presume you want us also to let some people go free?"

"Most definitely. The unpredictability of it will foster fear and suspicion. You have done this before. Just make the news media feel revulsion for your attacks. Force them to stick with each story for days. I'm counting on you."

"Do not worry. I won't fail you," Nanda said sternly.

"You will keep at this until the Americans have left or pulled back."

Zarqawi now had a question. "Do you know how long this will take? It affects how many safe houses we will need and how much money we will need on the street."

"Be prepared for 12 to 24 months, possibly longer."

Zarqawi was somewhat deflated by that. "That long? They'll stand up to it that long?"

The Doctor was very certain of what he said next. "No, not the Americans. Our other strategies will weaken them in a year. But once their forces are degraded in numbers and support from home, you will maintain and increase your attacks upon the Iraqis' attempt to establish law and order by themselves. I hold you personally responsible for preventing that, my dear friend. With the United States disabled and the Iraqis struggling with no internal protection, and with our forces possessing the weapons, Iraq becomes ours."

"How do you mean?" Zarqawi asked. He had truly not guessed the scope of this at all. He had assumed he would train fighters, establish camps, and then settle into Iraq as they had in Afghanistan, as a guest of a regime. This was a different picture. He must have looked confused because the Doctor spoke to him in an almost fatherly fashion.

"Do not worry about this. Your role is not political. Your role is creating the proper climate in the entire country. By the time you are done, the Iraqis themselves will welcome the political solution we offer them. The day of Al Qaeda being the guest of countries is ending. The tables are turning now and you must just play your part." And then, as if to sweeten it even more, he added, "I foresee that what you do in the coming years will make you more respected and admired than Usama himself. You will be the new face of our cause, and Usama and I welcome this."

It was the first time Usama Bin Laden had been mentioned in their discussions. Zarqawi had tacitly understood the meeting was directed by Bin Laden, and had thought nothing about it. Only when Zawahiri had mentioned him in closing did Zarqawi's attention turn to the man who had inspired him. He felt honored to be entrusted with the Great One's assignment. He spoke humbly, "Please tell him I wish him a long and healthy life, and that I will exercise the greatest ingenuity and creativity that I am capable of in the implementation of this plan."

The Doctor could see that they had picked the right man. He had no doubt whatsoever this cell leader would rack up a reputation that would become legendary in the community of terrorism; and his victims would quake at the mere mention of his name by the press.

No one wanted to stay longer in this meeting room than necessary. Their embraces were brief. Nanda and Zarqawi disappeared down the ladder and Ayman Al-Zawahiri exited the shop just as the merchants were closing up for the day. He knew they would be at prayers soon, so he hailed a taxi to his hotel and dressed for his evening meal.

A few blocks away, two men emerged onto the street. The younger man looked lost in thought as he made his way out of that part of the city. He was mulling over the last instruction he had received. It would become the strategy of his career. "Make the small appear greater than the large." That was all the Doctor had said. But he was getting it. He was already formulating a way to use small attacks to produce something greater than 9/11. Taking a deep breath, he guided Nanda to safety and the two commenced their plan.

CHAPTER 34

The day that George Nasser had ordered his usual pizza and opened the door to the expected delivery boy, only to find a stand-in for Andy, he realized he would need a better way to know where Andy was and what he was doing.

Counting out the change and gratefully accepting his tip, Bobby had explained to his customer that Andy had gone away for a few days. He vaguely remembered something about a birthday celebration somewhere and offered it up nonchalantly to Nasser.

"That's nice," Nasser had offered. But before he could think of an inconspicuous way to ask where Andy went for his birthday, Bobby grinned and headed for the door.

"Gotta run, we're having a busy night and the Boss's got another delivery for me right away. Thanks mister." And he was gone.

A few days later George Nasser initiated an email correspondence with Andy. He figured it was the best way to connect up with a student without flagging the attention of any nosy relatives. Happily Andy had answered right away. As it turns out Andy was feeling guilty about not letting Nasser know he was going out of town. The whole thing had come up so fast that he didn't really give much thought to the man alone in the hotel. When Andy had remembered Nasser, he felt he had treated him rather shabbily to not even let him know or say good-bye. He was genuinely relieved to get the email and took the opportunity to promise to take better care of Nasser the next time he visited the District.

Nasser had immediately responded that he was fine with it, but wondered if Andy wouldn't mind chatting a little about chess now and again. "I didn't want to impose on you when you were being gracious enough to tour me around Washington. But I recognized you from one of the magazines." He congratulated Andy on his many successes and explained that he was a fan of chess. "Nothing serious," he lied, "just a hobby."

Andy had not taken any offense at that, nor did he feel imposed upon. When the tournaments were on and he was achieving the notoriety for defeating Big Blue, he had flinched at the celebrity stuff. He sensed that most of the people didn't really know anything about chess; they just wanted their picture with someone they'd seen on TV. The few times he had gotten into conversations with someone, it had turned out to be some lesser player wanting to challenge him. He had jokingly referred to it as the "gunfighter of the West" syndrome. He totally understood how the gunfighters with the reputations were hounded by the "wanna-bes" who were trying to create a reputation for themselves. And he had braced himself for ambushes, just like a gunfighter.

But in the year of his absence from the limelight, he'd lost his edge. He didn't see this one coming. In fact he wasn't even expecting anyone to take an interest. Not even the tournament organizers called anymore. For all intents and purposes he was just another young man working his way through school. *Well, if I can just get to school anyway,* he reflected.

So he actually welcomed the opportunity to talk chess with Nasser. Nasser had been clever. He had approached Andy not from the standpoint of a challenger or hustler, but from a fan of the sport that valued Andy's insights and stories. He had successfully persuaded Andy to be his mentor in the game in order to help him play a little better. That was a role Andy was comfortable in, and Nasser congratulated himself on finding the right entrance point to the boy's confidence. *I really think I can be a field man,* he told himself.

Andy had never mentioned this to Kelly or James. His conversations with George Nasser were just another helpful thing that he could do as a no-brainer. And the man seemed genuinely interested in learning about the strategies of chess.

That was partially true. George Nasser already knew strategy. But what he was hoping to do was expose some of Andy's current activities. When he got the message that he had been waiting for in the chess site expressing interest in the CIA man who was hanging out with a Grandmaster, he was overjoyed that he had taken the initiative and already established a relationship.

His message back to the unknown originator was full of pride in his intelligence efforts. George Nasser had no way of knowing that the message had been read by Makkawi himself in a rare moment of quiet. Makkawi's instincts were that there was something there, and he authorized further probing and surveillance only. Although he did not know it, George Nasser had just been given an order by the Chief of Military Operations of Al Qaeda.

The Dictator looked at the message, which had been hand delivered. The border crossing into Jordan would be unprotected when his top echelon cabinet members would cross. With each of them traveling under French passport, a border guard wouldn't suspect anything even if he were trying to be diligent. The Jordanians were preparing for a mass exodus out of Iraq with the commencement of hostilities and they would especially be looking to help foreign nationals escape to their home countries.

Hussein had called a meeting for the following evening in his palace to give instructions and hand over the passports. At that point, the executive strata of Iraq would scatter in order to confuse the enemy. Uday and Qusay would be in charge of that evacuation and were holding the passports in their possession. It would fall to them to remain in Baghdad to present the appearance of a Central Command. Saddam Hussein had left his military leaders out of the loop on the plan to collapse the government, and allow the Americans and British to enter the country. As far as he was concerned, the less his own generals knew the better. Those loyal to him would find out later what the strategy had been and would re-form later when Saddam staged his return. Those who were not loyal would be identified by their surrender or assistance to the Coalition. That was something he actually welcomed. Frankly he'd been looking for a way to clean house and this whole plan would accomplish that.

It was a beautiful night in Baghdad. It was early spring and there was an unusual balmy breeze blowing off the Tigris. It was a soft night, a seductive night. Saddam Hussein had never been much of a literature buff. His education had been in the ways of war and domination, not in the world of Shakespeare.

While Saddam had studied Marx, Hegel, and *Mein Kampf,* one of his ministers, however, had become a man of letters. He was articulate, and smart, and had concluded now that Saddam Hussein had to be relieved of command. It was the Ides of March—a day of some significance in the life of Julius Caesar—and this minister chose that day to protect the people of a country he truly loved. Through channels long established by him, he sent a message to the President of the United States of the planned meeting for the following night. Then he quietly made preparations that would be unimpeachable which would justify his absence from the Cabinet meeting scheduled for March 21.

He knew very well that the Americans would attack in one week when their ultimatum expired. If his plan worked, they would decapitate the Iraqi leadership tomorrow and this nightmare would be over.

Uday and Qusay were, in fact, with their father. They had responded to an urgent summons from him and were a bit apprehensive of his needing to talk to them tonight. When they arrived, Saddam was in the process of explaining to them the double-cross he was about to pull on Usama Bin Laden. Knowing that assassins would be waiting at the Syrian border he informed them that his Cabinet would take the passports they were holding and exit through Jordan.

He then dropped the bombshell on them that he did not intend to leave the country but that he wanted Bin Laden to think that he had. Saddam Hussein had no intention of letting on to his sons, but he was certain the Americans wouldn't invade. Confident that the French, Germans and Turks would prevail at the UN and in back channels, Saddam Hussein never really expected the President of the United States to actually invade.

Part of the double-cross he had planned was to take the money from Bin Laden for the weapons, and then let the United Nations and some of its criminal constituents disgrace the United States. He did not foresee an invasion, but if one came, he expected to remain in Iraq where he would continue to receive kickbacks for the humanitarian aid projects and the oil deals. That money was already carefully laundered and he knew the flow would continue even in his absence. He was further confident that, even if the sanctions were lifted, he could squeeze money out of the other greedy countries that wanted a piece of Iraqi oil.

This was a no-lose situation for him, he reasoned. If the U.S. did not invade, he had double-crossed Bin Laden and made even more money. If they did, he would ultimately emerge on top using the plan his sons had been working on for their escape. He was smug now.

"That should keep Bin Laden looking over his shoulder, I should think," Saddam joked. "That phantom will wonder every night where this phantom is!" He relished the turning of the tables.

He would not answer when Qusay asked where he would be hiding. Claiming to want to protect his son in the event of Qusay's capture, he said only, "I will be close enough that I can resume command as soon as the Americans are forced out in disgrace."

"Do you know how long this will take?" Uday asked. The way his father looked at him, he guessed his father knew the true intent of his question. Uday was trying to figure out how long his sex and drug parties would be interrupted, and how much of a stash of cocaine he would need to provision. He was going along with this whole thing only because he knew his father would kill him if he refused. And he was cynical enough to know that the only way he would still be allowed the lifestyle he had grown accustomed to would be if Saddam were still in power. So, for purely selfish reasons, he wanted his father to remain safe.

"I would estimate at least a year, possibly more." Letting that register with his two sons, Hussein added, "So prepare yourselves well. Have you selected a destination in France?"

Qusay answered for them. "No, but we expect that by the

time of our meeting tomorrow night that will be…" Qusay never finished his sentence for at that moment the United States commenced a surprise air strike on the palace of Saddam Hussein. It was March 20, 2003 and the next day USA Today would report that bombers and cruise missiles both had been used in the assault on the Baghdad site.

Never fully trusting the reliability of the informant, the United States guessed that the meeting was, in fact, occurring that evening, not the next. Wanting the element of surprise and hoping for a quick decapitation of Saddam's regime, the new Gulf War began suddenly, one week ahead of the expectations of the pundits.

No one in the United States had any advance warning of the attack, not even the CIA. It would be the next day before they, along with the world's press, received initial reports.

The chaos this produced in Saddam's regime was significant. All three were wounded in the attack, but managed to escape for treatment. Not being able to communicate with either Qusay or Uday, none of the ministers received their French passports and were forced to scratch for what little safety they could muster in a few short hours.

For years they had participated in or sat by silently as Saddam and his sons had hunted and ravaged whole sections of their population. Now, in less than five minutes, they were all fugitives and were experiencing the terror of being hunted. Saddam's plans, however, had been completed and he successfully disappeared underground.

Loyal to the lifestyle of domination they had enjoyed for years, Qusay and Uday held the post at Central Command until it was too dangerous to do so. The man the press would come to call "Baghdad Bob" was ordered to remain in Baghdad and continue his propaganda broadcasts until the Americans made it physically impossible to do them. For the first few weeks, he did not notice that much of a change in his own lifestyle.

He had been lying to the Iraqi people throughout his whole career and this exaggerated reporting of the United States' forces being nowhere near the city of Baghdad came easily. He almost believed it himself.

The random and amateurish directions that were emanating

from Command to the generals in the field confused them at first. With no real intelligence at their fingertips to apprise them of the true situation in Baghdad, they were as confused as the Americans at the almost incoherent and sometimes nonexistent orders. Eventually, each concluded that Saddam had either been killed and some subordinate was manning the War Room, or he and his cronies had stealthily escaped, leaving his Army to fend for itself. And one by one, they made their own decisions whether to fight or fold.

The Americans had no one on the ground and had no real idea what had transpired in the wake of the first surprise strike. So they implemented their plan and began their invasion and advance, knowing full well that in a matter of weeks they would reach that Red Line and be vulnerable to the weapons Saddam had armed his military with.

The top echelon of the American Central Command sensed a trap. But they had no real idea what it was or where or when it would be sprung. They only knew that Saddam's central leadership should not have collapsed so fast, and they hoped for the best. They hoped it signaled that the man himself had been taken out, leaving his team in disarray.

Several thousand miles away, their adversary watched the events unfolding on television. "They're naturally optimistic, these people," he said out loud to himself. "That will be their undoing. They have never learned to be cunning." And with that, Ayman Al-Zawahiri was satisfied that the pain he had endured in prison was paying off now. He had learned that ultimately everyone can and will betray you, and to come out on top all you had to do was be the betrayer. He had accomplished that, for there was no one in or outside of Al Qaeda in a position to stop him now. He had outwitted them all.

Even more than watching what the Americans would do, he was delighted to know that the boorish man who once ruled Iraq was gone. Their assassins had not been needed. Sooner or later the U.S. or British forces would find him, if he were not dead already. He despised Saddam Hussein and had reasoned accurately that Hussein was ruining and plundering the natural resources of his land. *Al Qaeda will make much better use of the place.*

He'd had enough. Satisfied, he turned off the news.

CHAPTER 35

Andy was sweating profusely now. The window to his bedroom was open a crack, allowing a stinging air current to circulate in his bedroom. It was pitch black and he knew it was long before dawn. He had no way of knowing the events unfolding half a world away. The reports had not reached the West yet.

On the night the attack had commenced, Andy had no idea why he was in a sweat or why he was awake. He sat up and threw back the covers. Looking at the clock, the large red lights illuminated 2:20 a.m. His chest was pounding now, and he felt as if his heart were trying to push out between his ribs. Not in all the years he had played ball, not in all the years he had prepped for difficult chess tournaments, had he experienced the kind of anxiety he was experiencing at this moment.

He wanted to call James but he didn't know what he'd say to him. Somehow waking him to just say, "I'm scared," wasn't the appropriate behavior of a good partner. Andy knew that something had awakened him. Since it was not someone in the house with him, and since he had no recollection of a dream, he concluded his unconscious mind was signaling something. And whatever it was, it was plenty scary.

"Basics! Stick to the basics!" he could almost hear Coach yelling at him. *All right, I'm scared*, he told himself. *That means there is danger. So, Andy, look for the danger.* He decided that the best way to start was to pick up a book on dangers in chess. He knew there were several.

It was not even dawn yet, and he knew he couldn't wait for the library to open, so he logged on to the Internet and began a search. Finding some source books on chess and strategy, he found material on "danger." One of the books was downloadable and Andy was grateful tonight for these new publishing technologies. Since his breathing had started to normalize, he concluded he was on the right track. *At least I am doing something,* he told himself.

The book was a quick read for someone with Andy's experience. *I know all this already,* he complained to himself. And then it hit him. He *did* know it. There was something Andrew Weir always did instinctively in a chess match—so instinctively he never even observed it. Tonight it came into view with screaming urgency. *Put yourself in the opponent's shoes,* he admonished himself. *See it from his point of view; find a move that is good for him.*

Immediately, he felt an enormous pressure on his forehead as he scrolled to the next page. He wondered for a moment if this is what migraines felt like. It was so out of the ordinary for him. Nonetheless, he forced himself to read on. The book's conclusion revolved around the moment in a game when one sees victory coming. Andy was reminded that, at the moment of the imminent devastation of one's opponent, the player is most vulnerable. Expecting his foe to resign, the careless player often lets down his guard and eases up. Mentally, he's "in the showers." He puts his game on automatic. And that is where the danger lies.

As quickly as the pressure had come, it vanished; and the light in the room seemed brighter to him. Andy read several passages over and over again—scrolling forward and backward, forward and backward. Then, in an instant, he had a blinding realization. He had been reading the book and also playing the chess game downstairs in the basement as if he, Andy, were the opponent to Zawahiri. He knew he was not, but it was so easy to slip into it.

Grabbing his jeans and jumping into them, he stuffed his feet into his sneakers and headed as quietly as he could down the stairs. It was chilly in the room when he entered it. The heat was on; it should be warm, but it wasn't. Thinking it must be some kind of kinetic response to the chilliness of his thoughts, Andy did not notice that a window at the back of the basement was, in fact, ajar.

But for now, he shrugged it off and opened up the safe. Taking out the moves book and code book, he uncovered the chess game as he had left it and sat down. He didn't need his computer just yet. He needed to work the problem with the game in front of him.

Two things were rolling over and over in his mind. The first: find a good move for him as well. Taking out his notepad he wrote down the question, "What would be a good move for Ayman Al-Zawahiri at this moment?" Then he brought up another piece of paper and pondered the idea of the most dangerous moment being just before the victory is achieved. On the second piece of paper he wrote, "What victory is about to be achieved?"

He got it almost immediately and answered the second question first—the war in Iraq. Then he challenged himself to look at where the danger would lie. He concluded the same as the government and the press; it would lie in being attacked by chemical or biological weapons once the U.S. forces started north to Baghdad.

Andy stared at the dark TV screen for a few minutes. Then he picked up the remote and turned it on. The first channel to come up was WNG news. He left it there and just watched for a few moments. They were re-airing a debate between two "experts" on whether or not there were any weapons of mass destruction in Iraq, and whether or not we should have waited for the inspectors to finish their work before rushing into surprise air strikes. *Blah, blah, blah, blah,* Andy thought. He was about to turn it off when one of the talking heads belligerently yelled, "This is going to turn out to be the biggest 'I told you so' in history!"

His finger stopped on the "off" button. Picking up his pencil he wrote another answer to the second question: "the deposing of Hussein and the confiscation of weapons of mass destruction before they can be used." *All right,* he encouraged himself, *if that is the victory at hand and the greatest danger is at this moment, what move would be a good move for Zawahiri?*

He wished he had James with him now, for James' years of experience could probably answer it quickly. But he decided to muddle through as best he could. He posed an answer: "to have the weapons detonated amidst U.S. military personnel." That didn't seem right to him somehow. After all, it was too obvious. To think there wasn't danger in confiscating that type of weaponry would be juvenile. Besides, he couldn't see how Zawahiri would have control over that. So he was back to the question again.

"What would be a good move for Zawahiri?" he repeated to himself as if speaking it would somehow make it easier to find an answer. He got the idea that, perhaps, the answer had something to do with a different game. After all, he had concluded that Zawahiri was playing more than one game. Perhaps the greatest danger lay in a move he would make in another game. Frustrated, he still wasn't getting it until he looked again at what the "talking head" had said: "the biggest 'I told you so' in history." *What if it weren't? What if they weren't even there? Is there danger there?*

"Oh my God!" Andy exhaled. What he was looking at made sense. It was shocking, but it made sense. He answered the danger question: "to have assured somehow that there are no weapons of mass destruction; that it was a ruse." He wrote it down and then sat back and looked at it.

The next question was an obvious question. Why would that be a good move for Zawahiri, to have the United States and Britain occupying Iraq as well as Afghanistan? The answer wasn't as obvious. He could think of many reasons why Al Qaeda wouldn't want that. He could repeat easily what the news was reporting on it. Then he asked himself the question again and discovered something everyone else had missed. The question he had posed was not why it would be a good move for Al Qaeda, but why it would be a good move for Zawahiri? All of the intelligence and government agencies were talking about Al Qaeda. Now he saw it—why James had continued. James understood the opponent was not Al Qaeda. The real opponent was Zawahiri. The CIA was looking at Al Qaeda; James was looking at Zawahiri. He might be the only analyst who was.

At that moment he felt an almost desperate sense of responsibility. He wondered if it could really be possible that he and James were the only two who understood that the true opponent was this man with no face. His ability to figure this out might be the only chance we had.

Fighting the panic and the loneliness of it, he exhaled repeatedly. Reaching into the cooler for an energy drink, he popped it and guzzled down an herbal supplement of vitamin B and Rhodiola 110. Rhodiola was used by athletes to naturally enhance their performance. The effect on Andy that early in the morning was immediate. Andy said under his breath, "Dad, I'm going to be paying you a visit. We need to talk!"

Perhaps James would have spotted it faster than the Kid. Perhaps he would have missed it altogether. Andy slugged ahead. He could tell this was going to be a ground game. Maybe he'd get off a "Hail Mary" pass, but he doubted it. This one was going to be won yard by yard. Rolling up his mental sleeve, he posed an answer: not finding WMD, as the weapons were now affectionately referred to, would be a good move for Zawahiri. Why? He wrote, "Because it would make the United States look foolish?" Without knowing, Andy was closer than he guessed.

Shoving the pad and code book aside, he got out three more chess boards. Assembling the small support legs, he created four chessboards, one on top of the other. That was as far as he and James had gotten. For this to be a true three-dimensional chess game, Andy believed there would need to be eight games. So far, he felt he had identified four: Military, Public Relations, Intelligence and Religion. He knew somehow that there was a pecking order, an order of importance, but he hadn't figured it out yet.

Okay Andy, he teased himself, *if I were Zawahiri, which game is more important? How do they line up?* He stopped cold because they all seemed equally important to him. He realized his next thought flew in the face of conventional wisdom inside the CIA, but he just didn't think that the ultimate goal here was Religion. The others were looking through that looking glass, and to him, the goal of religious supremacy and world domination did not ring true.

To his young mind, it seemed like the excuse that everyone would buy as legitimate. It fit the history. But James had taught him they were not fighting an historian here. He reminded him the Israelis regarded him as the most dangerous man on the planet. James and Andy were both simple people. To them, that meant Zawahiri was "evil," not "ideologically inspired."

Nah, Religion is just a start point. Then he had it. *Each game led to the next. It led to the next game. There was a sequence after all! Only Zawahiri was playing them simultaneously which is why they all seemed equally important.*

Andy reviewed the four games he had identified and wrote each on a small piece of paper. Impatiently he rifled through a drawer looking for scotch tape. Religion. Intelligence. Military. Public Relations. There they were—the games. *Now which one leads to which one?*

Using his own gut instinct, he decided to try relabeling the games. He labeled the bottom game Religion. It had been the jumping off point, the point where people could rally 'round, or oppose. The opposition would obviously lead to conflict. He labeled the second game from the bottom Military.

He wasn't quite sure how the Intelligence part sprang from the Military, but he was quite sure the top game of the four had to be propaganda, which he fortuitously named Public Relations. Had Andy not had time in the limelight with agents wooing him and teams looking to sign him, he would have probably just called it propaganda. Because he thought more in civilian celebrity terms, he used another name. And that choice would prove pivotal in the outcome of the War on Terror.

Standing to stretch, he looked down at the four see-through boards. Then he opened up their code book and moves book and began to place chess pieces, with their labels, on whichever board was appropriate for the game they were playing in. The bulk of the pieces were on the Military game. But he had set up the other boards in anticipation of moves in the future.

Labeling the White Knights, "U.S. Military," he put them in position to strike and capture the Black Rooks, which he had labeled "Baghdad" and "Weapons Stashes," respectively. He still couldn't answer why that would be a good move for Zawahiri. And, if what he had heard on the news was correct, it looked as if the struggle to take over Iraq would be brief. So what did his opponent have to gain?

A fine line separates chance from genius. As bright as he was, tonight it was *chance* that graced Andy. Suddenly Andy experienced a charley horse in his right calf. Occasionally, he experienced them when he wasn't working out regularly enough and when his vitamin B intake dropped. He knew that standing on it and shaking it around would relieve the discomfort, so he stood up and started to stomp in place. Clumsily, he knocked the table hard enough to tilt the top game board off one of its pedestals. Pieces slipped off the other boards and tumbled on to the table. Andy removed the top board completely and set it level on the table. Picking up the pieces he placed them back on the gameboards where he had left them. He then placed the top gameboard gingerly back on its four pedestals, but inadvertently reversed the sides. As he looked down he noticed something astonishing. The change of vantage point had revealed something he had not noticed before.

"Holy shit! Holy shit!" he exclaimed, using one of James' expressions. "It can't be! Jesus, it can't be! Ayman Al-Zawahiri, you son of a bitch, I got you!!" Then, as quickly as he had said it, he knew that time was short. They had to intervene right now. Racing up to the bedroom he grabbed his cell phone and searched for James' pager number. The irony was that in the two years they had been together, nothing urgent enough had come up to require him to know James' number.

Tonight was different, however. Tonight, he needed to wake James. There was still time if they worked fast. A victory was about to be achieved and a terrible danger was about to materialize. He almost wept with fear.

James answered the page as soon as he heard the grinding sound of his pager on his nightstand. Andy's intention to reach him was so strong that the pager was vibrating violently. It was just about to fall onto the floor when James grabbed it.

Seeing the return number, James was on his feet, dialing and half-dressed, before Andy's voice came on the line.

"What's up, Kid? Are you and Kelly all right?"

"James, get over here right away. We've got to reach the White House!" Andy screamed into the phone. James knew not to interrupt. He had received calls like this in the night before. In the spy game, the night held the greatest surprises.

"It's a set-up, James. Get here as fast as you can. We don't have much time."

That was it, three curt sentences. James knew that his hunch was correct. He was there in less than 15 minutes. When he pulled up in front of the house, the streetlights were still on. There was a hint of light in the sky to the east, but it was still so early that not even one resident of this area was on his way to work yet.

Surprisingly, the door was ajar. He entered, quickly went into the basement, and stopped where Andy was standing at a cube that wasn't actually a cube—yet.

Andy seemed at ease now. Time was of the essence, but he knew that this was a major development, and he felt no more remorse for having forestalled his college years. Somehow delivering pizzas didn't seem as demeaning as he had once thought. For tonight he realized that only a chess player would have found this. He looked up at James and smiled.

"Hi, James."

"Hi, Kid. What's up?" James could hardly breathe.

Softly, Andy asked, "James, do you know what a 'skewer' is in chess?"

CHAPTER 36

James could see that Andy had set four separate chess sets out in the room, with chess pieces in various positions on each of the boards. Andy motioned for James to step closer and began his instruction. "A skewer in chess is an especially delicious move, when you pull it off. It's a no-win for your opponent. No matter what he does, he loses a major piece, and it usually catches him by surprise. The benefit of that is it demoralizes him and shakes his confidence."

"Sounds dangerous. How does it work?" James asked. Frankly, his limited exposure to chess years ago had never led him into any advanced moves. He was lucky to remember the pieces, let alone develop a strategy to trap an opponent. What games he *had* won had been due more to just dogged determination and persistence, and some luck.

Andy pointed to three pieces on the board that was sitting in the center of their work table. "Basically, all you do is move on one piece, forcing the opponent to defend by moving away. When he moves that piece away, it exposes a piece behind it. You capture that piece instead." James had that familiar frown of incomprehension, so Andy illustrated it for him.

"Let's say the Black Rook is on b7 and the Black Queen on c6," he patiently explained as he set the pieces on their ranks and files. "You move your White Queen to e3." He set the third piece on the board on its square and asked James, "Looking at that, what do you have to do?"

James could see immediately that the White Queen could make a diagonal move and capture the Black Queen. The Black Queen has to move. So James moved her. When he did, he could see that the Rook was now on that same diagonal and the White Queen could capture the Black Rook. "Neat. Very neat."

"Isn't it?" Andy checked to see if James' frown was gone. It was.

"So, are we being skewered?"

"Yep, I believe so."

"Then, Kid, you had better make damn sure and explain it to me really well," James challenged him.

"I will." Andy now reset that same board with the pieces he and James had been using in their analysis of the Military game they surmised Zawahiri was playing. The board was labeled Military. They had labeled one Black Rook, "Saddam Hussein" and one, "Weapons of Mass Destruction." The Rooks had been configured as "doubled up," a chess term for having the two Rooks of one side in either the same file or the same rank. It made them more powerful.

Andy and James had theorized that it was Saddam Hussein already having WMD that was prompting the preemptive strike and the intended toppling of his regime. Hussein's refusal to present proof of destruction of the weapons the United Nations knew he had had for years had caused them to conclude that he still had them. Thus two Rooks, working in tandem. And that was a real threat.

Now, Andy moved a White Knight into position to take one of the Rooks—the one labeled "WMD." He then asked James to move that Black Rook. As James moved it, the Rook labeled "WMD" was clear and safe for now. James looked puzzled. "I must not have gotten it, Kid. I don't see the skewer."

"I didn't see it at first either, James. I doubt the President sees it. Let me show you."

With that Andy lifted the other three boards onto the table and showed James the labels of each of the games. "I was just trying to work out which game is layered on top of which game, and labeling them, when I accidentally knocked one of the games a bit. It was when I stood up that I saw it."

Andy was stacking the games in the sequence he had them earlier when James interrupted him, "Hey, why would Religion be on the bottom? That would be on top, wouldn't it?"

Andy would not be diverted, "I don't think so James, but it doesn't matter where it is for what I want to show you. For now, let's set them as I set them. We'll argue later about the sequence." Something in Andy's voice signaled James that this was not the time to analyze or nit pick.

"Okay, okay; I'm mum."

Andy set the Military game board on the pedestals directly above the Religion game board, then the Intelligence game on top of that, and lastly, the Public Relations game. Reaching below to the Military game he reset the two Rooks and the White Knight and asked James to, once again, attack the Rook, forcing it to move away. James did so.

Then Andy asked James to stand up where he was and look at the board from the top down. This was something they had not done before. They had been using a two-dimensional board to play and analyze. But since Andy had figured out that Zawahiri was playing a three-dimensional game, they should have been looking at the game from the vantage point of looking down on it as well, not just viewing it from the side.

The instant James stood and looked down at the stack of games, the dynamics changed significantly. A piece that would have been out of harm's way in just the Military game might be exposed in the Intelligence game and so on. A piece on one layer could be threatening a piece on another layer, and it might go unnoticed.

"Holy, holy…" James exclaimed. "That sure complicates things."

"Yeah, I know," Andy responded emotionlessly.

Then James remembered he was to look for a skewer. He redid the move of saving the Black Rook from the Knight's attack. "Okay, so I've rescued the WMD from the Coalition attack upon the supposed stockpiles. The WMD are safe. But I just don't see the skewer, even looking down on it."

"Let me adjust the board as I did accidentally when I bumped it." Andy turned the top board, the Public Relations game, 180 degrees and secured it. The White pieces were now on the opposite side from where they are conventionally positioned. Then Andy smiled a little and suggested that James look again.

As James did so, he turned pale. He said nothing, just shook his head and stared down through the tiered games. Finally Andy asked, "Do you see the skewer?"

James felt his blood drain. If he hadn't had the discipline he did, he probably would have gotten sick. He now understood why his Israeli colleague had seemed so much off his intelligence game. Ben Gurion's face flashed before him and James could see the defeated look the man had in his eyes the day he had warned James about Ayman Al-Zawahiri.

Stepping back for a moment to get his bearings, James approached the table again, as if a second look would cause what he had seen to go away. At this point, James would have been relieved to have it all be a delusion. He closed his eyes for a moment, then opened them and looked again. It was still there. He took a deep breath and let out a long, loud sigh.

"Do you see it?"

"Yes, I do, Kid."

"What are you thinking?" Andy continued.

"Frankly, Kid, I was wishing I'd retired ten years ago. We're 'through the looking glass' on this one." He paused a moment before sucking in a huge amount of air. "And I'm thinking how the hell we get this to the White House in time."

It was sobering and daunting. What James had seen when he moved the Black Rook away to safety or obscurity was the White King "skewered." By reversing the Public Relations gameboard and literally "turning the table," the Military move made by the White Knight skewered its own King.

The White King sitting two layers above the Military game, safe in its Public Relations game, was suddenly under direct fire from its own Knight. The Knight was about to do something in the Military game that would destroy the King in the Public Relations game.

What frightened James the most was not that Zawahiri was brilliant enough to think it up, but this terrible sense of dread he felt that the Doctor somehow had pulled it off, that he had somehow turned the Public Relations against the United States. He felt almost helpless in the face of an adversary that could turn every military victory into a disaster through another means. He had no idea what this would mean in the coming war theater and he was stymied for the moment on how they were going to credibly explain this to Whitney in time to persuade the President of the trap.

This is so surreal I can hardly believe it myself, James thought. *How in God's name am I going to get this past the brick heads at Langley and up the line fast enough?* He knew the air strikes could begin any minute. How could he possibly defuse it now?

Andy for some inexplicable reason did not seem afraid or intimidated. James couldn't help but admire that fortitude. So he asked, "Kid, you don't seem the least bit intimidated here."

Surprisingly, Andy laughed. "I'm not. I'm a World Chess Champion, remember? I've finally figured out what he's doing. I can take him James, I know I can."

And for the moment, James believed him, because he needed to believe him. This young man just calmly worked the problem and worked the problem. James admired that in any human being, but especially in this curly-haired Irishman. He wished now that he'd remembered to wear green on St. Patrick's Day and vowed that he would from now on. He could see there was something to the expression "the fighting Irish."

"There's just one thing, James," Andy introduced.

"What?"

"I'd better figure out what these other four games are on this cube, or we're dead."

"Okay, balls to the walls! You handle that and I'll do my best to get this up the lines. Be ready when I get the appointment."

Hastily, James made notes on the boards and games and positions and raced out to an Office Max to get some transparencies. He knew that the only hope of having the Langley team comprehend this was to provide them the same birds-eye view he had. He could then use an erasable marker to illustrate the moves and the skewer from the viewpoint of Public Relations.

Neither he nor Andy had had time yet to address the obvious: if Zawahiri were capable of reversing the Public Relations, who was helping him? The urgency of the moment forced them to act before they had completed their analysis and that propelled James into a premature meeting. He would regret it.

While James and Andy raced to prevent a trap from being sprung, the secretary of an official in Paris placed a call to Bud Walker on behalf of his boss, accepting WNG's request for an interview. The interview was scheduled for some three weeks from the time the War in Iraq would commence.

Seeing that his turn at bat was coming, the French official inside the Ministry of Interior was looking forward to an opportunity to get out from under the blackmail of Ayman Al-Zawahiri. The thought of disgrace and prison was more than he could contemplate. And he knew he was too weak to kill himself. The thought had crossed his mind, but he knew he was too weak. So he had decided on the next best thing. He would help Ayman Al-Zawahiri, in exchange for a release of his obligation.

He had been told to set the meeting, and wait. Before the interview he would be given instructions as to what to bring up in that interview and what to do. Confident that he could effectively execute whatever plan Zawahiri wanted implemented, he found that his appetite returned. For the first time in months he called and made a reservation at his favorite restaurant on the Left Bank. He knew they would be happy to see him again, and he looked forward to one of Gerard's repasts.

A few blocks away, Samir received a phone call from Switzerland. The Doctor was reviewing Samir's "Fifth Column" list and had observed something unusual. He challenged Samir directly on it.

"I notice your list of 'Witting Fifth-Column' is fairly short, and your list of 'Unwitting' is much longer. Are you sure you have enough reliable resources?"

"Absolutely," Samir answered without hesitation. "I would always prefer to use the 'Unwitting.' They don't even know what's happening to them. The 'Witting' can always turn on you, or turn you in." Then he laughed.

"Why are you laughing, Samir?"

"Well, sir, I find great humor in irony."

"How so?"

"It has been my experience that the unwitting conspirator, if caught, not only denies it, but fights hard to persuade people he isn't involved. If pressed too hard, he counter-attacks. I find that ironic, but effective."

"I see. Well put, friend. Thank you for your information and I'm confident you're doing exceptional work. I just wanted to make sure you weren't undermanned."

"Thank you, Ayman," Samir spoke familiarly, "I appreciate your involvement. Please contact me at any time. I want you to feel comfortable in this undertaking." With that, the call was disconnected.

Whitney was irate about having to schedule an emergency meeting with James and Andy, and showed it. *Jesus, don't they think we've got anything else to do today with our invasion imminent?* The fact was that everyone at Langley was on edge about the impending commencement of hostilities in Iraq. The Director was near exploding at all times these days. No one in the Agency had anticipated the amount of resistance they were getting about these weapons. When the Administration started to encounter defiance from their allies, they began pressing hard on the Agency and its worldwide network to verify their intelligence interpretations.

Everyone knew that analyzing pictures and enemy actions or inactions were just that, analysis. Only actual intel on the ground would prove the enemy's capabilities and intentions, and they had none of that. Eyeball reporting was something they were sorely lacking. But Whitney was certain of the only logical explanation possible for the pictures and the belligerent actions of Hussein.

That didn't alter, however, Whitney's sense of dread. He knew something was not right, but he couldn't credibly put his finger on it. The weight of it was causing him to feel as if he were on a train hurtling downhill without any brakes. He hadn't slept well in weeks, and he looked it. Now, James said it was of the greatest urgency that he and the Kid brief him on something.

"This had better be good!" he shouted at James, not even offering them a seat. Noticing the rolls of transparencies and the bag over James shoulder he snarled, "What's that?"

"A visual aid," Andy responded innocently. Whitney shot James a withering look.

"All right, get to it. We're pretty goddamned busy around here right now."

To Whitney's surprise the knot in his stomach diminished during James' presentation of their theory. If Whitney had been a bit more in tune with his own body he might have drawn the conclusion that the truth has a tendency to wash away anxiety. Instead, he just assumed the antacid he'd taken had done the trick. Nonetheless, his belligerence abated and he asked insightful questions.

Something rang true, and James knew that Whitney recognized that. Whitney might be a bureaucrat, but he was not incompetent. What James didn't know was whether Whitney had the guts to stake his own job on something this explosive. And this is what he explained to Andy as the two left the building.

Andy had been around long enough now to get some sense of the paranoia inside that building. His only question was, "Is there anything else we can do?"

"We can just wait now, Andy." Then James added, "I've seen you pray before a game. I would suggest you pray." Andy looked affectionately at his friend and then looked away into the distance, something characteristic of him. Neither spoke.

Whitney was career CIA. He had been with the Agency his whole career. And he knew how things worked here. Once the Agency had staked out a claim on an issue, whether right or wrong, they dug in with their whole might to make it look right. The ramp up on the invasion of Iraq had been relentless. It was almost as if the Director and his top executives had found a way to redeem themselves after the failures preceding 9/11. They all knew their rapport and cooperativeness with other law enforcement agencies had been strained or non-existent since their inception.

Everyone there, though, did feel a kinship with MI-6 and the Mossad. And since the intel about Saddam Hussein's intentions and capabilities was consistent with intel from these two partners, and consistent with the Russians as well, there was a dangerous sense of euphoria at the headquarters. Egypt and Jordan also confirmed the weapons and urgency.

Whitney had a nagging feeling. It was the fact that there was consistency—too much consistency—that had raised the red flag to him. But he was realistic enough to know that he couldn't stop this now, even if there were an ambush waiting. The United States was in the process of draining the swamp, and the next pool down was Iraq. He further knew that if his superiors would turn a stone-cold eye at this analysis, the White House would never entertain it.

It was something that damned kid had said that bothered him the most. "It's a set-up. There are no WMD. They're looking to discredit us and the British." His years in counterintelligence told him this was probably true, that this kid had figured it out. What could be better than to discredit U.S. and British intelligence? That would render both agencies powerless in future entanglements. Everyone in intelligence sooner or later learns about "crying wolf." So, Whitney knew that there was something to this.

He also knew that he was not going to take this to the Director. The Director was committed on WMD; that was obvious. He would dig in and defend his position. And that would mean attacking Whitney if Whitney challenged the intel. Just two years from his retirement and his full pension, Whitney made a bean counter's decision. The U.S. stood to gain more by eliminating Hussein, than they stood to lose in a little PR flap, he concluded. He, on the other hand, stood to lose greatly, with very little to gain except a possible "I told you so." He counted the beans and made his decision. Rolling the transparencies up, tying them and stashing them in his office closet, he returned to the meeting he had interrupted to meet with James and Andy.

He was just asking his assistant for another antacid when the call came in. Whitney answered the internal line immediately, "Whitney here."

"We just hit Hussein's palace."

It had begun.

CHAPTER 37

Andy had begged off having dinner with James. He was still charged up about making the analysis and was nervous about the outcome. James could see that Andy was not one meant for waiting. As a quarterback and as a chess champion, he was very decisive, and the results of his decisions were immediately apparent. The idea of sitting by a phone waiting for it to ring was anathema to someone like Andy.

So Andy had said he wanted to get home, maybe take time to pick up his mom from her shop, and then get back to work on those next four levels. The game of intelligence was fun for him, but James knew the game of politics, and worse yet, corporate politics, would be too aggravating for the Kid.

"Sounds like a plan, Kid. I'll keep you posted."

Andy was jumping into his Jeep already. "Great. You'll call, right? No matter what time? We should hear soon, don't you think?"

James decided not to interrupt that run-on question, so he just answered, "Yes" to all three and let the Kid go. For someone as good at this as Andy was, he had never seen anyone so jumpy to get away from Langley. For a moment he experienced quite a wave of regret sweep over him. He had hoped this would be a short project, a few months to a year. Once it had become clear to him that their analysis depended upon the day's activities anywhere in the globe, James had accepted the reality that he would probably be at this 'til he retired.

But for now he was looking at the fact that Andy was delaying his life for this and the Kid didn't seem to be showing any awareness that that could be years. Al Qaeda was far more universal than James had known and Zawahiri was truly so far out in front that James had concluded the man would have to make a major mistake in order for them to catch up to him. And if James did any praying, it was for that—that Ayman Al-Zawahiri would make a mistake.

He hadn't had the heart to tell Andy that he didn't believe their analysis would make it up the line. If they had been just a few days earlier in putting it together they might have stood a chance. The President, it seemed to him, liked to evaluate upsides and downsides of impending actions. If he hadn't made his decision already, James believed that the President would have seen their report, laundered to appear as if it had come from the Deputy Director himself.

But the President had launched two days earlier than anyone had expected. James could surmise that he must have had some intelligence that indicated he had a chance to get Saddam Hussein right at the top. Why else would he have jumped the gun? Not only did it catch most of the world off guard, it effectively ruined James' chances of warning him he was about to be ambushed.

And he knew Whitney didn't have the stomach to walk into anyone's office after they had committed the resources and tell them, "By the way, you got it wrong. The whole thing was a sting operation." He reminded himself to let the Kid down easy, and to increase the demand for those next four levels in the three-dimensional model.

He resolved that he was going to demand that Whitney put the Kid on payroll. Surely they had some shadow category they could fit Andy into. Feeling a little better, he went home to catch the news. Truth-be-told he hated waiting, too. *Guess the Kid and I aren't much at bench warming,* he laughed to himself. The difference was the Kid was waiting to see the President of the United States change course because of their report; James was waiting to see for certain if their analysis was correct. They would all know soon enough.

Andy had made such good time on I-66 that he had a few minutes before his mom would be ready to leave work. So he decided to stop at home, do a little work on the Internet, take out the trash, and a few other chores.

The first thing he did was log-on. He'd been hoping for a communication from Brian. The two had kept in touch despite being in different parts of the country. Today he was envious of Brian being out there in Los Angeles at the University of Southern California. The April chill had nipped the cherry blossoms and he told himself that next fall he'd go out and see Brian play. USC was coming back after years of being nothing special and that was, in large part, due to his friend, Brian, and what he had brought to their team.

Both young men had limited means financially and both had acquired scholarships to the schools of their choice. Brian would graduate in his fifth year, having found that the demands of football and his scholastics were more than he could handle. His reduced course load had added an extra year, but he didn't seem to mind. Actually, he seemed to love being out there with what he said were the world's most beautiful co-eds. Andy wondered if he had settled on one yet, and really did look forward to seeing the Pacific Ocean.

There was nothing in incoming mail from Brian, but there was an email from George Nasser, which he opened and read. It was nothing special really, just a report on events at Columbia and an invitation again to come up to New York for the weekend. Andy had been invited repeatedly to enjoy the hospitality of a "native New Yorker," as Nasser put it. But he could never break away and wasn't willing to tell Nasser he didn't have the cash.

But, wanting to keep up the correspondence with his student, he clicked "reply." He was still pumped up with his breakthrough, and had to tell someone. Knowing that he could never discuss exactly what he was working on, he simply said, "I had a great day at work today. I made a real breakthrough on something and I'm pretty jazzed." Then he signed off, telling Nasser he had to run to pick up his mom.

Nasser was stunned and worried by the line Andy had written. Somehow he didn't figure Andy could be talking about a major breakthrough at Dominos. Certainly there was nothing exciting or earth-shattering about delivering pizza. He knew that, whatever it was, Andy had slipped up. For the first time, he had mentioned "work," and Nasser was very worried that Andy somehow was on to something with Al Qaeda.

Convinced that some operation had been compromised and that his colleagues and friends were in danger, he immediately added a chess move to the game and forwarded it to his "opponent." The move placed the Black King in check and George Nasser was certain it would generate a quick response.

Because the U.S. military was keeping their operations secret, Nasser had no way of knowing that Makkawi and the bulk of the remaining Al Qaeda army were shuttling back and forth across the Pakistani border. They were running for their lives most of the time. There was barely an hour or two separating them from detection and intervention by some Special Forces unit.

They had food, but the pressure and anxiety of it were taking their toll. Makkawi himself looked at least 15 years older. He and his men were exhausted, but still hopeful that this relentless pursuit would end or slow up now that the Iraq War was beginning. Makkawi needed a breather in order to go back down into Afghanistan and organize the Taliban and Al Qaeda remnants left stranded there following the surgical strikes of the U.S. military.

These forces would need to be focused and resolved in order to break down the impending elections. Makkawi himself had ordered the assassination of Hamid Karzai. If they could destabilize Afghanistan independence enough to thwart any possibility of free elections there, they still had a chance to maintain their bases in that country. But he needed to bolster the morale of men who had been living under the same squalid conditions he had been for a year and a half now.

Makkawi could see the Doctor's strategy of developing independent cells was working well. Though he was adjusting position and security daily, and sometimes hourly, other cells had successfully carried out attacks in Saudi Arabia and Bali. The hoped-for distraction from their arena had not materialized, but the Doctor had messaged him that he should consider those attacks as a vital part of their overall strategy. He had further assured Makkawi these would escalate in size and boldness, and soon the Infidel would be capitulating before Al Qaeda even showed up to attack them. "They are acting out exactly the actions their ancestors took a thousand years ago when faced with our assassins."

That statement from the Doctor kept Makkawi going. He prayed daily that the situation in Iraq would unfold quickly, so that Zarqawi could be unleashed. And he had absolute confidence in their ability to reroute their forces through Syria. As expected, Iran was getting jittery. The Mullahs had their own problems with the university crowd and were justifiably concerned about the United States' intentions regarding Iran. They were reluctant to exacerbate an already tense situation concerning their nuclear plans by continuing to allow Al Qaeda safe passage through their country. The Bush Doctrine seemed to have spooked them. He hoped Zawahiri could do something about that, as he personally believed Iran would make a good haven. For now, however, it was not proving fruitful.

Syria, on the other hand, had been totally willing to receive weapons being smuggled out of Iraq in exchange for the safe passage of Al Qaeda warriors. Once Zarqawi commenced his battle plan, Makkawi was certain they could supply him with the personnel to complete the last of this brilliant military plan. That is, if he himself could stay alive long enough.

With that on his mind, and in the absence of any technology except their satellite phones, the opponent's move in the chess game sat unexamined.

Before Whitney reconvened his meeting and called everyone back from their bathroom breaks, he had placed one phone call.

There was additional information that his gut told him was necessary now and he gave the official order for one of his specialists to acquire it. *There isn't going to be any mole on my watch,* he told himself.

Andy logged off and finished the tasks he normally did at this time of afternoon. Knowing that he had a few minutes to spare before picking Kelly up, he planned a surprise for her. She had been a really good sport about eating so many pizzas. It was one of the ways the store compensated him, one of the benefits of working for a pizza place. At the end of the day, you might just go home with a pizza.

Knowing that Kelly loved Chinese food, he hopped into the Jeep and headed for the Curry Bowl on his way to her shop. As his car turned the corner, the Orkin truck pulled up. Their neighbor, Mrs. Standish, was not outside to notice it. If she had been, she might have noted that this was the second time the truck had stopped this week. The regular day for the "bug sweep" was Monday. Today was Thursday.

This time the driver not only let himself in, but he went upstairs to Andy's room. He hadn't had much notice on this assignment. The phone call frankly caught him off guard, but the Boss was so insistent that he reprioritized.

He had gone into the basement first, but did not find what he was looking for there. He guessed that Andy would probably keep it in his own room, so he entered the private areas of the Weir household.

Guessing that he didn't have much time, he was relieved to see the computer sitting on the little desk near Andy's bed. The room was neat and immaculate, and that encouraged him. He figured now that the hard drive would probably be comprehensive, and that Andy had probably used only one computer for his various needs.

The man opened a heavy bag he was carrying over his shoulder. As he set it down, he thought he heard a car drive up.

Quickly, he peeked out the window, hoping he would have enough time. The car was still moving down the street, so he went back to his work. He had a special piece of equipment in his bag that enabled him to electronically duplicate the hard drive of Andy's PC. Without Andy knowing it, his whole computer life could be analyzed back at Langley. Whatever his security settings and passwords, they would have ample time there to probe it. And, whatever the Kid was looking at on the computer would be known to them as well. That was the order the Deputy had given him. He wanted to know the "what" and "who" of all of Andy's communications.

The process of the hook-up and transfer actually was quick. But it seemed to be dragging interminably while the driver waited to capture data. Sitting in someone's bedroom in broad daylight was not his idea of a good time. He had no idea how long he had before Andy would return, but he was very nervous about being caught in the family's private quarters.

Breathing a sigh of relief at the "finish" button that was flashing, he started to disconnect and pack up. He didn't know how it happened. Maybe he had been too focused on secreting the stuff in the bag. Maybe he let himself get rattled, but he heard it distinctly now. There were sounds of bags rustling and feet walking around in the kitchen below.

Shit! This is going to be close! he chastised himself. His pulse must have jumped to 180 given the jeopardy he was in, and the Deputy was in, if he were caught. Instinct took over and he made his move.

"I'll get the rest of this, Andy," Kelly said thankfully. She sounded relieved to be free of cooking tonight.

"Sure, Mom. I'm going downstairs for awhile."

"Before dinner?" she sounded disappointed.

"Yeah, if you don't mind. James and I had a real good day and there's something else I want to get a jumpstart on."

"I got it. Okay. I'll call you when I've set the table."

Andy was moving now through the little hall that connected the kitchen to the front foyer and the door to the basement. He had turned to hear Kelly's last remark and hadn't seen the driver stealthily descend from upstairs, open the basement door and move on to the basement stairs just in time to turn around and loudly clump back up the last two steps.

The door opening suddenly startled Andy and he jumped back shouting, "What the hell?" His reflexes were quick as they always had been, but the man emerged from the stairway before Andy even got the sentence out. Seeing who it was, Andy relaxed immediately.

"Geez, Fred, you scared the crap out of me!"

"Sorry, Kid, I didn't mean to."

"That's all right," Andy responded, catching his breath. "What day is it anyway?"

"It's Thursday, Andy. The boss wanted me to sweep twice this week, what with the Iraq thing and all. Everybody's a little edgy, you can imagine." It sounded good, logical. He expected Andy to buy it. And he did.

"Okay, sure, we just didn't see the truck is all."

"You didn't? I parked right out front," the man feigned surprise and concern for his vehicle. Opening the front door, he acted as if he were worried about his rig.

Andy interjected, "No, Fred; it's fine. Mom and I came in the back door. We turned into the alley around the corner. It's fine."

Having reassured the startled technician that his rig was fine, Andy thanked Fred for keeping an eye out for them and walked him to the truck. He even offered to carry Fred's cumbersome satchel. Distracted by the man's apparent concern for his truck, Andy's attention had been successfully diverted from the obvious question—how did the man get in?

It wouldn't have mattered. Even if he had asked, the man Andy knew as Fred was sufficiently in charge of his wits by that time to have offered up a good cover story. They shook hands and Andy went back to the house.

As Fred drove away, his only thought was, *Shit. That was close.*

CHAPTER 38

Zarqawi was under explicit orders to do nothing until Saddam Hussein was gone. The Doctor had been very clear that he wanted him to sit out the early stages of the invasion. Knowing that Zarqawi and his forces would be in the North, the Doctor was eloquent in his reasoning with Zarqawi. He deduced that the United States and Britain would attack from the North across the Turkish border, and from the southern part of Iraq.

They were expecting heavy fighting and that the invaders would kill many of Saddam's loyalists, as well as insurgents and terrorists who might be uniting. So he had ordered Zarqawi to just sit it out, to wait and watch. Although he was not to engage, he was to see who did. Beyond that he was to just train and organize and await his specific order to launch.

"I don't want you to get killed in the first fighting," the Doctor had said to him in their meeting in Syria. Zarqawi understood. This was not their fight; this was Hussein's. Their battle lay ahead and their resources needed to be preserved for the next phase.

A few weeks into the invasion of Iraq, it was clear to Zarqawi that Saddam was gone early on and that there was no significant resistance to the invasion forces. Further, once Turkey refused U.S. requests to use their country as a launching pad, the activity in the North had been mild. He and his men were totally safe, and hadn't even had to go out of their way to avoid a fight. He was ecstatic.

And that was the tone of the message that was delivered to Makkawi and subsequently to Zawahiri. "We missed the action altogether. Allah is great!"

When queried as to his strength and readiness, his report was electrifying to the command center of Al Qaeda. "I am at full strength."

Zawahiri looked forward now to the dual attack they would soon launch. He had confidence in the brilliance of Zarqawi and, more than that, he had confidence in his ambition. Though he was a thousand miles from the man, he knew that Zarqawi was anticipating the devastation he was about to wreak. And he knew that many a young man admired Usama Bin Laden and coveted his place in history.

Ironically, Usama was an expert in American movies. He had particularly enjoyed Westerns. The story of the gunfighter who was chased all over the West by young gunfighters seeking to enhance their reputation was a familiar plot in those movies. The Doctor recognized that that was not a uniquely American phenomenon. Every culture in every historical time had its young men who "would be King." Zarqawi was one of those and the Doctor intended to give the young man some room and let him stretch his wings a little.

Meanwhile, back in Iraq, sequestered in a remote area, Zarqawi was passing the time sharpening the blade of a sword. When no one was looking he practiced very deliberate swipes of the sword, cutting only the air. But in the shadows, if one could have watched his eyes, they would have seen that in his mind, Zarqawi's blade was connecting with something. Soon his practice would turn to reality and that blade and its masked wielder would become infamous.

Finished with his practice, he sat down to draw up a target list.

CHAPTER 39

James had been waiting at the house for more than an hour. Andy wasn't answering his pager or cell phone. Finally, he drove to Kelly's shop to see if she knew where he might be. Missing an appointment was very uncharacteristic of Andy, and James was worried.

It had been a few days since their desperate attempt to intervene and get Andy's theory to the President. Given the first strike against Saddam Hussein and the subsequent nightly bombings of Baghdad, it was clear the war had begun. And it was also clear that either no one up the line had taken the warning seriously; or it had, in fact, reached them too late; or it was never passed on at all. James had been in the war and avoid-war game for 30 years and he knew there was such a thing as momentum. There was always a turning point where rationality gave way to emotion; a point of no turning back.

When things went right the emotion was appropriate to the circumstance and when things went wrong, it was not. It was too early to tell in the Iraq War. These were things James understood well, but he knew Andy wouldn't. Andy's mind was clear and incisive and he had no doubts about the things he observed. Andy was also a fierce competitor and he was experiencing losses for the first time in his young life.

To James it was just another day, one to learn from and get prepared for the next one. He was confident now that he and Andy were on the right path, and the next few weeks would ironically prove it out if no WMD were found. As tragic as that fact would be, it would nonetheless confirm their thesis. James was, in fact, heartened. He felt the United States would win, under either scenario.

But he could tell his young friend had the impatience of his generation. His disappointment over not preventing the invasion was coupled with his impatience with waiting for news coverage on the march to Baghdad.

So, where is he? James asked himself. Entering the shop, he was trying to think of a way of bringing up Andy's absence without alarming Kelly. She looked surprised as she saw him enter. Then her brow furrowed in worry.

"What's wrong?" she asked, without even saying hello.

James had to remind himself that mothers responded differently, and that he had scared her anyway. Kicking himself, he replied, "Nothing. I just don't know where Andy is. I may have forgotten, probably did, but I thought we were working today."

"You were," Kelly answered. "He told me this morning that you and he were getting together." She paused for a moment, but seemed more relaxed somehow. "I think he was upset about something. He had that look he used to get when he fumbled a ball. He's had it for a few days."

"Okay. What did he do to get over the fumbled-ball-look?"

Kelly ignored the hint of impatience in James' voice. "He'd talk to his dad. He was just a little guy the last time I saw that look."

"Oh," was all James could think of. He felt a little sheepish now. After all, he was the one who had come looking, causing a bit of a scene. He had no business being impatient with Kelly. Sighing he added, "Well, when you see him, ask him to give me a call please."

"I will, James." Then Kelly added diplomatically, "I apologize. I know he wouldn't have wanted to waste your time."

"Sure, I understand."

With that James awkwardly excused himself from the salon. The smell was getting to him in there and he wondered how Kelly stood it all day. His mind was on something Kelly had said and he got an idea.

Twenty minutes later he was parked at Arlington Cemetery and headed toward the grave. He was pretty sure he'd remember it if he took his bearings off the Tomb of the Unknown Soldier. Turning left on the path he thought led to the grave, he could see him standing there at the headstone. Kelly was right. He had gone to talk to his dad.

Now that he was there, he didn't want to interfere. *Christ, the Kid doesn't need a babysitter,* he chastised himself. He reminded himself that Andy had a dad; he had a hero. Naturally he would come here if he were down. *Probably does him a lot of good.* No sooner had he thought that, than James experienced a sense of emptiness.

Watching Andy standing at the foot of the cross reminded James how disconnected he was from his own family. From the moment he had left Wisconsin and gone to Langley, he had never had much time for his mom and dad. They said they understood and he believed they did, but it didn't leave much to talk about when he did get a rare chance to come home. So much of what he did was under wraps that he realized now his parents knew no more of what he was feeling and experiencing than Andy's dad did of his own son. Alive or dead, if there is no communication, there is no understanding.

He debated for a while and then decided to approach. "How you doing, Kid?" he asked softly.

"Better," Andy responded simply. "How'd you find me?"

"Just a guess. Something your mother said." James waited.

"Yeah, well, I come here sometimes, when I need someone to talk to."

Oddly enough James felt a twinge of hurt, as if he'd been left out here, but he overrode it quickly. He knew he had no right. After looking at the cross for awhile he ventured, "You ready to get back to work?"

Andy didn't answer, so James pressed, "Kid, I know we're going to have to wait a few weeks, but you and I both know they aren't going to find the weapons. They walked into an ambush. We tried to prevent it, but we were too late. Now what we have to do is just get up and figure out the rest of the game this madman is playing."

Still, Andy said nothing, so James pressed harder. "Andy, I need you to get your head back in the game! You got it right. We were just a little slow, is all. Now let's get back to it, what do you say?"

Stepping forward and patting the top of the cross Andy turned to James and said, "Yeah, I know. I just wished it had turned out differently, that's all."

"What?"

"That tournament with Big Blue. If I hadn't won that, I'd be at MIT right now, doing what Dad wanted me to do."

"You don't think he'd want you to do this?" James asked sincerely.

"That's what I came here to find out."

"And did you?"

Andy's response was quick. "Yup, right as I passed the Tomb. 'The Unknown Soldier'—that's a good metaphor for me. I was just explaining to Dad why I had to do it." With that Andy turned to James and asked, "Do we have any milk at the house?"

James laughed and said, "I have no idea, but why do you ask?"

"Because I have a hankering for some Oreos and they just aren't the same without milk!" Smiling now, Andy patted the cross one more time and ended with, "See you, Dad. Thanks."

Andy was back in the game. And in Geneva, Ayman Al-Zawahiri was preparing a list of names to send to Samir. This list would travel by personal messenger, not by email. No one would think anything about a pouch being picked up in Switzerland for delivery in Paris. Pouches moved around the world in the world of business daily. Technology had not yet replaced the need for original papers and signatures. That fact made it easy for any front organization, as long as it was doing legitimate business, to send almost any kind of document to any other business linked to it in some legitimate way. A pouch from a finance and investment company to their public relations firm would go unnoticed in any sector, War on Terror or not.

Zawahiri knew this and decided, therefore, that Samir would receive this next list in a most obvious way. He knew the document would be most helpful to Samir in picking his targets.

Many countries were involved in fraud related to the United Nations and Iraq, but perhaps none more than France. And the corruption went to the highest levels of the French Government.

Al Qaeda's own intelligence officers had brought the list to Zawahiri when he and Bin Laden were still in Afghanistan. The Doctor had kept it in his blackmail file, knowing that one day he would use some or all of it to further the ambitions of his organization. Samir would be able to make good use of it. The kickbacks paid to Saddam for the humanitarian goods he bought would make a story in itself. That, coupled with the almost universal personal indiscretions of the perpetrators, made each of them a juicy target. He would leave it up to Samir to choose who would have the most influence over the French President.

The crimes were, in fact, so obnoxious that by the fall of 2003, an Iraqi investigator assigned to look into the "Oil for Food" scandal would be assassinated. No one in the world press would pay much attention to her death. To them, she was just another casualty of the ever-increasing violence in Iraq. And that camouflage would suit the Doctor perfectly. For today, however, he was content to just blackmail the men and women he needed.

If they choose to kill people, well, that's their choice. It certainly isn't on my conscience, he thought as he handed the pouch to the courier. What delighted him the most was knowing that the French ministers involved would exert influence on Chiraq and he, in turn, would press Putin and the Chinese. Zawahiri himself need have nothing to do with that. These special interests would take care of advancing his cause in their desperate attempts to advance their own.

Ah, what a gift it is to understand human nature, he laughed. He reminded himself to one day instruct Samir in this area. But that could keep, he reasoned. He would hold that until the time Samir might feel overwhelmed. *Why give up trade secrets, until one has to?* he decided. If that day came, and only if that day came, would Zawahiri condescend to elaborate on how one man without an army could, in fact, take control of the world.

The next day Samir eagerly opened the pouch and read the document. Expert as he was at smear propaganda, it stunned even him. The list of names of people on the take one way or another from Saddam Hussein was staggering. It reached to the very top levels of government and society. And the sheer hypocrisy of these people guaranteed his success now. Smiling, he noted the one name Zawahiri had highlighted in capital letters. He smiled because Samir himself had already identified this man as the best candidate to engage Bud Walker in Phase Two. From there, he knew the American press would duplicate Walker's efforts. He was especially proud of himself for having already begun the process. The interview had been set; the dignitary was eager to conduct the interview.

So Samir sat down at his computer and drafted the talking points he wanted the man to introduce into the interview. Not knowing how good his man was at impromptu, he included sample scenarios of how to insert one of their "buttons" into an otherwise innocuous answer to the journalist's question. He further planned a dry run with the man on the phone before the interview. The wording on the "cancer cell," as he called it, was impeccable and he wanted it delivered verbatim. Then he wanted to hear it verbatim on WNG news. He reviewed the draft and sent the email. He was ready.

Just after sending the courier to Samir, the Doctor sent another to the isolated asylum that housed Bin Laden. The pouch contained enough cash to run the facility for the next year. It had been almost one and a half years since his lieutenants had deposited their charge at the facility.

The Doctor received monthly reports through an intermediary regarding the condition of the patient. Never being one to trust the hospital's Administrator, the Doctor had employed the cook at the facility to keep an eye on the patient and to report to the Doctor. By the spring of 2003 the man, who never spoke, was reported to be doing well physically. The

Administrator had reported that the man's diabetes was under control and that his overall health was about the same as when he had first arrived. This was confirmed by the cook.

Recently, the Administrator had asked for more money. At first the Doctor suspected that the man might have guessed the identity of his patient and was beginning a type of blackmail. That was something he would not tolerate. But subsequent reports by the cook had indicated that the Administrator paid almost no attention to the patient, and that the demands for money were legitimate. The facility needed many things and the Administrator had no shame. He would vigorously seek money from anyone who might be willing to donate to a facility the government made no provision for.

Although the Administrator had continued the somewhat barbaric practices of lobotomy and electric shock, the cook assured the Doctor that nothing out of the ordinary was being done to the patient in question. He was regularly medicated, but as far as the cook could see, the prescription regimen laid out by the Doctor was being diligently followed.

The Doctor had concluded that the Administrator was in fact smart enough not to kill the goose that laid the golden egg. So he had decided to provide not only for his patient, but to give the Administrator additional funds to occupy himself with. By courier, the pouch would be in the man's hands in about one week. The Doctor felt confident he could keep this up until he needed Bin Laden again, if ever. He would decide later what the permanent solution would be.

George Nasser was very agitated now. His message with the important "check" move had gone unacknowledged. He still believed there would be an answer, but he now was convinced that he must be prepared to act, even if he received no direction. After all, he reasoned, wasn't that what "sleeper" operatives did? He had no idea what situations Ayman was dealing with, but he had vowed to himself that he would not let his friend down.

He just knew somehow that this Andrew Weir was involved with the hunt for Bin Laden and he could not let Andrew win. Direction or no, he would act. And inflated with that newfound sense of bravado, George Nasser asked a student of his if he knew how to go about getting a gun.

So as not to arouse suspicions, he had told the young man that his neighborhood was becoming dangerous, there was an influx of drug dealers from Broadway, and he feared for his safety on his train rides home from campus. He wanted to buy a gun and get trained on how to use it.

As it turned out, buying a gun in New York was quite simple. He didn't need to even do anything illegal. After 9/11, registration checks were exhaustive, but there was an implicit understanding of the fact that ordinary citizens might feel they needed a weapon. So it had been fairly easy for him to get a permit to own a weapon. Two weeks after he received his permit, George Nasser locked his Glock 9mm in his bedside stand and made arrangements to visit a shooting range two evenings a week following his last class.

CHAPTER 40

"The Director wants to know what happened here, and he wants to know now!" Whitney yelled at the team. He had called a meeting of all his analysts when it had become apparent that there had been an implosion at the highest levels of government in Iraq. From the first moment of the invasion, the level of confusion and apparent lack of command control had alarmed Whitney.

What had unnerved him the most was that he was getting data from CNN as he ate his breakfast. It almost made him retch to watch tanks rolling now into Baghdad itself with network news reporters in the armored vehicles reporting on what they were not experiencing.

The fact that the Boss had staked everything on his certainty that WMD were a "slam dunk," as he had put it, had Whitney literally terrified. He knew he feared for his job, but more importantly he feared for the Agency. Having misevaluated information prior to 9/11 and having failed to integrate intelligence from supporting agencies, the last thing the Agency could stand right now would be to have been catastrophically wrong with regard to the alleged weapons.

I saw the trucks myself, he continuously reminded himself. But Whitney was old-guard and he could smell when he had been taken. His long years in the Cold War had left him tired, but not inept. And today he felt not only fear, but remorse.

"Jesus, what a lousy fucking business this is," he exclaimed to his colleagues. "Here we are, desperate because our boys aren't taking fire. The Marines are in a cake-walk there and we're here wishing they'd driven into the city under fire wearing gas masks!"

No one on the team had seen Whitney like this in years, and they knew better than to say anything until he calmed down. They knew the stakes. As individuals, they were all relieved to see pictures on the TV of our forces rolling into Baghdad so easily, crossing the Red Line with no chemical attacks. But as CIA analysts who had reported the presence and intended use of chemical and or biological weapons was a slam dunk, they knew they had let their team down and had discredited themselves.

"I still think we'll find them as we go," one lone optimist piped up. He withered a bit when Whitney glowered at him. But he wouldn't quite give up on his perverse hope. "I mean, there is an upside to the implosion at the top, the disappearance. We were just too good, they gave up and turned on Saddam and left him with no option but to run."

The nodding of heads suggested that the others wanted it to be that simple. They wanted the coming weeks to unearth stockpiles of unused weapons. But in their guts each knew it wasn't going to happen. James was the first to speak, hiding his disgust.

"Look guys, that's wishful thinking, and we're not paid for that. Every one of us here knows that when Saddam and his Cabinet appeared to have vanished and there was no coherent communication going out to the commanders in the field, there was a reason. And it wasn't rebellion. They had no means to attack us."

Looking around, he could see they all were in agreement, so he continued. "I expect that in the next three to four weeks that will become clear to everyone—including the press. The good news is Saddam has vanished. The liberation of Iraq is a big enough deal that we may just skate past this. Personally, I sleep better just knowing the son of a bitch is hiding somewhere."

Whitney just listened. James was his most senior operative, even if he was fairly new to the analysis team. His instincts were exceptional. So, for now, he let James talk. It seemed to settle the team down. What James said next, though, was a graceful introduction to what Whitney really had called the meeting for.

"But that's not what the real problem is. So we had better focus on the real problem, and get ahead in this game, or there will be hell to pay."

Taking his cue from that, Whitney jumped in, "Right, James; that's exactly right." It was hard for him to phrase the next sentence. "The big problem for the next year will not be 'where is Saddam Hussein?' The big problem, and I do mean huge problem, is the army that 'disappeared.' I don't buy for one minute that they just had a change of heart and decided to lay down their arms and return to the bosoms of their wives."

There was general laughter at that image. "Some will, but the others are our problem. And we can't let the people upstairs down on this one. We had better get some good analysis up here on when and where they will attack, because they will attack, by God."

"Do you mean as a reconstituted army, sir?" one of the youngest on the team asked.

"No. Many have gone home. But don't let the dropping of their uniforms and weapons fool you, son. Now, the serious ones have faded into the environment. They look no different than the average Iraqi." He stopped a moment to let that sink in. "The next time we encounter them, they will be insurgents operating inside their own towns and neighborhoods. And what scares me, gentlemen, is that we don't have men on the street. It will be months, maybe years, before we have the intel we need to ferret out these scum."

No one said anything for quite sometime. Five minutes must have gone by. At least, it seemed like that to James. Finally Whitney laid the challenge on them. "You will bring me a solution. You're going to figure out how to find and liquidate these insurgents before they find a way to re-enslave the Iraqis. And you will do it, am I clear on that?"

"Yes, sir!" resounded in unison.

"All right, get to work. The Director is going to want to talk to me soon." The group started to fold up their laptops and slide out as quickly as they could. Before James could get out of there, however, Whitney barked, "James, I want to talk to you, if you don't mind."

James did, in fact, mind. He knew very well that Whitney had never even taken the warning up the line. No matter that Bush opened fire early; it still should have gone up the line. The White House at least deserved to know they were walking into an ambush. That way they could have cut their losses a bit. But ass-covering was all too familiar a thing to James. He understood it, but that didn't alter his feelings. So he stopped, but he said nothing. He just turned and looked at Whitney blankly.

For a moment, Whitney said nothing. Then, as he flinched, he asked, "What?"

"You never told the Director about the Kid's warning, did you?"

"No, I did not," Whitney answered defiantly. "But it was too late anyway. The order had already been given."

"That's bullshit and you know it, Whitney. The order was given…but if you'd at least told him, they might have been prepared for what you and I know is going to happen next."

"And what exactly do you think is going to happen next?" he retorted.

"I think there is going to be a firestorm, a real firestorm on this thing. We have enemies, in case you forgot. And they are going to come out of the woodwork." Then he delivered the last blow. "And the Director isn't coming out of this one. He's gone. And maybe you, too. So the next time the Kid brings you a warning, try to do what's right, not what covers your pension!"

He knew the minute he said it that he had gone too far. Surprisingly, all Whitney shouted back was, "Yeah, well, the next time, try to get the Kid to give me something in time!"

James waved it off with disgust and excused himself. He didn't look back, or try to lessen the tension between them. And he never noticed the look on Whitney's face. If he had, he would have seen suspicion. For Whitney, an old counterintelligence guy, was asking himself, *Why did the Kid bring it in too late?*

With that Whitney made a note to find out what they'd found on the Kid's hard drive, and to keep James and Andy out of the loop on whatever the team came up with. *That'll be easy; he doesn't like coming in here anyway. I'll just give him some rope on that one.* Logging on to his computer, he brought up Word and drew up an authorization for a surveillance team to be requisitioned. He didn't send it, however. He merely moved it to a pending folder and told himself, *I'll wait 'til the hard drive report.*

Feeling like he had a grip on things for the moment, Whitney called upstairs and asked to see the Director. He wondered if the

Director had any idea how much trouble he was in. This had been coming on for a long time. For more than a decade they had been behind in the game. And now it was going to surface. He almost welcomed it. A man could only live with so much of his life closeted off. One thing was for sure, Whitney had no intentions of toppling with this deck of cards.

CHAPTER 41

The vacuum created by the disappearance of Saddam Hussein's entire government had caught Al Qaeda by surprise as well. Makkawi was yelling orders into the satellite phone to the squads he had dispatched to Syria. Anticipating that the United States might strike early, the assassins had reported in without incident to the Syrian border. Waiting on both sides, they were prepared to intercept and kill Saddam and his two sons. Syria willingly allowed them to enter and wait as the government of Syria wanted to keep half of the $1 billion Saddam had bilked from the United Nations, which he deposited in Syrian accounts. Makkawi's orders had left it up to the discretion of the squad leader as to what he did with the likes of Saddam's Cabinet.

Personally, he felt no threat whatsoever from any of that Cabinet. Judging by how they cowed before the Dictator, he suspected they would be relieved to be free of the man. And if they had some of the Dictator's money to assuage their loss of position, the Doctor and Makkawi were confident they would yield.

The sons were a different matter, however. The Doctor had been very clear that they had to die along with Saddam. There was no way Al Qaeda was actually going to turn over that kind of money to Saddam permanently, and they were not going to leave Zarqawi to have to contend with Uday and Qusay. He had enough of an assignment as it was. The Iraqi people were not to be allowed to form a government; they were to be made to suffer and tremble and eventually accept the stability that Al Qaeda could offer them. That had been the plan.

The precipitous attack had caught them off-guard, however. They had successfully intercepted the money transfers. Saddam might have thought he had just earned another billion to add to the billions he had bilked from the UN, but Saddam really had no idea how much Al Qaeda and its supporters had infiltrated banking and banking systems globally. One might think he had secret off-shore accounts, but they, in fact, were known to Al Qaeda, if Al Qaeda wanted to know about them. And one might think they were impenetrable, but the reality was Al Qaeda had men on the inside of every aspect of the world's immensely complex money and banking systems. The night President George W. Bush attacked Baghdad, the money had already been retrieved.

Al Qaeda had lost no money whatsoever in its deal with Hussein, and now the organization stood to gain access to weapon stashes that would be almost limitless. Moreover, they were about to get a new home, replete with bunkers. All they had to do was wait out the retreat by the United States. That might take some time. But one thing Makkawi had learned by studying and working with both Zawahiri and Atef had been to be patient.

He was totally confident Zarqawi was the right man to take this fight to the next level. But he was shaken by the disappearance of Hussein. The Doctor had warned him that the Dictator and his sons, whom Zawahiri called the cur and his pups, would likely try to cross the border in Jordan. They were expecting the double-cross, but they were not expecting him to disappear inside Iraq. Or at least, Makkawi was not. It made him uneasy enough that he did not dare unleash Zarqawi without talking to the Doctor. He also didn't want the Doctor to hear about the interruption of their plan on the news. His own pride prevented him from accepting that possibility.

Swallowing his pride, he placed a phone call to the Doctor. Having no idea where the Doctor actually was, he was amazed at how clear and calm the Doctor's voice sounded. *Truly quiet-spoken,* he thought. *If I didn't know better, I'd think he was here inside Afghanistan with me.*

"You have something you wish to speak with me about?"

"The Americans attacked in Iraq earlier than you projected," Makkawi offered emotionlessly.

"I am aware of that."

"The cur and his pups didn't make it out."

"Are you saying they were killed in the attack?"

Makkawi hesitated for a moment. "No, sir, I'm saying they disappeared." He waited. There was no response on the line for what seemed like an eternity.

"That was not the plan."

Makkawi didn't know what to say. His instincts told him to say nothing. So he waited. After a moment, the Doctor continued, "Did they disappear inside Iraq, or did they make it out?"

"Inside Iraq," Makkawi answered immediately. Then he thought he'd better qualify that a bit. "At least, we're very certain they never made it out."

"How certain?"

The Doctor was testing him now; he knew it. "Very certain. We just don't know where they are in Iraq."

"Fine. I wouldn't worry about it. The Americans will find them. We'll make certain they do."

The Doctor had said that with such certainty Makkawi had an eerie feeling that the Doctor somehow was omnipotent. He remembered how mild Zawahiri had seemed to him when they had first met back in Egypt. He certainly was not the firebrand he and Atef were. But tonight, listening to this dry inquisition, he felt a bone-chilling apprehension. And for a fleeting moment, he feared the Doctor was actually in the next chamber.

He must have drifted off in fear too long, for Zawahiri interrupted him. "Friend, are you still there?"

"Yes, sir. Yes, sir."

"Good. I don't see a problem, just a change of personnel. Looks like the Americans will be doing some of our work for us," Zawahiri laughed. Continuing, he asked, "Have you given the orders to our man in the hospital yet?"

Makkawi knew the reference to Zarqawi was the real reason for his call. He was glad to answer. "No, not yet. I wanted to verify the timing with you first, given the change with the cur and the pups."

"There is no problem there. Tell him to go. Tell him we believe in him and we're counting on him. His activities should take some pressure off you."

Makkawi had no idea if the insurgency plans they had drawn up for Zarqawi would truly affect him in his military theater, but he hoped so. They had lost hundreds of their best-trained and most experienced men. No matter where they went, the Americans never seemed more than a few hours away. It was, in fact, the most dangerous and debilitating military campaign he had ever encountered. No one could prepare for the rigors of being on the run nearly 24 hours a day, while still waging war against the opponent.

Experiencing what he was now, he had no idea how Bin Laden had withstood it so long. He admired him for what he had gone through, but he couldn't help but think that Bin Laden had underestimated this enemy. The enemy was proving not only relentless, but also creative. And he knew it was only a matter of time. As he watched good men die, he truly did hope the Doctor's strategy in Iraq would give him some respite.

But Makkawi was not a maudlin man, nor was he given to self-pity. He had a temper. But he also had a no-quit attitude, and that is why Atef had picked him. While there was still life in his body, he would be on the mission.

"It will take some time, my friend," the Doctor said kindly. "I am confident you will outwit our adversary long enough that you'll get a bit of relief once the counter-insurgency takes a grip on the people and the military. Samir is ready. As soon as you unleash Zarqawi, Samir will act. He will be effective. But he cannot launch until Zarqawi launches, so don't delay."

"Understood. Thank you."

"And one last thing. I want to see Nanda's film footage on the news almost immediately."

With that, Makkawi had been given authorization to begin a type of warfare not seen in almost a thousand years. Nanda's film footage, as the Doctor put it, would so shock the viewers in Europe and the United States that they would begin to doubt their own reality. And like their ancestors of a thousand years ago, they would question whether it was worth it.

Four days later, a message reached Abu Zarqawi in a camp in northern Iraq. He was given the go-ahead. Less than 24 hours later, he and his men staged their first assault. It went almost unnoticed by the press. It was actually a mortar attack, and a short one at that. They escaped unharmed and had inflicted only one casualty, an American Marine.

The Marine's commander wrote a heartfelt letter to the young man's parents that evening. He had no idea what had just commenced. For Abu Zarqawi was implementing a strategy of making the small appear large. He had learned from his mentor that the brilliant flashy gigantic strike only served to unite the enemy, and it was also quickly forgotten by the enemy. The mind made it small, over time.

But a small attack repeated over and over again with no relenting became large in the mind. The mind could never escape it. It had no rest from it. And over time, the small became huge. It took discipline; it took patience. And Abu Zarqawi was developing both.

There was a part two to the strategy. This he relished the most. It would be some months before he would implement it, but he was preparing himself. His blade was ready. His arms were strong with practice. And his heart desired the blood that would flow. And his mind savored the fear and terror his actions would arouse.

Knowing that he would have to wait, he contented himself with making his list. He had been scouting locations, and he had been scouting categories that would be vulnerable. The military was an obvious one, though more difficult. The press was another, though riskier. The civilian contractors seemed plentiful—and easy. He had decided to pick the easy ones first. And at the top of his list was a name of the one he would do first. The name was Nicholas Berg.

CHAPTER 42

Samir had been watching the news reports out of Iraq closely for several weeks. He had no real concern about Saddam Hussein, or the whereabouts of U.S. forces. He was tracking, wherever he could, the annoying fly-like attacks of some counterinsurgents. It was necessary that they be noticeable and frequent enough that the button would play and be pressed in the French Minister's interview with WNG. To do the interview too soon would risk the issue having no significance for the interviewer. He had to pick just the right time. Fortunately Samir had years of experience with American journalists in particular. He knew their bias and their blindness. Part of their blindness was to their own bias. And he was going to exploit that now. He knew their ambitions. The word Pulitzer was bait to any serious journalist. He also knew they were impatient. WNG had expected the interview earlier. But Samir had arranged for the Minister to delay it.

He knew Walker would send one of his best. And he knew one of his best would be one of his most ambitious, and probably one of his most arrogant. Samir wanted a true believer, a true "in the public good" journalist. As he waited, he smirked at how nicely the WMD issue was setting itself up. Truthfully, he wasn't going to have to do much to tilt that.

If he handled it right, it would be an easy transition from "there aren't any WMD in Iraq" to "there never were any WMD in Iraq." And with just another little bit of "grease," that would slide from an "intelligence error" to "deliberate misrepresentation." And that would open up an exciting and devastating game. His work, if he did it right, would cause the United States to nearly devour itself. Like a mother eating her young, he could envision a downward spiral into complete confusion. *This truly will be my masterpiece.*

By summer, the European press was reporting a body count high enough that what had been just an annoying fly was now a deadly viper. Singly, and without warning, the viper would strike, and fear was festering in the heat of the summer. It was time.

Alicia Quixote had been selected to do the interview with the Minister of Interior. At age 29, she was a rising star in WNG. Short, pugnacious, and brilliant, Walker was grooming her to be the counterpart to CNN's Christine Amanpour.

Right now she was based in the United States, and only rarely traveled abroad. Walker hoped to change that by letting her cut her teeth on some serious interviews with government heads and top officials. Because of his strong relationship with the government of Jacques Chiraq, he had decided she was ready to interview one of the top people in the Ministry of Interior in the Chiraq government.

Since France had so vociferously opposed the American and British move into Iraq, and since they were withholding support of any kind in a Coalition effort, Walker felt her interview might offer an illuminating insight into not only France's point of view, but Europe's as well. *After all, the White House doesn't need another mouthpiece. The people deserve to know how all of this is viewed by others. They need to see the other side of the story,* he told himself.

Moreover, he expressed that to Alicia when he gave her the assignment. Alicia took the cue. This was her chance to attract attention as well as provide a service. She knew what to do. All journalists did. They thrive on controversy and it is one of the key elements a journalist looks for in a story that has "bite." Surely, given what was happening, she would be able to exploit this controversy and create a great interview.

And this was to be her first big on-camera interview. She didn't look anything like Paula Zahn, but she could see herself in that category quickly. So Alicia had a makeover at one of New

York's top salons, purchased a new wardrobe with the advice of WNG's costume designer, and flew to Paris.

Using the flying time to her advantage, she developed her questions and enjoyed the sherry and luxury that first class on Air France provided. She felt truly lucky to be in this position and proud to be on such an expense account. Bud Walker took care of his people. That was for sure.

Smiling, she relished the moment she could call her parents in El Paso and all her girlfriends there as well, and announce the air time of her first major interview. She vowed to herself that she would do so stellar a job that Walker would not only have to use it, but would use it in a prime slot.

Samir met with the French Minister personally. He wanted to verify that the man was properly briefed and coached. Rather than risk anyone overhearing their talk, the meeting occurred in the offices of ST Associates, Samir's Paris-based firm.

Samir had just drilled the official on the imperative of inserting a button into the interview. Knowing that Alicia Quixote would ask questions about Iraq, Samir instructed the man to answer the question she asked in any way appropriate.

"After all," he assured him, "you represent your government and the answers must reflect that."

The man nodded and seemed relieved. Samir continued, "However, you are to add at the end—did you get that—at the end?"

Again, the man nodded his agreement.

"At the end, you add almost as an aside, 'we hope this doesn't turn into another Vietnam for the United States,' and then drop it."

"And if she asks me to elaborate?" the man challenged.

"Then respond superciliously with something like 'I'm sure you can easily identify the parallels. You know your history better than I do.' It doesn't really matter; just challenge her ego a bit. She'll take the bait. Understood?"

"Yes."

"Good, now on the matter of weapons of mass destruction, you are to say something to the effect that you and your administration feel vindicated. With no WMD found even months after the invasion, it's obvious, or should be to the world, that they didn't exist."

Samir looked up to see that the man was tracking with him. Then he added, "And if you can draw the inference that it was not just an intelligence failure, but rather something more sinister, that would be ideal."

To his surprise, the man was now quite animated. "Yes, I have given that some thought and I plan to insert, again at the end, 'Of course, far be it from me to impugn the motives of the United States.'"

"Perfect." Samir closed his folder and was prepared to show his guest out when the man, still seated, dropped the bombshell. The process somehow had emboldened him. Although he was the one being blackmailed for crimes he had committed and he needed to be released from the threat of the exposure of these crimes by way of his cooperation in the interview, he had analyzed the whole situation and had reached an alarming conclusion.

Right now, the only ones who knew of his crimes were Bin Laden and Zawahiri. But he realized that if the Americans uncovered documentation in Iraq of the Oil for Food scams and pay-offs, he would still be in jeopardy.

Recent French intelligence reports had crossed his desk. Quietly, an investigation was beginning in Iraq conducted by a man named Karim. He headed the Iraqi Finance Ministry's audit board and he was beginning to snoop in the area of possible fraud related to the United Nations' sanctions.

This had shocked him. "*What the hell? They don't even have a government yet; their courts aren't even back up. How the hell are they mounting an investigation? And why?* he asked himself.

He could only conclude that whatever incipient government or leadership was emerging out of the collapse of Hussein's government, it had access to information. He had further concluded that, whoever that was, was blindly accepting the delusion that they could be free and independent. Apparently the man had no idea the world would never let his nation be free. He doubted if Karim even knew the can of worms he was opening.

As he stared at Ehsan Karim's picture, he made his decision. This information could never see the light of day. It had to be quashed before it attracted any serious media or government attention.

Now, with Samir satisfied that he was going to effectively help them, he made his move.

"There is one more thing, Samir."

"Yes?"

"I will do all of this and I will do it well."

Samir jumped in, "Yes, I am confident of this."

Without hesitating, the man continued, "But I want you to take care of this man for me." He pulled out a folder with Karim's picture and handed it to Samir.

Samir looked at the unassuming man in the picture but was genuinely puzzled. "Who is he?"

"He is the one who has been assigned to investigate the United Nations' Oil for Food program."

Samir was stunned. "There is an investigation already?"

"Yes, just beginning. Right now, it is on no one's radar screen. And I need to keep it that way."

"What are you suggesting?" Samir queried, although the quivering in his stomach told him already.

"I'm suggesting that your people take care of him—permanently."

Samir was speechless. *The audacity of the man! We're blackmailing him and he turns around and puts demands on the blackmailer.* All he could think was, *That is not how extortion works.*

Slowly he responded, "And if they don't?"

"Then I will do the interview, minus our insertions."

"I'm not sure you are in a position to make demands on us," Samir said somewhat sinisterly.

"Quite the contrary. Who better?" the man smiled. "This is just an extension of our negotiations."

"How so?" Samir remained unflappable, giving no visible sign of his disposition.

"You promised not to expose me in exchange for my helping you with the Americans. I agreed. Your end of the bargain requires that I not be exposed. To do that, this infant investigation has to cease."

Samir nodded and opened the door to the outer office. "If you will please wait, I would like to handle this right now."

Once the Minister had exited, Samir reached the Doctor immediately. The Doctor overrode his resentment at the brazen negotiation. Obviously this man did not know how long or patient the arm of Al Qaeda was. If he did, he would not risk this. But for now he could see that the man was just afraid. And his fear had made him bold.

"Tell him he has a good point. We appreciate the information on the investigation and he can consider it done."

"Yes, sir, I will tell him."

The message was conveyed and the Minister returned to his office feeling as if a thousand pound weight had lifted. He would honor the bargain and be free of this unseemly incident with Saddam Hussein and his tawdry offers. *With luck, I'll even keep my job until retirement.*

As expected, Alicia Quixote conducted her interview in the posh offices of the Minister. In addition to the magnificent Louis XV furnishings, the interviewee demonstrated remarkable charm and candor in his answers.

Once the film of the interview was returned to New York, Bud Walker was supervising the editing personally in the editor's booth. His girl had done well, no doubt. She had pressed the man on all the issues he felt the American people would want to have answered.

Two almost offhand remarks, however, caught his attention and he instructed the editor to not only leave them in, but feature them.

"Are you sure? They seem like added personal opinions to me."

"Exactly. And that's what's so important about them."

His man was a total professional and Walker knew that, but Walker also felt he knew the street better. Assuming almost a fatherly tutorial position he lectured, "When you're dealing with government types they always have an angle. They always have a pat answer."

"Yeah?"

"A great journalist will get them somehow to slip up and say what they really think." Walker stopped and had the editor replay the clips he was interested in. "See there, Alicia has what it takes. She has the makings of one of the great ones. See? He is so comfortable with her that he opens up."

Slapping his editor on the back, Walker exclaimed with pride, "Now, we have something new here, a fresh angle. Get the viewers thinking!"

The editor didn't see it, but he was not in a position to challenge the Boss. So he edited the piece to include and highlight those two remarks.

Bud Walker then decided to run his protégé's piece in his prime news show. The director of that show was told to write some copy for their anchor that would set the piece up well. And he was further told to write it in such a way that the audience would hang in during the commercial, just to hear this interview.

"Wait 'til you hear what our allies think the United States has gotten itself into," was the script. It caught the young anchor's fancy and he punched it with enthusiasm. The viewing audience was large at that time of night. WNG planted two seeds in the airing of the interview.

In addition to millions of viewers, other news networks picked up the "buttons." The duplication process began like a chain reaction. In the next few months, the imagination and creativity of ambitious, open-minded people would escalate those two small "buttons" into a shrill chorus.

Zawahiri was watching the broadcast from his office. He smiled as he saw how skillfully the bureaucrat had slipped in his extra comment. He knew the press and he knew without even watching that the bait was in the water and that it would be grabbed repeatedly now.

"Make the small large; make the untrue true," he reiterated his mantra. "Repetition. Repetition. Ah, the blessings of a competitive market. Each will top the other."

He was proud of Samir. In addition to congratulations he transferred $100,000 into the account of ST Associates. Labeling it with his accounting software as Public Relations expenses, he brought up his three-dimensional model and illuminated the top four layers of his game.

It took almost a year for Zarqawi to catch up to Karim and to time the assassination so that it would not attract much attention. Early in the following summer, a car bomb exploded, killing the inconspicuous member of the Iraqi Finance Ministry's audit board. The assumption would be that insurgents were targeting government officials in an attempt to prevent a provisional government from forming and that it was a terror tactic to scare off would-be officials in a free Iraq.

His death would barely achieve a mention on the news. Zawahiri would be watching closely to see how it was handled. His death would be incorporated into a story that focused on how violent and dangerous the environment of Iraq was following Saddam's fall, and how tragic it was that a dedicated bureaucrat was suffering the consequences of the new policies. The journalist would have no apparent interest in why the man had been killed. He would seem content to just use this as yet another example of the anarchy within Baghdad.

Uncharacteristically, Zawahiri did not wait the year for proof of the man's death. Just giving the order was enough for him. He knew Zarqawi would accomplish it. So he removed a pawn on Level Two. The elimination of that pawn took some pressure off one of the Rooks on Level Four.

On the day the interview had aired, there was someone else watching WNG that night. Actually he and his staff were watching all major cable networks, trying to figure an angle, a way of getting him in the game as a candidate.

"I just hope this doesn't turn into another Vietnam for the United States." When he heard it, the Candidate shouted to his aides. "Get on WNG's site. I want the transcript of the Alicia Quixote interview today."

This was it and he knew it. It would become his way of getting in the game and mounting a serious assault for his party's nomination. Politicians, good politicians, know when they have a window of opportunity. If their staff is exceptional, they know how to exploit it.

"Gotcha!" That was all the Candidate said, but somehow everyone in the room knew that that one word, said with such gusto, meant they were going to the "Show."

CHAPTER 43

The next months were a frantic build-up of rhetoric and suspense. Accusations were hurled in governments and households. Alliances were fractured or fracturing around the world.

While Coalition forces struggled to secure a nation whose endemic hostilities were unleashed by their sudden freedom, they were surrounded by a firestorm of criticism, and all this while emerging Iraqi leaders jockeyed and struggled to do in one year what would normally require a generation.

Accusations were rampant. Newspapers, news programs, and talk shows were full of experts with opinions who talked about everything from Iraqi zoos to weapons of mass destruction. To the bewilderment of the United States, the inability to find WMD had transferred somehow in the public's eye to the idea that they had never existed at all.

Perhaps the possibility was just too terrible to contemplate, or perhaps the direction of the chatter on the news was more than logic could bear. But the one question that should have been asked was never asked.

"Where did they go?" Andy yelled at their TV in the kitchen. "Ask that question, you fools!"

Kelly turned from the stove where she had been frying pork chops and suddenly switched off the television. Without saying a word, she went back to preparing dinner.

James, too, had been a little taken aback by the vehemence in Andy's tone, but he was reluctant to speak. Kelly's action said it all. Watching her closely, he could see she was upset. He decided to use these few minutes. "Kid, let's take a walk."

Before Andy could say yes or no, James gave Kelly a look that said this was not negotiable. As Andy rose James reassured her, "Don't worry, Kelly, we won't be long." She waved her hand as if to say "whatever" and turned back to the chops.

"Okay, Andy, spit it out," James said as they came off the front porch. "What's on your mind?"

"It's the WMD, James. The news. It's driving me crazy. I tried to warn them!"

"I know."

"Can't they see, James? Now, they're attacking us!" Andy had included himself with the CIA, something he had never done before. "Can't any of those jerks see anything? I can see it. Why can't they?"

Andy's frustration had brought him to the edge of tears. His face was red and the vein in his neck was pulsing. Walking helped, but James felt the need to calm his partner.

"Okay, okay. I know how you feel," James paused. "The news, it drives you crazy, I know. I don't know why they write like that, Kid. Maybe it's just because negative sells."

Andy stopped abruptly. "That's not what bothers me, James."

"What, then?"

"The fact that those idiots can't see is not what bothers me. It's that they don't know they can't see. That's dangerous. It's dangerous in chess, it's dangerous in football and it's dangerous in life."

James just listened. Looking James in the eye, Andy added, "What scares me, James, is that people sound like they are actually starting to believe this crap. I just don't know how that could be. But their anger, their emotion…" his voice trailed off as he looked up at a street light that was coming on at dusk. "You can't win a game, James, when there is this much emotion. I can't win with this much emotion."

"What are you saying?"

"I'm saying, I think Zawahiri has cleaned our clock in the Public Relations game. I lost this one. We've become our own worst enemy now. I sure don't call that a victory," Andy finished sarcastically.

The two men walked silently for the better part of a block. Wanting to encourage his protégé and friend, James remembered something from the days shortly after 9/11. "Do you remember, early on in the war, Rumsfeld telling us all that there would be good days and bad days?"

"Yes."

"Well, he was right. Not finding those weapons is one of the bad days for us, for the United States. Paying the price in the media—that is one of the bad days."

Andy looked skeptical as if to say, "Is there some good news in here?" James put his arm around his friend's shoulder and continued, "But there was a good day too, Andy."

"Yeah? When?"

"You were too late to stop it. But this craziness on TV proves you were right about the Public Relations game. You were right about his using this to discredit us, to isolate us. You were right."

"James, I love you, man, but I just told you I lost this game."

"I know, I know, but that's not what encourages me," James offered kindly.

"What does?"

"The fact that my partner even spotted it—that encourages me. At night, when I get afraid, I remind myself that Zawahiri has met his match. He doesn't even know you figured out he has a PR game. He doesn't even know you exist."

"And that gives you comfort?" Andy laughed, shaking his head. "I get my butt kicked by a world-class bad guy and you're comforted because at least I know there was a game?"

"No; I'm comforted by the fact that you showed up to play knowing what the stakes were, and how hopeless the thing looked." James loved this kid and he hoped he hadn't been too sappy.

"I didn't know you got scared, James," Andy changed the subject.

"Oh yeah. Always have. That's why I'm good at what I do. I always know that we could lose. Keeps me motivated."

"What are you scared of now?"

There was no delay on the answer. "The possibility that Zawahiri might outrun us; that he could bring us down before you figure out those other four layers—that scares me."

That was a sobering admission for both of them. There was a bond between the two stronger even than blood. James had experienced it before when he was in the field, but he hadn't expected to feel it again once he came inside. It was comforting somehow. As bad as things were, it was comforting.

"James, I just want you to know that I appreciate the faith you have in me. I really do."

James smiled.

"I won't let you down; I won't."

"I know. America's having a bad day right now; so is intelligence. But you had a good day. And when you isolate the top part of that cube, Zawahiri will have a really bad day."

It was said with such conviction that any doubt Andy had about this work they were doing maybe being just an "exercise" vanished. James had done it again. He had transferred to Andy his belief that somehow this was the route that would win the thing and Andy would be the one to throw the "Hail Mary" pass.

Andy felt blessed. *Dad, Coach, now James. All three have taught me to get up one more time.*

As if he had read Andy's mind, James joked, "Hey, Kid, do you know the only thing it takes to win?"

Andy smiled. He did, in fact. "Just get up one more time than you get knocked down."

They had returned to the front steps.

"Ready to eat?"

"You bet. Mom's pork chops are awesome."

The two partners knew how imperative it was to identify the top four layers. They knew the stakes. But they also knew that Kelly deserved a quiet meal. As they opened the door, they heard her call out, "Supper's on."

CHAPTER 44

Ari Ben Gurion was in Geneva investigating a lead into a supposed financial empire that was financing Al Qaeda and other terrorist organizations, and laundering money for them. To Ben Gurion it didn't really matter the name an organization called itself. He had disdain for the emerging American view that somehow the only group they should be seeking was one labeled Al Qaeda.

He had been in the anti-terrorism business most of his life. Talk was beginning to mount in Tel Aviv that the U.S. President would be toppled. Judging by the man's words, he doubted if Bush would back off his word and that left only one option. Al Qaeda had to topple him somehow.

No one had noticed that Israel was absent from all discussions about Iraq and the so-called "preemptive strike."

What a blunder that was, he thought. *Don't the Americans know yet they have already been attacked?* He wondered why no one was paying heed to Henry Kissinger. Kissinger had pointed out that, for the first time in modern history, a private party had attacked a nation.

Now that man has it right. It's a new world now; no nation to subdue; no one leader to topple; no army to surrender. Just an amorphous cell-like obscenity housed in sixty countries, he told himself.

He wondered if anyone could stop it now. Israel had had its hands full for decades. Now the United States, its best ally, was besieged by a new generation of terror and extortion. He doubted that the people of the United States had the stomach for it, and if they didn't, Israel, too, was doomed. To win now would mean handling, one way or the other, every country who harbored these vermin. That task was daunting.

He'd been in the game a long time and Israel still existed. He had some hope. He was a praying man and every day he prayed that everyone involved would go the distance.

Today, however, was a magnificent day. He settled in at a table near the water's edge and ordered a small lunch. *No harm in a little respite.* He knew the combined agencies were going to bring down a big fish in Lugano. His mission was to tie a box manufacturing company that was laundering terrorist money to the financier in Lugano. Once that was done he would move to Lugano. The whole mess felt oddly like Zawahiri to him. Layer upon layer; the complexity was discouraging intelligence. And for that reason, he suspected the presence of Zawahiri.

He couldn't help but wish the United States had gotten him in Afghanistan. And he wished his friend, James, had understood how serious he had been in warning him what seemed like a millennium ago.

Well, he must know by now how right I was, he told himself. *Right hand man to Bin Laden. What a joke! No way; he's the Man. He's always been the puppeteer. The United States is learning that the hard way.*

"Would you like to order, sir?" his waiter asked.

Snapping to, Ben Gurion nodded. "Yes, I would like your fattest almond croissant, please, and a bit of raspberry preserves."

Before his waiter could acknowledge the order, the maître d' approached the table next to Ben Gurion and spoke to the gentleman sitting alone at the table.

"Monsieur Monet?" The man looked up.

"*Oui.*"

"Your office called. There is an international phone call coming in for you in 30 minutes. They requested that you return to take the call."

Ben Gurion was too busy adding sugar to his tea to notice that the man at the table looked startled by the maître d's message. By the time Ben Gurion looked up, the Doctor had regained his composure and was gathering his briefcase. In order to get past Ben Gurion's chair in the crowded outdoor seating area, Phillipe Monet paused for a moment and politely asked Ben Gurion to move to the left.

"Sure, no problem."

"*Merci*." For a brief moment the eyes of the two men met as Monet passed narrowly by the table. Ari Ben Gurion had no idea he was looking into the eyes of Ayman Al-Zawahiri.

Thirty minutes later, the Doctor took the call on his encrypted phone. He had paid a fortune for U.S. technology on encryption. But it had been worth every dollar. Al Qaeda's cell phones, satellite phones, emails and faxes were encrypted totally. Even if someone could listen they couldn't trace. Over the last year, the Doctor had come to feel quite secure with communications from Geneva. He felt that way today as he received a call from Makkawi.

Zawahiri assumed Makkawi and his inner circle had moved into southern Waziristan, a region in northwest Pakistan where they were protected not only by mountains, but also by indigenous people who operated completely separately from Pakistan. These Pashtun tribesmen were fiercely loyal to the Taliban and to Bin Laden. This was the territory not even the Pakistani army dared venture into.

Makkawi was to get his men there and refit. There they could retrain, plan and redeploy. More than 20 square miles of concentric circles of defenses would protect them and provide early warning. That had been the plan and Zawahiri expected the call was coming from somewhere inside Pakistan. He hoped the call was to tell him of the assassination of President Pervez Musharraf.

Instead it turned out to be a disconcerting call. He knew it was possible, but he had hoped it wouldn't be so extreme. The voice on the other end of the call sounded fatigued. *Not defeated,* Zawahiri noted, *just tired.*

"I regret, sir, that we will need to meet." That was what Zawahiri heard first.

"Has something come up?"

"Yes, sir. I wouldn't ask if it weren't urgent."

Zawahiri needed to know the worst of it. There was no change in his voice. He matter-of-factly asked, "I've been seeing on TV that large numbers have been killed or captured. Is that true?"

The man, though fatigued, answered immediately, "Yes."

"Do you have an estimate?" There was a long pause with only the shrill sound of interference on the phone. Then came the answer.

"I do. I will meet you at the location you designated." Zawahiri knew exactly where he meant.

"Are you there now?"

"Yes, I was able to get passage."

"Fine," Zawahiri acknowledged. But he was angry and Makkawi heard it in his voice. "Twenty-four hours."

Makkawi didn't care at this point. More than 50% of his men were dead or captured, and the count was rising. His money sources were drying up and he needed to meet with the Doctor to open up new lines. He frankly didn't care if Zawahiri was angry. He needed money to complete the plan. Makkawi always favored military options and he resented somewhat that so much money was deployed into areas like public relations, bribery, and other so-called "investments." Atef was the one who had brought him into this, not the Doctor. He wanted to make sure the Doctor understood that military actions require money and personnel. He was short on both.

Twenty-four hours later Phillipe Monet checked into a hotel in Istanbul. Less than one hour later, room service delivered his evening meal. No one at the hotel noticed that the waiter stayed in Monet's suite for more than an hour. When he did leave, he looked like a man who had enjoyed a good meal himself.

"Come in," the Doctor said invitingly.

"Sir," Makkawi pushed the room service cart into the room as the Doctor closed the door. Not knowing what to do next, he just stood by the cart like a waiter standing by for instructions on where to set up the dinner.

Zawahiri looked at Makkawi for a moment and concluded he was fine. The fatigue he had heard in his voice was just that. But he could see in Makkawi's eyes that his head was still in the game. That was encouraging. Once again he was reminded how astute Atef had been in his promotions: first Makkawi, then Zarqawi. *Let's hope Makkawi has that same talent,* he thought.

"Please, eat, my friend." He motioned for Makkawi to sit. Makkawi did so without reluctance. He was weary to begin with and the journey had made him more so. He relished the eggplant salad and devoured the lamb. Sitting back he began his report.

"More than 50% are dead or captured."

"So, the news media is reporting accurately?"

"Yes. I have made numerous promotions. So far we are replacing the men, but…" his voice trailed off.

"Yes?"

"I promised you Musharraf. We have tried twice, both unsuccessful."

"Yes, I am aware. The pompous ass told the whole world about it. What were the consequences to you?"

"Unsanitized?" he asked. The Doctor nodded and Makkawi continued. "It could be devastating." Makkawi didn't hold back. He knew the Doctor needed the whole picture. "He is planning an offensive inside southern Waziristan. He is stationing a force now near Wana, and that is something they have not done before."

"That's not good. Will our hosts fight do you think?"

"Yes, sir, I do. But I also believe he will use his Special Forces, his best men, not the lackeys we've seen before. His intelligence is improving despite our efforts to kill anyone informing to either the Pakistanis or the Americans."

"What do you need?"

"Money," Makkawi said flatly. "With enough, we can buy the loyalty we need. We can also buy the armaments needed. But our sources are dry. They are closing down our money laundering operations everywhere. Every week they have found a new one. And the charities are being hit the worst."

"Yes. I know. They clearly took the gloves off."

"I want to remind you, Ayman, that our security will not be won by public relations in this region of Pakistan. It will require a military solution," he commented brazenly. The Doctor seemed to take the implicit criticism well enough, so he continued. "I have one more negative report. Then I'd like to turn to my plans and what we can accomplish if you can open up a new source of money."

"Proceed." The Doctor could feel the resentment Makkawi had about his allocation of funds and prioritization of resources, but that was not uncommon in a military commander. Their job was war, and they always fought for every bit of money they could get, and every bit of armament and manpower. Subtleties were not their strong suit. Atef had been able to combine both, but he was gone. Makkawi was competent militarily, but he clearly lacked the executive viewpoint necessary to run the whole operation. His criticism was to be expected, given his losses. *Nonetheless,* the Doctor reminded himself, *I won't let him pursue this attitude long.*

Makkawi continued, "I sent a twelve-man team out yesterday to make the third attempt. They were harboring in a safe house in Peshawar. Only one came back."

Zawahiri was interested in this. The *one* intrigued him. "The other 11?"

"Killed or captured. If captured, I'll have to scrap several missions they were developing."

"What does your survivor tell you?"

"He said they never saw it coming. They were resting for two hours. They heard only some gravel rolling down the roof, and a small rock falling in front of the door at the same instant it was kicked open. The American spoke…"

The Doctor interrupted him here. "Did you say, 'the American'?"

"Yes. That's what he says. The American spoke, shouted actually, and then opened fire. They never even got their guns unholstered." Makkawi stopped. He knew what Zawahiri was thinking.

"And your survivor, how did he get out?"

"They let him go, after stuffing a card in his shirt written in Arabic. The card read, 'From the President of the United States.'"

Suddenly Zawahiri laughed. "I see they're true to character." Makkawi looked confused so Zawahiri elaborated. "Santa Ana did that at the Alamo. He left survivors so they would tell the rest of the people of Texas about the massacre. He thought it would frighten them so much they'd abandon their goal of independence."

"Did it work?" Makkawi asked innocently.

"Did you ever hear of the state of Texas?"

Makkawi shook his head. He really had no knowledge of United States history or geography.

"Well, they got their independence from Mexico and became a state later. The current President is from Texas. You should keep that in mind, Makkawi."

Makkawi mulled it over a bit; then offered, "Well, it didn't work on us either."

"Funny though, isn't it?"

"What?" Makkawi asked.

"The Americans thinking they can terrify a terrorist!" With that the two men laughed heartily. It felt good to laugh. Makkawi hadn't found humor in much of anything for more than a year now, and just the simple act of laughing was restorative.

When their laughter abated, the Doctor asked sincerely, "What do you need?"

"About $15 million. Pakistan may become untenable. If it does, I will need money to move our base, but $15 million, I believe, will allow me to complete my plans."

With that Makkawi laid out his plan to isolate the United States. He complimented the Doctor on the brilliance of the Iraq plan and on its effectiveness in discrediting the United States and Britain, while ridding the area of Saddam.

"I presume you retrieved the money used to lure Saddam?" Makkawi was counting on that being the case in the hopes of diverting some of it to his operation.

"Not only that, but Saddam sent more than $1 billion of money he scammed in some sanctions scheme into bank accounts in Syria. He expected to escape through Jordan and retrieve the money through corporations."

"What happened?"

The Doctor seemed pleased to confirm this for Makkawi. He knew the man was isolated from current news. "Well, Saddam disappeared after the first strike back in April. Frankly we don't know where he is, but he never made it out. So we struck a deal with the Syrians to split the money."

"Phew. So much for his plan to return to power," Makkawi gloated. Then he added, "What do you think he planned to buy with that money?"

The Doctor debated whether to say anything, and then he responded, "The same things we are going to buy with the money!" Redirecting the conversation he then asked, "You'll have the money in a few days. Is it going into Iraq?"

"Some. But frankly, Zarqawi is all right now. He's promoted five new men into his inner circle. He's well-armed. Former Saddam loyalists and Bathists are protecting him. He's all right."

"Good."

"We'll use the money in Bali, the Philippines, Korea, Italy, Spain, and Chechnya. We have plans developed for all of them."

"I'm particularly interested in Spain," The Doctor interjected. "Can you do something major there? I have a political goal in mind and I feel your activities could help them see their way more clearly."

"Yes. All of these will be big. Our intention is to fracture resolve and to cause these countries to step back. If you like, I'll increase the size of the attack in Spain. I planned one bomb; we can do three."

"Do three. Let them live with it. I'm looking for one precedent. So do your best. Spain asked to be part of this. So let's give them what they've been asking for."

"It's done. Meanwhile, Abu is ready to take it to the next level."

Makkawi rarely referred to Zarqawi, and never by his first name. The Doctor noted that, but decided to say nothing. Instead, he appeared quite interested. "Who's first?"

"He's got quite a list. The strategy is that I'll isolate them globally and he will break them locally. I know these people. They will not be able to stand up to this."

The Doctor repeated, "Who's first?"

"Oh, sorry. Some guy named Berg, Nicholas Berg."

"American?"

"Yes, definitely. He's first."

The Doctor thanked Makkawi and embraced him. The momentum was on their side now and he could feel it growing. He actually looked forward to 2004. By the time the year was done, the United States would feel like they'd been in the center of a ring with 20 kickboxers attacking from all directions.

He was satisfied and ready to excuse him when Makkawi added, "One last thing. I don't think it's important, but I wanted you to evaluate that, not me."

"What is it?"

Pulling a piece of paper from his breast pocket, Makkawi handed the Doctor the message from the chess game. "Your person in New York sent that through several months ago, just before the United States launched Iraq. I didn't get it until yesterday."

"The chess move he's entered?" The Doctor pretended not to know.

"He's indicated the Black King is in check. Do you want me to respond?"

The Doctor hesitated for a moment, wondering who could be after him; then he let it go. He concluded quickly that there was no way Nasser could actually know anything, at least not anything that would put any of them in jeopardy. So he dismissed it.

"No. Not now. I'll do it myself if I feel the need later." The Doctor explained to Makkawi that Nasser was a bit of a dilettante, but the Doctor hadn't wanted to offend him. He had thrown him some scraps in order to let the man feel involved in the movement. Monitoring chess games for CIA involvement seemed like something he could do well enough, and it was something the Doctor felt certain would have no long-term ramifications on their activities. In short, the Doctor felt Nasser could do no harm there, and yet, could stroke himself for being involved with Al Qaeda.

"Very well." Makkawi was secretly a bit indignant about the luxury the Doctor felt he had with personnel. Makkawi himself had no such leeway. A man was either in this thing or not. There was no room for dilettantes in northwest Pakistan.

The two embraced one last time and Makkawi left with the dinner cart. The Doctor headed to the steam room to relax and enjoy the luxury of a Turkish bath.

CHAPTER 45

He could hear them coming for him. Almost diabolically they slammed the outer door signaling their approach on the corridor. He could tell by the boot steps there were four of them.

That meant they were prepared to go at him for six hours, maybe eight. His whole body started to rack with fear. Trembling, he stood naked and afraid.

There it was, the cursed voice of Egypt's primary interrogator. "Ayman? Are you awake? We're coming for you. We have a few questions."

He jolted to consciousness, not knowing for a moment where he was. His pulse was racing and he was having trouble getting his breath. As he struggled to get to his feet, he felt the cold, clammy sheets. He had sweated so much their wetness was causing him to have chills now.

Then he felt a burning pain in his esophagus. Hearing the familiar carillon he pulled himself from the clutches of the nightmare of his torture in Egypt and reminded himself he was safe in his home in Geneva. He took a hot shower and shook off the dream.

Eerily though, he couldn't shake off the feeling that someone was coming for him.

Forget it, the Doctor told himself. He took a tranquilizer to take the edge off. *It's just a dream.*

CHAPTER 46

Nasser was glued to the television screen. He was clicking his remote to see if all news channels were covering the story. They were, although some placed greater significance to it than others.

When Fox News advertised that one of their most popular talk shows would do a fair and balanced piece on the man, Nasser felt a terrible surge of jealousy.

He remembered in the fall of 2002 when the man had been arrested in Tampa. There had been news coverage, but frankly, no one knew how significant an issue it was for a well-respected university professor to be suspected of aiding Al Qaeda from inside the United States, and from his campus.

It seemed so implausible to most Americans that they wondered if this was just Homeland Security run amuck. Later, as pictures surfaced of the man standing near the President at a political gathering, bureau chiefs took the arrest a little more seriously. The most astute found it chilling that an alleged Al Qaeda operative had gotten within eight feet of the President of the United States. Whatever personal suspicions they had about the man were quickly suppressed however as they reported the other story. The news focused on the fact he was an alleged conspirator, and then cartwheeled off into privacy and Constitutional issues. And there they had stayed, in the abstract, until today.

What had upset Nasser was not that the man had been caught. Like most professors, Nasser guarded his status zealously. It was not the man's status within the academic community that grabbed at Nasser. It was his status within Al Qaeda.

After all, I know Ayman Al-Zawahiri personally, he told himself repeatedly. *Why did they give this man such an important position and assignment?*

That question had been plaguing him for months. Nasser didn't even notice that his eating and bathing habits had changed. Compulsively, he spent his evenings on the Internet. Every day he expected an answer from his last chess move. And every day, when none came, he became more worried.

Finally, however, he became angry. "I bet they didn't let your messages go unanswered!" he yelled at the man's image on Fox. "I bet they believed in you. You're not better than me. Why did you get a good assignment and I drew playing babysitter to international chess tournaments? Didn't they think I was qualified?"

Nasser knew he was smarter than this professor. He knew he could handle more responsibility than the other man could. The fact the other had gotten caught seemed proof enough to him.

"Who was it that was invited to Langley?" he said out loud to himself and the TV screen simultaneously. "Who was it who figured out the Weir connection, huh? Who was it that's now on the inside with Weir? Huh? Huh?"

With that he clicked the TV off and threw the remote onto the sofa. He decided then that he would show them. For whatever reason, his friend Ayman had offered him a lower level post. He would prove to Ayman that he was worthy of a much higher position inside Al Qaeda. He would show them he was intuitive and creative and brave, all attributes he ascribed to the top echelon of Al Qaeda.

To him this Tampa professor looked like a wimp. He didn't strike Nasser as the kind of man who would be willing to die for the cause, let alone protect Ayman and Usama Bin Laden. *George Nasser will, though. I'm no wimp.* Nasser stood up tall and threw his shoulders back. His disheveled appearance was overridden by the momentary presence of a proud warrior standing in the line of fire for his leader.

The Fox News story of the Tampa professor was not the only story Nasser had been tracking. On his worst days he assumed the "no answer" was a slap at him, a way of telling him he and his assignment weren't important. His mind did play tricks with him now and again. But on his best days, he assigned a more sinister and frightening reason to the lack of communication. George Nasser believed Ayman Al-Zawahiri was in trouble.

Whenever the Administration reported the number of Al Qaeda killed or captured, George Nasser was affected by it. He knew the reports were propaganda but, fictitious or true, he wanted to believe it was all fiction designed to discourage warriors like himself all over the world.

But the longer his chess game move went unacknowledged, the more credence was given to the idea that his brothers were in trouble. His self-importance had grown to the point that he believed himself now to be on an even keel with the Doctor, and entrusted with a vital mission.

He feared his friend was in trouble. He feared also that it was what Andrew Weir and James Mikolas were doing in that house that was causing so many of Al Qaeda to be killed and captured.

And that conclusion led George Nasser to the step-off point. Someone had to stop what was going on in that house. Al Qaeda cells were autonomous. He knew that by reading articles in the New Yorker.

Well, I'm a cell, and they will expect me to do what is necessary to insure victory. With that George Nasser sat down to send a hastily written email to his department head. Claiming a sudden family illness, he said he would need an emergency sabbatical. Then, very graciously, he recommended his best graduate student, at Columbia on a full fellowship, to take his place for a year or two. He knew he would receive the leave.

Once the email was sent, Nasser started to feel much calmer. He was breathing calmly now and he began to flesh out his plan. He was going to do something about Andrew Weir. Not being trained in this type of thing, no immediate ideas came to mind, save one. That was to purchase a used car. He would start with that and decide later what would come next.

Nasser was quite sure a plan would come to him, so he prepared himself by getting his own car. He caught a cab in front of his apartment and asked to be dropped at the Port Authority. From there, he made his way anonymously into the crowd and boarded a bus for Hackensack, New Jersey. He had picked

Hackensack from a car dealer's bus stop advertisement he had seen. That looked like as good a place as any to buy a vehicle.

It was a beautiful Saturday as the bus came out of the tunnel. Nasser made a point not to look back at lower Manhattan where the World Trade Center Towers had stood. Across the aisle from him was a woman with two children. She was pointing out where the towers had once stood and describing how beautiful it had all been. She was looking back. He looked forward instead, and steeled himself for what he knew he had to do.

CHAPTER 47

The measure of success for a terrorist is not how many homes they have, or how many windows their office has on a top floor, or what exclusive restaurants hold special tables for them. The measure of success of a terrorist is the amount of bounty on their head.

During the Afghanistan campaign, the United States had placed a $25 million reward each for the capture of Usama Bin Laden and Zawahiri. They had placed lesser amounts on the other Most Wanted Terrorists they were pursuing.

Once in Iraq they followed suit with Saddam Hussein and his two sons, and placed similar bounties on his top echelon Cabinet members.

Now, one more name was elevated to superstar status. Abu Zarqawi. His campaign of insurgency, suicide bombings, and hijackings had racked up a large-enough body-count to qualify him as a star. The United States wanted him and they wanted him badly.

It was one of his lieutenants that gave him the news that he now had a $25 million reward on his head. The news was a cause for celebration and every member of the team shouted, "Allah be praised." They were puffed up with pride, for their leader was now on par with Usama Bin Laden and Ayman Al-Zawahiri.

Shortly, some astute news agency caught the implication in the reward. It wasn't long before Europe, the United States, and the United Kingdom had television news touting the idea that Usama Bin Laden had disappeared and that Al Qaeda now had two leaders—Ayman Al-Zawahiri and Abu Al-Zarqawi.

That fact caused a bit of consternation in Makkawi. It lasted only a minute, however. He was smart enough to recognize that the man with the greatest bounty is the most hunted. For a while at least, he would enjoy a respite.

Many attacks were now completely planned. The money and men had been deployed. And he was especially relieved to know that the Doctor was funneling some of the Saddam windfall to Zarqawi. He was confident the man would know what to do with it.

Zarqawi did know what to do with it. He was using the money to recruit fighters from neighboring countries to inflate his numbers and to attack the power structure in Iraq. He expected to have major battles before the end of 2004 and he was amassing an army of terrorists large enough to quash whatever incipient army the Iraqis might try to train.

He had done this, however, without the permission of Zawahiri and Makkawi. And that would prove to be a catastrophic mistake. Perhaps it was his pride; perhaps he was drunk on the rush of his recent successes; perhaps it was the fact that the U.S. press had stopped covering Rumsfeld daily. But for the moment, Abu Al-Zarqawi forgot that Donald Rumsfeld had told the American people that the strategy was to drain the swamp.

Neither the press, nor the people, nor Zarqawi had bothered to illustrate for themselves how that might be accomplished, nor what it might actually look like as it was shaping up. Assuming the United States military to be dull and hamstrung with regulations, Zarqawi was cocky. It never occurred to him that someone might try to use his cockiness against him.

So for months he continued recruiting. And men left the relative safety of their own country's mountains, their own neighborhoods, their cave compounds and came out into the open in the valleys of the birthplace of civilization.

Meanwhile, back in Washington and at Langley, a team of "counter-hackers" was educating the United States on the term "sucker hole."

Zarqawi had never been much of a computer man. His specialty was killing. Sated with money and manpower, and drunk with the success of his attacks and suicide bombings, he prepared to escalate his own brand of terror.

"Samir has done a masterful job with what we gave him," he told his inner circle. "No one in the world can turn on their television without seeing bodies and U.S. soldiers and destruction. What we do now, I believe, will result in the expulsion of the Americans from the area. Samir has moved the Americans themselves to the point of being a powder keg. It has a long fuse. And we are about to ignite it. Once that fuse is consumed, you will see the people of the United States blow themselves up and we will then complete our mission unimpaired."

Zarqawi did not have the charisma of Bin Laden, but his passion was unmistakable. And it transferred successfully to his inner circle. He did have Bin Laden's ruthlessness, however, and that, in kind, was duplicated.

The next day they picked up their first kidnap victim with a goal of turning him into a reverse celebrity. His name was Nicholas Berg.

The beheading of Nicholas Berg after all efforts to save him failed was a blow to the gut of all the people in the region. The United States, Britain and Europe, however, had the worst reaction.

It was not his death that triggered the fear and revulsion; it was the filming and the televising of it. Samir handled the "peoples' right to know" issue magnificently. Networks that would never in the past even have thought of airing something so gruesome were intimidated by the Internet release that was viewed by millions. Fearing an erosion of audience and feeling an obligation to their shareholders, they too gave the incident coverage. Using the defense of freedom of speech and freedom of the press, Samir took the U.S. Constitution and turned it into a weapon against the United States. The fine document on which America's freedom was anchored cut so thin and so delicately, however, that no one spotted for some time that they were even bleeding.

One person who did not take it well, however, was Nanda. Up until the moment of the actual decapitation, this was nothing more than another staged propaganda piece. Nanda, himself, had never committed a violent act. He was disassociated from the things the Doctor had done. He had never felt a connection to any of the violence. In his mind he was just a filmmaker helping his client set the audience on edge with fear. To him, he felt like he was a documentary filmmaker, and a maker of thrillers. His specialty was suspense, deception, and fear—not murder.

The blood gushing from the man he was filming reached the camera and Nanda himself. Using the blood-coated lens as an excuse to go outside, he dashed out into the bright sun. The camera fell to the ground as Nanda retched. His heaving was so intense that eventually he fell to his knees and nearly fell face forward into his own vomit.

A strong arm prevented that and held him up. "Are you all right?" The voice belonged to Zarqawi. He pushed Nanda back up into his kneeling position.

"Are you all right?" Zarqawi repeated, pouring water from a canteen onto Nanda's head.

"Yes. Yes," he lied.

"The first one is hardest, Nanda. I didn't know you were a virgin!" Zarqawi laughed at the irony of a member of his killing squad never actually having killed anyone.

"Anyway, I need you to check the film right now; make certain we got it."

"We got it." Nanda whispered.

"Do you know what to do with it?"

"Yes."

Twenty-four hours later, Usama Bin Laden's contact person at Al-Jazeerah received the footage. It marked the beginning of a new chapter in the 21st century remake of the days of the Hashshashin.

Whitney placed a call to Professor Nasser to get his input on the latest horror on Al-Jazeerah. He dreaded such obscenities reaching U.S. air waves, and he wanted input from the country's leading expert on the Hashshashin. Simultaneously, he contacted a Constitutional law expert to get his input. He heard from the lawyer, but he received no response from the professor.

A few days went by before he called again. This time Whitney tried calling Columbia University. He was informed by them that Dr. Nasser had returned to Egypt to handle a family illness of a grave nature. He was on a one year sabbatical.

Thinking nothing of it, Whitney took another approach. Once he found the information he needed from another source, he set Dr. Nasser aside in his mind and didn't give him another thought.

CHAPTER 48

There was quite a list now. Zarqawi had kidnapped and executed many people. Some he let go; some he killed. There seemed to be no particular reason for the sparing. Not until the sensational bombing of the train station in Madrid in March of 2004 and the subsequent toppling of that government, did Nanda put it together.

Zarqawi had been setting the stage—first with sheer terror and grief, now with extortion. From that moment on Zarqawi wanted something in return for the life of the victim.

Nanda secretly prayed that the demands would be met. He couldn't do this anymore. Serving a cause to save himself was one thing, but losing his father and now participating in murder was another. He desperately longed for a way out.

One victim in particular haunted him. He was watching a replay of the execution. Zarqawi had not released this one for the news. It involved several Italians who had been kidnapped. They had all been defiant rather than submissive. Most victims were submissive and tearful, but not this group. And not one man in particular.

They were filming them in a row. The Italians were on their knees facing the camera. Their arms were bound behind them, but they were not hooded. Zarqawi and his men stood in a row behind them. They were hooded. Zarqawi was in the center and held the sword that was now becoming infamous. Zarqawi had selected the ringleader of the group to be his first victim. The man was defiant and brazen, and the others seemed to follow his lead.

The man, who was a common laborer, could feel the malevolence oozing from the hooded man behind him. Many men know when they are about to die and they have no fear. This Italian was one of them. He could feel that he was to be killed and he was not going to go out cowering, crying, or begging. The camera wasn't going to capture the look of shock in his eyes at the moment of decapitation. He would end this on his terms.

Just as Zarqawi stepped forward swinging the blade, the man spun around on his knees facing Zarqawi and shouted, "Let me show you how an Italian dies!" A fraction of a second later the blade connected and the man's body crumpled.

Horrified, but equally defiant, the others spun in place and were executed with backs to the camera. Nanda had caught it all on film. Zarqawi had scrapped it, never expecting it to see the light of day since it didn't accomplish what he wanted.

To him it was just a bad "take." They would get another in a few days. But to Nanda, it was a chance—a chance to show the world the other side of the story. He kept the film, edited it only slightly, and forwarded it in the pouch to the go-between. Secretly, he hoped it would inspire resistance and greater defiance. He saw no other way out for him but for the Coalition and Iraqi forces to remain steadfast and to ultimately kill Zarqawi.

At that moment he didn't even care if it meant his own death. He knew, in the dark quiet moments, that God would never forgive him for what he had done.

Al-Jazeerah aired the tape. In his office in Geneva, Phillipe Monet saw the film and the subsequent coverage of it by other news networks. It sparked debate and each agency clamored to get two experts on to discuss both sides of this abhorrent death. There was a tug of war emerging on the screen in front of him. Defy or not defy? That was the question of the day.

Eloquent, brilliant men and women expressed strong forceful arguments for both approaches. One side demanded more creative solutions, and wondered where this path would end. The other saw resistance as the only way to break down the will of the enemy.

There were many variations. Watching them, however, was like watching a tennis match that is tied up. No matter who scores, the opponent evens the score. And the viewers around the world found themselves talking to their television, "Yes, that's a good point. But yes, that's a good point, too." Then back again. "Yes. No. Yes. No. Yes. No. Yes. No. Oh, the hell with it. Let's watch 'Friends.'"

The Doctor was delighted. The unholy trio of Samir, Zarqawi and Nanda were undoing a thousand years of history. The 200-year-old enemy would soon be disabled and dismembered. Stuck in a quagmire of right/wrong dichotomies, Zawahiri knew the enemy would implode.

And he had Nanda to thank for that. On an encrypted phone he called Nanda to do just that.

"Well done, Nanda."

"What do you mean?" Nanda asked, suspecting Zawahiri was setting him up. He couldn't tell if he heard any sarcasm. But he was expecting it. Criminals always get caught eventually. Surely Zawahiri would have spotted the betrayal. He had known the Doctor too long and he was far too cunning to have missed it.

"The Italian execution, Nanda, it was a stroke of brilliance. Samir is gaining major ground in the public relations area with this contrasting film."

"I'm glad," Nanda lied. The Doctor heard the lie. He always heard the lie. Atef had slipped; now Nanda.

What a pity, he thought. "I was wise to leave this to your judgment. Zarqawi can be counted on to get the hard jobs done. You can be counted on to get the right shot at the right time," he said sincerely.

"Thank you. I try." Nanda could barely breathe.

"I'm still counting on you, Nanda, to know what to film, when to film it and when to release it. You're the mogul. Remember that. It's your show," the Doctor admonished like a pep talk.

"I will sir. Thank you for the call." Nanda's hurry to end the call cinched it for the Doctor. He had lost his man. This time Nanda's actions had worked to their advantage, but what of next time? To be absolutely certain, however, he tried one more test. Just before he hung up he added, "Oh, by the way, I was wondering, though, why did you do it?"

Nanda didn't answer right away. He was trying to figure out the hidden meaning in the question. That lag would cost him dearly. For the Doctor knew Nanda's response should have been instantaneous. Whatever his reason had been, he should have responded immediately. The fact that he did not told the Doctor that his man was searching for a plausible story to cover his sin and that he, in fact, had lost a good man.

When the conversation was over, Nanda started vomiting again. The one thing he had done that was right still turned out to the Doctor's advantage. *It is hopeless,* he grieved. *No matter what move you make, the Doctor turns it into a move for him. No one can win.*

The call to Zarqawi was more explosive. He first had to settle him down. Zarqawi was livid about the Italian footage and wanted to make certain the Doctor understood he would never have approved.

Patiently, the Doctor explained to him that it was, in fact, not only the right thing to do, but it was the most effective piece they had had. The Doctor knew that Zarqawi was not tracking with all of this. He had his part to play and Samir had his.

"Do you remember, Abu, when we told you what your mission was and that you were to create a body count that would be revulsive to Westerners?"

"Yes, sir, I do. We are doing that."

"Yes you are, and brilliantly. Your work has advanced the plan, and it has also drawn attention away from Makkawi. But if you'll remember I indicated Samir would take what you gave him and run with it."

Zarqawi did remember, but he had no real idea of what Samir did or the size of role he had played in the events as they were unfolding. He certainly had no idea how it would all play out. He trusted the masterminding to the Doctor.

"Just remember, Abu, that our goal is to drive our enemy into confusion. In confusion he will be uncertain; he will be insecure; he will be stupid."

He took the tutorial well. "Sir, I can see an advantage to that," Abu commented.

"Exactly. But this can't be accomplished militarily. I'm sure you have noticed the American military is not confused."

"That is correct."

"But the ones who send those men can be made confused. And that is Samir's assignment. He has chosen to attack their very certainty on right and wrong. He intends to flip it and, at the same time, bring their reasoning down to a level of nothing is more right or more wrong. When they have evenly balanced all arguments in their minds, uncertainty will set in." And then, as if to drive the point home, "And that will spread like a cancer. It is my intention that they experience the same fate as those who encountered the Lorelei on the Rhine."

Zarqawi understood the reference. While he was a student, he had traveled to Europe one summer and had taken the boat down the Rhine River. To this day all boats stayed clear of the powerful eddy that had sucked in and sunk so many vessels. Legend had it that a beautiful maiden beguiled them. Whatever the reason, no boat could escape the force of the current.

"That's quite an image, sir. I'll remember that. Samir's job is the Lorelei and mine is to drive the boats close to the eddy." The two chuckled for a moment. Both knew it was an odd conversation to be having. The Doctor let that settle for a moment and then added, "Ironic isn't it? By trying to be balanced, by fair play, they will be thrown off-balance." A moment later he added, "One final thing."

"Yes?" Zarqawi queried.

"Nanda did the right thing, but I'm sorry to say he did it for the wrong reasons."

To the Doctor, Nanda had now acted like an enemy and, in the frame of mind the Doctor was in, all enemies had to be destroyed. His survival depended on it. He felt no remorse whatsoever in giving the next order. He further knew that Zarqawi was now a stone-cold killer. He would follow the order.

For a moment he reflected on the men who were gone. The last two years had been hard on their numbers. And he knew Zarqawi would not come out of this alive. He didn't know where, and he didn't know when, but he knew Zarqawi's fate would be to perish in the struggle.

Atef had seen from the very beginning that this was a young man who would never have a family and who would never see old age. He had a role to play, and it would be a brief one.

"Sir," Zarqawi interrupted, "Is there an order there, sir?"

"Yes. Make it quick."

"Yes, sir."

Three days later the body of a man was found in an ally in Fallujah near the police station. He had been executed with a single shot to the head. No identification was found on or near the body.

A hasty fingerprint search turned up nothing either and no one filed a missing person report. The Iraqis didn't expect anyone would. They had decades of people disappearing or turning up murdered. Saddam was gone, but the dangers of their city, obviously, had not.

So they made almost no inquiry and simply stored the man at the morgue under the Arabic name for John Doe. No one at the station had the slightest idea that the man in the box had started his life with dreams and ambitions of making wonderful movies to delight audiences throughout India. Clearly, he had made a wrong turn somewhere.

The Black Knight on Level Two bore the label "Zarqawi." Removing the label, the Doctor pasted it on to the Black Knight on Level Four, and had that Knight capture the Black Bishop on the same level. Somewhat reluctantly the Doctor sent the Black Bishop to "trash." This piece could not be used again, so he eliminated it altogether. With a heavy sigh, the Doctor logged off and began his nightly regimen.

CHAPTER 49

He had read the reports three times. Iseli's staff had prepared the year-end figures for 2002 and for the first quarter of 2003. The numbers were up so dramatically that Rudi Iseli was certain there had been an error in computation. And he certainly didn't want to issue any press releases with embarrassing misinformation in them.

His usually tranquil demeanor was transformed that morning into one of truculence as he insisted the numbers be rerun. But when his chief financial officer reviewed the numbers with him personally, he was finally satisfied with their accuracy. Once certain, he could give way to the sense of euphoria he felt.

Not only were their pharmaceutical sales up, but profits and earnings as well. And all of this was apparently due to one division. He had Monet to thank for that, and he was waiting now for his investor to arrive so that he could give him the good news personally. He decided to break out a 150-year-old bottle of champagne, and to accompany it with a sumptuous spread of cheeses, crab and caviar. He had no idea whether Monet enjoyed this food, but he did remember the man's bout with ulcers. So he had his chef prepare some milder quiche and papaya in the event Monet was reluctant to try the other.

"You might even want to have a glass of buttermilk standing by," he instructed his chef. The thought of it made him almost retch, but he had heard it often helped with acidity. His secretary stepped in to announce Mr. Monet and then went into the outer office to personally escort him in.

The Doctor entered the offices of Decu-Hehiz having no idea why he had been summoned so urgently. One glance at

Iseli's grin let him know that whatever it was, Rudi was excited about it.

"My dear friend," Rudi exuded as he embraced Monet with the customary kiss on both cheeks. "I am so glad you were able to join me on such short notice, but I wanted very much to celebrate with you, since you are responsible for this."

"I'm honored by your kind words, but I must confess you have me in a mystery here."

"Yes, I expected that may be the case. I have wonderful news for you—for us all, actually—regarding last year and this first quarter."

Suddenly the Doctor knew what Rudi was aflutter about. *It's not like this velvety dandy to be so apoplectic,* he mused. "I gather my advice has produced a good result."

"You have no idea. No idea. Extraordinary results. Extraordinary."

The Doctor already knew the stock prices were in a steep upward graph and he had already calculated how much wealthier he had become given the quantity of stock he owned in Decu-Hehiz. What he was eager to hear was in what divisions they had made the most gains. Since Rudi had invited him here personally and singly, he could only guess that his recommendation to concentrate on psychotropic drugs had triggered the surge.

Iseli offered him a champagne toast, but his guest demurred. The buttermilk, however, proved to be the right choice, and both men laughed as they indulged in a bit of the spread Rudi had prepared. "I have something to show you," Rudi confided as he opened up the report. Quickly he pointed out the dramatic rise in revenue and then what he was most proud of, the rise in profits and earnings.

As Monet reviewed the numbers, Iseli grew impatient and turned the page. "This is what I want you to see."

There it was, proof that his plan was working. The report documented a dramatic upturn in the sale of anti-depressants and sleeping pills. Consistent with Decu-Hehiz's thoroughness, the analysts had broken the categories down and identified not only the top locations for the sales, but tracked them against a time line.

It was clear that the upsurge began after 9/11, but only slightly. In business, any upturn is good news, so the attacks on the United States had indeed been good for business. What was most gratifying, however, was the identification of the markets. Sales in Europe had remained at their flat pre-2001 numbers. The increases had all occurred in the United States. And the most dramatic upward graphs were in New York City and Washington, D.C.

"Very interesting."

"Yes, indeed," Rudi affirmed. "But there is more. Turn the page."

It was the next page that corroborated his strategy. The graphs showed that the upturn in those two cities had been marked as much as 22%, but that it had leveled off after a few weeks. Then, in 2003 they had begun another steady climb. That climb was sustained right up to the last weeks of the report and included all other areas of the United States.

"It was your idea," Rudi pointed out very sincerely. "You were correct to spot that the Americans would be suffering from anxiety, and fear, and depression; and we should turn our resources toward that market and give them some aid."

"Yes, it appears I was," the Doctor said modestly.

"It goes beyond that, my friend. We not only changed our R&D allocations, but we took your advice and hired ST and Associates in Paris. That man, Samir, is absolutely brilliant, and he showed us exactly how to penetrate and capture the U.S. market." Rudi was gloating as he poured his second glass of champagne.

Zawahiri knew Rudi. He was eager to brag a bit on his business prowess, so he encouraged him to fill him in. "Tell me."

"Samir showed me that the consumption of prescription drugs had been increasing steadily in the United States since 1987. Really. Every report showed the same type of increases. What Samir showed me was that this was not just an increase in expenditures driven by rising costs of drugs, but rather an increase in expenditures driven by actual increased consumption."

"Remarkable, isn't it, in a country with such a medical establishment?"

Rudi laughed. "Yes, friend, but with all their own manufacturers competing with one another, we had precious little of the market. That's where Samir was magnificent."

"How so?"

"He drew up a marketing strategy that involved direct-to-consumer advertising. His advice was to take our message directly to the consumer. They are hurting and their doctors were not listening to them. You were right, Phillipe, the events of 9/11 and this subsequent debacle of their multiple-front war has left the people fearful and anxious. They need these psychiatric medications."

The Doctor really had no interest in a long dissertation on how markets are picked. He wanted Rudi to get to the heart of it. "And how did Samir accomplish this?"

"Yes, of course. Well, first he persuaded me to place our entire budget into television advertising and magazine advertising. Then he created a series of brilliant ad campaigns that went straight to the consumer in his home promoting his depressed or anxious feelings and our empathy for those feelings. The ads then offered our products as the best possible solution to their worries. You would have loved them, Phillipe; they were a work of art!"

"I'm sure," the Doctor answered politely.

"No, Phillipe, I'm not engaging in any hyperbole here. They were beautiful. By the time I had watched them, I wanted to take the medication just so I could look or feel like the people on the screen. And I'm not the least bit anxious; never have been!"

The Doctor could not help but laugh at this picture. "Who did you target?"

"All ages actually. Oddly, we expected the most from adults, of course, but we were staggered by the increase in sales of medications for young children."

"Why is that, do you think?"

"I have no idea. Samir is theorizing that the parents are very sensitive about their children and don't want them disturbed or terrified by the news and state of the world. But frankly, we don't know yet. He is studying that."

"Am I to understand that you directed these TV commercials at young children?" the Doctor asked incredulously.

"No. That's the odd part." Rudi stopped momentarily. He was clearly puzzled by this. "We didn't place any ads on children's shows. We were trying to help only the adults. So we advertised, at Samir's recommendation, only on the news shows. Samir was very specific about that."

"Interesting."

"Yes, isn't it? I tell you, Phillipe, I had such misgivings. *Mon Dieu!* I hardly slept for weeks. Imagine! Placing your entire marketing and advertising budget into such a tiny basket—one type of show only." Iseli seemed pained by even thinking about this now. He continued, "But that's what they pay me for, making the tough decisions. And by God, I made this one. News shows only. And that did it. We got both the parents and the children. And the market is settling in with continued prescriptions. It's part of their life now."

"Just out of curiosity, Rudi, what made Samir so certain that you should select news shows instead of nightly programming or daytime programming?"

Rudi laughed. He was shaking his head in disbelief. "That is the best part. That is why I am so grateful to you, not just for suggesting the direction our manufacturing should go, but for almost insisting that I use this firm. Thank you."

"You're welcome, but what did Samir base his recommendation on?"

"Research. Research he had done in the 1970's at Princeton, of all places. He had done a paper on what shows sell what products. Pain relievers, stomach aids, and sleep aids sold the best on the nightly news and he had concluded that was because of the content."

"I'm not following you," the Doctor lied.

"The content of the news in the United States is predominantly negative and upsetting. It upsets people or makes them afraid. Apparently, the U.S. drug companies had figured this out, so they advertised their products exclusively on the news programs that would produce a demand in their audience. It worked. Sominex and Pepto-Bismol. All of those products did very well back then."

"I get it. Samir just graduated it up to the 21st century and its news! Beautiful! I knew he would be the right one."

"It is so gratifying, Phillipe. When the news is grim or it's a bad day, our sales jump. So we simply placed our ads on the shows that tended to point it out the best. Simple really. We wanted to help the Americans and we found a way to reach them directly. And we found a way to alleviate their depression. I see no limit here."

The Doctor could not tell whether Rudi Iseli actually believed this, or whether he had worn the schmoozing CEO hat so long that it just came out of him as if he believed it. But there was no doubt in the Doctor's mind that, above all, what Rudi Iseli was enjoying were the bottom-line figures. His company was now number one in pharmaceuticals in the world. And the game was just beginning.

Regardless of his sincerity or not, the Doctor was grateful to him for being such an ambitious and manipulatable executive. *It's all about money,* he reminded himself. Finishing his lunch, he stood and prepared to make his departure.

"But you are not leaving yet, surely."

"Yes. But I do appreciate your advising me of our success."

"But I wanted you to be with me when I inform the press in one-half hour. I can think of nothing better than to have our number one investor and the man who pushed us in this great humanitarian direction standing there with me."

The Doctor was completely taken aback. He made a point of avoiding the press and never letting his picture be taken, lest it appear in some newspaper somewhere or in the thousands of pictures the intelligence agencies reviewed, looking for prey. He lived a quiet, inconspicuous life and he couldn't let Iseli change that now.

"You are most kind," he began apologetically. "But I have another appointment that cannot be broken; much as I would like to, I can not. But I am confident you will represent us brilliantly. After all, Rudi, I merely suggested a few ideas. Your leadership has taken them to fruition and to our ascendancy. So, my apologies, and at the same time, my congratulations."

With that, he excused himself and darted into a cab immediately outside the building. It was beginning to drizzle, but he didn't care. He was eager to get to his computer. He wanted to reposition some pieces on the top two game levels. *What a day!*

CHAPTER 50

The smell of jasmine was everywhere. That balmy breeze that accompanied the blossoms warmed him and comforted him. He could see her silhouetted against the bushes. She looked as she had before the children. There were others with her, other lovely young women who seemed to laugh and enjoy each other's company.

Suddenly the sound of horses' hooves shattered the tranquility and the girls scattered in fear as the sound bore down on them. Before he could even sit up, he could hear the sound of the hooves on the cement floor. He did not know where he was at first. The girls had seemed so real. But now the stench of urine and defecation displaced the jasmine, and the floor of his cell shook with the approach of what sounded like a beast approaching.

Always before, there had been guards and interrogators. There was the sound of chains and cursing and keys. Today, there was none of that. And he felt such fear. Something was stamping at the door, hurling itself against the old hinges and lock. There was nowhere to hide as the door broke loose from the hinges and crashed to the cement in front of him. And through the door came a white horse with no rider.

The Doctor bolted out of bed this time. He was furious at these nightmares. But Ayman Al-Zawahiri was a disciplined man. *It's only in my mind,* he reminded himself, *only in my mind.* The Doctor knew enough about the mind to manipulate it, but he had no pretenses of knowing everything. These dreams were a nuisance to him, but he knew there was no deep significance to them no matter what Jung might have thought. If this was the only curse he had to bear for the years of torture and violence, he welcomed them.

Shaking it off, he quickly showered and made preparations for his trip to Paris. It was time to review plans with Samir, and to turn over the inventory of films Nanda had created. The United States was doing exactly what he had expected them to do, and he was more than prepared to meet them in the propaganda area. But he no longer felt it was safe to store the films in the theater of activity. The greater the rewards offered by the enemy, the more vulnerable he felt his go-between would become. Ayman Al-Zawahiri had learned through time to trust no one for the long-haul. He had complete confidence in himself; everyone else was a tool.

To be sure, the productions and scenarios created by Nanda had contributed enormously to the success of their plan. They had only used a few of what they had filmed and taped to date. For the most part they had needed just a few taped recordings by Zawahiri spread out through 2002 to keep the forces inspired. Bin Laden's material had been used once or twice, but nothing on video other than Bin Laden in Pashtun robes descending a cedar and rock-covered slope in Pakistan. Most certainly that had perpetuated the Intelligence community's belief that Bin Laden was somehow still in that region of Pakistan. The Doctor felt certain, however, that sooner or later, they would need more and he wanted these secured. If worse came to worse, he could visit Bin Laden in the asylum and crudely record some message. But for now, no one seemed to be expressing any serious doubts about Bin Laden's whereabouts. Samir would know how to handle them.

The drive from Geneva to Paris was one he enjoyed. Avoiding airports as much as possible, he had discovered that driving through the small villages that dotted the Burgundy area of France gave him cover. He drove a modest car and took pains not to draw attention to himself. To the casual observer, he was just another traveler passing through.

Leaving his car garaged outside of Paris, he took the Metro into the city and checked into a small hotel in Montmartre. Their meeting was scheduled for mid-afternoon at the carousel.

"Would you prefer to sit at the café around the corner?" Samir asked as he approached Zawahiri from behind.

Showing no signs of being startled, Zawahiri answered, "No, I think this is best. I've been watching the children and tourists on the carousel. It seems the spring air has brought them out in great numbers."

"Yes." Samir sat down next to the Doctor and faced the carousel as well. The two men looked like any other Parisians enjoying a little sun on a beautiful day. Both were adept at carrying on conversations without looking as if they were even conversing with one another.

Samir had hoped to sit and have a lunch at a café where he could keep an eye on the artists who were habitually setting up their easels. Tourists from all over the world stopped by to watch them work, and to occasionally commission their own portrait from one of the street artists. Clearly, they were not the best the city had to offer, but they were sometimes the most interesting. And Samir knew the noise factor in the area would make it easy for the two men to talk safely.

But, given the number of people lining up for the ride, this site was equally fine. Setting his brief case down on the bench, he created a space between himself and the Doctor and thereby took up the whole bench.

"Let me congratulate you on your meteoric rise, Samir," Zawahiri complimented him sincerely. "Your firm has grown faster than any other public relations and advertising firm on record, I believe."

It was true. In the wake of 9/11 and the subsequent three years of the United States' War on Terror, Samir had grown from being a one-man insider of Al Qaeda to the owner of a multi-national firm. He had offices in New York and Paris and was about to expand into London as well.

"How have you set up your branches?" the Doctor queried.

"The New York branch is strictly public relations and advertising. We handle all advertising of pharmaceuticals out of that office. Decu-Hehiz is, of course, our primary client, but we recently have added some prominent U.S. manufacturers of more mainstream, mundane products. It's affording a great cover and tremendous profits."

"Are any of our men there with you?" the Doctor asked, referring to a cell of Al Qaeda who had specialized training in propaganda.

"No, none. I wanted the New York operation to be squeaky clean. As far as my staff there is concerned, they feel privileged to be working with such a cutting-edge firm and look forward to the prestige that adds to their resume. I pay them well. Turnover is low."

"Excellent. The others, then, are in Paris?"

"Yes, all of them."

"Are there any outsiders?" the Doctor pressed him.

"No. It was not possible, too much danger. I needed them all to feel free around one another."

The Doctor was pleased with this arrangement. He had had some concerns about having regular personnel anywhere near his elite squad. Unlike any other cell, these were trained commandos in the area of propaganda. Samir had personally selected each man and had trained them personally. All deception propaganda would emanate from this team.

What the Doctor knew about the affairs of men, and it appeared the rest of the world did not, was that, if a conflict won't resolve between two individuals or groups, there is someone hidden that is fomenting the conflict. That hidden person has only one goal—sustained hostility. Zawahiri had observed it often in his dealings with Bin Laden. It was one of the reasons he had to occasionally take out an ally. If he found they had the ear of Usama and were feeding him lies or distortions about someone, Usama would end up in prolonged conflicts.

The Doctor had trained himself to investigate to find out who had the ear of both parties in such a conflict, and to eliminate that person as the source of contention. He called it the "Iago Effect" in deference to the special role Iago had played in the destruction of the loving relationship between Othello and his bride Desdemona. Time and time again, the Doctor had found truth and treachery in the works of Shakespeare. His guards had allowed him to read. His studies at University had included literature and poetry, and he had a gift for it.

So he took the lessons he learned in these great pieces of drama and learned to apply them into contemporary life. While directors in theatres across the world congratulated themselves on making Shakespeare relevant to the contemporary audience by updating their costumes and setting them in the streets of a modern city, he had perfected the art of actually bringing the drama into the day-to-day life of people all over the world.

And to do that, he needed Samir and his commandos. Their job was to foment dissent, to foster and prolong disagreement, to escalate conflict and, in general, to fracture alliances. They were in fact a new breed of mercenary. Each was educated in propaganda by Samir, but all had a background in journalism and marketing. They came from different parts of the world, and all had substantial connections into business and government. Some held degrees in economics; some in government. In short, they knew their way around and were eager for assignments.

"I thought you might want to see the offices," Samir offered.

"Not with them there. I am to have direct contact with only you, Samir. As far as the rest are concerned, I'm in Pakistan. Is that understood?"

"Perfectly." Samir felt reprimanded, though the Doctor's tone had been mild. He felt the need to justify his suggestion. "They are all out of the offices today. I felt it would be safe."

"Hmm." The Doctor said no more. The squeals of children overrode their conversation for a moment.

"I have a strategic question for you. This one I did not want to decide on my own."

"Yes?"

"How much do you want us to influence the United States' actions with regard to trials of the combatants and cells they have captured or detained? It seems to me there is a great deal we could do to tangle that up."

"I don't want you to involve yourself, at least not now."

The answered startled Samir. He was tempted to turn and directly confront the Doctor, but instead looked straight ahead. Trying not to sound defiant or in disagreement he asked, "May I ask why?"

"I believe they are taking care of that themselves."

Samir wanted more, but decided to let the Doctor offer it up. He did. "Remember, Samir, use their strengths against them. Remember I told you of their reverence for their Constitution and their sense of justice?"

"Definitely. That's why I asked."

"Well, from what I have been watching on television for most of 2003 and 2004, they have already started to wrap themselves up on that. It seems you were right. They had their own fifth column, already in place, albeit unwitting. The ACLU is already confusing the issue in the name of Constitutional rights. Their lawyers and judges are already screaming 'justice.' I would just let them do themselves in."

"But…" Samir never got the sentence out.

"There is no 'but,' Samir. It's already clear they can't differentiate between an ordinary criminal and a combatant. That fact alone will keep them tied up and in bitter controversy and conflict for at least two years." He paused to assess Samir's agreement here.

Samir nodded his understanding.

"It should be entertaining, to say the least, to watch them argue in circles on that. In fact, I think you can expect the discourse to deteriorate to angry verbal assaults before long. I want to see them devour themselves. If it goes well, they will be calling each other traitors, and will forget about us."

Two years ago Samir would have scoffed at the possibility of such a thing. But, in truth, he was seeing signs of that fracturing already and he had not done much work in that area. He suspected they were getting a boost by the revving up of the political candidates. A carefully placed "suggestion" in the mind of a political operative working a presidential candidate had caused them to turn from attacking the other candidates to attacking the incumbent. He marveled at the simplicity of the power of duplication. As soon as one candidate turned, the others did. As soon as they did, the press did.

Both men knew the enemy would not forget about them. But enemies can be deceived and they can be distracted. Samir knew he had been effective in that area. It was clear the United States was reeling in the wake of the bombings in Spain and the ousting of their supporter. His replacement was unwittingly playing his part magnificently. *If the people of Spain only knew how stupid they were!* Samir had reflected. This certainly made his job even simpler now, for he had unwitting allies.

In truth, he despised cowards. His work, when it hit the mark, surfaced cowardice. When it surfaced, he and his staff would celebrate by spitting at the image of the coward. Then they would drink a toast.

"You see now how evil their freedom is, Samir?" the Doctor broke the silence.

Samir said nothing. He was looking at that.

"Look how the momentum is building in all the areas we have attacked. They are polarized on education issues, on abortion issues, on military allocations, on mental health, on trials, election irregularities, and military tribunals. They are weighing all these things in balance. And why? Because they have the freedom to do so. I applaud you, Samir."

"Thank you." Samir didn't want to appear to need praise.

"They are angry now. They are despondent now. They are embittered. And they are pointing to each other as the one who victimized them. Their freedom has turned them all into bickering victims. And in that morass of accusations, we will defeat them."

Samir could not help but hear the swell of disdain in the Doctor's voice. He clearly hated these self-righteous people and was truly relishing their fall.

"Are there any areas you do want me to focus on now?"

"Yes. Given what I have seen appearing on television, for the next six months I want you to hit the political area. Use the military efforts anywhere. Press the "Distraction" button. Given how confused they are already, they should fall for that one quickly. I will direct Makkawi to keep the pressure on internationally, and Zarqawi will give you much to work with in Iraq. We are repositioning him now. Remember, too, that the Americans have a button on 'Failure.' Punch it wherever you can. Their press will assist. It is one of the components of a worthy piece. So they'll boost you. Keep the pressure on the 'Vietnam' and 'No WMD' buttons until your street interviews show the man on the street repeating them."

"Right, we're polling like that now in New York. They are starting to repeat the headlines and talking points, but it hasn't gone rote or verbatim yet."

"When it's verbatim and automatic, you know you're done."

With that, one of the simplest and most devastating aspects of mind-control and brain-washing was authorized and augmented. The strategy would prove so successful that within six months a nation would come to the verge of a psychotic break. World leaders would hover in fear of what might happen. Its birthplace was in front of the carousel on Montmartre, while children and tourists snapped endless photos. The two men stood, without once looking at each other, and went their separate ways.

It was time for the Doctor to begin the final four-game conclusion. If successful, the conclusion of those last four layers would place in his hands the most dreaded weapon in the arsenal. And then he would begin the games again. It would be the last game a free people would ever engage in.

CHAPTER 51

The next morning the Doctor arrived at his office early. He was feeling buoyed by the speed and efficiency of Samir's campaign. Before his secretary would arrive, or he would be interrupted, he wanted to evaluate the last steps.

Opening up his encrypted file, the familiar cube appeared. The bottom four layers were highlighted in a metallic blue. The upper layers were almost invisible unless illuminated. Since no one in Al Qaeda had any knowledge of the existence of the top four games, he was confident no one would ever guess his master plan. Even if his top lieutenants were compromised, they could shed light on only one or two of the game layers.

Only Samir was aware of materials in play on the higher levels. But he had already pigeon-holed them into the area of public relations. *That is his game after all,* he mused. Samir was brilliant in his arena, but he was not the strategic thinker that the Doctor was. He was also not a terrorist. He had been chosen because he was ambitious, and without morals. Samir liked to win; and he liked to destroy. The Doctor and Usama both had recognized this in him. It was never a matter of a cause for Samir. It was always about destruction. The amount of money steadily flowing into his bank accounts was more than a sufficient enticement to keep him steady.

So the Doctor was confident that not even Samir would ever guess his true intention. Quickly, he highlighted the top four layers in hues of gold. The top layer glowed like gold bullion. He began to place pieces in the games and move them. As he looked at the configuration, he began to smile. The smile broadened and soon he was laughing. He was absolutely fascinated at how this looked on the board. It had been developed in his mind. He felt his plan would work. But on the board, it was stunning. Seeing it in front of him produced a sensation of electricity throughout his body. *I've done it!*

With the data Samir had provided the Doctor and the exhilarating report from Iseli confirming it further, he prepared to log off. "Perfect," he said aloud. As the screen started to fade, the last pieces to disappear were the White pieces. On all four top layers, the White pieces were facing toward the White King. They were turned on their own King.

"You cannot allow a government to form in Iraq!" he shouted into the encrypted phone.

"I understand, sir, and I believe our kidnappings are weakening the support of the partners. It is my hope that the great success we've had with the bombings at the enlistment centers is weakening the resolve of the Iraqis." Zarqawi sounded a bit blustery.

"Don't delude yourself, Abu," the Doctor responded tersely. "They are returning by the hundreds the very next day. You must adapt now."

"What do you suggest I do?"

"I would bring your fifth column in from the Afghanistan prison, and I would add a little variety to the news out of Fallujah."

"The one I can do easily. One beheading, two beheadings. After awhile, even they seem repetitive. This next assault will be thrown in their faces. I have a bridge operation in mind. That should make it easy for the man on the street to see. This Allawi is a tougher adversary than I expected. He's expelling Al-Jazeerah from the country. I was relying upon that to get the videos out. I'll just have to go live with a live event."

"Fine, I leave it up to you. Now, back to the fifth column."

Zarqawi was reluctant to do this. He had no qualms about the event, or giving the order for it to happen. But he had reservations about the repercussions. For a second he debated whether to discuss this with the Doctor or ignore it. Confident as he was in his new-found celebrity status, he knew he was not in the same league with the famous Ayman Al-Zawahiri. *Now, if the order came from Bin Laden himself, I would feel more comfortable.*

"What is your reservation?" the Doctor asked.

"I know you think a prison scandal would be helpful to discredit them right now, but I'm reluctant to use the fifth column."

"Why?"

"The deaths in Afghanistan are being investigated, but so far no one has spotted our man on the inside. His unit is now in Iraq…"

The Doctor cut in, "Exactly. That's why I suggest you use him."

"With respect, sir," Zarqawi proceeded with caution, "if I create a blow-up right now, and investigations begin under scrutiny of the press, as you suggest, they will eventually notice that it is the same unit that was responsible for the prisoners in the Afghanistan prison. Sooner or later, they may put it together that there is an inside man setting them up."

"That is a risk we will have to take, Abu. We have to turn up the heat on the Americans. Their election is drawing close and I want the maximum pressure from us. Samir can work with that."

"I'm sure he could, but what about me? I need this man on the inside for us. He's the only way I have of identifying just exactly how much they have learned. That's how my men and I know when to move. I'm frankly concerned about compromising the integrity of our operations if the man is caught."

"I repeat: this is a risk we will have to take!" The Doctor was emphatic. He did not anticipate what came next.

"I would feel more comfortable if this order came directly from Bin Laden himself."

The Doctor didn't let even a second lapse. He hissed, "You are to deal with me. I speak for Bin Laden."

Brazenly, Zarqawi fired back, "Bin Laden himself commissioned me in Afghanistan. He gave me my orders, and I would prefer to hear from him directly on this." His fame had emboldened him. No sooner had he uttered the challenge than he knew it was a mistake. But there was no way to take it back now. He waited.

The Doctor's mind was, in fact, immensely faster than Zarqawi's. He knew the man to be a firebrand. Bin Laden and he had chosen this man for his volatility. Therefore, it did not really surprise him to hear Zarqawi flexing his muscles and flashing on the phone. He knew also that Zarqawi would have regretted it the moment it came out of his mouth. So he let him dangle there for a bit. He let him sweat a bit about the insubordination.

It worked. The silence was painful for Zarqawi. And the Doctor knew it would be. The next man who spoke lost. There was nothing but mild static on the line as the two men remained in their stand-off on the phone. Finally, Zarqawi broke the silence.

"I apologize for my impertinence. I mean no disrespect."

Again, the Doctor paused to let him twirl just a bit longer. Feeling the man had been humbled, he responded calmly, "None taken." Then he kindly added an explanation he knew Zarqawi would accept. "If you remember, Abu, Usama actually told you to go to Iraq and wait. He told you that, after Saddam was gone, you would be told what to do and that you were to do nothing until that time. Do you recall this?"

"Yes."

"On Usama's orders I came to you after Saddam disappeared. At that time I informed you that I would be your contact person. And that is how it will remain. I'm sure you can imagine that Usama will not break cover for any reason. He will not expose himself to location detection for any reason. And that includes handling any misgivings you may have. You are going to have to work that out for yourself, understood?"

Softly, Zarqawi responded, "Understood."

"Good. I'm glad we cleared that up. I want you to understand, Abu, that we feel you have performed brilliantly. You have done more in this short period than any other field commander we have had. But with the expected capture of Saddam and this stiff determination the enemy has to complete the hand off from their Ambassador to the Provisional

Government by the end of June, we must amplify our interference with this process."

"May I ask if you have any concerns about Saddam?"

"None whatsoever. The man is a coward. He has always been a coward. He will not give up the deal he struck with us because it would prove to the Americans his direct involvement with Al Qaeda. And that will mean his certain death. No, he'll take his chances on his own people failing to form a government. He expects chaos and the return of his strongmen. He'll quietly wait out what we do. But it won't save him in any case. We know that. He's a spot in history now, nothing more."

"I understand. And I can assure you, you will see some fireworks soon."

"I look forward to it."

His next call to Makkawi was short and to the point. The more he dealt with this man, the more he respected him. There were some disagreements, to be sure, and perhaps some resentment. But so far, their relationship was building. Nothing could replace the decades-old partnership of Zawahiri and Atef, but Atef's failings at the end had at least occurred after he had picked a worthy successor.

The Doctor wanted to make sure that Makkawi would follow-up the Madrid bombings with other debilitating attacks. Makkawi assured him that he would and, in his estimation, he could expect the Philippine government to reverse itself and withdraw from the Coalition as well.

That forecast bolstered Zawahiri's spirits. Now if they could just get the Australians to cave as well, the balance would tip for sure.

Calling Samir, he coached him, "Samir, if the hand-off occurs in Iraq, I want you to talk as if it is a puppet government. Discredit it. Remember, the Americans are especially vulnerable on 'Vietnam' now. However you did it, the ghost of Vietnam in the midst of their elections is creating havoc. Keep it up. Keep the equation going: a puppet regime in Iraq equals the puppet regime in Vietnam. Their own past guilt and regret will do the rest. Before you're done, I want them to see the number 58,000 every time they look at the death count in Iraq. They will superimpose it, if you help them."

"That is easily done," Samir responded confidently. He was comfortable with his experience now. He was totally professional.

"Will you use the Minister in France?"

"No. It is not necessary now. I have established such a successful firm in New York that I am a frequent guest at the parties Bud Walker and his wife throw in the city. He has even invited me to go hunting with him at his ranch in Idaho."

"Really?" the Doctor smirked.

"Yes. Seems he appreciates my 'unjaded viewpoint.'"

"You're joking."

"No. He says I'm refreshing and he's open, frankly, to my interpretations of world events, especially since I sit well in Paris."

"Congratulations, Samir. That is…remarkable."

"Funny, isn't it? Anyway, all I have to do is drop in 'puppet regime', 'Vietnam'—whatever—he'll echo it."

"I have no doubt. So, just be watching for Makkawi's next moves. Zarqawi's are obvious. Makkawi's less so." And with that admonition, they ended the call.

CHAPTER 52

He could hear their voices—Americans, for sure. Judging by the dirt falling around him, there were many of them and they were very close. He had never really expected it would come to this, but he had already made his decision as to what he would do if they gave him a chance.

It was cold and dark, and his body was already protesting the constrictions of the almost tomb-like hideout. His sons were dead, but he had survived. With the help of loyal townspeople and colleagues, he had managed to escape them since April. Saddam knew that he had skimmed and hidden more than $20 billion during the time of the sanctions, and he knew the men around him and the men they worked with at the United Nations would never give him up. They were in too deep.

Years would go by before they found the more than 200 front companies he had used. But that would never happen, he reassured himself through those long months of hiding. With billions of that money allocated to armaments and tactics, he knew his generals and aides would eventually throw the United States out of his country. He had heard of this man Zarqawi's rise to fame, but he knew the man was not bright enough to survive once Saddam gave the order. But for now, Zarqawi seemed content to spill the blood of his own men, and that was just fine with Hussein.

I will be captured and I will await a trial. What the Americans do not know is that there never will be a trial, because there never will be a new government. Zarqawi will see to that, and the men and nations that owe me will see to that. My people will come for me and I will have my country back.

That had been his mantra these last few sordid weeks, and he repeated it once again to himself as he waited. It was so cold now that he feared his very breathing might attract attention.

It went quiet up above and he knew this was it. A second later the camouflaged trap door to his hole swung open and the sunlight flooded in. Blinded momentarily, he struggled to focus his eyes. When he could finally see again, he was staring into the barrel of a gun. The disconnected voice of a translator a few feet away shouted into the hole in Arabic to surrender and come out.

I won, he congratulated himself. *I gambled and I won, once again. I would have killed me, but not the Americans—it's not their style.*

And with that thought, Saddam Hussein surrendered his weapon, and crawled dirty and emaciated into the daylight.

CHAPTER 53

He had been staring at the cube for some time. The events around the world since the fall of Saddam Hussein in Iraq had stunningly affirmed not only the validity of his strategy, but the accomplishment of it as well. The extraordinary interdependence of each of the games was gratifying. "A perfect zero-sum-game!" he said aloud.

Every time the Coalition forces achieved a military victory, Samir and his cell had managed to offset it with a public relations loss of a comparable magnitude. Even when the Americans did something right, his team had turned it to make it look wrong. He took deep pleasure in hearing of a battle where a number of insurgents or loyalists had been killed or captured, only to see it offset by nightfall as journalists reported on how many had escaped.

Even the public relations victory of the United States in the capture of Saddam Hussein had been zeroed out by the Madrid bombings. Like a magnificent teeter-totter, the military game and propaganda games counter-pointed each other.

The handover of authority to the Provisional Government in Iraq had been a public relations loss for Al Qaeda; but it was quickly offset by the brutally brilliant escalation of beheadings and slaughter that Zarqawi concocted. *They are quite a pair, these two warriors of mine. The world will know the one. Let him enjoy his fame. But they will never know the other.*

Zawahiri had already concluded that Zarqawi, although brave, would make a mistake and be captured or killed. He could see the man was reading his press clippings and that the American military would eventually outsmart him. For Zarqawi was not submissive. He did not seek a mentor and that would undo him.

Samir, on the other hand, had sought the mentorship of the Doctor. Like Bin Laden himself, he had been a willing and appreciative student—not just of war, but also of deception. And the Doctor had already decided that Samir would be with him as the games continued. As long as Samir remained submissive and effective, the Doctor would school him little by little.

He came out of his reverie when the top four layers of the cube flashed at him on the computer. Any loss by the U.S. in the Military or Propaganda games resulted in an off-setting win for him in the Drug and Money games. Often the games reflected the zero-sum-game as well. If the enemy found money, it was offset by weapons gone missing. Extraordinary, really! There was no way for the United States to totally win. He would ensure that. For if the United States succeeded ultimately in the Military and Propaganda games, then the Doctor would lose in the top two games. And that was never going to happen.

In order to rule the world, he could never allow it to happen.

What was perhaps the most gratifying aspect of this whole thing to the Doctor was the confirmation of something he had theorized years earlier as he began to study the mind.

Ayman Al-Zawahiri had theorized that it would be possible for one man to rule the world, and that he would not even need an army. All the man would have to do, he theorized, was be truly observant of the behavior and motives of men. Then one could predict and thereby manipulate their actions.

What the Doctor had, in fact, theorized was that each man has an agenda, something that drives his actions. Nations are comprised of men; nations, therefore, would also have agendas. In the absence of a true spirituality, man would behave on a base, reactive level and could be counted on to pursue the accomplishment of his own agenda.

The Doctor agreed with Pavlov and the early psychiatrists that man was an animal and would respond much as any other animal would to stimuli. If something happened to him, he would react. If it happened often enough, his reaction would become automatic. What the Doctor had discovered for himself was that a person's motives or agenda were tied to this automatic response. The motives were derived from it. The person's intention could be good or bad, it did not matter. It only mattered that men thought their agenda was important enough to pursue. Although they might not know it, their motives were linked to something more "base." Therefore, all the Doctor had to do was reactivate that base response in someone and they would go forward from there to accomplish their own goals.

The only thing necessary, then, to actually rule the world would be an indirect mind-control in the form of controlling the ambitions of men. It was a basic marketing challenge, actually. Find a way to invigorate their ambitions, to empower their ambitions. Simply, get them to do what they already wanted to do and then take advantage of it. Punch the button and then let them act it out. Like an invisible master puppeteer, he could then oversee the actions of nations until they eventually all sank into slavery. And at the same time, he could remain above it all, getting wealthier and more powerful by the minute. By the time he revealed his identity, it would be too late.

They would be so dependent on their games that they would submit. The Doctor saw evidence of that in the successful manipulation of the press that he and Samir had already pulled off. The ambitions of Bud Walker now dictated the actions of his counterparts. The base desire that Samir had punched was Walker's need to be accepted and recognized. The ambitions of nations ran even deeper. For centuries they had succeeded or failed in forcing their agendas on other nations. The easy handling of France, Spain, and Russia in the beginning of the 21st Century bore out his theory. They were doing what they had wanted to do all along. Their actions in the War on Terror were just a response to situations similar to those they had encountered in their past history, and they were solving it now the way they historically did.

The list of substantiating documentation went on and on. He had known exactly what Decu-Hehiz would do based on the ambitions of the company. And he knew other drug companies would follow suit. Educators, doctors, lawyers, lawmakers, ministers, human rights organizations—they all fell victim. And he could see the chaos they were creating. And that chaos allowed him to remain invisible. As long as he kept their focus on themselves and what they wanted to do, they would never look up. And if they never looked up, they would never suspect his watchful eye monitoring and planning their every move.

Ayman Al-Zawahiri was in fact planning a worldwide coup. His tool was his incomplete, but powerful understanding of the mind. No one would know that he was controlling their minds. Instead, they would all pride themselves in how much they were exercising their own creative process as they took actions that moved them inexorably closer to a world of complete Shari'a.

But this was not going to be Mohammed's Shari'a. No. Islam, too, would succumb in the Doctor's plan. From that point forward in mankind's history, Ayman Al-Zawahiri would be recorded as the complete and absolute ruler of the world. Certain that he would evolve as well in his abilities to manipulate, he was confident there would be no other.

All he had to do was remain faithful to the workable actions that were devouring the West. Once the West and its pathetic freedom had been vanquished, then he would rid the world of the other ineffective civilizations. Only then could he be assured that the sordid and immoral behaviors that he had witnessed would be purged.

Before 9/11 he had assumed this plan's accomplishment would take 20 years. He would be an old man by then. But since 9/11 and his resuming control of the game, he could see now that the whole plan would take less than ten years. He would be in his late sixties, he calculated. There was still plenty of time to enjoy his victory.

Ayman Al-Zawahiri had been raised without wealth. To this day, he did not care much for material things. He lived as well as his status in Geneva required, but that is not what inspired him. What gave him greatest pleasure was watching the destruction of the whole corrupt playing field. The new timeline afforded him an extra ten years of that satisfaction.

And once his life was done, there would be no further history for man on this planet. His rule would be the final rule. At his end, he and his weapons would deliver all good men to Allah, and all others would perish.

But back to the immediate task, he admonished himself. *One step at a time. First, the West. And that means England, and it means the United States.*

The Doctor had a real problem with Blair and Bush. Knowing that men reenact their pasts, he wondered if these two were replaying World War II again. Either way he despised them both and concluded that to bring down Blair, you bring down Bush. The British people would do the rest. *There it was again; just get people to do what they wanted to do in the first place and make sure it matches up with your ultimate goal.*

It was a quiet Sunday everywhere in the world as the Doctor logged off. The people of Great Britain and the United States had no idea what was about to be unleashed on them. How could they? They had never learned that you can use freedom to kill freedom. Perhaps if they had all been doctors they would have spotted it. A cancer grows freely by creating a new body within a body. And the second body devours the first. This was an area Dr. Ayman Al-Zawahiri was expert in.

Unfortunately, they were not doctors and they were locked in now. He wondered if the Americans even had any idea what was happening to them. He wondered if the President he would soon topple felt by now that he was boxing with a shadow.

CHAPTER 54

He would rather have relived the Los Angeles earthquake of 1971. He had been in the heart of the mid-Wilshire district that morning when the 6.8 earthquake hit. It was the closest thing he had experienced to the explosions and confusion of a war zone, until now.

What he was experiencing inside the walls of the CIA reminded him of the tremors before the quake. The President was mad as hell at the flap he was taking over the weapons of mass destruction. Everyone, including the British and Russians, was looking for someone to blame. The vitriol that was spewing into American living rooms every night from the news programs, as they covered the most psychotic political campaign in decades, was causing everyone in command to quake. "How could they have been so wrong?" was the question asked endlessly everywhere in the world.

The answer one received depended largely on who was giving the answer. If it came from the BBC, you got one answer. If it came from Fox News, you got another. Any way you cut it, however, leaders and aides everywhere were trying to explain logically how they got it wrong.

Nowhere was this more evident than at the CIA. The hours he spent there on other projects had become agony for him. Personally, he felt that people had heard what they wanted to hear; they had seen what they wanted to see. And they had based their decisions on that inherent bias. But to him, this *mea culpa* crap was just that—crap. Why on earth anyone would apologize for toppling that murderous beast was beyond James. *That's why I would never have made it in diplomacy.*

Having spent the years in the Balkans that he had, he felt it wouldn't matter if they had invented the evidence. Taking that guy out was imperative. He had not spoken to Ari Ben Gurion, but he could almost feel Israel breathing easier. But James didn't like weasels, and he just couldn't stomach his superiors up the line scrambling to avoid taking the direct hit when the shit hit the fan.

He had never seen Whitney and the other deputy directors so frantic. He'd see them pass his office, or he'd run into them in the men's room, and they had that "deer in the headlights" look. They'd almost freeze for a surreal moment, and then dash away. Back at their desks, they would shudder at each phone call.

The prospect of going up to the Hill to testify was horrifying to them. And personally, he knew the Director was going to resign. He could see the disdain in the man's eyes when he was summoned like a school-boy to answer questions about what he did or did not know.

He couldn't blame them though. The anxiety and paranoia that was oozing in the halls of Langley was matched only by the out-of-control anxiety that seemed to be raging across the country at-large.

James had been out of the country most of his adult life in areas where absentee ballots could not be delivered. Voting was not something he took for granted. He was actually looking forward to voting until this election process took on what he called "Alice in Wonderland" qualities. The whole nation seemed to be on an emotional roller-coaster—frantic, fearful, and dangerously critical.

That was shocking and distasteful enough by itself, but the fact that this kind of barnyard fighting was occurring on our own turf, barely three years after 9/11, was keeping him awake at night. He made up his mind that he and Andy were going to have to break this thing. Tonight he would tell him they had to wrap this up. Otherwise, he feared they would all be sucked over a cliff.

Maybe I'm making too much of it, he told himself as he parked the car behind Andy's. *I've been watching too much news on this damned project.* "Let's end this thing," he said to the doorbell as he waited for Kelly to answer.

Kelly had been polite but he had known her long enough now to know something was bothering her. She gave him one of those "I'll deal with you later" looks as he passed her to go downstairs.

"Hi, Kid, what's with Kelly?" Then, not wanting to appear critical he added, "Was it me or you?"

"Me, mostly."

"What's it about?"

"Honestly, I don't know, James. She's just generally agitated these days. She was upset about some fight that broke out in her shop yesterday."

"A fight?"

"Yeah, two of her clients came to blows over Bush and Kerry. They were really screaming at each other about this Vietnam record stuff. I guess they even broke up the place a bit."

"Is this a joke?"

Andy was quick to answer, "No, I wish it were. I ordered up my absentee ballot today."

"Why'd you do that? You'll have time to go to the polls."

Andy's answer surprised James. "I don't think I want to, James. I don't want Mom to go, either."

"Why not?"

Andy looked away for a moment and then shrugged it off. "Don't know; just don't feel it's safe."

James was about to just change the subject when Andy added, "We need to finish this off, James. And we need to do it before this election." There they were again, on the same page. *He's something!* James reflected.

"Right. I've got an idea about something. This craziness in the news gave me an idea."

Andy sat down at the work table, brought out his pad and said, "I'm all ears."

"Something's wrong, Andy, here in the United States. I get totally how you and Kelly feel. I've been losing sleep myself. It feels like a juxtaposition of being sucked along into this storm on the one hand, and being in slow motion on the other. One minute I almost see all of us just stepping in place going nowhere, and the next minute I feel like the storm engulfed us and we're in a whirlwind spinning out of control. I found myself this morning asking, 'When did America lose its common sense?'"

Andy said nothing. He just furrowed his brow. James continued, "It's like a time warp. One minute I feel the election has already happened and gasp that I missed it, and the next minute I feel like it's two years away and we're walking in molasses. It's all upside down somehow. We were attacked. We should be attacking, not apologizing for attacking, right?"

"Right."

"I keep reminding myself we were the victims. Somehow, the world out there is acting like we were the victimizers. I wake up each morning afraid to turn on WNG."

"Why's that?" Andy perked up.

"Because I'm afraid I'm going to hear that someone is seriously suggesting *we* flew the planes into those buildings; that we should be apologizing for all the terrible things we've done; that somehow Bin Laden's a victim." He paused. "To be honest, Kid, there are days I think I went crazy."

Both men just sat there nodding their heads. After a long moment, Andy broke the silence, "Well…I'm glad I'm not alone." That broke the tension and they released their nervous laughter. It felt good to laugh.

"So, let me tell you what I was thinking as I was bringing myself back to sanity."

Andy got out the ledgers and was setting up the video to play the clips James was removing from the safe. Every day or so he brought the latest videos edited at Langley. These news reports were a basis of their analysis. That is what had given James the idea.

"Today, Kid, we're not going to watch clips. We're going to watch this stuff live, as it is being aired. Because I think you are closer than you think, and I think we can speed this up."

"I fail to see how watching the whole thing, commercials included, can possibly speed things up. We need it distilled."

Now James was excited. "No, that's where we went wrong, Kid. That's why Langley didn't get it right, either. It hit me like a ton on my way over here."

Andy just squinted at him, so James continued, "We're looking for eight games, right?"

"Right."

"And we've identified four, right?"

"Well, I was reminded of something I observed in Wisconsin during the Vietnam War, and which I observed again in the Los Angeles riots in '92. I think we'll get the next four if we just step back and broaden our area of search just a little."

"Broaden, in what way?"

"You know how the news is full of all these anti-war protestors and arguments, and how the rhetoric and now even the issues are about Vietnam, not the current war?"

"Yes…" Andy seemed pensive.

"Well, that's what gave me the idea. I went to school with guys like this, actually just like this Michael Moore guy. In my University of Wisconsin days there were protests, and violence, and riots. I remember watching one anti-war march in particular. I saw these other guys, these outsiders. And I knew that the real agitators didn't give a rip about our war. They had another agenda. And our war demonstrations were achieving their agenda."

"Did you figure it out?"

"No. Not at the time. But I remembered the effect it all had on everybody. It made you feel helpless—and cynical. Most of the guys I ran with just started smoking dope and making love, as if somehow that would stop the madness. They just gave in to hiding. I thought it was stupid. You don't just smoke the problem away. You don't love it away. That's no antidote."

"What does that have to do with our game?"

"I'm not totally sure. But it feels to me now like it did then. The same guys are at work. Or at least, the same tactics are being used. We're being had now, like we were then."

Andy looked at that for a moment and simply said, "Interesting. Where do we go from here?"

"What I was just describing Andy was a factor of sociology or society; not war or propaganda. The war and the propaganda about the war produced an effect in society. I have a hunch that sociology in some way is one of your levels. Get out your list and let's take today and look not just for war data or propaganda data or religious data. Let's broaden the evaluation to include sociological phenomena. Because Vietnam and our failure there was not just military; it was more sociology."

"War by Sociology. Interesting." The theory bit. It had some muscle. Andy got out his list as they turned on the TV. Normally it would be on CNN, but they decided to watch instead a network that was climbing in the ratings wars in the last year.

"All right," Andy began, " we've got game number one-Religion; game number two-Military; game number three-Intelligence; game number four-Public Relations." At that point he started to erase the public relations and substitute propaganda. James caught him doing it and interrupted him.

"What are you doing?"

"Changing the label. Given what you described, this game seems more like Propaganda, like we encountered in the Cold War. I'm labeling it like the military would think it."

James exploded, "No. That's just it. That's how we missed it. That's how Langley missed it. They think military. They use conventional analysis. They were born in the Cold War. Some of those old farts were born in World War II. You say 'military action,' they say 'propaganda.'"

"Yeah? Is that wrong?"

"Not for 1941, Kid. Not for 1963. Not for 1988. But for 2004, I think you got it right. I love you, Kid. If you weren't 21 and could beat the crap out of me, I'd give you a big old kiss on the lips."

The levity startled Andy. He was studying this as if preparing to go onto the football field and launch a new play that they had never practiced, trying desperately to duplicate what Coach was telling him. "You lost me."

"You're the new generation, Kid. And you are a star. That's why you got it right. You have colleges pursuing you, Grandmasters pursuing you looking for a match; you're famous at a young age. And fame brings Staff, and that Staff we call, in the real world, Public Relations!"

Andy was beginning to get it. James pressed it. "This is the real world. This war is not being waged on some battlefield somewhere. What was it Kissinger said recently about this being the first time a private party has attacked a nation?"

"He did say that. Mom commented on that last week."

"Right. That private party lives in at least 60 different countries, camouflaged as just your 'Average Joe' in his country. He's attacking us where we live, not some chosen military battlefield. Where we live! And that is sociology, my young friend. And that enemy uses public relations to do his propaganda. He's got to look like the normal guy. You had it right. The rest of us had the dinosaur version."

The image of that was amusing to Andy. He really loved his colorful partner. But it made sense. It might have been a fluke. But hell, he'd take any break at this point in the game. They were down by ten with a two-minute warning looming.

Four hours later James and Andy had hammered out another two layers. They "trialed and erred" their way through a few options like Technology and Espionage and Education and Weapons of Mass Destruction. A lot of the list was of no value to them. They just couldn't make any of these fit into a sequence. So, most of their ideas ended up in the shredder, as they had for months. One proved productive. They shortened it to broaden the scope of the game and Andy liked that. So, one of the new labels that went onto the board and into the computer was Weapons; the other was Sociology.

Arguing back and forth, they decided not to break Sociology down. James was adamant that the solution lay in a broader investigation, not in a narrow one. The "Sociology" label certainly was broad enough. They were still missing two. But Andy was gaining confidence that he had the sequence. He and James argued back and forth about the sequence, but he held his ground. The sequence they ended the day with made sense to him. He, as a chess player, could think with it. And one led to the next. He couldn't wait to label the boards again and begin plotting the next day's data pieces.

As he logged off that night, his three-dimensional chess board was layered and labeled:

8-unknown
7-unknown
6-Sociology
5-Weapons

4-Public Relations
3-Intelligence (Counter-intelligence)
2-Military
1-Religion

He had lots of question marks on the Weapons layer. He didn't know whether that was just weapons of mass destruction or whether it included the whole arsenal of military weapons. So he just left it as Weapons.

Andy didn't know it. But he was close, very close. His adversary did, in fact, have a Weapons layer, but it was not the type of Weapons that Andy had in mind. Missing that layer would cost Andy and James dearly.

But for the first time in a long time, Andy had hope. He felt that great adrenalin rush he always felt just before he let the ball leave his hands when he was about to throw a game-winning pass.

CHAPTER 55

George Nasser had been holed up in his apartment for months now. He knew he had to stay out of sight as much as possible to avoid being seen by anyone from the University. He didn't mind if neighbors saw him, although he did wonder why they seemed to take a double-take when they passed him in the hall or met him coming out of the elevator.

Any casual neighbor observing him would have noted the changes. Nasser himself was so preoccupied with the events unfolding around the world that he hadn't really looked in the mirror lately. Normally, he was meticulously neat and always wore a crisply pressed shirt and jeans with creases in them. His beard and mustache were always immaculate. And his hair above his collar was always neatly trimmed.

But in the last few months he had let himself go. He was still bathing and tending to some personal matters, but his hair was longer and creeping over his collar. There no longer was a clear demarcation between his cheeks and his beard. And his complexion, always somewhat pale, had become pallid.

The absence of the walks he used to take to campus had not only robbed him of the little sun he did get, but had also left him out of shape. His energy and motivation were low and he was aware that the longer he sat in front of the television, the worse he felt. But he didn't see any alternative.

Nasser was desperately afraid that his friends were being killed. And he scoured the networks for any signs of their successes and failures. He waited for any news of Bin Laden, even if it had to be reported to him by the U.S. press rather than through his encoded lines via the Internet.

Twice since he took his leave of absence from his courses, he resent the message regarding the Grandmaster who had dropped out of sight and who he knew was working with the CIA. Each time the message went unanswered. He had no way of knowing that Makkawi had received both transmissions, but he had already left the response in the hands of Zawahiri. And one thing Makkawi knew was to never crowd the Doctor. The man's capacity for information and projects and management was legendary. As far as Makkawi was concerned, if the Doctor did not want to answer the communication, then it was none of his business.

Nasser had been careful to tell the University to send all mail to his apartment and that he had arranged for it to be picked up and forwarded to him in Cairo periodically. This would enhance the ruse that he was in Egypt and allow nothing to flag the attention of anyone at the university.

After the national political parties' conventions in New York and Boston, Nasser's tensions increased. The President and his challenger were preparing for debates, and the news was reporting the ever-increasing number of Al Qaeda that had been either killed or captured. Nasser was more addicted to the news than most women are to the daytime soap operas. He would get up and find out from each network when the President or Secretary Powell or Secretary Rumsfeld would be speaking live, and organize his day to monitor all their talks in hopes of gleaning something about the fate of his friends.

One day he caught the President stumping in Ohio. During his address to a Veterans of Foreign Wars luncheon the President had commented that more than 75% of Al Qaeda had been killed or captured. This was devastating to Nasser. It seemed that every time he turned on the news—WNG, Fox, CNN—they all were reporting the same: the count was rising.

He had no idea whether the reports were true. Logic told him they were probably exaggerated. Certainly the current administration had a vested interest in overstating their successes. Had it not been for the mysterious absence of response to his urgent chess move, he probably wouldn't have been so agitated. But weeks and weeks of inactivity and waiting had sapped him, and he felt so helpless.

They gave me the assignment. They must have felt it was important, he argued over and over in his mind. "They're in trouble; they must be," he had deteriorated to talking to himself aloud. "It has to have something to do with this Andrew Weir." Pouring water over his head to sharpen his senses, he added, "They are in trouble. They may be dead. I can't wait for an answer. If they are alive I must help them."

After a sleepless night of sitting out on the fire escape in the steamy late-summer weather, he made a decision that would change the course of his life forever. He packed a small bag of clothes, secured the Glock 9mm he had purchased, and arranged for a neighbor to pick up his mail. Not wanting to attract attention to his absence or arouse the super's suspicions, he paid his rent three months in advance, and sent an ample check to the utilities and phone companies to keep the apartment operational.

He removed his car from storage and made one last check to make certain he hadn't forgotten anything. Confident that no one in the building other than his reclusive neighbor would know he was gone, and even more confident that if someone checked they would think he had gone to Cairo, he crossed the George Washington Bridge.

His cover was in place. As he got closer and closer to Washington, he felt his anxiety waning. *This is the right thing to do.* "Hold on, friends, I'm coming," was the last thing he said to himself as he pulled into the Holiday Inn parking lot at the Fair Oaks Mall.

CHAPTER 56

No wonder we're so damned ineffective sometimes! Whitney thought critically. *We spend more time criticizing each other than we do anything else.* His observation of the CIA was true, in general. Over the years the Agency had been degraded to the point that self-examination had become self-flagellation. No one on the Hill trusted Langley to properly monitor itself. And recent leaks and betrayals hadn't helped.

Every time something leaked out of Langley, the White House went ballistic. "Don't you guys get that we're running a war here?" was how the chastisement usually went. The fact was they did know, but everyone inside had been so shaken by 9/11 that they were second-guessing themselves. The sense of defeat was so thick you could cut it. He didn't know how they even survived the Iraq WMD debacle. The only consolation was that the other agencies they were tightest with—Israel and Russia, and especially MI-6—had also gotten it wrong. *Hell, even Egypt and Jordan got it wrong.*

As he looked out his window at a rather dreary September afternoon, he wondered if his counterparts were catching as much hell as he was for the misevaluations. "Juvenile!" That's what the Director had said when he realized they had fallen for those photos of trucks around the alleged weapons caches. To Whitney, they had just been outfoxed was all. He wanted to tell the whole damn lot of them to shove it. Didn't they understand that war was about misinformation and deception? You try to deceive the other guy and he does the same to you.

Sure the enemy had shafted us good this time, he reflected, *but that didn't mean we had to turn on ourselves.* He, for one, was not going to doubt everything he had ever learned just because the New York

Times didn't like what had happened. And he was not going to do cartwheels every time some Senator from Massachusetts or any place else tried to bust his balls.

The only ones around Langley who seemed to have any certainty whatsoever were James Mikolas and that brainy kid. And they were under investigation for having been *"right,"* he admonished himself. *What an irony! I finally get one team that got it right, and they're the ones I'm investigating! Christ, what a lousy business this is sometimes. The suspicion, it makes you crazy!*

That was what made what he had to do next stick in his throat. Taking a deep breath he opened the door and yelled down the corridor for his deputy to get into his office.

"Is this all of it?" Whitney asked his technology team. He secretly called them the "flat-food people" because the whole bunch of them were like new-age spooks, just plain weird. But he had to give it to them; they sure knew their stuff.

The report he was reading detailed everything they had captured from Andrew Weir's computer. The "Bug Squad" handled the surveillance of the place. Nothing unusual had turned up there. If anything, the conversations showed a logical, systematic approach to analysis.

But Whitney had ordered an examination of Andrew's hard drive right after the Kid, as Mikolas called him, hit it right on the head with his theory that the weapons were gone. Given that everyone else in the whole field of intelligence, as well as the Department of Defense, had missed it, Whitney figured he'd better cover his ass by having a real good explanation as to why one of his amateur guys could have gotten it right.

It seemed like normal traffic to him. They had found nothing encoded or encrypted. Finishing it off, the last section was a breakdown of the email traffic to and from Andrew Weir. The report was thorough. He was provided the dates, the names, the addresses and subject lines in sequence.

Andy had emailed his Coach; his buddy, Brian, at the University of Southern California 12 times; a flower shop once; and a Professor Nasser seven times. Whitney was about to close the report and put it in his files when something caught his attention. He asked for more detail. One name rang a bell. That was Professor Nasser.

"Who's this?"

His deputy was prepared with background on all of the names on the sheet. It took only a minute for him to page through to his notes on Professor Nasser.

"Professor George Nasser, sir, of Columbia University. Seems he's a tenured professor in Mid-Eastern history."

Whitney knew immediately who he was. And Whitney was too experienced to believe in coincidences. He remembered all too well that he had hired Nasser to come out to Langley, of all places, to brief his team on the Hashshashin. And now, here he was turning up on Andrew Weir's emails. *I need a scotch,* he lamented as he braced himself for what would come next.

"What else you got on the Professor?" he asked tersely.

"Seems he's quite a chess aficionado. Not a player, as far as we can tell, but he's a groupie on the United States Chess Federation circuit. He's a fan for sure. And it seems he took quite a fancy to Andrew Weir. The content of the emails is definitely consistent with that of a fan."

Whitney was discouraged now. The odds of one of his reliable experts on ancient terrorism also being a chess player and seeking out a relationship with one of the CIA's assets were too long for him to take. He waited a moment and then matter-of-factly asked, "You don't happen to know where he's from do you?"

"Yes, sir, it's in his biography with Columbia University. He is from Cairo, Egypt. His father is a doctor."

"Where did he go school? Is that there, too?"

"He attended the University of Cairo in the early 1970's. He's been in the United States for almost 15 years."

Whitney paused for a moment to sip some water. His mouth was dry and he wanted just a moment to formulate his next move. Setting the report down deliberately on the end of his desk, he walked around behind it and sat down. His two deputies were standing still, waiting for some instruction.

"Good report, gentlemen."

"Thank you, sir. He seems okay, doesn't he, sir?" one of them asked with a hopeful sound in his voice. No one wants to be looking into one of their own.

"Afraid not. I want you to get the Homeland Security people on the line and I want them to get you one of those special search warrants the Patriot Act allows us. And I want you to get up to New York to the Professor's apartment and capture Nasser's computer just like you did Weir's."

Just before the two exited, he called after them, "And I need it done and reported on in 48 hours."

He couldn't help but wonder what Mikolas' role was in this. Was he in on it too, or was he being used? What did he have to gain? *Maybe it wasn't money; maybe it was access,* his mind wandered cynically. *Shut up and wait,* he admonished himself. Then he did indulge in a good strong scotch. A loud knock jolted him out of his malignant reverie.

"Come in," he shouted as he poured the remains of his drink into the sink in his private bathroom. A moment later, Fred entered.

"Boss, we have the preliminary on Nasser."

"Give it to me," Whitney said, bracing himself.

"We got into his apartment pretty easily and grabbed the content of the computer. He'll never even know we were there. Frankly, the place was a mess. Anyway, Bo here had the feeling the Professor hadn't been there in a while. So he asked around a bit while I was doing my work."

Whitney turned to Bo. He was a smooth operator. People would tell him anything.

"The neighbors say they haven't seen him in a few days; the super either."

"So, we went next to the University to get into his computer in his office, too. That was something. Man, those people are suspicious up there."

"How so?" Whitney asked.

"Well, let's just say you don't want to say 'Homeland Security' to them! We had to decide whether to break in and do it, or try the power of persuasion."

"I can guess," Whitney joked a bit.

"No. We decided to walk in straight up. They were resentful and gave us an earful, but a warrant is a warrant, even on the upper west side of New York."

Bo then added seriously, "Thing of it was though, boss, they said he left months ago."

Whitney leaned forward and thrust his jaw out. "Then you had better get me a real bio on this guy. I want to know everyone he's been connected to since he was in diapers and I want to see what he's been doing on those computers. Understood?"

"Yes, sir, but that may take cooperation from Cairo."

"You'll have it."

James had left his car in the shop near Andy's and had taken the subway back into the District after Andy had given him a lift to Arlington Cemetery. Andy, then, had gone to see his dad's grave. Dropping down the two flights to the subterranean tracks, James had to wait a few minutes for the train.

Once he got on the train, he was grateful it had to make only a few stops. The stridency of the conversations on the train about the elections and the war was just too much for him. Everywhere he tried to sit, someone was arguing loudly with someone else over some headline or another.

Even when he got up and out of there, he could see and feel anger and tension all around him. He reminded himself that he was just sensitive to that kind of stuff. He had had to be to stay alive when he was in the field. But this was worse than that. People seemed to be spilling out of the stores on their way home and exploding into frustration and debate. He stopped into a bar on the corner but darted out quickly when he saw their split screens were on WNG and CNN.

He was so sick and tired of talking heads that he wanted to take out his pistol and shoot out the screens. Then he argued with himself for awhile about why anyone would need to have four TVs in one bar, and better yet, why they would have them all on different channels.

The cacophony of shrill voices tromping on each other's sentences, refusing to allow anyone to complete a thought, had him frazzled. The inside of his apartment had never looked so good to him. For once, he didn't mind the silence when he came in. Without even turning on a light, he collapsed on his sofa and went unconscious.

"We traced Nasser to Cairo University." Bo was the one to give him the news.

"Tell me something I don't know," Whitney demanded.

"Let me cut to the chase. Cairo confirms he knew Ayman Al-Zawahiri, took a few classes with him. Turns out they keep pretty accurate records in their universities, too."

That was the one thing Whitney did not want to hear. This was such a nightmare. "You got any more bad news?"

Bo shook his head no, but his partner ventured, "Actually, yes, well maybe…"

"Let me have it."

"Nasser logged onto the Internet often. The most frequently visited site is a chess site where he has a game going on. But there's something odd about it."

"What?"

"Well, I almost didn't notice it, but I did. So I included it there for you."

Fred waited and then continued on his own, "He made a move and sent it."

"So?' Whitney didn't follow.

"There was no answer. That's what caught my eye. So, he repeated the move again. He did it a total of five times: five moves, but all were the same move."

"What's your take on that?" Whitney wasn't certain he was following this. He wasn't really up on the protocols of Internet chess so he didn't know if this was unusual or not.

"Either he doesn't have a game partner, and he's playing one-way chess, which I doubt, or…."

"What?"

"His partner is unable to respond."

"I don't suppose you can identify where that Internet communication ended up?" Whitney asked.

"No sir, regrettably not. But it must be important though, because he logged on to this site far more often than just the moves he made. If you'll look at the pattern of his logging on, it was daily for many months, then it trended up to multiple times daily. Look at the last two weeks though, sir."

What Whitney saw caused his flesh to crawl. Nasser had been logging in to the site every hour for more than two weeks. It was the consensus among the analysts that whatever he was expecting was very important and that he was anxious about it. They were most concerned about the last thing in the report—Nasser had stopped logging in six days ago. That coincided with the last time the neighbors remember seeing or hearing him.

Whitney asked only one question at that point, "Did someone answer his move?"

"No. Not by computer at least. He may have gotten a message some other way."

He'd deceived the University. He'd deceived the building super. He was gone. He'd gone to ground. Whitney was decisive in his next orders. "Get on to his credit cards and bank accounts. Trace any transaction since the last login."

"Do we notify Mikolas?" Fred asked. "Maybe we should warn him, you know, give him a heads up."

"No." Whitney's answer startled the two men. But they'd been in the game a long time, and they knew not to question. "Put HR on it." "HR" in their lingo meant, put human resources on it, and that meant a field operative.

The next day an ordinary-looking man who said he was an engineer on a one-month project in the District took an efficiency apartment in the building across the street from James Mikolas' apartment. He was very specific that he needed an apartment with a view of the street.

CHAPTER 57

Makkawi's call had been disturbing to the Doctor. Apparently Atef had not properly explained to Makkawi that the War in Afghanistan could not possibly be won, and that the one in Iraq would be very costly. In fact, the only way they could win there was if Samir's campaigns produced the ultimate objective in the ideal time. The Doctor had learned through the years not to count on "ultimates" and "ideals," but he did have to admit things were going better than planned.

What was confusing was whether or not Makkawi had briefed Zarqawi properly. The man seemed to be operating independently. Zarqawi's announcement that his terrorist group was linked to Al Qaeda certainly came as no surprise to anyone, except a few rabid politicians. But his timing was dreadful. They had the White King where they wanted him, losing on all matters of public relations. Now Zarqawi shoots off his mouth and Samir has a new problem to deal with.

Fortunately, the tone of argument in the United States and Britain had escalated to ferocious personal attacks, and what might have been a bright spot in public relations in the United States was almost ignored altogether. The Doctor ascribed that to the stellar job Samir had done in co-opting the U.S. press. He shook his head in amusement every time he heard some anchorman or interviewer give deference to anything the French said. The press was now starting to copy verbatim some of the questions and answers given in the foreign press, and the American people were copying the United States press. *And to think, all it took was an exploitation of human nature.*

He preferred it, however, when Zarqawi just stuck to warfare. With Nanda gone, there was no one there with judgment to reign in this man's lust for attention now. They knew when they promoted him that this would be his weakness. *If only Nanda hadn't lost his backbone. I could use him now.* But at least he knew Zarqawi had his head in the game. The Doctor would tolerate his flamboyance since he knew the time was drawing near when the United States and the Iraqi military would launch an assault on Fallujah.

The handover of authority to the Provisional Government and the assumption of control by Allawi were forcing some military battles. Zarqawi had failed so far to have Allawi assassinated, so he was in his fall-back plan now to prevent, at all costs, the elections from happening.

To the Doctor's surprise, the murder, mutilation and hangings of the security agents from the bridge in Fallujah had not slowed down the juggernaut at all. Zarqawi's immediate answer was to increase the frequency and brutality of the kidnappings and beheadings. He was applying pressure to all governments who had personnel in the area. Still, the resolve of those governments did not seem to be weakening.

It was then that Zarqawi took one of his most reprehensible steps. He kidnapped Margaret Hassan as a warning to governments, aid agencies, and civilians alike that no one was exempt from the insurgency. This is what had prompted Makkawi's call. He had informed the Doctor that she had been forced to make a video and that she had been killed. Makkawi felt this was a mistake and that Zarqawi would suffer for it when news of her death came out.

The Doctor agreed, but there was nothing he could do about it now. Assuaging Makkawi he ordered him to prepare Zarqawi for Coalition assaults upon his strongholds and for the loss of many men.

"How many?" Makkawi had asked.

"Fifty-percent in the first assault. Make certain Zarqawi and his top lieutenants have left the area. They are not to fight at Fallujah. Use the same war plan we used in Tora Bora. It worked and the Americans still haven't figured it out. Only this time, I want his attacks in other cities to be multiple and simultaneous. He will lose another 25 percent when the enemy counterattacks. Be sure he understands this."

Makkawi had been silent for a moment.

"Are you still there?" the Doctor asked.

"Yes. The reality is just setting in. Muhammad told me this was inevitable; he wanted me operating in another theater."

"Yes, Muhammad Atef was perhaps the most brilliant military strategist I have ever had the privilege of working with. Your time is yet to come, my friend. You have a mission yet to fulfill, but it will involve weapons that will guarantee the success of our overall mission. You will not see this kind of slaughter of our men again. In the future, the ones falling by the millions will be the enemy. I assure you."

That seemed to have done it for Makkawi. He resigned himself to what lay ahead and returned to his planning of attacks on multiple continents. Frankly, he was relieved not to be carrying the responsibility of what was about to happen in Iraq. His war plans required he turn his attention to the establishment of alternate bases for Al Qaeda and the training of the men who would begin the softening of each of those areas.

Personally he liked the dry, forbidding mountainous terrains that had harbored him for so long, but he had the feeling he was about to have to acclimate to more tropical climates. He hoped their overall war plan would work and the Americans would withdraw from Iraq, leaving the country in chaos. If all went well, they would then have Iraq and all its resources at their disposal. If not, he would be prepared. Realistically, they had many choices of location. It was just a matter of money as to what it would take to ramp up. And the Doctor had assured him money would be no problem. As good as their enemy was at finding their financial sources, there were still money lines the intelligence agencies neither knew about nor suspected. By the time he and Ayman had finished talking, he was back in the game. His next phone call was to Zarqawi.

The Doctor on the other hand was confirming in his own mind that the war plans were in fact still viable. He recalled the Chinese definition for crisis: opportunity riding a dangerous wind. That definition was particularly significant for him. These times were indeed a crisis for Al Qaeda, and for the elimination of the degradation and debauchery of the West that their movement represented. But they were also the times of their greatest opportunity. And for him, personally, it was a great opportunity. He would not have another like it. Confident that he could ride out the dangerous wind, he concluded the plans were viable and braced himself for what was to come. The only concern he had at the moment was the acid reflux reaction he was getting from his agitated ulcer. The burning was particularly painful today and it broke his concentration a bit. He was just turning off the lights in his office when his private line rang.

Taking the call, he was surprised to hear Rudi Iseli's voice on the other end. It was a bit late in the day for him. Iseli was famous in Geneva for knocking off early. He liked fine dining and he liked the casinos, so he and his staff wrapped up their days early.

"To what do I owe the honor, Rudi?"

"I'm so glad I caught you. You will receive a written invitation, of course, but I wanted to personally invite you to a reception the World Health Organization is holding immediately following their convention."

"Thank you, I appreciate that," the Doctor said, having no intention of going.

But Rudi Iseli knew his investor too well. "Now see, that's why I called you directly, Phillipe. I knew you would find some excuse to miss this and I really feel it's important for you, for us. I need you there to assist us in capturing the loyalty of these bureaucratic department heads when they need medications in the future. You know how fickle they can be. And I believe we deserve a bigger share of their business."

Phillipe Monet agreed to attend, in order not to alienate or offend his business associate. The reality was that he was making most of his money from the United States. The greatest demand was for their psychiatric pharmaceuticals and that demand was limited primarily to the United States. He had designed it so; and through the efforts of Samir, they had accomplished it. He frankly didn't really care about the rest of Europe, with the exception of Britain. For that reason, he decided to accompany Rudi Iseli to an elaborate, exclusive black tie affair in a chateau on the edge of Lake Zurich. Had he not been distracted by the severe and stabbing burning in his esophagus, he might have made a different choice.

Andrew Weir had told James that sooner or later his opponent would make a mistake. In deciding to attend the event, the Doctor had made his first mistake.

CHAPTER 58

It was a magnificent fall evening on the banks of Lake Zurich. The three-day World Health Organization's conference had ended just hours earlier. Attendance was mandatory for government agencies from every signatory nation and included all humanitarian aid agencies as well. Scientists, bureaucrats, administrators, and the "Angels" that supported the programs were all there.

Though it was true that governments of the wealthier nations contributed handsomely to the research and humanitarian projects the WHO embraced, some of their greatest financial contributions came from private citizens or corporations.

Decu-Hehiz not only secured contracts from the WHO, but it also gave generously to the organization. Under Rudi Iseli's leadership the company had risen to the pinnacle of publicized corporate responsibility. Rudi felt it was just good business to contribute to the very organizations that turned around and then offered you contracts. There was no quid pro quo. There didn't need to be, in his mind. His company was the best, after all. Why wouldn't WHO buy from Decu-Hehiz?

Monet had agreed to ride in Iseli's limousine from Geneva. This was uncharacteristic of him. Usually he drove himself so that he could leave whenever he felt he needed to. But Iseli had promised to review some business reports with him on the way, and to make the ride a truly pleasant one. Against his better judgment, he accepted the invitation.

The party was well-started when Iseli's limousine arrived. He knew there would be dignitaries and socialites as well attending the soirée and he expected there to be a crush of limousines at the beginning of the evening. Rudi Iseli had a flare for drama and he wanted to make sure he and his illustrious guest did not arrive anonymously or unnoticed.

In fact, as they pulled up, the valets quickly helped them out onto the red carpet that had been laid for special dignitaries. The local Zurich press was there and flashbulbs were going off constantly.

Wanting to stay away from the camera, Phillipe Monet quickly made his way up the carpet and into the party where he felt certain there would be no reporters or paparazzi. It was definitely quieter inside. Most of the guests were standing in clusters of three or four, talking to each other in the kind of hushed voices that people of pretense often adopt in such circumstances. No one wanted their vocals to stand out. They took great pains to stand out in their apparel and overall bearing, but no one wanted to embarrass himself by calling attention to himself needlessly.

The dinner was served buffet-style with elegant candle-lit tables dotting the property. The chateau dated back to King Ludwig's time and looked truly remarkable in the candle light. Torches lighted the outer terraces and lined a walkway down to the lake so that the guests could enjoy the sunset.

Typically, a quartet was situated in the ballroom, providing a delicate enhancement to the festivities. Phillipe Monet fit in. No one in the room would have noticed him. Perhaps the only thing separating him from the other guests was the fact that he did not drink. He had asked the waiter for a glass of ice water and had spent the evening nursing a clear drink.

He had been enjoying the view of the lake and the sound of the rustling birch leaves as they traded green for yellow in the autumn breezes. Out of the corner of his eye, he seemed to note a flash or two and heard a surge in the laughter inside the chateau. He seemed to also hear muffled applause, but he wasn't sure of that. Passing by on the lake was a dinner boat that toured Lake Zurich during the summer. It was closed for seasonal traffic, but was entertaining one last group—a private party from some local insurance company. It was the distinctly loud laughter emanating from that boat that masked the sounds from within the chateau.

The Doctor made his way back in just in time to have Rudi seize his arm and say loudly, "There you are. I have someone I want you to meet."

Before the Doctor could dodge the social ambush, he found himself being pushed forward and slightly to the right by Rudi. Reaching over, Iseli tapped another man on the arm and turned him around to face Phillipe and himself.

In the next instant, Phillipe Monet was introduced to the Director of one of Zurich's largest financial institutions. Its 14-story building was visible anywhere in Zurich. Through its doors passed billions and billions of dollars of business. The Director was one of the pillars of Zurich society and one of the most respected financiers in the area.

What the Doctor did not know was that a photographer had been hired for the party. His assignment was to get pictures of all the prominent people in attendance and get the pictures ready for the society page or front page, depending on how interesting the news was.

At the moment Rudi thrust Phillipe Monet and the Director together the two men shook hands. Under the command of the photographer, the Director deftly turned the Doctor to the camera and smiled. There was a flash.

It had happened so fast, the Doctor didn't have time for his reflexes to take over. Having his picture taken was bad enough, but it was not the greatest of his concerns. The second he was introduced to the Director, he recognized him as the man Bin Laden had selected to head up one of their largest money-laundering operations. The entire financial operation was a front for Al Qaeda.

Up until now there seemed to be no awareness of the man's affiliations, let alone his company's. But the Doctor knew that it was only a matter of time before investigators in the United States or Britain would trace the money lines back to this institution. Some of the greatest, though least publicized, successes the West had had in their War on Terror had come in the financial arena. Interpol was cooperating totally and was very effective. No one in Al Qaeda linked directly to money-laundering operations was safe.

The Doctor had taken great pains, however, to secure his own financial dealings in totally legitimate businesses that would never come under scrutiny.

He felt a sudden burning in his esophagus as his ulcer acted up. Adrenalin was flowing and his pulse was racing. He had just been photographed with a man he knew would end up being arrested. It was only a matter of time.

Knowing the intelligence community as well as he did, he knew the minute the Director was implicated, analysts would be pouring over pictures of every known associate or contact the Director had. The identities of anyone photographed with him for any reason would be sought. Investigations would commence on all of these people. That's how they pulled the string, followed the money, and ultimately found the financial lines. One face led to another.

Trying to calm himself, the Doctor excused himself quickly and headed into the rest room. He needed a moment to think. He knew the man, but the Director, of course, did not know what Zawahiri looked like. If asked about Ayman Al-Zawahiri, he believed what the rest of the world believed—that Nanda's father was Zawahiri.

He felt safe from identification as Zawahiri by the Director. But he knew he was vulnerable now to someone identifying him as Phillipe Monet. If an investigator dug deep, they would discover that Phillipe Monet's background was sketchy. And that should raise a flag.

It was all so unexpected. *Why did I come?* he whined to himself. Then the paranoia that ruled Zawahiri flared. He began to wonder if Rudi had somehow set him up. The Doctor, for some time, had seen everyone as an enemy. He knew that sooner or later everyone would reveal their true colors and he debated now as to whether Rudi had turned.

But rationality prevailed. He concluded that Rudi Iseli had no idea about any of this. It had just been an accident, an unfortunate accident. What he had to do now was present some reasonable excuse why he couldn't rejoin the party and run the risk of being photographed again. Had he driven himself, he would have just left. But as Iseli's guest he was dependent upon Rudi to leave the party. Beckoning an eager valet, he asked the man to tell Mr. Iseli that his friend was suffering from an attack of one of his ulcers and that he would be lying down until it was time to leave.

As he expected, Rudi excused himself immediately and graciously offered to drive his friend home. Pretending to be sick was not difficult. The situation with his ulcer was real and he welcomed the medication he could take once he returned home. This had caught him off-guard and he had to decide what to do. It was a long ride home in the silence and darkness of the limousine as it glided through the Swiss foothills.

CHAPTER 59

George Nasser was comfortable in his hotel room. Because the desk team knew him from his previous stay with them, and addressed him by his name, they did not even notice that he was paying with cash. Rather than use his credit card where his location could be traced by transactions, he had withdrawn money from his accounts before leaving New York.

The bulk of the cash was on his person, in envelopes containing $100 bills inside his coat pockets. The rest was in his room. He was nervous about that as he had no idea whether or not he could trust the maids at the Holiday Inn. When he saw that he had the same lady he had had the last time he stayed there and, better yet, that she recognized him, he relaxed a bit.

He was quite certain no one would know where he was. And he also believed deep down that there would be no reason for anyone to be looking for him. *After all,* he reassured himself, *I'm not on anyone's radar screen. I'm just a professor.*

Feeling secure, he called Domino's pizza to inquire whether or not Andrew Weir was still delivering pizza. He was told he no longer worked there, but they would send someone else if he wanted to order pizza. Frankly, pizza was one of his least favorite foods and he was grateful not to have to force himself to eat it. His budget was limited. *Not like those other guys who had millions to work with and airline tickets whenever they needed it. No, me they put watching chess matches—and on my own dollar as well! Well, they will soon learn just how they underestimated me. I'll be one of the great heroes of this war. I just hope I'm in time.*

CHAPTER 60

"I can't do this." That was all he said.

James just leaned back in his chair and looked at Andy. Something in Andy's demeanor made James reach for the remote and turn the television off. Watching it live had had its advantages, but it also had its drawbacks. They were subjected to all forms of negative and an almost constant chatter.

This relentless barrage of bad news was affecting them both. Watching TV, one could almost feel each news item reverberating through the public. One could almost experience a shock wave. James had felt it too. He wondered if this shaking and trembling was what they felt in the World Trade Center that morning, before the unthinkable happened. He wondered if they had any idea the towers were collapsing, or if they thought it was just a bad shock they could ride out. Recently, he had come to fear his own country was falling apart. And he had no idea how this had happened. He tried to push these doomsday thoughts out of his mind, but the truth was James felt in more danger now than at any point in his life. He had hoped the Kid hadn't noticed. But it seemed now the Kid was ravaged by it too.

He reminded himself that analysts look at pieces of data, outside the total context. Most of the story is actually missing. They have interest in certain isolated pieces of data and often work them into a new context. With the TV on, their ideas and thoughts were being influenced by the tone and content of what they were hearing. Their work had magnified it. That was all.

The room was quiet now. The only sound was Andy tapping one of his feet on the floor, a habit he had developed recently. James was sure it was nerves. They had placed an arbitrary deadline on themselves and that deadline was approaching. Try as they did, they had not isolated the top two layers of Zawahiri's game. Nothing they thought up made any sense, least of all in the context of the other six games.

Andy was starting to get scared that he had missed it altogether.

Finally, when he felt he might get an answer, James ventured a question, "Can't do what?"

Andy's lip started to quiver first, then his shoulders would rise and fall as he seemed to be struggling for breath. It was as if he had had the wind knocked out of him and he was struggling for breath. That was apparently the case, for Andy was in fact struggling for breath. He felt as if he couldn't breathe; as if he were under water and unable to surface. And he felt he was slipping and in danger of letting go.

"Andy, what?" James nudged.

Andy's voice cracked. "I can't solve it."

"We're close, Andy, I can feel it. Just a little farther."

"Bull! We're not close and you know it." The outburst startled James. They had never come to blows in the three years they had worked together. But he felt somehow that the Kid was looking for a fight.

"Have you been watching this crap, James?" Pointing to the television he shouted, "The insanity that's out there. One of these guys just suggested the War on Terror is a metaphor, like the War on Poverty! What an idiot! What news is he watching? Didn't he see that they took that poor woman? What about those 40 soldiers that were massacred last night on their way home from boot camp? Is that a metaphor? What fantasy world are these people living in?"

James knew he needed to blow off steam, so he just waited for the explosion to dissipate.

"And the woman, what's her name?"

"Hassan. Margaret Hassan?"

"Right. Is she a metaphor too? My dad was a young man when Johnson created his War on Poverty. We talked about it. But no one was being murdered by these beasts in the War on Poverty. This is no goddamned metaphor! These people are brilliant beyond belief and all we can do is argue with ourselves. Have all these people on television gone crazy?"

Andy was serious. Weeks of having to watch the news channels had started him spinning with visions of Americans arguing with Americans. "My God, James, they act like we're the enemy. How are we supposed to help anybody that dumb? How can anybody that dumb survive?"

"It's crazy Andy, I know. But you can't let it get to you. We can figure out this game, I know it. And we can put this guy out of business."

"No, no we can't, James." Andy's voice was choking now. He was struggling to hold back tears. His face was red and flushed with rage. "Zawahiri's playing a game that doesn't even exist except in science fiction. He's playing 8x8x8 three-dimensional chess with rules he's made up. For all I know he's playing with the ghost of Herr Doktor Ferdinand Maack!" Tears were starting to flow down his cheeks now as he grimaced.

"He moves any piece, anywhere, anytime. It's like he takes all the opponent's pieces and turns them into his own. He doesn't capture pieces like in a normal game; he commandeers them. Let me show you."

Andy took James over to the eight clear glass boards that represented the three-dimensional game they were hypothesizing. He pointed to the Military game, second from the bottom. "You see that?"

"Yeah, I see a Black Knight."

"Right. See how he's sitting in the middle of the action. A Knight can leap. It doesn't bother him to be in the midst of other pieces. That's Zarqawi right now. He can be anywhere. He leaps out of the cities he's been in, leaving our troops and his own scratching their heads wondering where he went."

James just listened. "But look at this. Now he's a Rook in the Intelligence game. Zawahiri moves him to a different game and now Zarqawi's a Rook. He's a damned tank rolling over any opening we get in intelligence. He kills anybody who's even thinking of talking to us or the Iraqis. He's shut down the intel. Now watch this…the Public Relations game. See, Zawahiri moves him up to that game. But here Zarqawi's a pawn. It makes no sense. This man makes any piece into whatever piece he wants them to be in whichever game he decides to engage. It's crazy."

Andy had violated one of his own operating policies. *You can't win if you're overcome with emotion.* Too much association with hysterical emotion had brought up emotion in him. If his head had been clear he would have been able to see that he was on the cusp of it. Andy had presumed there was just one set of chess pieces being moved around to different layers of game boards. His perspective was off; Zawahiri actually had complete chess sets on each layer. He had also accepted James' theory that Zawahiri was in fact playing chess. That was also not true.

Zawahiri was using chess boards merely to keep track of the personnel in the various theaters of operation he was creating simultaneously. Only that. The players didn't change identities. The Doctor was simply moving their name tag to the chess piece they represented in the maneuver he was working on.

Andy was right. Zarqawi could be a Knight in one game and a Rook in another. It was not, however, Zarqawi's chess piece that was moving. It was simply the label "Zarqawi" that was moving. Andy was so close to identifying what Zawahiri was doing that only his irrational emotion short-circuited his resolving the problem right there. But he was too far gone into the emotional indulgence that had also seized his nation. He missed it.

"I see." James didn't, but he could see Andy was in a lot of pain.

"It gets worse, James. If that wasn't bad enough, there are also no rules. Three-dimensional chess. Pieces changing identities. I could handle all that, until this." Andy grabbed James and pulled him around to his side. "I want you to look at this from the top down. You see all those White pieces there on the various levels?"

"Yes. What of them?"

Pointing to some prominent chess pieces on the board Andy spat out, "These are the Bishops, James. See their label—"the Press." Remember? They're the standard bearers of truth and information. These are the Rooks, James. These tanks should be out there mowing down anyone assailing him. It doesn't matter whether the Rooks are his press corps or his generals or members of his party. They should be protecting him. They're not. Now, look at the Knights. They should be defending something. But they're Abu Ghraib. They are AWOL marines that turn up God knows where. They are Cabinet members who defect. They are news shows lying and distorting. Whoever the hell they are—however we labeled them—they aren't doing their job!"

James was beginning to feel uneasy now. He had a terrible wave of fear hit him. Andy continued, "And look at the pawns. Look at those soldiers that are going to be put on trial. Pawns. But they are attacking their own King. Look at the Sociology game. We identified the pawns as the people. The Knights, Bishops, the Rooks are all opinion leaders. That's when I got it."

"Okay, Kid; you got my attention."

"Every single piece we placed on this board from the data we are retrieving from live television is facing in one direction and one direction only." James looked down and it nearly took his breath away. From the top down, there were pieces covering squares on the various chess boards. Half were Black, poised for attack. It was the White pieces that caused James' heart to almost slow down. They were all facing their own King. They were squaring off with the White King.

"He has somehow commandeered every White piece on the board and is using them to augment his own forces and materiel. Look at the White King. He's completely surrounded. He has no move he can make. He's stuck."

"My God..." James exhaled.

Andy's tears of frustration had deteriorated to sobbing now. "I feel so helpless, James. I can't play an opponent that plays a game that doesn't exist with rules he makes up. There's nothing I can do." It was all he could say. Andy sat there in total defeat.

And there was nothing James could do. He himself did not know where to turn. He never thought the game would manifest itself like this. He didn't know what to do, so he just sat and listened to Andy drain his reservoir of frustration.

After awhile Andy started to fold up the game. Layer by layer he took it apart. James decided to leave him alone for a few minutes and just give the Kid some room. They'd try again tomorrow. He went upstairs to the kitchen to get a glass of water. Kelly was sitting at the kitchen table, soaking her feet. She looked worried.

"You look like him now," she commented unexpectedly.

"What?" James asked.

"You look as bad as Andy does. You know, these three years, I've never asked what you were doing down there. You promised me this would not be dangerous. I want you to tell me now it is not dangerous, James; I want you to tell me that." Her voice was tremulous and there was desperation in her tone. She feared for her son and she had every right to demand reassurance from the man who had put him in harm's way.

"It's not…" James couldn't bring himself to say it wasn't dangerous. How do you define the value of hope and optimism and confidence? Andy had had all of those traits. And the young man downstairs had lost them all. It was dangerous, after all. He didn't know what to tell her. Finally he just whispered, "He'll be all right, Kelly, I promise you that."

"You promise?" Kelly asked through her tear-filled eyes. She wanted to believe. She needed to believe.

A moment later they heard the front door slam. Andy was gone.

CHAPTER 61

Nasser had been watching the house for three days. Andy's car wasn't there and each night he didn't return. By the third night George Nasser was desperate. In the absence of information, he assumed the worst. He had dubbed in that Andy and his man, James, were plotting right now and involved right now in the death or entrapment of his friends.

Determined to help them, he returned to the hotel one last time. Checking out of his room, he was careful to leave an excellent tip for the maid. He quietly paid his bill. The young man on duty was new. George had never seen him before. It was October 29, his mother's birthday. He wondered if she would be proud of him.

In his car, he loaded the Glock 9mm with a full clip and pulled out of the parking lot.

He missed the breaking news that Usama Bin Laden had released a video tape.

Samir took the call when his secretary said it was an urgent call from Phillipe Monet. He had no idea what the Doctor was talking about when he brutally dressed Samir down for such a blunder of a PR move.

"I have no idea what you are talking about, Ayman. Slow down."

It took a few moments for Zawahiri to realize that the tape of Usama Bin Laden venturing his opinion about the United States

President had not come from them. He had seen the script for it. He had seen Usama tape it. In fact, they had taped it repeatedly, substituting different names for the Democrats they felt might end up running against Bush. They had contrived it from the history of the Afghanistan War with the Russians. Using rhetoric like "rising death toll, quagmire, black gold, and collapsing economy" they had assumed that the United States would experience what the Russians did. So they had scripted a generic address to be used to their advantage at some time during the war.

Different countries that might end up as the second theater of operation had been written into versions two and up. Nanda had said they would do a "one size fits all" type of tape and just change the color by changing the countries and the personnel. The Vice President's name was even included in one in the event of the hoped-for death of President Bush. They had a version for Tony Blair and Britain as well.

Once Nanda had been killed, Zawahiri had ordered that all copies Nanda might have had of any videos be sent to Samir. Samir had retrieved all of the ones that were with the go-between. So, either the go-between had decided to release it, or Zarqawi had. Those were the only two options. He knew, without asking, that it was Zarqawi. The fool was a military man, not a public relations man. Only someone as headstrong as he would be out of touch enough to think this video would frighten anyone.

The Doctor had a right to be livid. Samir had the enemy right where he wanted him. The United States was on the verge of holding the most dangerous and disruptive election in its history. The press had jumped all over his button about election fraud and machine malfunction. That was easy. The event he was drawing upon to fuel the upset was, after all, only four years old. He could almost feel the psychosis come up, even in Paris.

Thousands of lawyers were poised to make a living hell out of the coming months, and strangle the United States in its own freedom. The people were afraid. Doctors were prescribing medications in huge numbers to handle the anxiety.

One famous news anchor had gone so far as to poll his audience to see if they felt the United States should ask an international body to step in and monitor the election process.

Ten years ago the man would have been considered a traitor, or laughed off the air for being insane. The fact that he got the go-ahead to ask such an absurd question, and the fact that Americans scrambled to their computers to respond to it, was proof to both Samir and Zawahiri that they had them.

And now this. The Doctor knew in his gut that this would produce the opposite effect. This was going to boomerang.

All he could do right now was say, "I'm sorry, Samir. I apologize for even thinking you would have been so stupid." Then, not wanting to tip his hand, he added, "It seems one of our team feels you need a little help. Rest assured I'll straighten him out."

Samir was relieved to be off the hook and didn't even notice the sinister tone in his mentor's last remark. The two parted cordially.

Chapter 62

"What do you make of the latest video?" Whitney asked as James passed him on the way to his office.

"What video?" James had not turned on the television since Andy walked out. He had had enough, and was frankly worried about his young friend. He'd seen this kind of collapse before. Some men came back; some did not. But he was kicking himself for bringing someone without training or experience into such a long assignment. He honestly hadn't thought it would be that dangerous mentally. But who knew?

"Usama Bin Laden released a video."

"Let me guess, he says he loves George Bush and we should all support him now," James murmured sarcastically.

James always did have a sense of humor. "Not quite." Whitney was reluctant to get into too much of a conversation with James given the suspicions he had. He needed to keep a clear head about him. So he asked what he thought was a Chatty-Cathy type of question. "What are you doing in here so early?" He was stunned at James' answer.

"Actually, Boss, I came in to talk to you. The Kid disappeared three days ago. He just got overwhelmed and couldn't handle it. I don't know where he is."

If James had been on his game, he would have seen Whitney pale in front of him.

I can't believe this is happening to me, Whitney despaired. Nasser had disappeared; and now the Kid. And James was telling him, rather than keeping it a secret. It really made no sense, unless James was setting up a cover for himself. Whitney knew that he had to tread very carefully here.

"How's his mother taking it?"

"Not well. She's worried sick."

"Did you try the usual hangouts, the usual friends?"

"Yeah. Nothing. So I thought I'd come in here, see if I could be any help on anything else."

"Right. Good idea." He was winging it now. "See what comes to mind on this Bin Laden thing."

James seemed to accept that as a way of getting his attention off his missing partner, so Whitney took the opportunity to withdraw quickly to his office and make a phone call.

CHAPTER 63

It was Monday, November 1, 2004. Andy walked in the front door, looking the worse for wear. He was unshaven and disheveled, and his eyes were bloodshot. The first thing he did was to dart into the kitchen and give Kelly a kiss on the head. She was so startled she didn't even know how to speak

"Don't worry, Mom. It's going to be all right. I'll explain later, I promise." Before she could object, he added, "I'm sorry for disappearing like that. But right now I've got to reach James." The next second he was gone into the basement.

James was in a meeting with three other analysts when he got the page. It was Andy's special number, followed by 911. That was their code for an emergency. James was out of there and had Andy's number dialed before he even cleared the door.

"Yeah, Kid, what's up?" He didn't want to sound too anxious.

There was true exhilaration in Andy's voice. "Get over here, James. I figured it out. I know where to find him!"

James drove as fast as the traffic in D.C. would allow. He was so preoccupied with that last sentence of Andy's that he didn't notice the car parked across the street from Andy's house. And he didn't notice the car that had been following him.

George Nasser had been relieved to see Andy drive up. He had planned to give it one more day and he congratulated himself on his patience. Seeing James racing up the steps and into the house was exactly what he had hoped for. He had them both where he wanted them. He knew, though, that the mother was in the house as well and he regretted what he was going to have to do. But he just didn't see any other way.

Carefully, he placed the pistol in his coat pocket and settled back to wait until dark. He, too, failed to notice a burgundy sedan pull up, slow down a bit, and then disappear around the back of the house.

"I've been thinking about what you showed me last week, Andy. Sure makes you appreciate what they must be going through over there at 1600 Pennsylvania Avenue," he joked feebly.

"Yeah!" Andy grinned and James could see he was back.

"You look like hell, Kid. What have you been doing?"

"Watching TV." Andy said nothing more, but he still had that grin on his face.

"For three days?"

"Yup. And I found something very interesting. While you were on the way over here, I tried it out on the board and it fit. I was just ready to put it into the computer."

"Okay, step me through it slowly. I haven't had much sleep. I was worried about my partner." James knew Andy would take the gentle reproach properly. He did.

"Sorry. But you'll be glad I did blow my cork. If I hadn't, I wouldn't have found it."

"I'm starting to get excited over here, Kid. Let's have a look."

"First, let me explain what happened. I was pretty bummed out if you remember," Andy asserted, setting the stage. James nodded he did. "You know, I've been living in this box for three years. There are days I feel like a mole and I've got nothing to show for it. So I took off and checked into a motel to get away. I had some hair-brained idea I'd 'veg out' and watch a bunch of John Wayne westerns on cable."

James laughed. Andy continued, "But when I got there and had paid already, I discovered they had only cable news. Bummer, right?"

"Right."

"No. Wrong. But I didn't know that. So I lay back on the bed and just stared at the news. I think it was WNG. I wasn't really watching any of it. It was just more blather like we've already overloaded ourselves with. So I would only perk up when a commercial came on. Did you know they crank up the volume on those things?"

"No, not really." James had never paid attention to them frankly, and he had no idea where Andy was going with this.

"Well they do, trust me. Even if I had been trying to sleep, they would have awakened me. Now here's where it gets interesting see. I'm just kind of catatonic during the news, but I wake up for the commercials. Then I'd change channels and the same thing would happen. So pretty soon I'm watching commercials—only commercials."

James still had no idea where this was going, but he hadn't seen that look in Andy's eyes since he won the Conference title three years ago. James just sat down and listened. The next question, however, was totally unexpected.

"James, when did they stop advertising toilet paper and cereal?"

"You lost me, Kid."

Andy continued, "I remember TV. They used to advertise cute little kids and funny people with their toilet paper and cereals and hair spray. When did that change?"

"I don't know, Kid, my recollection is that they have different commercials for different types of shows. You know, the show sells the product. That's why the advertiser picks the slot."

"Bingo!" Andy exclaimed. "You got it."

"What?"

"The show sells the product. So what does news sell?"

James knew the answer to that. "It sells stuff like Pepto-Bismol and Bayer and Sominex. Once you've watched the news you need that stuff because you've got an upset stomach, a headache, and you can't sleep." James thought he was making a joke, but the look on Andy's face said he was in earnest.

"Not bad for an old guy. But I would say you haven't watched a commercial since Carter was in office."

"What's on there now?" James asked innocently.

"Pharmaceuticals—kind of like over-the-counter on speed. It's hardcore stuff, James. Most of the ads promote anxiety and depression, and great products on how to not feel so fearful and anxious. It's not limited to news either. I changed to some of the nighttime soaps, some of Mom's favorites, and it was all the same. 'Tell your Doctor you need....' It was all the same basically. Take a drug. It was all about drugs."

Andy paused for James to digest this. James struggled a bit. "Are you saying the news and television sell drugs?"

"I'm saying their content makes people feel they need a medication. They might have felt okay at dinner, by the time they watch their favorite news show, they feel awful and the ad reminds them they need something."

James was feeling a tiny adrenalin rush and the shortness of breath he recognized. It was a welcome feeling right now.

"James, I didn't do as well in history as I could have, but I remember most of what my dad talked to me about. He told me one day what it meant to guard the Tomb. The Unknown Soldier represented the anonymous soul that preserved our freedom. He taught me about communism and how they would take and brainwash and drug their people to keep them submissive. And he used a term I hadn't thought about in a long time. Then I got it. I just got it."

James knew what was next even before the Kid asked. "Do you know what a fifth column is, James?"

There was more than a tiny amount of adrenalin flowing now. "Yes, I do. It's the man on the inside who is supposed to help, but he betrays instead. He destroys the solidarity of the main team and makes it possible for the enemy to successfully attack."

This was a sobering conversation. Andy continued, "Right. That's when I figured out the top two layers. Suppose it wasn't about religion or war or anything else. Suppose those were just steps to the real goal."

"The real goal?"

"You had it months ago, James. I don't remember. We might have been eating pizza, I don't remember, but you said, 'when all is said and done, it's all about money.'"

"I said that?" James honestly had no such recollection. But the Kid seemed certain. Andy smiled now, a knowing smile.

"Let me show you."

Taking out paper, he sat down next to James. "Here's where I was when I gave up. I had figured out that one of the games was Weapons. What I hadn't figured out was that was any kind of weapons, including fear."

"Fear?"

"Yeah, think about it, James. Fear is a great weapon. It gets people to do things. Hell, look at what happened in Madrid."

"Oh, I got it. I did say to look wider. But it never occurred to me…fear as a weapon." He looked at that for a moment and added, "Nice abstract."

Reassuring him, Andy added that it included WMD and conventional weapons as well. They were like the material thing that produced the mental phenomena. "But I didn't get the fear thing right away. Watch."

He continued, "So I had:

Weapons

?- a still unidentified game

Money

Sociology. That's when I popped a cork."

James smiled at the reference.

"Then I watched TV and I spotted it. The other level of game is Medication or Medicine or Medical. So now I had all eight, but I didn't have the sequence. I tried:

Weapons

Medication

Money. But I couldn't get one to lead to the other going north. It was frustrating; but a good kind of frustration. I used to feel that way sometimes in a tournament."

James was just watching now. The Kid was doing the analysis.

"Then I remembered what you said about money, so for the heck of it I put money on top. It fit. This is my final alignment." He showed James a simple list arranged in a sequence.

Money
Medical (pharmaceutical)
Sociology (reactions of people, i.e. anxiety)
Weapons (including fear)
Public Relations
Intelligence
Military
Religion

James was still stuck on the sequence and which one should be on top. "You really think Religion is on the bottom?"

"I do. I know that's not what the rest of the world thinks. But they are wrong. But James, it doesn't matter. Don't get hung up on it. He can work this in either direction—bottom up or top down. Each one leads to the next no matter which way you run the scale. Each game promotes the next game. No matter which direction he starts, he wins."

James looked at the board and, dimly now, he could see a masterful threading from top to bottom.

Turning the light on the table, Andy revealed the game boards set up again, only this time the top two were labeled. "Game number seven is Drugs. It's pretty simple, actually. Much simpler than we thought. The Weapons game leads to fear and breaches the Social fabric, leading to anxiety. That leads to Medicine—specifically psych meds. And that leads to the top game—Money. You said it all along. It was all about money."

"He's doing this *for* money?" James asked himself. He was putting it together. "He's not seeking money for other things? He's actually doing them for his own personal gain?" James must have sounded incredulous.

"As implausible as that sounds, I think so, James."

"But why?"

"I don't know. Maybe he wants to be King. But I'm very certain he is an opportunist, not an idealist. Everyone has it wrong about him."

Surprisingly, this resonated with James. He laughed abruptly. His years of experience had taught him it usually was simpler than intelligence wanted it to be. And it never was romantic.

Nodding his head he exclaimed, "That's why they couldn't figure it out!"

"Who?"

"The Mossad. Their best men, all their intelligence analysts. They were looking at it through the filter of intelligence, through the standards and practices of intelligence. Me, too."

There was a long silence. "Right, but if you think about it, James, who could sabotage us? Only an insider. Who is trusted? Medicine, the doctor."

"Are you suggesting these people know they are doing this?"

"No, not necessarily. That's all the more interesting. I would call it more an unwitting involvement. Anyway, here's the bottom line. Who makes the drugs? Who profits? Look there and you will find him." Andy could see that this was pushing James to the edge of reality. But he was very certain of this. It played out on the boards and it made sense. You just had to look. A truth so fantastic that it is dismissed as a lie.

"One will find Zawahiri wherever you find his pharmaceutical company. He will be the owner, or on the board of directors, an investor, stockholder—something. Look there. Tell your people to look there. He will be there. And one thing more…"

"What?"

"He won't be wearing a turban." Suddenly they both laughed. It was the laughter of relief. They had gone down the rabbit hole and found its depth, and they had returned.

"Are you sure?"

"Yeah, absolutely."

"We'd better pull all this together real coherently and get it to the Boss. Are you up for it?"

Andy straightened up tall. "Absolutely."

"You're certain?"

"Dead certain."

James was just starting to dial Whitney to ask for a meeting the next morning when the doorbell rang upstairs. They could hear Kelly walk across the floor to the hallway. Then she seemed to go into the living room and sit down.

Whitney was in a meeting James was told, so the two started to diagram this analysis and log it and enter it into the computer. They looked forward to tomorrow. It had been quite a journey, but James' mind was already filling in the gaps. This was the one scenario that fit all the various games as well as all the current events. The more he evaluated it, the better it looked. The more questions he raised, the more they were answered. In analysis usually things look worse the more you scrutinize the thing. This one looked better and better. It was radical, but he was convinced it was true.

"James, are you hungry?"

"Yeah, definitely."

"I'll go get us something to eat. You want me to get Mom to make us a burger?"

"Whatever…" and Andy was gone up the stairs. He left the door ajar.

The HR man, Ed, had been following James under Whitney's orders. When Ed pulled up near Andy's house he noticed another car with a passenger in it and New York plates. It caught his attention.

Once he pulled around the corner he said out loud into his wireless head set, "I have a car outside Weir's house with New York plates."

The voice that came back was Whitney's. "Give us the plate and stand by."

Having given them the license number, Ed moved to a corner of the house where he could observe the car from the shadows. To his surprise the car's passenger had just left the car and was ringing the doorbell at the Weir residence. The door opened and, after a brief exchange, Kelly Weir invited the man inside.

Just as the door closed, Ed relayed what had transpired to Whitney. "Whoever he is, he just went into Weir's."

"Invited or uninvited?"

"Looked normal to me, Boss."

It had only taken two minutes for Whitney to ID the car. The suspect who had disappeared on them was now inside the Weir house.

"Ed, the man is George Nasser. He is a suspected terrorist we've been looking for. He gave us the slip."

"Well, he's in there now. Do you want me to enter?"

"No. See if you can look around, see what they are doing. We're trying to identify his connection with Weir and Mikolas."

"All right. I can't see anything here from the front. The shades are drawn. So I'm going around to the back."

He then slipped back into the shadows and made his way around the backside of the house. Squatting, he could see a long, narrow window just above ground level. It was ajar and there was a light shaft visible, so he approached the open window. Looking in, he saw a semblance of a room with a cluttered table in the middle. Although the window was at the rear of the basement and seemed to be in an area no one ever came into, he had a clear line of sight into the room. The room appeared to be empty.

At the same time Whitney and a three-man team in a van dispatched from a garage nearby and were followed by a black ambulance.

As Andy came out of the cellar he could see that Kelly had a guest in the living room. Wondering who had come over, he stepped in and was startled to see his friend Professor Nasser sitting on the sofa.

"Professor Nasser, what a surprise. Mom, this is the professor I was telling you about. I used to deliver him pizza."

"Yes, he was telling me," Kelly answered easily.

"Good to see you, friend; where you been?" Andy asked as he effusively shook the professor's hand. It felt a little sweaty.

"Working mostly. But I was in Washington for a conference and I thought I'd stop by and say hello, see how you were doing."

Andy didn't remember giving Professor Nasser his address, but he was about to dismiss it when James emerged from the basement saying he wanted pickles and tomato on his burger. Seeing they had company, he eased into the room.

"Sorry," James apologized for interrupting.

"Naw, James, let me introduce you to a friend of mine. He just stopped by to say hello. Professor Nasser I'd like you to meet my partner, James Mikolas." James was stepping forward when he heard the man's name. It rang a bell. As he shook his hand and looked Nasser in the eye, he recognized him from the hallway at Langley.

Unlike Andy who was basically a good, trusting kid, James was a paid operative of the CIA and had been for years. His instincts hadn't deserted him. He didn't wait to logically put it together. *An expert on the Hashshashin, a guest at Langley, now here in Andy's home. Something is terribly wrong.* As fast as he was thinking, his body was even faster. His body went onto automatic.

James' reflexes were good, but before he could reach for the weapon he always wore concealed, or warn Kelly or Andy, Nasser had drawn the Glock and grabbed Kelly around the throat. Using her as a shield, he held the gun to her head and shouted, "Get down there. Get down there right now or I'll kill her."

The whole thing was so sudden and so unreal that Kelly showed almost no fear. Her eyes showed more disbelief and confusion than anything else. Andy yelled and tried to lunge for her, but James pulled him back and took control of the situation.

"All right, all right, we're going."

James went first, then Andy, and then Kelly, awkwardly being pushed down the stairs by Nasser.

"I don't see anything but a lot of papers and what looks like a stack of chess boards," Ed reported. He was just about to change locations when he heard noises inside. He looked to the stairs just as James, Andy, and Kelly were forced into the room by Nasser.

"Someone's coming." He waited, trying to assess the scene. "Boss, we got a hostage situation here. I got the man in the car holding a gun to the woman and using her to hold Mikolas and Weir at bay. What are my orders?"

James could see that Nasser was sweating and not a professional. Nasser was quivering and that made James even more nervous. He couldn't for the life of him think why this scared nerd was threatening to kill them, but he could see that the man was strung out. He tried to speak non-threateningly, "I don't know what you want, Professor Nasser, but please put the gun down. I know you don't want to hurt Mrs. Weir. You're frightening her."

Nasser said nothing. James knew if he could reach his revolver he could get a shot off, but with Kelly in the way it was too risky. The look in Nasser's eyes scared him however. He had seen that look before, many times in Bosnia. *Nasser is desperate and he doesn't believe he is going home.*

"Put the gun down, Professor," Andy pleaded. "Whatever you want, please don't harm my mother."

"I can't do that, Andy. I'm sorry. I didn't want it this way. It was supposed to be just you and him. But you came home too late. She was already here. I'm sorry."

"What do you want?'

"I'm going to have to kill you." He had said it so matter-of-factly they almost thought he was joking.

"Why, in the name of God?" Andy pleaded.

"Because I can't let you find Usama. It is my duty..."

"Jesus, guys, I need confirmation! Ed says it looks like Nasser is holding all three of them hostage. Can you confirm?"

Instantly the response came in to Whitney from the team that was monitoring the bug planted in the Weir basement. "Yes, sir, we confirm. There are three—repeat three—hostages and one hostage taker. He just said he's going to kill them."

Upon hearing that Whitney had no choice. "Do you have a shot, Ed?"

"Yes."

Whitney gave the order.

Before Nasser could finish explaining his duty James lunged at him, instinctively knowing that this man wasn't going to talk; he was going to shoot. Kelly screamed. Suddenly there was a deafening explosion from the rear of the basement. The explosion created a tremendous flash of light in the small concrete area. It was followed by another round, fired at close range. Then another. The last shot knocked out the light. There was too much screaming and yelling for James to know anything other than that he himself was not hit. In the darkness he could just make out Kelly on the floor and Andy was silent.

What the hell happened? he asked himself. *Surely Nasser couldn't have fired that soon.* And it was all over before James got a shot off.

Suddenly a man's voice penetrated the darkness and warned them through the window at the back of the basement, "Don't move, any of you. I'll shoot."

James had no idea who was outside that window, but he suspected he was the one who must have fired first. He hoped the man had taken Nasser out. "This is James Mikolas. We can't see in here. Help us."

"They'll be there in a minute. Just stay where you are. And sound off."

"Kelly, can you hear me?"

She could. She was on the floor near the stairs, crying, but she could hear. "Yes."

"Are you all right?"

"Yes, I think so. I can't hear anything in my right ear. And I've got blood all over me."

"Is it yours?"

"I don't think so, no."

The voice outside interjected gruffly. He was talking to someone. "All right, I've got Mikolas and the mom." James realized then the man was relaying information to someone else. He could hear cars pulling up out front, but no sirens. "What about Weir?" the man asked.

Andy didn't answer. James couldn't see well enough to know where he was. He was starting to panic. "Get us some goddamned light in here. The shooting's over, and I don't know where Andy is!"

"I'm staying right where I am. They're coming in the front door now."

Just then the area was flooded with wide, bright flashlight beams as several men thundered down the stairs. Kelly was helped to her feet and taken upstairs. James was screaming, "I can't see Andy, for the love of God!" James couldn't see this, but the men were verifying that Nasser was killed.

"He's dead," one of the men reported.

"No!" James screamed, not knowing they were referring to Nasser. "Andy, no!"

"Nasser is dead." He recognized the voice. It was Whitney's.

"Whitney? For God's sake, help me. Get a light around here. I've got to find Andy."

Whitney did just that. In a matter of seconds one of his men replaced the light bulb and the room was normally illuminated. "Jesus, that was some shot, Ed. You got him right through the temple."

"Ten-four," Ed responded through the window opening. "Where do you want me now?"

"Out front. An ambulance will be by. It won't have lights or sirens on. Flag it down and bring it around back. The press on this one is coming from us and only us."

Just as he finished James heard Andy moaning. Even with the light back on he had been hard to see. The table with the eight chess boards had crashed and fallen on him, knocking him down. The weight of all that had cut him pretty badly and knocked him out, but it had also saved his life.

Glass chess boards are dense, and these game boards were one-inch thick. Fortunately for Andy, the top boards had saved his life when Nasser had fired off two reflex rounds before his own body hit the floor.

Kelly came running down the stairs again. She had gotten away from the men helping her and was desperately seeking news of Andy. Oblivious to the blood she was soaked in, she ran to her son and cradled his head. "Is he all right?"

"He will be, Kelly. He's just coming around now. We just need to give him some air." James touched her gently on the shoulder.

Now that she knew he was all right, she let down her guard and looked around at her own circumstances. "Is this…?'

"Yeah, it's Nasser's. Let's get you back upstairs so you can clean up."

They were all upstairs now, including Andy, who was woozy but starting to focus. From his perspective, it seemed like his house was full of people and he couldn't imagine why. He didn't remember anything except the sounds of gunfire.

"James, why was Nasser trying to kill Andy?" Kelly asked it pointedly as one of the men ordered her to get into one of the cars outside. Whitney had ordered that all three of them be interrogated separately. It was standard procedure and he didn't want them concocting a story. James tried to answer, but she was already being shoved outside.

Just as the bagged body of George Nasser was brought up out of the basement and carried out the back door to the black ambulance in the rear, Whitney turned to James. He was disgusted that they had to take Nasser out and that he couldn't be interrogated.

"I'll see you back at headquarters," he spat the words out ominously.

"Yeah, sure," James answered. He knew they would all be debriefed first. Then they could get to what he and Andy wanted to talk to Whitney about.

Andy was resisting getting into any of the cars. He had received first-aid, but still appeared disoriented. Knowing that his partner wouldn't understand being interrogated, James shouted to him, "Andy, just do what they tell you. It'll be all right. I'll see you at Langley."

Andy seemed to get it, but insisted on going in his own car. The more Whitney refused, the greater Andy resisted. Finally, Whitney relented and had a government agent accompany him while the government car followed Andy's.

The small caravan pulled away from the Weir house just as the sun was coming up. The polls were opening. It was Election Day.

Kelly was the first to be released. It was evident very quickly from the audio surveillance and from Ed's testimony that she knew nothing about why she was being held hostage.

Despite her protests of wanting to stay with her son, she was driven home. By the time she got there, all signs of a struggle and all blood had been cleaned up. The house and basement looked as they had before the incident. No one in the neighborhood had even been awakened.

James was next to be released. He had been cleared by the surveillance tapes. Without Nasser alive, Whitney knew he couldn't prove any connection between Mikolas and Nasser. If the three of them had been in on it together and Nasser was double-crossing his accomplices, they couldn't prove it. Whitney was more than disgusted, but he didn't really have any other choice.

He and James were standing now on the same side of the double mirror where they were the first day James had brought

Andy in. Andy's interrogation was complete and they were running a check on the data he had given them. Until a determination was made, he was told to just sit in their conference room.

Looking tired and in pain, he sat calmly at the table and seemed oblivious to the fact that he was being watched. *I've got to practice the sequence of data if Whitney is to understand this,* he coached himself. Andy knew he had been in a dangerous situation, but he was so intent upon getting his findings up the line that he didn't really get the fact that he was under suspicion. Whether it was naiveté or optimism, he just sat there, calmly thinking and planning how to convince Whitney that he had figured out how to find Zawahiri.

"You caught a break tonight, James."

"How so? I would've got the guy."

"I'm not talking about the shooting. I'm talking about the fact that we bugged the place. That's what saved you."

James was startled by what Whitney had said. "You were bugging the place?"

"Yes. We have been since the Kid's discussion about Zawahiri being several games out in front of us. Then there was the warning about the WMD. It seemed too conveniently timed for us. We were suspicious. And we'd already been looking for an Al Qaeda cell which intel said was operating in Manhattan. We suspected there might be a connection; that someone might be trying to get on the inside and procure information. We're grateful we got this guy, James. Turns out he was a loner, a real 'sleeper.'"

"George Nasser is Al Qaeda?"

"Seems that way. We're pulling everything off his computer now. Of course, there isn't going to be any trial with this guy. Ed's shot was it for that bastard."

"I just don't see that." James was finding this hard to believe. "Why? What was he planning?"

"Beats me. Maybe the computer guys will turn up something. But one thing is for sure, he was planning to kill you tonight. If it hadn't been for our watching the Kid, we wouldn't have found Nasser, and we sure as hell wouldn't have been at the house tonight."

James was stunned. He could feel his temper rising. The only reason he kept a lid on it at all was the realization that Andy was still locked up in there; he was, in fact, being interrogated, not just debriefed.

Seething inside James asked, "And the guy following me?"

Whitney didn't answer right away. He still had residual bad feelings about this whole thing and he wasn't sure how to put it. "We thought the Kid was part of the cell. He just seemed to know too much. There's no way some chess player's 'exercise' outsmarts our best analysts. He had to be in on it. We had to find Nasser. Once we did, we had to find out if Nasser was using Andy to get to you, or if Nasser and Andy were using you to get to the CIA. Or—and this is hard to say, pal—if Nasser, Andy and *you* were using us."

James knew the game. Whitney was firing a warning shot across his bow. If James knew he had been under suspicion too, they were gambling he'd just slink away, grateful to keep his job. They expected him to drop the whole thing right now.

"You son of a bitch..." His voice was menacing.

A runner handed Whitney the report. Reading it quickly he tapped on the glass for Andy's interrogator to release him. Apparently the report corroborated Andy's story. James couldn't tell whether Whitney was relieved or disappointed, but he knew what Whitney would do next. He would discredit Andy and his work, to justify having suspected him. He would cover his own ass. James just stared at him.

"What are you looking at?" Whitney asked belligerently.

"I'm looking at an asshole. How many years have you known me? Huh? You're the one who brought me in here, remember? And I'm the one who sought out the Kid. He didn't seek me out. If this guy Nasser was Al Qaeda, which I doubt, Andy was the victim. Listen to the tape. He wasn't using Andy to get to the CIA. He said he had to stop Andy from finding Bin Laden."

Whitney said nothing. He was beginning to stonewall and he looked menacing.

"That's the only thing that makes sense," James insisted. "The Kid has figured out the chess boards. Andy thinks he knows where you'll find Zawahiri. I don't know how, but Nasser must have known that, and that's why he came for us."

Still Whitney said nothing. He was twirling the report in his hand.

"It's obvious if you'd just get your head out of your ass and admit that your best analysts don't know shit!"

He hadn't meant to explode, but this was exactly why they had failed before 9/11 and after 9/11. He almost spat the next statement at Whitney. "Instead of asking this young man stupid questions about some alleged 'sleeper,' you should be asking him where to find Zawahiri, and how he figured it out. But no, you're determined to stay as ignorant now as you were then. No wonder Bin Laden thinks he can win this thing."

That was all Whitney was going to listen to. He was not totally convinced of James' and Weir's innocence, but he had nowhere to go once Nasser was killed. But he wasn't going to stand here and listen to this insolence. James needed to be put in his place.

"If you want to make a big deal about this, I can start a full investigation. We can look into why the Kid was feeding Nasser information, using chess codes. I don't know, after all, what you and the Kid talked about when you were not within range of our bugs. I don't know what information you may have given him that he later relayed to his colleague. We do know Nasser was trying to reach someone repeatedly on the Internet and it had something to do with his coming here tonight. We are certain of that."

James knew when to fold. Like it or not, the stakes were too high now. Judging by the vein throbbing in Whitney's neck, he knew the man would do it. He didn't want Andy to endure anything more for the Agency. Three years of his life was enough. As it turned out, the work had been dangerous. James was grateful they had all made it out alive.

"Fine. Have it your way. I'm out of here. But don't ever say we didn't try to tell you where you could find Zawahiri." *The smug bastard actually thinks that twit Nasser was somebody. They're going to settle for him, and pat themselves on the back for a job well-done.*

He brushed past Whitney and thrust the door to the hallway open. Walking through it he took a deep breath. Andy was just coming out of the conference room door and the two met.

"Did he get it?" Andy asked enthusiastically. "Is he going to look for him?"

All he ever wanted to do was help, James stifled his anger. *How do I tell this man who was doing his duty that the Agency viewed his theory and discoveries as, at best, an exercise, and at worst, a suspicious exercise? Either way, they wanted no more from Andrew Weir.* He looked away and Andy pressed him on it again.

Just tell him the truth; he deserves that much.

CHAPTER 64

Andy didn't take it well. James didn't really know how to tell someone so brilliant, who had sacrificed so much, that his work would be discredited and rejected. He looked back over the last three years and was profoundly moved by the distance they had covered. He remembered the promise he had made to help the President in the wake of 9/11. He remembered the rush he had gotten when that 18-year-old young man had solved his puzzle and validated his theory.

They had come a long way. Andy had become a man right before his eyes. Never once did he complain. Never once did he waiver in his sense of duty. He had lost a lot. But the only thing he seemed crushed about now was his inability to get anyone to listen to what he had discovered. Andy was absolutely certain that Ayman Al-Zawahiri was not playing chess. He was merely using it as a way to keep track of players and events in a worldwide theater of engagement. Rumsfeld had said it, "This is a different kind of war." The chess game was just a tool—a code system. But in unlocking that secret, Andy had stumbled on what he felt was the real location of the world's most dangerous man.

"I feel betrayed, James." Andy had said it quietly, but there was a deep sadness in his voice. "I feel used and betrayed. And I do not want to speak of this again."

"Fair enough, Kid. I owe you that. I'm truly sorry it turned out this way."

"I know." Andy inserted his key and slipped into his Jeep. They were back in the visitor's parking area at Langley where they had started.

"What time is it?" Andy asked. It was already dark. They had been in interrogation all day.

"Seven p.m." James answered, squinting at his watch. He noticed it had blood on it. *Probably that asshole Nasser's,* he thought.

"You see now why I wanted an absentee ballot? I told you it was too dangerous this year."

James laughed. *The Kid never lost his sense of humor. Or was it irony?* "Can I do anything for you?" he asked.

"No." And with that, Andy drove away.

When James returned to his office, the last message he took before turning in his own resignation letter was a confirmation from MIT that they were still waiting on Andrew Weir. *At least he didn't lose that.*

CHAPTER 65

He had been disappointed when he saw the newspaper. The headlines, of course, told of the shocking victory of the incumbent President in the United States. He knew that was a possibility. But he was not that disappointed about the outcome. He wanted to take the man down, but he knew it didn't really matter. He would win in the next round.

What disturbed him was his own picture with the Director. The printing of his picture with the Director in a prominent Swiss newspaper was just bad luck. Had they printed someone else's smiling face he wouldn't have to do what he was about to do. But he knew from his own intelligence reports that it was only a matter of weeks before they were going to bring the Director and his financial institution down.

It was time to move once again. He was not in a hurry. The morning after the picture appeared, he had commenced a complicated series of financial moves which redirected all of his financial holdings into other accounts. One new account was also opened in Panama. Believing these to be untraceable, he was free to take the identity of the new accounts' holder. Creating a new identity was not difficult. He had always had several to choose from.

What was a little more disturbing, however, was the fact he was going to have to use a surgeon to perform plastic surgery. After reflecting on it for a day, he had concluded that the changes he contemplated were subtle enough that he would use a regular plastic surgeon. The risk of one of Al Qaeda's doctors being aware of what he actually looked like was too dangerous at this point. He felt it was actually safer to just use some doctor that was already performing surgeries for celebrities. He would stay under wraps for a few weeks, and then journey on to his next base.

He had told Makkawi he would be changing locations and that he would be difficult to reach for about three weeks. Makkawi was confident they could go at least that long without needing to communicate. So was the Doctor. His money was waiting for him and appeared secure. His weapons development team was waiting for him and they also appeared secure. It would not be long now before he would be able to introduce that team to Makkawi. The Doctor was renowned in the terrorist community for his belief that biological and chemical weapons were the next great step Al Qaeda should take in its conquest. Little did anyone know just how far he had advanced with those plans. *Just a slight delay in the game,* he told himself. *What I have planned next will give the United States something to really be anxious about.*

He left his offices open and staffed. It would be some time before anyone realized he wasn't coming back. And it would be easy to just send a telegram along with their severance. But for the time being, he wanted the city of Geneva to think he was just away on another of his lengthy trips. As for Iseli, he had turned him over to Samir under the ruse that Samir had a line on another investor who could help Decu-Hehiz skyrocket in the current climate.

Iseli had said he would miss his friend and advisor, but he was most appreciative of the referral of another major investor. Samir would be the go-between. Smiling, he looked forward to the challenge of funneling funds and information through Samir to Iseli without Iseli having any real idea who his investor was, let alone where he was. This game had been fruitful. He had sufficient money now to insure his ultimate victory.

There was just one last little detail to attend to before he departed. He had never answered George Nasser's urgent chess moves. The code indicated the King was in check. He had no idea what that referred to, but Nasser, frankly was not qualified to be making evaluations in the field. The best thing he could do right now for his friend, since he wanted to fade into the shadows for awhile, was to send a very clear message to him. He typed in a very specific instruction which to a chess player would say, "Do not engage."

"There, that should satisfy him." And with that, he turned off the lights and locked the door. Minutes later he boarded a train.

CHAPTER 66

The Administrator had begun reducing the Thorazine drip three weeks ago. His patient seemed to be responding normally to this gradual reduction in his medication. The instructions that accompanied the latest prescription from the man's personal physician had been very specific. He wanted his patient to be very gradually weaned. The Administrator knew that the man could have been brought around much faster, but far be it from him to countermand the orders of this other physician, whoever he was.

Today for the first time, the patient seemed to actually have some awareness of where he was. Instead of the stupor he usually sat in, he was looking out the window and actually appeared to be focusing on various objects outside in the yard behind the asylum. It was the end of November and there was really nothing to look at back there except an occasional pile of leaves blown by the wind. Nonetheless, the patient seemed to be fixated on something below. For a moment the Administrator thought the man was going to speak. He moved his lips as if he were, but then changed his mind and sat down again having said nothing.

At least he's coming around, he thought. *I was concerned for a moment we might have medicated him too long.*

"I thank you for having taken such good care of my friend," the Doctor said sincerely. His entrance into the sun room had gone unnoticed by the Administrator and his voice caused the man to jump.

"My goodness, sir, you startled me! I didn't hear anyone come in." The man seemed truly surprised.

"I'm sorry to have done that. My apologies…I can see by my patient's alertness that you followed the regimen very well. If you do not mind, I would like to examine him in private."

The man was falling all over himself to accommodate his benefactor. This was the only paying customer he had and he wanted to make sure the man continued to do so. They all had benefited from the funds this mystery man had provided.

The Doctor could almost read the man's mind and abruptly addressed the Administrator, "I apologize for having sent my associates with my friend here. You see, I was ill at the time myself and required extensive hospitalization or I would have come personally to see that he was comfortably settled in."

"I understand completely," the man responded obsequiously. "I can assure you your associates took great care of your friend, and they made certain your wishes were carried out. I, for one, am also most appreciative of your promptness in sending money. As you can imagine, running a facility with such sick people requires a great many resources."

"Yes, I see that." The Doctor paused a moment and then reminded the man, "His room please, that I might examine him?"

"Oh, yes, of course. Follow me."

It had taken the Doctor an additional two hours to bring Usama around to the level of alertness he needed for his next step. Usama recognized the Doctor when the effects of a massive vitamin B shot took hold. He smiled and reached out his arms to his friend and colleague.

"Ayman, it is so good to see you." The two men embraced in their customary fashion. Just as Zawahiri was about to step back, Usama clutched his sleeve. "Ayman, tell me what happened and where I am. I have been experiencing the strangest phenomena in my mind and I have been frightened."

"I understand, Usama. You have been very ill. We brought you here where you could receive the quality of medical care you needed and where no one would ever find you. You went into insulin shock during our arduous escape from Tora Bora and I was forced to take the drastic measures of evacuating you."

Usama Bin Laden trusted his doctor. He always had. He had no reason to suspect the real truth of what had happened to him. For now, he was relieved to be talking to Zawahiri and eagerly accepted the briefing Zawahiri did to bring him current with the state of affairs. The effects of the medications caused his mind to jumble the timelines, but the Doctor gave him some relevant data regarding their successful attacks. He told Bin Laden nothing of their defeats for fear of actually triggering a psychotic break. There was still too much residual danger from the meds.

The Doctor had brought a crude tape recorder with him. As the afternoon wore on, he coached Bin Laden through some rough recordings. The brilliant filmmaking and recording Nanda had done in their state-of-the-art studios had been almost foolproof—almost. The few times they had needed to release a tape over the last three years, the world's press and intelligence agencies had readily accepted the tapes as proof of life of Bin Laden. Once they authenticated his voice, they seemed to accept the content. The scripts had been so imaginative that they had the ring of truth and seemed contemporaneous.

One of Nanda's strokes of genius had been recording Bin Laden in a way that would later be described as "poor quality." He had left careful instructions to release those recordings by way of telephone so that the telephone interference coupled with the poor recording quality would cover any edit they might want to make to insert a specific so current as to be an unchallengeable proof of life.

They had skated by on the release of the Bin Laden video just prior to the American election. The Doctor was confident they wouldn't have a repeat of that insubordination and that any future video releases would be controlled by Samir and his Paris team. But the Doctor wanted to give himself some options with regard to tape releases he might want to do between now and the elections in Iraq. His opportunity to further influence the American elections was over, but the Iraqis still seemed hell-bent on holding theirs. That could not be allowed to happen. And he felt he might need to reinforce Zarqawi's efforts by a pep talk from Bin Laden himself. To do that believably, he would need

Bin Laden's voice discussing precise candidates and recent locations of terrorist attacks. These could then be edited into some of the poor quality recordings Nanda had done for just such a ruse.

Bin Laden obliged. Even though he was somewhat incoherent, the Doctor got enough of his ramblings on tape to suffice. Once he had gotten what he wanted, he informed Bin Laden that he would be changing his medication now that he was out of his coma. To reassure Bin Laden, the Doctor said he would administer the first dose personally to make certain it worked as he desired. With that, he administered his unsuspecting friend another dose of the medication he had used to induce the near catatonia.

When he left, the Administrator walked him to the end of the leaf-strewn lane. The Doctor turned and handed the man an envelope. A quick peek inside revealed a series of prescriptions and a large sum of cash.

The Doctor addressed the Administrator before he could speak, "For your continued exceptional care of my friend." With that, he was gone.

As he boarded the train to his new location, he was contemplating just how he would explain these "extremely realistic" recordings of Usama to Samir and Makkawi. They were the only two top Al Qaeda commanders still alive who believed Usama Bin Laden to be dead and cremated in the hills near Tora Bora. All other members of Al Qaeda, including Zarqawi, had accepted the same propaganda that the intelligence community and the news media community had accepted.

He concluded, ultimately, that it was best to bring Samir and Makkawi into the loop. After all, they would concur that moving Bin Laden secretly was a brilliant way of saving his life and still allowing them to proceed without the encumbrance. Down the road, if need be, he would eliminate Usama and he was certain they all would accept it as the inevitable outcome of an illness as serious as his was.

The Doctor smiled as he looked out the train window. It was picking up speed now through the countryside. He was happy. He had solved his Bin Laden problem.

CHAPTER 67

Ari Ben Gurion was preparing to begin the interrogation of the director of one of Switzerland's largest banks. Ferreting out this front for Al Qaeda had required the cooperation of all major intelligence agencies in the world. It had taken four years, but they were quite certain they had them, and their assets.

He looked forward to being the first one to have a go at the man, to see how much he might offer up. Meanwhile, he was preparing himself by studying what looked like a very complete file. Photos of the Director and all his associates were included along with every other photo Mossad could find that contained the Director of the institution.

It had long been a policy of the Israelis to look at every person who appeared close to one of their marks. So they were almost compulsive about this scrapbook approach to flushing out cohorts. As he looked through the photos, he recognized many of the people. They were already on watch lists and were under surveillance of some kind. But there were several photos of people he didn't recognize. One of those was a photo taken very recently at the WHO bash following their convention.

"Do you know who this is?' he asked as he showed his associate the picture of the Director and Phillipe Monet. "I don't recognize him."

"Me, either. What do you want me to do with it?"

"Find out who he is, of course, and get me his history."

The man working with Ben Gurion was new. His next question revealed his naiveté. "And if he doesn't have one?"

"Then that would be a red flag." The young investigator nodded and stepped out of the room eager to attack his first assignment.

EPILOGUE

James had to admit his Mustang looked great. As he looked outside at the slush that was throwing the Beltway into chaos, he was reluctant even to take his new showpiece out. For years he had threatened to restore his first car from the V8 out. Somehow there had always been a greater priority. Decades went by, but every time he went to his garage the thought crossed his mind: *When I retire I'll bring this baby back to life and move to Phoenix.* Frankly, he never expected to retire. In his line of work in the 1970's, most guys never had to contemplate what to do in their "golden years."

Two months ago though he had hung it up. When they closed down his operation and sent the Kid home, he decided it was time for him too. The Agency was too calcified for him now. He knew that, even with the new leadership, if they didn't change their approach, they would never be able to keep up.

Whitney had not taken it well. Something about, "Stop sulking. You're acting like a teenager who got dumped by his girlfriend. When you suckle at the breast of Government, you'll always be rejected sooner or later; you know that." And on that pathetic metaphor, James had quietly turned in his retirement papers. It had really mattered this time. This time the enemy was smarter than they were.

In the weeks since the election, there had been a massive change at the Agency. The new Director's presence was being felt. And by the end of November, Whitney and the chain of command above him had all resigned or been forced to resign. The team that had brought James inside, and then ignored most of what they brought him inside to do, was replaced. He did not know the new team, and they did not know him. It was the right time to leave. His only regret was that no one had wanted to take his ideas seriously, let alone go to bat for them. He hoped the new boys would have the mental flexibility to carry it off.

He was a bit nostalgic about being in the game but, it was just a twinge, and he was looking forward to a new life.

He was reviewing a roadmap in order to enjoy the surprise break in the weather the South was enjoying. He had just decided to take I-95 south and pick up I-10 west in Jacksonville, Florida, in order to avoid a lot of weather from the Midwest, when the idea flashed. He tried to shake it off. He reminded himself that he was out of the game now. But this idea he had was seductive, and persistent. "Son of a bitch," he laughed. A minute later he was on the Beltway, scribbling something onto a small piece of paper he had recovered from the floorboard.

Meteorologists were predicting a cloudy and cold day for the Inauguration. Washington's news channels kept the citizens posted every few minutes on the weather forecasts and were debating what the conditions would be like for the inaugural parade. The consensus was that it would be cold, but dry and that everyone could enjoy the city's festivities.

Taking advantage of the surprisingly decent weather, Andy was loading the last of his cheap canvas bags into the back of his mom's car, when he heard what had to be a "muscle car" nearby. He was scheduled to start at MIT at the end of January, three years later than originally planned. They had held his scholarship for him. Despite the honor that represented, he had little joy or anticipation in him this morning. He regretted that the Agency had rejected his work. He knew he had solved the problem, but they didn't like the answer. He had to admit, from the Sociology game on up, the White King had nowhere to go. What he had discovered was a checkmate move.

Shaking it off, he put his attention once again on the project ahead. *And what excitement could MIT possibly offer after the last three years?* he lamented. No, this was not his best day.

"Hey, Kid," a familiar voice interrupted. Andy knocked his head on the trunk standing up quickly. He was so startled to hear James' voice. He stood up, massaging his head, and came around to the front. He was wowed by the car in front of him.

"Hey, yourself. 'Sweet' car!"

"Yeah, she still turns the heads, man," James laughed.

Andy hadn't expected to see James. "I'm just heading off to school. I got a week before classes begin."

"I heard." Seeing that Andy looked puzzled, he added, "Your mom told me. She seems relieved to have you getting on with a real life."

"Yeah." It was a sore subject, one he didn't want to discuss. "I thought you were going to Phoenix."

"I was. I swear I was, Kid," James said sheepishly. Patting the dashboard, he added, "In fact I was headed out this morning. Yes, I was."

Andy couldn't help but notice the tense James was using. "And?"

Smiling, James reached into his pocket and pulled out the folded scrap of paper. "I had an idea." He looked up at Andy and smiled that smile.

"No, no, I've had enough of your ideas." He almost shouted as he went for the last bag.

"Sure, sure I know, Andy. But I think I know where we failed. We had the game right, but we missed something." Andy hesitated for a moment, which emboldened James. "We had the White King wrong." Andy stopped; his back still to James. "We based our analysis on the assumption that Zawahiri's opponent, the White King, was the President of the United States, or the U.S. Government. That was our mistake." James knew that if Andy took the bait now, they were still in the game. He waited.

"It wasn't the President?" Andy asked without turning.

"No."

"Then who the hell was it? Surely not France!"

"Very funny! Now that's where my theory comes in," James grinned. "You want to see it? I wrote it down on my way over here, and I think it's a good one. This one I think explains every game he's been playing."

This was too much for Andy. He had invested so much in trying to prove James' last theory. He dropped the bag and walked briskly to the Mustang and almost snatched the little piece of paper from James' fingers. He unfolded the paper and read it—studied it was more like it. Then, characteristically, he looked into the distance and smiled slightly.

"So Bush was the White Queen?" He was making certain he got it.

"You got it, Kid. That was our mistake. We assumed he was the King!" He let out a huge sigh as if the weight of the world were off him. "I was listening to the Inauguration news on the way out of town when it came to me. The President is the Queen."

Andy was trying to follow James' thought pattern. Like so many times before when they synchronized, he picked up the thread, "The Queen protects the King. She has more power and more reach. She is unrestricted in her movements, whereas the King has the same movements, but limited." Suddenly he got it. "Son of a bitch!"

"That's when I got it Andy. Who is it the Queen protects? The King, right?" Andy nodded. "And who is it the President protects?"

"The people of the United States," Andy stated simply, still looking at the hastily scribbled note James had written while listening to some commentator review the upcoming inaugural address.

"The people have authority over the government, Andy. They are the King. And they don't even know it."

"What, that they have authority?"

"No, son, that they are Zawahiri's true opponent." James let that sink in for a moment. He couldn't quite tell what Andy was thinking. He looked morose.

"Okay, okay, I can think with that—the drugs, the money. But what am I supposed to do with it?" Andy challenged. "They shut us down, remember? You're retired. You don't even have a plastic card to Langley!" he scoffed.

James grinned from ear to ear now. "I don't need one kid. It's not our job to convince bureaucrats or military careerists. We're *civilians* now. We can talk to anyone we want. So, I was thinking we should stop at my fishing camp on the Cape Fear River, you know, and figure out how to tell the White King he's been playing chess games, and losing them."

He had said *we*.

Andy chewed on his lip for a minute, dropped his last bag into the back seat of James' Mustang and said, "I'd better go tell my mom."

ACKNOWLEDGMENTS

Grateful acknowledgment is made to Suzette Howe for her creativity in the cover design of the first version, to Kathleen Kaake for her patient and thorough assistance in the editing process, and to my publicist, Jeff Hodgson, for his discernment and wisdom.

I am especially appreciative of the current cover design by Linda Gipson, gipsonstudio@rcn.com, and of the interior book design and layout by www.integrativeink.com.

Along the way, numerous friends and acquaintances gave their enthusiastic recommendations of the book—going "above and beyond" to see that it would be read widely. Thank you Rich DeVos, Marcy Sanders, Linda R. Newman, Eileen Batson, Terry Foust, Sharon Johnson, Rex & Judy Nichols, Steve & Jeannie Luckey, Liam & Shannon Leahy, Paul & Pam Reeb, Steve and Jeannie Nichols, and Jeff Hodgson.

And lastly, a special thank you to friends Karen Paul and Tanya Meyers for their help at my first book signing, and to Theresa at the Eureka Book Store for a truly invigorating and productive evening.

About the Author

Lee Kessler is a television actress, playwright, and stage director. Her career in Hollywood and New York spans 28 years, and includes dozens of guest starring roles in episodic TV, mini-series and movies-of-the-week. She had reoccurring roles in the series "Hill Street Blues" and "Matlock," and was submitted for Emmy nomination twice for her starring roles in the movie "Collision Course," and the ABC special, "Which Mother Is Mine?" She co-starred with Peter O'Toole in the movie "Creator."

Her play, "Anais Nin—the Paris Years," was produced in New York and Los Angeles, with a subsequent tour on the West Coast. She also directed the West Coast premiere of A.R. Gurney's "Who Killed Richard Cory?"

Since 2000, Lee has invested much of her time and energy in human rights projects designed to protect children in dangerous environments, and has transitioned from primarily an acting career to one in writing.

In addition, during the development of her entertainment industry career, Lee became a successful entrepreneur, a pioneer in Internet commerce, and today owns an international Internet business which operates throughout the United States. She currently resides with her husband in Florida and Montana.